Zoë Barnes was born and brought up on Merseyside, where legend has it her skirt once fell off during a school performance of 'Dido and Aeneas'. According to her mum, she has been making an exhibition of herself ever since.

Her varied career has included stints as a hearing-aid technician, switchboard operator, shorthand teacher, French translator, and the worst accounts clerk in the entire world. When not writing her own novels, she translates other people's and also works as a semi-professional singer.

Although not in the least bit posh, Zoë now lives in Cheltenham where most of her novels are set. She shares a home with her husband Simon, and would rather like to be a writer when she grows up.

Zoë Barnes is the author of seven best-selling novels including BUMPS and HITCHED. The others are HOT PROPERTY, BOUNCING BACK, EX-APPEAL, LOVE BUG and JUST MARRIED, also published by Piatkus. Zoë loves to hear from her readers. Write to her c/o Piatkus Books, 5 Windmill Street, London, W1T 2JA or via email at zoebarnes@bookfactory.fsnet.co.uk

D1335768

Split Ends

Zoë Barnes

PIATKUS

First published in Great Britain in 2004 by
Piatkus Books Ltd of
5 Windmill Street, London W1T 2JA
email: info@piatkus.co.uk

This edition published 2005

Reprinted 2006

The moral right of the author has been asserted

A catalogue record for this book is available from the British Library

ISBN 0 7499 3468 9

Set in Times by
Phoenix Photosetting, Chatham, Kent
Printed and bound in Great Britain by
Mackays Ltd, Chatham, Kent

With many thanks to Tracie Philips,
for all her hair-flair!

For Mum,
My keenest critic and my staunchest fan.
The world's just not the same without you.

Prologue

'Oh Nick, I love it. It's perfect!'

Hannah Steadman's new husband scratched his ear doubtfully. 'You don't think it's a bit—'

'No, it's wonderful. Wonderful. Can we have it? Can we?'

As utterly entranced as a six-year-old in a Disney store, Hannah stood in the overgrown garden that could have staged 'Jurassic Park: the Musical', and marvelled as she took in the mess that was number 19, Foley Road. Even if you overlooked the small tree growing out of the roof, the dead piano upside down on the lawn and the several million rats that seemed to have taken up residence in the doorless shed, it wasn't exactly in the running for ideal home of the year. In fact it was obvious that the house hadn't been anybody's home for some considerable time.

But she could see from Nick's face that he felt it too: the pull of the place; the inescapable charm; the potential that oozed from every cracked brick and length of rusty guttering.

She looked down at the sleeping baby in her arms and smiled in a way she'd never have thought she'd ever smile again, if you'd asked her six months before. 'It's a real family house, Nick,' she pleaded. 'Just think what it could be like if we restored it.'

Sensible as he always was, Nick paced thoughtfully around the outside of the house, narrowly avoiding spearing himself on a pile of discarded bedsprings. 'We'd have to be sure it was structurally sound.'

'Yes, yes, of course.' He sounds like my dad, bless him, she giggled to herself, idolising him all the more. All sensible and gruff. 'But look how much space there is.'

'And we'd have to do nearly all the work ourselves. It'd probably mean living in a caravan in the garden for . . . oh . . . I don't know, maybe even years.' He swung round and chucked baby Lottie gently under the chin. 'And with this little one to think of . . .'

Hannah clutched at his arm. 'She'll be fine, Nick. *We'll* be fine. We already talked this through, remember? It's the only way we'll ever afford the kind of house we really want.'

He flicked a fly off his nose and ran his hand through a mop of brown curls that could only loosely be described as a hairstyle. 'It'd mean work. A lot of hard, physical work.' He was trying to sound cautious, but she could tell from the sound of his voice that he was already won over.

'It's so beautiful. And it's huge. We could turn that second spare bedroom into a nursery. Maybe even do a loft conversion. You could have your own study.'

'Have you ever tried your hand at plastering a ceiling?'

'I'd never tried my hand at marriage until I met you,' she retorted. 'Nick, we have to do this! Everything about it's right, including the area.'

Nick shook his head in an affable, OK-you-win kind of way, and slid an arm round her shoulder. 'So what do you reckon, Baby Lottie? Is your mum a few marbles short, or what?' Lottie merely stirred in her sleep, clenched one tiny fist and blew a few bubbles. 'Oh I get it, taking the Fifth Amendment are we? Talk about women sticking together.'

As Hannah turned her face towards him, he moved in for a kiss. But Hannah was glancing behind her. 'Look, he's coming back.'

'Who?'

'The creepy estate agent. So what are we going to tell him?'

Nick gave a crooked smile. 'Dunno. What do you think? Shall we ask him if he's knows anyone with a second-hand caravan going cheap?'

Chapter 1

Almost nine years later ...

It was Friday – maddest day of the week at the Split Ends salon –
but there was always time for a quick chat amid the chaos. Especially when you and your best friend actually ran the place.

Maxine Judd wiped the leave-in conditioner off her hands and
took the photo from Hannah. 'She's the image of Nick,' she commented. 'You'd never guess she wasn't his, not in a million years.'

'She practically is,' pointed out Hannah, reflecting that Lottie
had only been a couple of months old when she married Nick.
'As far as she's concerned, he's her daddy.'

'You know, I can hardly believe she used to be that tiny pink
blob. Just look at her, nine already! She'll be a stroppy teenager
before you know it.'

Hannah groaned. 'Don't! Let me fondly imagine she'll be a
cute little moppet forever.'

'Can I have a look?' asked the dripping client in the chair.

'Oh sorry, Gloria.' Hannah held the photo over the woman's
face, immaculate make-up contrasting rather vividly with the
rat's-tails of dyed wet hair. 'It's just a photo of Lottie and Nick on
that big new ride at Alton Towers.'

Gloria was one of Split Ends' most valued customers – so
much so that Maxine always washed her hair personally. Not
only did Gloria's lurid romantic exploits bring in some of the
juiciest gossip in town, she was also a high-maintenance woman.
There wasn't a single hair treatment or beauty therapy she hadn't
tried, at least twice. Whether it was the treatments or all that ath-
letic sex, it was hard to say; but she sure as heck looked good for
forty-three.

3

'Pretty little girl,' commented Gloria. 'Is there something wrong with the film though? Your Nick's face is all green.'

Maxine snorted. 'Go on, tell her Hannah. Tell Gloria what a big brave soldier he is.'

Hannah stuck out her tongue. 'Nick and roller coasters don't really go together, that's all. He's green because he'd just thrown up.'

Gloria chuckled. 'Not that he's a wuss or anything.'

'He's not!'

'Why didn't you go on with Lottie then?' asked Maxine. 'I thought you liked travelling at a hundred miles an hour upside down.'

'Try telling that to a little girl who thinks her daddy walks on water. Believe me, we were going on that ride with Daddy or we weren't going on at all.'

Maxine smiled. 'Ah well, Daddy has special powers – he knows how to walk on water *and* plumb in a bidet.

'So does Mummy!'

Gloria looked deeply sympathetic. 'Yes, I suppose you must do love, after all these years of doing up that house of yours. No wonder your poor cuticles are all ragged.'

Hannah looked down at her hands in surprise. Gloria was right. 'Ah. My cuticles.'

'You ought to get those sorted out dear. Not good for business! Not when you're a beautician.'

A voice called over from the reception desk at the front of the salon. 'Hannah? Your half-past two pedicure has just arrived.' A lanky youth with tortured eighties' hair indicated a girl so immensely pregnant that she was clearly having to lean over backwards to avoid falling on her face. 'Shall I send her up?'

'It's OK, Jason, I'll take Mrs Donohue up myself.'

'How *is* the house anyway?' enquired Maxine, a styling comb between her teeth. 'Finished the damn thing yet?'

'Oh, you know . . . nearly.'

'Gawd help us Han, how long's it been – seven years?'

'Eight.'

'You could've built your own bloody castle by now.'

The enormous, whale-shaped hulk that was Mrs Donohue waddled across the salon and Hannah hurried to her side. One of these days we've really got to get somewhere with a downstairs therapy room, thought Hannah as she helped the mum-to-be up two flights of stairs. Or a lift. Or one day soon I'm going to be playing midwife on the landing.

But that was only what was going on at the front of her mind. At the back, the same two words were spooling past, over and over, endlessly repeating like some disturbing mantra:

Nearly. Finished. Nearly. Finished. Nearly. Finished.

Yes, the house was nearly finished and soon she and Nick and Lottie would have the perfect family home they'd been striving for, for eight endless years. She ought to be punching the air and putting the champagne on ice.

So why did she feel just plain . . . uneasy?

When Mrs Donohue had gone, leaving behind her a potent smell of patchouli oil, Hannah kicked off her Scholl clogs and stole a crafty five minutes on her own massage couch.

Beauty therapy hadn't started out as Hannah's dream profession. Frankly, it had never even occurred to her until she was twenty-three with a biology degree and an unplanned baby. If someone had told her at eighteen that at thirty-one she'd be waxing bikini lines and massaging knotted deltoids for a living, she'd have said there was more chance of her driving a dodgem car up the M1.

As a teenager, she'd always imagined herself working as some sort of scientific researcher. Making amazing discoveries and benefiting humanity, all that idealistic stuff. But things you think are set in stone have a habit of changing, and suddenly you have to change with them. And even if you've found yourself a lovely, steady bloke like Nick who wants to look after you and wrap you up in love, you still have to have something to do with the time when you're not changing nappies or cooking casseroles. Not to mention money to finance the never-ending house improvements. And so she had answered the advert in the local paper on a whim, got the bursary, and before she knew it she was back at college.

Which was where she'd met Maxine . . .

Well, not so much met as collided with, sending Maxine's jumbo rollers and bottles of perming lotion bouncing down the stairs from the training salon. She'd apologised, Maxine had sworn inventively, and they'd been the best of mates ever since.

5

Now, Maxine had drive, flair and a fistful of hairdressing NVQs, while Hannah could tweeze out the stubbornest eyebrow hair. So when Maxine's husband Jay announced that he was looking for a business to invest in, the solution was obvious.

And Split Ends was born.

As she dried her hands and wiped off the last of the massage oil on a fluffy white towel, Hannah let out a long, low sigh and flopped back onto the couch. Her whole body seemed to deflate, draining the tension from her shoulders, back and arms, and for the first time that day she allowed herself to feel the ache of all those hours spent on her feet. If only someone could come in now and give *me* a massage and a facial, she thought. A nice tall Adonis with perfect abs and the tiniest of thongs . . .

Fat chance. More likely it would be Nick at bedtime with a tube of Ralgex.

Her mobile rang just as she was debating whether or not George Clooney's medical experience might run to shiatsu massage.

'Hi. Nick?'

'Yep, only me. How're you doing?'

Hannah stifled a yawn. 'Not too bad. What's up?'

'Nothing, just wondered if you could pick up the cake on your way home, only they've roped me in for the after-school homework club.'

She sat up and swung her legs over the side of the couch. 'What – again? But you promised *you* would.'

'I know Han, but I couldn't really say no. I mean, some of these kids don't have anywhere to do their homework properly at home, and if I told you what kind of homes some of them come from—'

Something between a growl, a hiss and a despairing sigh escaped from between Hannah's clenched teeth. It wasn't just the fact that collecting Lottie's birthday cake would mean a twenty-minute detour in the rush hour; it was the fact that her husband had Done It Again.

'I don't care if they live in jam jars in the middle of the A40!' she cut in, with excessive relish. 'You're not the only teacher in the world you know – just the only one who can't say no. Let somebody else take on the responsibility for once.'

'Next time,' he promised; and she knew he meant it, just as he had meant it on the last fourteen occasions. She'd lost count of the number of times his dinner had dried to a brown husk in the oven. 'See you later.' Then he added, almost as an afterthought, 'Oh – er – love you.'

'Yeah. Right.'

Number 19, Foley Road shone in the autumn sunshine like a perfectly cut gem, its fresh blue and white paintwork reflecting the golden light from every sharp, clean brush stroke.

A lot had changed in eight years. If you'd placed two photographs side by side, one 'before' and one 'after', most people wouldn't even have recognised it as the same house. Where there had been holes there was neat brickwork and a brand-new roof. Where there had been a decaying, back room held together with dirt, there was a lovely new kitchen, leading into an Edwardian-style conservatory with genuine stained glass panels.

The transformation didn't just extend to the building, either. Where there had been jungle, there was a cool, stylish modern garden that Maxine's rather talented husband had designed for them, just managing to keep it on the right side of pretentious. Mind you, the space-hopper and the row of hutches, where the rabbits and a couple of ferrets lived, tended to take the edge off the egg-shaped concrete pergola and the mirrored water feature.

Hannah nudged open the front gate with her bottom, handbag strap over one arm, shopping bag in one hand and the cake perilously balanced in the other. Now would be a nice time to come to my rescue, Nick, she thought, but of course Nick couldn't because he was nursemaiding a bunch of kids through their algebra homework. She felt slightly ashamed of her own resentment, but hey, everybody was entitled to be unreasonable sometimes.

She staggered gamely up the three stone steps to the rather grand front porch, complete with ancient bell-pull and a brass letter box that actually had the word 'letters' embossed on it. It took all her ingenuity to get the front door open without dropping anything, but she felt a flush of achievement as she finally kicked the front door shut behind her and dumped the cake on the hall table.

'Lottie?' No answer. 'Lottie, are you back?' Good, she had time to hide the cake before Lottie got in from school. Her daughter might be exultant about making it to the grand old age of nine, but nobody was ever too old for nice surprises.

The answering machine was flashing petulantly. Against her better judgement, Hannah pushed 'Play'.

'Hiya, Granny and Grandpa Steadman here, calling from La Belle France. Just ringing to say happy birthday Lottie, nine years old today! Whoopee!' There followed an out-of-tune chorus of 'Happy Birthday' that sounded as if it was being sung by a couple of six-year-olds, not Nick's mum and dad. Hannah shook her head in amusement. Trust Julie and Clive not to realise that Lottie's birthday wasn't till tomorrow. Nice they might be, but you could never accuse them of being organised.

The other message was from Hannah's own mother. 'Hello love, it's Mum. I'll be round tomorrow morning at eleven, in case you want me to make some sandwiches or jellies or something. Give our little princess a kiss from Gran and Grandad, and tell her we'll see her tomorrow.'

'Jellies?'

Hannah turned round and nearly jumped out of her skin when she found Lottie standing right behind her, a pair of stereo headphones hanging round her neck.

'Mum,' said Lottie firmly, 'only little kids eat jellies! I'm not a little kid any more. I'm *nine*.'

No, thought Hannah with a tiny pang of regret. You're not a little kid. And you're growing up so fast that in no time at all you'll have children of your own and I'll be wondering what happened to the rest of my life.

'Grandma just wants you to have a nice birthday,' she said. 'And when Grandma was a little girl, jellies were what you had at birthday parties. Jellies, fairy cakes and meat paste sandwiches.'

Lottie wrinkled her freckled nose. 'All her birthdays must have been horrible then.' At one day off nine years old, she was already strongly reminiscent of her mother: same dark hair that flamed red when the sun burnished it, and pale, almost translucent skin, cobalt blue eyes framed by long, fair lashes, and a mouth whose shape seemed to combine sweet good nature and bloody-mindedness.

The funny thing was that Lottie managed to be the spitting image of Nick too – and he wasn't even her real father. Beloved daddy or not, it wasn't Nick who'd fumbled the condom and got her pregnant halfway through her second year at university. Nor

8

was it Nick whose influential dad had promptly whisked him off to an American university, quicker than you could say 'nothing to do with me, guv'.

But it was Nick who'd come along, just when she was at her lowest ebb, and stepped into the big black hole that Rhys's departure had left; Nick who had been everything to Lottie that her biological father never would. So perhaps it wasn't so very surprising that she was growing up to look like him too.

'What's in that box, Mum?'

'What box?'

'The one you've thrown your coat over. You're not very good at hiding things, Mum; you'd be no good as a spy.' Her eyes lit up. 'Is it my birthday cake?'

'Who says you're getting a birthday cake?' teased Hannah.

'Mum!'

'Well, there might be anything in that box. It might be full of . . . oh, I don't know . . . people's toenails. Or dead frogs.'

'Mum, that's so gross!' Lottie tried to peek underneath Hannah's coat. 'It's not a Thomas the Tank Engine one, is it? Or a My Little Pony?' Dismay registered on Lottie's normally perky face. 'Grandma Maddrell didn't buy it, did she?'

Hannah tapped a finger lightly on her daughter's nose. 'Never you mind. You'll have to wait and see, won't you? The big day's not till tomorrow.'

Lottie pouted. 'I'll ask Daddy when he gets home. I bet he'll let me have a look.'

'Ah well madam, that's where you're wrong. 'cause Daddy's not going to know where I've hidden it.'

The Megaplex on the outskirts of town might look like something out of pre-1990 East Berlin, but it was a godsend for anyone with a bunch of eight-and nine-year-olds to entertain on a rainy Saturday afternoon. The latest animated feature, a dozen family buckets of popcorn and some blue, raspberry-flavoured Slush Puppie packed with E-numbers, and you had the recipe for an effortless birthday celebration. Even the alarmingly precocious Melanie-Anne was apt to stop boasting about her designer shoe collection if you gave her enough ice cream to eat.

Hannah and Nick sat together at one end of the row, ostensibly watching the film but not really taking it in. Cartoon pirates and princesses had never been Hannah's thing, they had both been woken up by Lottie at five a.m., and in any case Nick was so tired after all the extra hours he'd been working at the school that he could hardly keep his eyes open.

Hannah nudged him in the semi-darkness. 'Nick,' she hissed.

'Uh?'

'Wake up, you're missing the film.'

'Am I? Sorry.' He rubbed his eyes with the back of his hand, and stretched out his long legs. Oh God, thought Hannah with a rush of embarrassment, I hadn't realised he was wearing *those* trousers.

'Where did you get those?' she demanded.

'What?'

'Those horrible cords.' She plucked at the balding grey fabric, so old and baggy that in places it had gone as shiny as a taxi driver's backside. 'I was sure I'd put them in the charity bag.'

'You did,' confessed Nick. 'I took them out again.'

'But they're vile!'

'I don't care, I like them.' There was a tiny note of petulance in Nick's normally easygoing tone. 'They're comfortable.'

'Yes, and they're also two inches too short, and what about the—'

A small voice from halfway down the row gave a disapproving 'Shhh!' and they promptly shut up like guilty fourth-formers. On the screen, the character voiced by Tom Cruise was romancing the princess, and a dozen little girls were gazing open-mouthed at the screen, dreaming that next time they'd be the one.

But Hannah was still looking at Nick.

At eight years Hannah's senior, he was just a few months shy of thirty-nine. Still young in a lot of people's books; but if Nick was a book he was definitely no cutting-edge blockbuster. More like an ex-library copy of Charles Dickens, with the covers hanging off.

Thirty-nine going on fifty, she thought as she took in the disorderly assortment of jumble-sale items that constituted Nick Steadman's apology for a wardrobe. He mightn't look too bad if he'd just take a bit of care over his appearance, she mused. His untidy hair was naturally wavy and a glossy shade of nut-brown, and his face – though not remarkable enough to be classed as handsome – exuded the kind of genuine amiability that made people feel warm and safe. The very characteristic that had drawn her to him all those years ago and which now, in dark moments she didn't even admit to herself, provoked a feeling akin to drowning in warm milk.

But that was unfair and she knew it. Not tall but not short either, not muscle-bound but no wimp, Nick would certainly never have made it onto the books of a model agency, but he could really have looked quite presentable . . . if he could have been bothered. And Nick can never be bothered, thought Hannah wistfully. Even on their very first date, he'd turned up wearing an old jumper with a hole in the front where he'd dropped something corrosive on it. But that, she mused, was what you got when you married a chemistry teacher – and one who cared far more about the rest of the world than he cared about himself.

It was, Hannah supposed, a virtue. Sometimes though, she found herself wishing that he could separate her from the rest of the world and single her out for a bit of special attention. It was uncomfortably like waiting in line as the biscuit tin was passed round, only to get your turn at last and discover that someone else had had all the chocolate Hob-Nobs.

'Chocolate?' She nudged him with the box and he dipped in a hand and took one.

'Ta.'

'The kids seem to be enjoying it. So much for saying it was "too babyish".'

'Yes.'

'Mum should be waiting at the pizza restaurant, with the birthday cake. It's a pity yours couldn't make it.'

'Bad time of the year for them. What with the grape harvest. But I'm sure they'll get over later.'

For the last couple of years, Nick's parents had been living their dream: running a smallholding with its own tiny vineyard, in the depths of Périgord. To be honest, it seemed like more of a nightmare to Hannah, what with vine weevils, suspicious locals, forest fires and a thousand and one other mishaps; but the Steadmans seemed to thrive on it. Sometimes Hannah thought Nick saw his life's mission as being to atone for his parents' own brand of happy chaos.

Hannah sat back and gazed up at the giant figures on the

screen. I wish I was a princess, she mused. Not a real one though – that'd be horrendous. No, a fairy-tale one like you, you lucky . . .

'Cow', she said aloud as the Pirate King scooped the princess up in his arms and whisked her from the ballroom floor, away to his waiting galleon and a crew of hot and cold running cutthroats. 'Bet you wish you were him,' she commented, turning to look at Nick.

But Nick didn't answer. Head thrown back, mouth open, popcorn spilling all over his knees, he was snoring peacefully.

'Charlotte! Where's our little birthday princess then?' beamed Erica Maddrell, throwing open her arms and enveloping Lottie in her huge overhang of a bosom. It was a good job Lottie's face was hidden, because it was bright red with the embarrassment of being shown up in front of her friends. Being loved to death by your gran in a pizza restaurant – even an expensive Cheltenham one like Pizza Bellissima – was distinctly uncool. Especially when your gran was only in her early fifties but favoured floral polyester and sensible shoes. And having her call you Charlotte, which nobody ever did, wasn't much cop either.

If anybody had been glad to hit middle age, it was Erica. She'd struggled all her life to be slim and chic, had mostly failed, and the minute she hit forty she had taken it as a green light to eat Battenberg cake and embrace her inner self which, rather like the Tardis, had turned out to be somewhat larger than the outer one. As her husband Derek never noticed what shape anybody was, even when they were in the nude, there were no dire domestic consequences.

Consequently, Erica was plumper, dowdier and infinitely happier than she had ever been in her entire life. And the crowning joy of that life was her pretty, clever, adorable granddaughter.

For her part, Lottie adored her grandma too. She was lovely and soft, and jolly, and never told her off when she picked her nose at the dinner table. It was just that there were times when she just didn't seem to understand the intricate subtleties involved in being a cool nine-year-old.

The pizzas were great, and even Melanie-Anne was impressed by the cake: a blazing inferno of candles atop the most amazing sugar-craft model of Hogwarts Academy. Mum and Daddy didn't

12

say or do anything embarrassing, nobody threw up or needed their asthma inhaler, and it was all going beautifully until Grandma and Granddad handed Lottie her present.

'I do hope it's big enough, Grandma said anxiously. 'I had such trouble getting one in your size, I can't think why.'

Lottie could. As she tore off the paper and revealed the contents, a titter ran round the table. Lottie just wanted to sink underneath it. Her mouth opened and closed like a stranded goldfish's.

'It's a Barbie sweater,' prompted Grandad proudly, seeing that Lottie was too overjoyed to speak. 'We know how much you've always loved your Barbie.

Hannah exchanged looks with Nick. Lottie turned a despairing gaze on her daddy, and saw the pleading look on his face. She swallowed. 'Thank you Grandma, it's lovely,' she said, with a perfect stage-school smile. 'Isn't it?' she added with a note of ferocity as Melanie-Anne snorted in amusement. In surprise, Melanie-Anne inhaled a currant and had to be thumped on the back, which just about gave Hannah time to whisk away the fluffy pink jumper and change the topic of conversation.

She had to hand it to Nick, he was good with kids. Really good. She wondered where he'd learned a routine of magic tricks so slick that even Martin, the cleverest boy in the school and didn't he know it, kept his mouth shut and his baffled eyes saucer-wide.

The look on Lottie's face said it all. 'She's really proud of her daddy,' commented Hannah, breaking off one of the Hogwarts turrets and biting the top off.

Grandma Maddrell nodded and smiled. 'Such a shame she doesn't have her real daddy though,' she sighed.

'Mum!'

'It's true, dear. Every child needs its father, isn't that right, Derek?' Derek was too busy laughing at the egg that had just appeared in Martin's mouth to hear. 'Well, I'm sure he'd agree with me, anyway.'

'But Nick *is* her father,' protested Hannah. 'All right, maybe he's not her *biological* father, but so what? He's definitely her daddy. She loves him to bits.'

'Of course she does,' agreed Erica. 'And he's a very nice man, is your Nicholas.' There was a definite 'but' in her voice – not in any way malicious, but it still annoyed Hannah. If anybody was going to criticise Nick, it was her and nobody else.

'Why do we always have this conversation on birthdays and at Christmas?' she asked wearily.

'Do we?'

'You know we do!'

'Ah well dear, I expect it's just that it brings it home to me how different things could have been if . . . well, you know.' She gave Hannah a maternal pat on the shoulder. 'Still, you're happy and settled now, aren't you? That's all that matters at the end of the day.'

'Of course it is,' agreed Hannah. Normally she'd have put the whole thing out of her mind, the way she did every year. But that night, as she clumped wearily up the stairs to bed, she was still thinking about it. And wondering.

Chapter 2

'Delbert Mackenzie, if I see that one more time it'll be confiscated until the end of term. Got that?'

'Yes sir, I'm putting it away sir.'

The boy shoved the Game Boy Advance back into his rucksack and legged it down the corridor.

'And don't run!'

The words bounced off the walls and disappeared into the seething hubbub of a typical Monday morning at Alderman Braithwaite Comprehensive.

'He's not a bad lad, but you want to watch him – give him an inch and he'll have the whole rope off you. Can't half talk as well. I've never known anyone come up with such creative excuses for not doing their homework. Come on, Colin, I'll introduce you to the rest of the department.'

Nick strode off down the corridor towards the staffroom. The young man by his side was a good three inches taller, but looked small and apologetic by comparison. He might as well have had 'this is my first day' stamped in large capitals across his forehead. All the same, the zeal of the newly hatched teacher shone out of his well-scrubbed face.

Normally, new staff started in September, but after Mr Sparrow had been found in a compromising situation with Miss Raeburn, there had been two urgent vacancies to fill. They were astonishingly lucky to find a well-qualified science teacher like Colin Rooney halfway through the autumn term, and Nick knew it. As acting deputy head of science, he intended to make sure that his new protégé liked the place well enough to stick around.

The staffroom was the usual crowded hovel, the floor more

coffee-stain than carpet and the noticeboard completely obliterated by adverts for second-hand Fiestas and 2CVs.

'Well, this is where it all happens,' announced Nick. 'Help yourself to a coffee and I'll run through your timetable with you.'

Colin wandered over to the table where the coffee machine stood. 'Any particular mug?'

Nick was distracted by the glowing comments on Colin's teaching practice reports. 'Hmm? No, whatever.'

'Not zat one!' snapped a short black woman with a pronounced French accent, whisking away a Wallace and Gromit mug. 'Zat one ees mine. You will 'ave to bring your own.'

Colin's face fell.

'Don't mind Claudette,' advised Nick, taking his own spare mug out of the bottom drawer of a filing cabinet marked 'SATS' and handing it to Colin. 'She's all bark and no bite, aren't you, Claudie?'

'Huh. You weesh!' sniffed Claudette, but her expression softened.

Nick lowered his voice. 'And she knows where all the secret stocks of stationery are kept, so best keep in with her. Now, how do you feel about Year Nine general science first thing on a Monday morning?'

'Er . . . fine. Great.'

Nick smiled ruefully. 'You might not say that when you've met them. There's one or two right little buggers in there. Maybe I ought to swap you with Graham and then you could have that nice GCSE chemistry set.'

Colin shrugged with equanimity. 'No need, just throw me in with 'em. Got to face the difficult ones sometime, after all.'

Nick laughed. 'You sound just like me when I started. All bushy-tailed and idealistic.'

'Don't worry,' cut in Graham the physics specialist, brushing jam off his brown tweed tie. 'We'll soon knock that out of you.'

'So when did you start teaching then?' asked Colin, sipping his coffee.

'Not as long ago as you might think,' replied Nick. 'Actually I was a dentist before I took up this lark.'

Colin's jaw dropped. 'A dentist! You mean you gave up all that for . . . this?'

16

'All that what?' laughed Nick. 'You mean all that stress and boredom? Ah, you're talking about the *money*. Believe it or not, it really isn't everything.'

'If you say so,' said Colin, clearly unconvinced.

'It's OK, he's insane,' said Graham, walking past with a model of Clifton Suspension Bridge.

'He must be,' sniffed Claudette, gathering up her pile of French books. 'He works 'ere.'

'Anyhow, I only did it for a couple of years before I realised I'd made a big mistake, Nick went on. 'This is what I was meant to do – for my sins.' He glanced at the clock on the wall, and slammed down his mug. 'Come on, I'll show you round the department while the little darlings are still in assembly.'

He set off along the corridor and up the stairs, with Colin panting in his wake like an unfit spaniel, and wondering if he was going to last out the morning. As luck would have it they never actually got as far as Science Room 1, because just as they were turning the corner by the jar of pickled tapeworms, there was an almighty bang.

The next thing they knew, the fire alarm went off. And then all hell was let loose.

Hannah laughed so much that she choked on her Wagon Wheel.

'Exploded?' she coughed, wiping the tears from her eyes with chocolatey fingers. 'You're having me on.'

Nick's expression demonstrated that he was definitely not in the mood for having anybody on. 'It's not funny,' he said.

'What? A flagon of illicit home-brew explodes in the science stockroom and the entire school gets evacuated? It's bloody hilarious.' She heaved breath into her aching lungs. 'For God's sake lighten up, Nick, it's not as if *you* got into trouble, is it?'

It was after dinner, and they were sitting in the brand-new kitchen at home, one on either side of the scrubbed-oak table, like opponents in a chess match.

'That's not the point,' protested Nick.

'So what is the point?' demanded Hannah, though she knew exactly what he was going to say. These days it seemed she always did.

'The point is,' belaboured Nick, 'that I am deputy head of science—'

'Acting deputy head,' interrupted Hannah, more to annoy him than anything else.

'Whatever. Anyhow, I'm responsible for what goes on in the department. Didn't I tell Graham and the lads making home-brew in the stockroom was irresponsible?'

'Of course you did,' muttered Hannah, wishing she'd never started this conversation.

'Didn't I tell them it was bound to lead to trouble?' He didn't wait for an answer. 'But did they listen? Do they ever? And now look what's happened. Broken glass everywhere, and everything stinks of beer. And what if someone had been in there when it happened? A kid for example.'

'Pupils aren't allowed in there,' Hannah reminded him. 'And nobody got hurt. Hey, drink your coffee, it's going cold.'

Nick grunted, and took an ill-tempered mouthful. 'I might have guessed you'd think it was all a big joke,' he commented.

'Yeah well, we're not all emotionally constipated, you know.'

That hit home. Nick prickled like a pissed-off porcupine. 'Oh. And what's that supposed to mean?'

She laid a hand on his, as a mother might to do a troublesome schoolboy. 'Look, I know you feel you have a lot of responsibility with the job you're doing, but there's such a thing as overdoing it.'

'I don't overdo it!'

'Yes you do, you feel responsible for everything. And I mean everything. You'd feel responsible for the sky being blue if you thought you could get away with it.'

She'd hit the nail on the head and Nick knew it. He drained his coffee mug and stood up. 'I'd have thought you'd understand,' he said sullenly, 'what with running a business yourself.'

'I do understand, that's the problem. Just try and relax a bit, will you? Before you drive everybody round the bend – yourself included.'

He looked at her and their eyes met, for the first time that evening; in fact, for the first time in quite a while. They didn't go in much for love-struck gazing into each other's eyes any more; not that they ever really had. It had never been that kind of relationship. For a moment, Hannah thought ... no, was afraid ... that he might say something meaningful. But she ought to have known better.

'Got to go and pick up Lottie from your mum's. It's past her bedtime.'

Hannah watched him shove the car keys into the pocket of his styleless jeans and walk out, leaving the house filled with an atmosphere of unfinished sentences and questions never to be answered. It was like that all too often, she mused. Too many times they talked without saying anything; or had conversations that scarcely fulfilled any purpose, since both of them knew what the other was going to say before they opened their mouths.

Feeling suddenly tired, she put the coffee mugs on the draining board, and went upstairs to take off her make-up. As she crossed the landing to the main bedroom, she couldn't avoid looking at the half-finished staircase that was meant to serve the loft conversion – the last major job left to do on the house, and one that, for some unaccountable reason, they still hadn't started yet.

She laid a hand briefly on the pine steps, and felt a pang of something poignant and sad. All at once it seemed utterly aimless to her, the way those steps wound pointlessly upwards into mid-air like a string of unfulfilled promises, towards the hole in the ceiling that she and Nick had somehow never done anything with.

Just like the baby they'd never got round to making.

Later that evening, Hannah went into the boxroom and turned on the computer. There really wasn't that much else to do. Lottie had fallen asleep in the middle of complaining that she wasn't tired, and Nick was doing his lesson preparation in front of some late-night TV talk show. She could have put a skimcoat of plaster on the ceiling of the new utility room, but that would have demanded an enthusiasm and energy she just didn't feel.

As usual, most of the emails in her inbox were spam. 'Get generic Viagra DIRT CHEAP!' 'Ashamed of your manhood? Add inches NOW!' Oh, and a new one: 'Need urgent assistance with the transfer of 25 million US dollars in gold bullion.' Yeah, right. What couldn't I do with 25 million dollars though, she thought wistfully. Pay for a plasterer to come in and finish the bloody ceiling, for a start off.

Her spirits rose when she saw that there was a message from Reba. They'd been at school together, then college; but when

19

Hannah had moved back to Cheltenham, Reba had stayed on in Edinburgh.

Reba was one of those impossible women who manage to accomplish ten things at once and still find time for a French manicure. The kind who drop a sprog in the morning and are back at their desk, breastfeeding the angelic infant, by lunchtime. Unmarried, with three children by a selection of obliging friends, Reba had risen swiftly to a senior management position and firmly believed in living her life the way she planned it: without extraneous complications. And those extraneous complications included live-in lovers.

She was also the sort of woman who liked to keep her ear to the ground. 'Knowledge is power,' she would declare with a grin, carefully noting the fact that the chief executive had a weakness for busty brunettes, or eavesdropping on someone from a rival firm in a restaurant.

More than that, though, Reba loved gossip. You didn't need Friends Reunited if you had Reba: she seemed to have a direct hotline to everybody they'd known at uni, from the weird guy who peeled oranges in his pockets one-handed to the jewellery heiress who'd been kidnapped and started the third year with half an ear missing.

But, most of all, to Rhys.

'Hiya Han,' the message began. *'Your turn to write but if I wait I'll be dead before you get round to it. You OK down there? Finished that house yet?'*

Hannah's throat tightened. She wished people wouldn't keep going on about the house. It made her feel tense; she wasn't quite sure why. Skimming over that bit, and Reba's account of the twins' chickenpox, her eyes were drawn by a single word: *Rhys*.

'You'll never guess what he's into now. Mind you, he was always going to do whatever he wanted, what with his dad being who he is and with all that money behind him. Anyhow, he's on TV now! Presenting a weekend kids' pop show on cable with this fluffy blonde bit called Priscilla. Actually he's not half bad at it. Even if he is a smug bastard.

'I was on the phone to Jacqui Newman the other day, and she told me that red-haired girl with the squint from Natural Sciences is standing for Parliament . . .'

Hannah read the rest of the message, but it didn't really sink in.

Only the name 'Rhys' really registered, and that burned like acid into her flesh.

Of course, hatred was a kind of acid: a corrosive thing that ate away at you unless you could find a way to protect yourself from it. Hannah's way was to avoid thinking about the bloke who had planned her seduction like a military operation, conned her into thinking he loved her, then vanished like a pantomime villain the minute he heard about the baby.

It was an old story. She should have been less naive, but at twenty was anybody not naive – apart from cold, calculating, head-squarely-on-shoulders Rhys?

There'd been no contact between them since then, and she hadn't wanted any. In fact if she'd found herself in the same room as him she'd probably have grabbed a sharp object and inserted it into his nearest orifice. But for all that the very thought of him made her sick, she had a curious addiction to Reba's emails, a horrible fascination with the little, disjointed snippets of Rhys's charmed life. Perhaps she hoped one day to learn that something horrible had happened to him, not that it ever would. He just wasn't that kind of a guy.

One thing was for sure. If she'd ever hoped that one day he'd get in touch and ask after the child he knew nothing about, she'd long since grown out of that. Even when she was a struggling student she'd had far too much self-respect to think of asking him for money, and frankly she'd been almost relieved when he didn't get in touch. Nowadays, she was just profoundly grateful that he never had, and never ever would.

Turning off the computer, she crept into Lottie's bedroom and stood for a few minutes, watching her daughter sleep in the moonlight, a little dark-red curl straggling over her clever, stubborn little face.

Then she planted the lightest of kisses on her brow and tiptoed away.

Nick came to bed late. Hannah lay very still, feigning sleep, but he knew her too well.

'Are you awake?'

Hannah bit her lip.

'Hannah.'

She sighed. 'What? It's really late.'

He wriggled up close to her and slid an arm round her waist. Oh no, she thought, her toes curling. Not now.

'I've been thinking . . . about what we said we'd do when the house was finished.'

Hannah's mouth went dry. She played it stupid. 'What do you mean?'

Nick's hand moved to her belly. 'About having a baby. You can hardly have forgotten, we've talked about it often enough!'

She squirmed at his touch – too familiar, too brotherly, too utterly unsexual. 'Now's not the time.'

'But it's been eight years!'

'Besides . . . I'm still not sure. And we said not until the house was finished, remember?'

'But that's what I'm saying – it *is* finished!' Exasperation roughened the edges of Nick's voice. 'As near as dammit.'

Calmly but firmly, Hannah removed his hand from her stomach and rolled away. 'No it's not,' she said, clutching her pillow as if it were her only life-raft in a hostile sea. 'Not quite yet.'

Chapter 3

By the time a grim, grey dawn broke over the suburb of Tivoli, Hannah had already been up for two hours, drinking cups of tea and cleaning out the rabbits. In truth, she'd hardly slept at all. And all the time she'd been lying there next to Nick, listening to the rhythmic rise and fall of his breathing, her brain had been turning somersaults and tying itself in knots.

She sat at the kitchen table, staring out at the hutches containing all Lottie's waifs and strays, and the kennel where Doom the three-legged Rottweiler slept, his massive bottom poking out into the fresh autumn air. I love him, I love him not, she murmured to herself. I love him, I love him not. A mental flower lost its petals, grew them back and started the whole destructive process all over again. And still she was none the wiser. About all this, about her life, about Nick.

Or was it just that she wasn't admitting it to herself?

Her fingers drummed restlessly on the table top. I must have loved him when I married him, she told herself firmly. But something at the back of her mind retorted: 'Says who? Plenty of people get married for all the wrong reasons, why not you?'

There had certainly been lots of wrong ones, though she'd denied them all at the time. There she was, alone with a baby, deep in debt after struggling through college on handouts from her parents and a few hours a week at the burger bar; and suddenly there was Nick. Big, strong, dependable: the kind of man who wanted to bundle you up in his big blanket of love and make all the bad things go away.

Safe.

Hannah tried hard to think back to their brief courtship; to the way she'd felt when he'd proposed, the first time they'd slept together, the day she'd become Mrs Nick Steadman. But somehow she'd managed not to retain any really strong memories of that time. Could that be because she'd never had any in the first place? The ironic thing was, she had violent, vivid memories of every second she'd spent with Rhys: memories she didn't even want. And sometimes it took all the strength in her to keep them from resurfacing.

A big lump of lead plummeted from the heavens and landed in the pit of her stomach. I was never in love with Nick, she thought. That's the truth of it. Not even on the day I married him. I thought I was, but I thought a lot of things that weren't right. I was confused, lonely, looking for someone to rescue me . . .

Then she felt guilty and started telling herself that couldn't be so. Of course she'd loved him; she wouldn't have taken advantage of a nice man like Nick, not like that. Surely.

Maybe she had loved him and maybe she hadn't. Perhaps there was just no way of knowing, so many years on from the event. And anyway, she told herself, what really mattered was the way she felt now. The trouble was, that was something she tried not to think about.

Or possibly she was looking at this the wrong way. Maybe she had loved Nick – even loved him still. It was just that she'd never been *in love* with him. Not, at any rate, in the way she'd been in love with Rhys.

In any case I've changed, she thought. In fact I've changed so much in the last eight years that I hardly recognise myself. I'm more confident, independent, ambitious – and I'm fine with that.

The trouble is, Nick . . . She glanced across to the wedding photo on the pine dresser. The trouble is, you haven't changed at all.

Philomena Carson was not a happy woman, as was obvious to anyone who spent more than a couple of minutes at the salon. Her short, dark, fortyish Irish frame positively sparked with suppressed anger and resentment; in fact, she even managed to cut hair angrily. Everybody said spiky styles were her speciality.

The cause of Philomena's discontent was close to home. In fact it was currently spreadeagled in its favourite armchair in front of the television, can of lager in one hand and *The Racing*

Post in the other. Its name was Bernard, it claimed to have a bad back, and it hadn't done a day's work in ten years.

Worse, when suppressed tension turned to anger, Bernard had a habit of arguing with his fists. Mind you, Philomena argued right back – and she had an impressive left hook for one so small. Still, you couldn't call it anything but a turbulent marriage, and that was if you were being charitable. People often wondered why she didn't just pack her suitcase and get the hell out. Perhaps because there was nothing to get out for.

But there was one thing that kept Philomena going. The one great love of her life: gossip.

By the time Hannah had dropped Lottie off at school and driven to work, Philomena was already on her second cut and blow, deep in excited conversation with Gloria, the fount of all scandal. With her colourful love life, encompassing just about every single male in town and quite a few of the others as well, Gloria was in fact a sort of one-woman Reuters of gossip.

'So I told him, "Sweetie, I wouldn't touch that with rubber gloves and tweezers; for God's sake put it back in your pants".'

Philomena's eyes widened. 'You never did!'

'As I live and breathe.' Gloria took a drag on a black Russian cigarette. 'Honest to God Phil, some of these blokes wouldn't know a bar of soap if it walked in and unwrapped itself.' She went misty-eyed. 'And he was drop-dead gorgeous, too.'

'With his clothes on,' Philomena reminded her.

'Well, yeah. But what a waste.'

Hannah went through into the staff restroom and hung up her coat. She couldn't help smiling at the sight of all the salon staff – not to mention the customers – straining for details of Gloria's latest adventures. Of course, for the full low-down they'd have to wait till later, when Philomena would spill the beans over coffee and a vanilla cream doughnut. Hannah sometimes felt gossip was the only way Philomena had of exerting some kind of control over the world.

Please God, don't let me end up like you, thought Hannah, slipping on her white uniform tunic and emerging from the restroom: trapped and hopeless and living on other people's lives.

It was another busy morning, and the salon door seemed to clatter and jingle continuously above the background hum of

25

conversation, the click of scissors and the drone of Chelt FM, the local radio station. Hardly surprising really, since Thursdays were half price for pensioners and a plate of fancy biscuits thrown in. Consequently this was the day you would always find Miss Fabian, Mrs De'Ath and Mrs Lorrimer under the dryers, having identical shampoo and sets in preparation for their weekly night out at the bingo.

'This tea's cold,' commented Mrs Lorrimer, waving her cup at Claire, the large, jolly and extremely Welsh senior stylist, who was in charge of the hair salon whenever Maxine wasn't around. If life was a game of Monopoly, as Nick was apt to say, then Claire was definitely the Community Chest. It loomed up before her like the figurehead on a galleon, and seemed to precede her into any room by a good two seconds. Not that Claire minded. Her heart was as big as her chest, and when it came to parties she was always the one leading the conga.

'Of course it's cold, you've been gabbing for half an hour!' Claire swiped the cup in mock exasperation. 'I suppose you'll be wanting a fresh one now?'

'If it's not too much trouble. And some more biscuits. They are still free though, aren't they?'

'Well, seeing as it's you.'

Miss Fabian drained her cup and held it out like a winsome Oliver Twist. 'I'll have some more too.'

'And me,' agreed Mrs De'Ath. 'No Jammie Dodgers though, they gum up my plate.'

'Off to the bingo tonight are we, ladies?' enquired Jason the junior as he sashayed past on the end of a broom, trying to look cool and failing.

'Course we are, dear,' beamed Mrs Lorrimer. 'Every Thursday for ten years we've been going, never missed a jackpot night.'

'Never won anything much though, have we?' sighed Miss Fabian. 'Apart from that weekend in Torquay, and I had to pay a single room supplement.'

'No, Clarice dear,' Mrs Lorrimer corrected her, 'We *all* paid your single room supplement. Share and share alike, split everything three ways, that's our motto.'

'Just like the Three Musketeers eh?' chuckled Jason, trying to edge away. 'Only ... er ... prettier.'

'Oooh, did you hear that? He's such a cheeky boy, isn't he?'

simpered Mrs De'Ath as Miss Fabian discreetly pinched Jason's bottom. 'Give us a kiss and bring us luck, eh?'

'You never know,' giggled Miss Fabian as the three of them mobbed the unfortunate Jason, 'tonight might be the night.' The wink she gave him left him in two minds as to what she was talking about, and he turned crimson to the roots of his highlights.

'Yes, well, good luck then.' He wiped a smear of dribble and pink lipstick off his cheek, thanking his lucky stars that at least Mrs Lorrimer had kept her tongue to herself.

Hannah suppressed a grin. Jason was such a babe in arms, bless him; and the three old dears were more than a match for him. She supposed she'd better rescue him.

'I think you've missed a bit,' she said, tapping Jason on the shoulder and pointing to a minuscule tuft of hair on the tiled floor.

He peered at it vacantly. 'Oh. Oh yes.'

'Don't you think you'd better get on with your work?' hinted Hannah. 'Sorry to whisk him away from you, ladies, but we can't have the salon looking untidy now, can we?'

Jason escaped with a look of gratitude, and Hannah checked the appointments book at reception. A couple of neck and back massages, a hot wax treatment, another electrolysis session, and . . . ugh. Councillor Plowright. She looked up as Philomena went past in search of more red hair dye. 'Gee thanks. Councillor Plowright for a full body massage. Christmas is coming early this year.'

Philomena shrugged. 'He likes you. What's wrong with that?'

Hannah lowered her voice. 'He's a creep, that's what.'

Philomena gave a small, dry laugh. 'Hannah love, if I had ten quid for every creepy client I've had, I'd be running this place, not you. Don't you worry about him, he's harmless. Just make sure he gives you a nice big tip.'

Hannah was still thinking about the delights of an hour with Councillor Plowright as she finished off the hot wax treatment and peeled off her disposable gloves. Maybe she ought to find some excuse not to treat him any more. On the other hand, maybe she was just being oversensitive . . .

There was a knock at the door and Hannah started. An hour early? Even Councillor Plowright wasn't *that* keen.

'Come in.'

The door opened a little way and a head of plaster-dusted dark hair thrust its way inside. 'Hi. Thought I'd better knock, in case you had somebody with you.' Jay came in, brushing the white dust off his trendy black suit.

'Hi Jay. What happened to you? You look like you fell in a bag of flour.'

Maxine's husband gave the broad, open smile Hannah liked so much. Nothing was hiding behind that smile. In fact Jay never hid anything. Others might call a spade a spade; Jay would actually pick it up and dig a hole with it. 'Oh, just popped over to see how the lads are getting on refitting that shop on Clarence Street. One thing leads to another, and the next thing you know I'm up a ladder nailing on plasterboard.'

'But you're supposed to be the boss!'

Jay shrugged good-naturedly. 'Ah well, does me good to keep my hand in once in a while, remind myself where I started out. Besides, the shopfitting business is so dependent on how the economy's doing – you never know when you're going to need a trade again.'

Hannah raised an eyebrow as she laid snowy-white towels out for her next client. 'You're sounding a bit doom-laden. Something bad happened?'

'No, just been on a routine visit to the accountant. She always makes me nervous, that woman. Like she's the police and I'm about to be caught with my hand in the till.'

'Did you mention – ?'

Jay raked a hand through his thick hair, dislodging an avalanche of powdery white dust. 'No point. The salon's doing great so far, but when it comes to spare capital . . .' He blew out his cheeks. 'Sorry, Hannah, but I'm not even going to think about investing in a new salon at the moment, it's way too risky. Unless you've got a spare twenty grand you haven't told me about?'

'Ha, ha, very amusing.' Hannah whisked a clean towel away from Jay's far-from-clean hands. 'Have you seen the price of school uniforms lately?'

'That's the other thing,' Jay went on. 'Maxine's started talking about having a baby again. Next year maybe.'

'Yeah, I know. It'd be nice for you guys to start a family.'

'I guess. Maxine says she wants to have kids before her bits drop off. Myself, I reckon it's just 'cause she wants to buy all those cute little baby outfits. What's this?' Jay wriggled uncomfortably on his chair and extracted a bent CD from underneath him. 'Oops. Didn't know it was there.'

Hannah took one look at the state of it and threw it in the bin. 'Jay, that was my "Andean Rapture", you can only get it by mail order! Now I'll have to give Councillor Plowright "Moods of Meditation", and that always jumps when it gets to track six.' Serve him right, she thought.

'Sorry. I'll buy you another one. Hey, didn't you say you and Nick were thinking of having a kid once the house was fi—'

'Not you as well!' snapped Hannah. 'Why is the whole world suddenly trying to get me pregnant?'

'Ah.' Jay blinked, rather taken aback. 'Mother-in-law pushing for more grandchildren is she? Started sending baby magazines so Nick can leave them round the house?'

'What, Julie? Good God no, she's so laid-back she's horizontal. No, it's Nick. He just gets this bee in his bonnet from time to time . . .'

'And he's got it now, right?'

'Right.'

'Suppose you can't really blame the guy,' mused Jay. 'I mean, I know he's accepted Lottie brilliantly and all that, but he's bound to want one of his own, isn't he? Carry on the proud family name and all that.'

'As far as he's concerned, Lottie is his own,' replied Hannah, more than a tad defensively. 'He's the only dad she's ever had.'

'All the same,' Jay insisted, finding a boiled sweet and popping it into his mouth, 'every man's got this thing about having a little boy to take to the match.'

'Nick? Go to the match?' laughed Hannah. 'More likely take him to the Natural History Museum and show him the parasitic worms collection.'

'Well, whatever floats your boat.

The cool blue phone on the soothing green windowsill chirruped gently into life. 'Hannah? It's Claire. Your half-past is here, shall I send him up?' A barely suppressed giggle entered Claire's lilting voice. 'He says he's been looking forward all week to seeing you again.'

Clarence Plowright's moon-shaped face spoke of the many sumptuous lunches he had enjoyed during his career as a litigation solicitor and, latterly, a town councillor. He was the sort of man who could never manage to look casual, no matter what he wore, and today's Hugo Boss leisure ensemble made him look like he'd just walked off the set of some Californian soap.

'Hannah, darling!' He held out a gift-wrapped box. 'Just a little something for you.'

She looked at it, aghast. 'Really Mr Plowright, I—'

'Clarence, please. I'd like to think we're friends. Good friends.'

'You really don't need to give me presents; in fact I'd rather you didn't, I'm just doing my job.'

He laughed indulgently and patted her shoulder. 'Of course you are. But every woman likes presents. You open it later; I think you'll be pleased with it.' He winked. 'If not, you let Uncle Clarence know and Santa will fetch you something else, just you see if he doesn't. Believe me, he can't wait to fill your stocking.'

He rubbed his hands together and began peeling off his tie. 'Now – how'd you like me?'

'Down to your underwear as usual please, Mr Pl—Clarence. I'll just pop outside and mix up some oils while you get undressed.'

Something that was more of a leer than a smile spread across his face. 'No need to leave on my account, Hannah. Actually I'd quite like it if you stayed . . .'

Pervert, thought Hannah, with a backward glance at the box on the back seat of the car. As a last thought she threw it into the boot and locked it. She didn't like to imagine the misunderstandings if Nick found a red nylon basque on show for all to see.

First thing tomorrow, she told herself as she walked up the front path, she would wrap the horrible thing up again and send it right back to Clarence Plowright, with a curt note about his manners. He might be 'harmless', but one more incident like this, and she was going to have to ban him from the salon.

When she got inside, she found Lottie bopping around the hall, more like a mad pogo stick than an old lady of nine and three days. 'Mum, guess what, I'm the Angel of the Lord!'

'What?'

'The Angel of the Lord! In the Christmas play. Miss Grimshaw said she was going to give me the part because I've got a nice voice and then Portia Williams said it wasn't fair her only being Mrs Innkeeper only it is because she always gets what she wants and I was only the donkey last year and the outfit smelt funny and—'

'Whoa there, slow down!' laughed Nick, coming in through the back door and dumping a stack of coursework on the kitchen table. 'What's all this? You're going to be an angel? What d'you reckon, Mum, typecasting or what?'

'Oh I don't know about that,' replied Hannah straight-facedly. 'I think angels tidy their rooms occasionally.'

'I tidied my room!' protested Lottie. 'I did! Once,' she admitted as an afterthought.

Nick tousled her hair and tickled her in the ribs until she was breathless with laughter as well as excitement. 'You know what? I think this calls for ice cream.' He reached into his pocket and took out a five-pound note. 'What flavour? Salt and vinegar? Cheese and onion? Steak and chips?'

'Noooo!' she giggled in mock-horror. 'Chocolate! Double chocolate chip. With sprinkles.'

And she knew from the look of pride on her daddy's face that whatever she asked for, she would get.

'She's really bright, you know,' remarked Nick later that evening as he and Hannah sat side by side on the sofa, ostensibly watching something about agoraphobic dolphins.

'Hmm?' Hannah turned to look at him across the six-inch gap that always seemed to open up between them, no matter how small the sofa.

'Lottie, she's a bright girl. Doing really well at school. And she's especially gifted in music. I was wondering if we ought to get her some specialist tuition.'

'Maybe.' There was doubt in Hannah's mind. 'But I don't want her pushed too hard.' That's what happened to me, she thought, and look where I ended up: jumping into bed with the first man who said he loved me, and struggling to bring up a child before I'd even finished university.

'No, of course not. But we have to be responsible parents, don't we? Do the best for her.'

Responsible, thought Hannah. That word again. Doesn't he ever think about anything but responsibility?

'Yes, and maybe the best for her is just having a happy childhood.'

'Not if it means she wastes talents that would make her happy later on in her life,' pointed out Nick.

'Nick, that's not going to happen. You said it yourself, she's doing well at a good school and she's happy. What more could we ask for?'

The clock on the wall clunked noisily onward, notching up a few more tedious seconds. On the television screen, a dolphin was having a panic attack, while a bunch of scientists stood round arguing about who knew best, and whether they could psychoanalyse it by means of its clicks and squeaks. There was a long silence, not so much tense as flabby, with no real expectation of being filled. Hannah supposed that was what happened when old married people got a bit too familiar with each other.

'The new guttering's looking good,' she commented.

'Yes.'

'What do you think – pale blue or primrose yellow for the rendering?'

'Dunno. Pale blue I guess. We don't really want to live in a house that looks like a giant lump of cheese.'

More silence. From up above, they could hear the floorboards creak as Lottie tried to tiptoe around her bedroom, playing whatever kids played when they thought no one was listening.

'About last night,' they both said at once.

'Go on,' said Nick.

'No – you first.'

'Well, OK. I didn't mean to pressurise you, I'm sorry if I did. It's just ... oh, you know. This baby thing ... I guess it needs to be talked through, doesn't it?'

Hannah's fingers clenched, the nails digging into her palm. 'We've talked about it loads of times,' she hedged.

'I meant properly.' He took her hand in his, for the first time in ages, and it felt strange – like the hand of a very distant uncle, or a friend you hadn't seen since schooldays. 'We are a family, aren't we, Hannah?'

She cocked her head on one side and looked at him oddly. 'Of course we are. Why?'

'I just ... worry sometimes, I guess. With Lottie not being mine. And being a dad, well, it's a difficult job at the best of times. I want to be sure I'm doing it right.'

She gave his hand a squeeze. 'Hey, listen. You're doing a great job. Lottie worships you. You're her daddy, for goodness' sake. I bet she'd hardly notice if I disappeared in a puff of smoke tomorrow, but not her beloved daddy!'

'You reckon I make an OK job of being a dad then?'

'Uh-huh.'

He let her hand fall back onto the sofa cushions. 'I just wish I could be so sure.'

'Nick, nobody's ever sure. That's what being a parent's all about.'

Oh God, thought Hannah, in an agony of guilt; did I ever really know this man? Did I? Here I am, owing him this massive debt of gratitude, and all he wants from me is one little baby, and somehow I can't do it . . . I just *can't.*

Or maybe you could one day, said a quiet voice inside her head. Just not with him.

Saturday was the only day when Nick allowed himself a small dose of hard-won laziness. On Saturdays Hannah often worked right through, after dropping Lottie off at her weekend drama class, while Nick had the whole day off.

For once Nick had nothing to do – if you didn't count marking, washing the car, putting up the new garden shed and feeding the menagerie – until lunchtime; so he padded around the house in his dressing gown, dropping toast crumbs and reading *Fortean Times.*

The minute the envelope came through the letter box he knew it was from his mum and dad. There was no mistaking his dad's crazily sloping handwriting and the French stamp was a bit of a giveaway, along with the faint smell of goat dung.

He tore it open eagerly. Other parents might send their offspring emails, but Clive and Julie would have stuck with goosefeather quill pens if they could have got away with it. Besides, the electricity supply to their isolated French smallholding was erratic at the best of times, so until somebody invented a clockwork computer snail-mail and the occasional phone call would have to suffice.

Dear All, he read, *Weather a bit of a washout and rain damaged part of the grape harvest, but we managed to rescue enough to have a laugh treading them with the locals. Your mother's feet are still purple and that was a fortnight ago.'* A note underneath, in different handwriting, ran: *Don't believe a word your father says, he's been "testing" cider all day!*

Nick sat down on the sofa, smiling as he read the latest instalment of his parents' new life. They'd come a long way from civil service jobs in Shepperton, but this had always been their dream – long before *A Year in Provence* made that sort of thing fashionable. Along the way, they'd instilled their own love of the country into Nick; and, as he read, he felt the lavender fields and the big, sunburned, empty spaces tug at his heart.

Ah, holes in the roof, no mains sanitation, chickens pecking around the kitchen floor . . . He glanced around the chic, sensible home he and Hannah had spent so long creating and felt a small pang of regret. He knew in his heart that Hannah had a point. Even so, there was something to be said for chaos, when it came accompanied by beauty, freedom and a lot of love.

He imagined his mum and dad hugging and giggling, and generally behaving like irresponsible teenagers. So different from the way he'd become. But maybe not so different from the way he could be, if . . .

The letter resting on his lap, he gazed into the far distance. It would be so good to get away from the rat race. And what a fantastic experience for Lottie, not to mention the new baby.

The baby. His pulse quickened.

Well, all he had to do was persuade Hannah. Surely it couldn't be that difficult.

Chapter 4

'What's up?' said Maxine for the third time; and this time it just about registered on Hannah's consciousness.

'Hmm? Oh, nothing much.'

It was Friday lunchtime and they had escaped from the salon to the relative calm of the High Street, to sit on the benches outside the Regent Arcade, eat their sandwiches and have a therapeutic moan. Only it was no fun because Hannah wasn't moaning. In fact she wasn't doing a lot of anything, just gazing apathetically at the toes of her white work shoes.

'Nothing much?' Maxine took a bite of peanut butter sandwich. 'That means something. Come on, out with it. It's not Councillor What's-his-name again, is it?'

'No.'

'Lottie then?'

'Lottie's fine. She's playing an angel in the Christmas play.'

'Aw, cute! So why aren't you smiling?' Maxine wiped a crumb from the corner of her mouth. 'You and Nick haven't had a row, have you?'

Hannah let out a faintly exasperated sigh. 'No, we haven't had a row.'

'Good, because you two *never* have rows.'

'Maybe we should then.' Hannah picked her cheese roll to bits and threw lumps of it into the little mob of pigeons at her feet.

Maxine looked ever so slightly concerned. She'd known Hannah for a long time, and she'd never been quite like this before. 'Look, it's OK if it's something you don't want to talk about,' she began, 'but sometimes bottling things up just makes you feel worse. Like the time that bloke attacked me in the churchyard and Jay didn't know a thing about it until I burst into tears in Mcdonald's. The thing is—'

'Nick wants a baby,' cut in Hannah quietly.

'O . . . k.' Maxine cocked her head on one side. 'But that's good. Isn't it?'

'If you'd asked me a while back I might have said yes, but now I'm not sure any more.'

'But you've been talking about having a baby for years! I thought it was Nick who was putting the brakes on.'

Hannah slumped back onto the bench, crumpling the empty paper bag in her fist. 'It was. "Yes, it'd be lovely to have another one," he used to say, "but not until we're more secure financially, not until the house is finished, not until Hell freezes over." And then all of a sudden it's "Let's have one right now, 'cause I want one and bugger what you feel about it."'

'Oh, I'm sure he never said that.'

'It's what he meant.'

'Maybe he's just realised you can't be cautious all your life. He's coming up to forty, isn't he? That can really make a bloke, you know, *think*.'

'I guess,' conceded Hannah. 'But the thing is, when we got married I was desperate for us to have a baby – I wanted to give him a child of his own, something we could share. And then Nick kept saying no. And the more he said no, the more I thought, OK, if I'm not going to be playing stay-at-home-mum . . .'

'You'd better get yourself a life?'

'Exactly. So what happens? I get myself trained, build up something I really care about – and suddenly it's drop-every-thing-and-repopulate-the-world time. Just because Nick says so.'

Maxine held out a bag of chocolate buttons. 'Here, have plenty,' she said. 'You sound like you need them more than I do.'

They munched in silence. 'This is something you can talk about though, isn't it?' ventured Maxine. 'You know, negotiate?'

'We could,' replied Hannah, 'but we won't. We don't talk properly any more, not about anything that matters. I'm not even sure we can remember how.'

Maxine was starting to feel uncomfortable, suspecting that she'd thrust her unwary hand into a wasps' nest. 'Well, that's the thing about being married, isn't it? After a while you don't need to say stuff any more, you just sort of . . . know.'

Or in Nick's case, you think you know, mused Hannah darkly. Not that it was really his fault. If she'd not let the pair of them fall into the habit of him leading and her following, maybe things could have turned out differently. As it was, each of them was acting on assumptions about the other that were probably well wide of the mark.

Maxine said the first thing that came into her head, just to break the silence. 'Jay and I are thinking of starting a family.'

'Good for you,' said Hannah.

'Next year, before my ovaries start packing up. It runs in the family you see, early menopause.' She lowered her voice to a dramatic stage whisper. 'My mum's shrivelled up at thirty-four, you know. The consultant said they were like two dried-up sultanas.' It suddenly occurred to Maxine that Hannah wasn't that far off thirty-four herself, and she added hastily, 'Not that that's going to happen to you or anything . . .'

'Great,' sighed Hannah. 'First Nick and now you.'

'What?'

'Look: if I want a baby I'll have one, and if I don't—' She stopped short, feeling angry tears prickling the undersides of her eyelids. This was silly, so silly. Her fingers fumbled in her handbag as a tear escaped and ran down the side of her nose.

'Hannah? What's the matter, what are you looking for?'

'Nothing,' she sniffed. Then: 'A tissue.'

'You're crying!' Maxine took a packet of tissues out of her jacket pocket and handed one to Hannah.

'No I'm not,' Hannah retorted feebly. Then she buried her face in Maxine's shoulder and sobbed her heart out.

That evening, Hannah did the ironing and watched TV while Lottie challenged Nick to endless games of 'Operation'.

'I win!' she exulted as Nick's hand shook and the buzzer went off yet again. 'That's fourteen jelly babies you owe me, Daddy!' Her keen eyes narrowed. 'You're not letting me win, are you?'

He poked her in the ribs and made her giggle. 'Would I do a thing like that?' he asked innocently. 'Would I?'

'You always let Mum win at Scrabble.'

Nick and Hannah's eyes met; it was an uncomfortable sensation for a split second, then Nick smiled. 'No I don't, your mum's much better at spelling than I am.'

'We haven't played Scrabble in ages,' Hannah observed quietly. She was remembering all those the nights they'd spent in the caravan – snuggled up together and wrapped in blankets against the cold, playing board games all night because Lottie was teething and nobody could get any sleep. They'd been perfectly happy then, she was sure they had – well, in their own low-key way. But now . . .

She had a feeling Nick was remembering those times too. He looked away. 'No, well . . . Come on, let's play again. Double or quits.'

Watching them play, Hannah felt a dull ache in her chest. An ache that reminded her of the way she had felt when her best friend at school had died. The sort of ache that filled a lonely space where something precious had once been. He's such a great father to her, she thought, caught between sentimental pleasure and sadness. Of course he wants to be a dad himself, why shouldn't he?

You can't hurt him, her conscience urged her. You know you can't. He picked you up and cared for you when you and Lottie had nothing. You owe him everything. And you care about him too, you know you do. All he's asking is for you to make him happy.

Is that such a difficult thing to do?

'What's it like, Mark?' asked Nick over lunchtime pie and chips in the greasy spoon café opposite the school gates.

His friend and colleague Mark Newman forked the straggling end of a chip into his open mouth. 'The pie? Bloody horrible. Know what they used to call this stuff when I was at college? Space Pie – a pie with a space where the meat should be.'

'Not the pie! God, do you ever think about anything other than food?'

'Not often,' Mark confessed, his rather pudgy physique testifying to his love of carbohydrates and hydrogenated fat. Mark was a simple soul, devoid of ambition, for whom near-perfect happiness could be summed up as a full stomach, a cosy armchair and a nice soft woman. He shared quite a few of Nick's pet likes and dislikes; perhaps that was why they'd hit it off straight away when Nick came to teach at the school. 'Besides,' he mumbled through a mouthful of food, 'I've got to keep my strength up. So what were you on about then?'

'I meant what we were talking about before – you know, you and Caroline and the twins. What's it like being a new dad?'

Mark considered for a moment. 'Bloody knackering,' he concluded. 'You think you're tired at the end of the summer term, after all the exams and the marking? Forget it. This is tired with a capital T. Think no sleep for a month, and somebody constantly screaming in your ear.'

'So you don't recommend it then?'

Mark grinned. 'Are you kidding? It's great. I never thought being a physical and mental wreck could be so much fun. Why?' He lowered his voice though there was nobody within earshot. 'Hey, Hannah's not pregnant, is she?'

'No, not that.' Nick toyed with a baked bean. 'It's just . . . oh, I guess I've been doing a lot of thinking lately. Do you ever have . . . doubts?'

'All the time. What about?'

'Yourself and . . .' He swallowed, wishing he'd never started this. 'And your, er, relationships.'

Mark scratched his head. Psychology to him was a question of whether to wear the red socks or the blue ones. 'Well I suppose having a couple of babies in the house disrupts the old sex life a bit,' he admitted, 'but I expect that'll sort itself out. And Caroline gets a bit weepy.'

'What about being a dad? Do you think you're a good one?'

Now Mark looked really perplexed. You could almost see his brain trying to bulge out from underneath his thinning blond hair. 'I've only been one for three months,' he pointed out. 'But I'm quite good at wiping bottoms. Why?' he wondered, rather belatedly.

Nick shrugged. 'Oh, no special reason. It's just that sometimes I think, what if I'm a bad father and I just don't realise?'

'You get on great with Lottie, don't you?'

'Well, yes . . . but I'm not technically her dad, am I? What if we have a baby and then everything gets worse instead of better? What if a baby's not the thing that's missing?'

'That's a lot of what-ifs,' commented Mark.

'I know.' Nick prodded at his pastry unenthusiastically. 'The thing is – look, you won't say anything to anyone else, will you?' He knew Mark wouldn't; he trusted him implicitly. But somehow he had to go through the motions of asking.

'Me? What do you think?' He stopped chewing. 'Why, what's wrong?'

What's right? thought Nick. But instead of saying so, he tried to explain about all the years he and Hannah had talked about having a baby and never got round to it. About all the pathetic excuses he'd made – the unfinished house, the lack of money – when all it had really boiled down to was fear. Fear that adding to their family would damage or even destroy what they had.

And now, he wasn't even sure there was anything much left to spoil.

Mark was gobsmacked. 'Nick, mate. Surely you're not saying ...? But you and Hannah, you get on so well!'

It's true, thought Nick, we do. Never a cross word. Trouble is, never a passionate one either. 'Oh, we'll be OK,' he said, with more optimism than he truly felt. 'It's just that now I've decided there's nothing to lose and we should go for it and have the baby, I think Hannah's got cold feet, God knows why.

'And now even I'm beginning to wonder if I'm making the right decision.'

'Bad day?' asked Hannah, taking Nick's coat when he staggered in out of the autumn drizzle, laden briefcase in either hand.

'Not great. Everybody's getting uptight about the Christmas resits, and the way Harry Turnbull's going I'm not sure he's even going to last out that long. They've given him RE with 3B on a Friday afternoon.'

Hannah made sympathetic noises. She'd only met Harry once, and he'd struck her as the sort of nice, middle-aged ex-research scientist who ought to have more sense than to decide suddenly that he wanted to teach in a comprehensive school.

'RE? But he's a science teacher!'

'Tell that to the deputy head. Apparently we all have to muck in now we're one and a half members of staff down.'

'It'll be two and a half if Harry Turnbull gets eaten alive. Can't you swap him with somebody?'

'Only Colin Rooney, and the lad's so new you can still see the price label on the back of his head. No, looks like Harry'll just have to cope.' He flopped down into a chair in the front room. 'Like the rest of us.' Belatedly, he added, 'How about you?'

She shrugged. 'Had a bit of a headache. Did my last leg-wax and then shut up shop early for the day.'

'Lottie?'

'Over at Melanie-Anne's, her mum's bringing her home in an hour or so.' She sat down in the armchair opposite him. Her mouth was dry. 'Shouldn't we be talking or something?' she asked after a few moments' silence.

'What?'

'Talking. Shouldn't we be having a conversation, like people do?'

'Oh. What about?' Picking up the TV remote, he turned on the news.

'I don't know, anything.' Anything but babies, she thought. And then she thought again, maybe we should be brave and talk about just that; then perhaps we could sort things out between us, clear the air. 'You know what you were saying, the other night?'

'Hmm?'

'I just wanted to say I'm sorry I ...' She could tell he was barely listening, and that irritated her. 'Are you listening?'

'Of course I am.'

'No you're not. What did I just say?'

He looked at her. 'I dunno, something about the other night?' He rubbed his temple with the heel of his hand. 'Look Han, is this important? Only I think I'm getting a headache too. Can't it wait until some other time?'

Chapter 5

At seventy-six years old, Herbie Flowers had done it all; and anything he hadn't done, he'd watched, listened to or heard about. In any event, that was what he reckoned. And Herbie reckoned a lot; he had opinions on just about everything, and wasn't sparing with them either.

Consequently, just about everyone on C Wing in Her Majesty's Prison Stonehill knew that Herbie thought he'd never see the outside world again – unless you counted viewing it from the inside of a wooden box. Herbie 'The Touch' Flowers was class, see. Thirty years ago, he'd been one of the West of England's most successful jewel-thieves – or he would have been if he hadn't kept getting caught. And the authorities knew it; that much was obvious. They knew you couldn't set a man like Herbie Flowers free; that would be like dropping a lighted match into a barrel of dynamite. Society just couldn't cope with the one-man crime wave that'd ensue.

Not that he was entirely unhappy in prison. Thanks to a couple of sympathetic warders and a bank robber down the landing who had a soft spot for him, he had his home comforts – even a budgerigar called Reggie Kray, who hated people who wore uniforms, and could swear any East End gangster under the table. More comforts, in fact, than he would have had if he'd really been at home, since on her infrequent visits his prim and proper daughter had made it quite clear he was an embarrassment to the entire family.

Well, stuff 'em. He was quite OK here, thank you very much.

He was putting the finishing touches to his latest matchstick model when there was a dainty knock and the cell door swung open. It was Sharon, that nice young social worker.

'Hello, Mr Flowers.' Nobody, but nobody called him Mr Flowers. Come to that, nobody knocked before they came in either. It made him feel positively important. 'Gosh, that's nice,' she gushed. 'What is it? Stonehenge?'

'Er, yes,' he replied, although it was supposed to be the Albert Hall. You had to encourage them by doing this rehabilitation rubbish, even if you were crap at it.

'Aren't you clever? Guess what, Mr Flowers – you've got another parole hearing coming up, isn't that exciting?'

That was a bit of a bolt from the blue. 'What? But I thought after last time—'

'Ah well, you see, somebody put in a good word for you, didn't they?' she beamed. 'And do you know what?' His heart sank even before the words emerged from her mouth. 'This time, we all think you've got a really good chance of getting out.'

'I don't believe it!' exclaimed Claire, rushing into the salon brandishing the lunchtime edition of the *Cheltenham Courant*. She was so animated that her bosom was quivering in her low-cut T-shirt like an enormous strawberry jelly. 'Have you seen this? Have you?'

Heads bobbed up. Gloria stopped reading *Heat* under the dryer and strained to listen.

'Go on, what is it now?' asked Maxine through a mouthful of hairbrush. 'They're turning the Town Hall into a lap-dancing club?'

At this, Jason left off shampooing; his scraggy head spun round with interest. 'Hey, they're not, are they?'

'Don't be daft, bonehead.' Claire held up the page one headline for everyone to see: CHELTENHAM PENSIONER SCOOPS JACKPOT. Underneath it was a picture of a dazed-looking Clarice Fabian and her pug Bertie, flanked by Mrs De'Ath, Mrs Lorrimer and a man with an orange tan and a cheque almost as big as himself. 'Look: it's one of our old ladies! She's only gone and won the national jackpot at bingo.'

'Well, good luck to her,' said Philomena, managing to make good luck sound like a mortal sin.

'How much?' demanded Jason, swathing his client's head in a towel and bounding over to snatch the newspaper with soapy hands. 'Wow! Have you seen this? Do you reckon she wants a toy-boy?'

'Well, you'll be looking for another job if you don't mop that water off the floor,' replied Maxine sternly. 'Have you never heard of health hazards?' She looked him up and down. 'Speaking of which, when's the last time you washed that T-shirt?'

'It's supposed to look like this!' he protested. 'It's distressed.'

Before Maxine had thought of a suitable riposte, Claire had started reading out chunks of the article. '"It won't change my life," said Miss Fabian—'

'Yeah, right,' snorted Jason.

Claire glared at him and went on. '. . . enjoying a celebratory sherry with her close friends June Lorrimer and Lavinia De'Ath . . .'

Gloria wrinkled her nose. 'Lavinia? Poor cow. As if being called Mrs De'Ath wasn't bad enough.'

'According to Mrs Lorrimer, the three friends have been playing at the Sunlight Bingo Hall every Thursday night for fifteen years, and have a pact that if any of them wins anything, they share it between them.'

'That's nice.' Philomena nodded approvingly. 'Don't you think that's nice, Mrs Kenworthy?' The client in the chair ducked as Philomena swung round and her sharp cutting scissors whisked past one ear.

'Miss Fabian puts her big win down to—' Claire bounced excitedly, knocking a stand-up ad for hair colour off the reception desk. 'Hey, listen to this! 'Puts it down to her lucky chair at the Split Ends hair salon in Cheltenham! "Whenever I sit in that chair, I always win something," she says. "Even if it's only a few pounds."'

Maxine burst out laughing. 'I've heard some rubbish,' she commented, 'but that takes some beating. Still, what does it matter? As long as the old dears are having a good time.'

'Maybe we should do something nice for them next time they come in,' mused Claire, easing the waistband of her trousers up to cover the overstretched pink lace of a minute thong. 'Get a cake or some wine or something.'

'If they haven't all moved to some posh salon, now they're in the money,' pointed out Maxine. 'Somewhere where they don't fall arse over tip on a wet floor,' she added with a pointed look at Jason, who was staring dreamily into space with a mop in one hand. Claire jabbed him in the ribs.

'Oh – what? Oh, right.' Belatedly, he started mopping while Claire rescued his soggy client. 'Do you think if I sat in the lucky chair I'd make enough to pay that back rent I owe?'

'Dream on, Jace,' cut in Hannah, coming down the stairs from the beauty suite. 'Didn't anyone ever tell you magic only works in fairy tales?'

Magic wasn't something Lottie believed in any more. She might have done when she was seven, maybe even eight, but definitely not now she was nine. Nine was nearly ten, and ten was practically a teenager, which was the next best thing to being completely grown-up.

The trouble with being almost an adult was that you started feeling responsible for things – things you couldn't control. Like Mum and Daddy. You wanted them to be happy and lovey-dovey all the time, but sometimes you could tell that they weren't, and that started you thinking. Were they unhappy because of something you'd done and didn't even realise?

That night, she was having trouble sleeping. For a long time, she lay on her side watching the street light outside shining through the curtains, picking out dark faces in the patterned fabric. She wasn't scared; they were friendly faces. When you were an only child you needed to people your world from your imagination, otherwise there were times when you were uncomfortably aware of your own one-ness.

When she got bored with that, she listened for interesting sounds: foxes in the allotments across the way; people coming home late from doing exciting and glamorous things. But all she was really aware of was the drone of voices from downstairs.

It was only Mum and Daddy talking. But something in the tone of their voices tied a little knot in her tummy, like the feeling she got before she did her dancing exams.

Creeping out of bed, owl hot-water bottle under her arm, she padded silently out onto the landing, avoiding the squeaky floor-board that would give her presence away. Very, very quietly she descended to around halfway down the stairs, crouching down in the darkness and pressing her face between the banisters.

Downstairs, a strip of orange light outlined the slightly open door of the front room. Something was playing quietly on the CD player – one of those boring albums really ancient parents liked, with all the soppy love songs and nothing at all you could dance to.

'It's not my fault,' said a voice. Mum's voice.

'I never said it was.' That was Daddy. Both voices sounded strange; not exactly miserable, but not exactly happy either. Sort of flat.

'Then whose is it?'

Lottie's heart quickened. I don't know what it is, she thought, and I don't know why, but maybe it's my fault. If they're not happy, maybe it's me that's making them that way.

'It's nobody's fault,' said Daddy. 'We're just not seeing things the same way any more.'

'And why's that?'

'You tell me.' Now there was something else in Daddy's voice, a sort of tiredness that was a little bit angry at the same time. 'Oh for God's sake, this is just plain stupid.'

'No it's not.' Mum's voice sounded calm, but in that strained way mums had when they were trying not to let you know that the plane left in half an hour and Daddy had left his passport in the car. 'This isn't just about us and what we want, you know. It's about Lottie too.'

Lottie's little fingers clenched the banister rail until her knuckles went white. I knew it, she thought. I knew it had something to do with me.

She couldn't bear to stay and listen to any more. Afraid of what she might hear, she clutched her owl hot water-bottle very tightly and crept back to bed, where she lay curled up under the covers until she was too exhausted to stay awake any longer.

Chapter 6

In the dark of the very early morning, Nick rolled across the bed until his body was in contact with Hannah's.

'Are you awake?'

'No,' she said flatly.

'Thought so. I couldn't sleep either.'

She took a deep breath and rolled over to face him. It took a big effort; all she really wanted to do was curl up into a little ball of misery. 'Look, I'm sorry,' she said. 'About earlier. I didn't mean to . . . you know . . . lose my temper.'

'Nor did I. I expect it's because you're overtired,' he added, stroking her shoulder.

She bristled. 'What?'

'You've been working too hard, taking too much on – you said yourself you had a headache the other day. Maybe you should ease up a bit, spend some more time at home.'

That kindled a spark of annoyance. 'Hang on, we have an argument so it's me that's "overtired", not you being unreasonable?'

'Hey, who's being unreasonable now?'

'Oh, right. And the solution for this is for me to jack in my business and play house so we can be up to our knees in little Steadmans before the year's out? Is that it?'

He rolled onto his back. 'Well, it's not the worst idea I've ever heard,' he said curtly.

'That's funny, 'cause to me it sounds decidedly shit.'

They both lay on their backs, glaring up at the invisible ceiling.

'We're doing it again,' said Hannah quietly.

47

'I know. And we never argue.'

'So why does it keep happening all of a sudden?'

'I don't know. We're probably both tired, I guess.'

'You don't think it's more than that?'

'Like what?'

She swallowed hard. 'Like ... we're just not getting on any more?' There was a short silence. 'No, you're right, that's stupid. We get on fine.'

'Better than fine,' Nick said firmly. 'You're the best friend I've ever had in my entire life.'

'Friend?' There was something alarming about the word, something horribly out of context.

'And the sexiest lover, of course,' he added, a trifle too hastily to sound entirely convincing. 'Why shouldn't you be my friend as well? Married people should be friends, shouldn't they?'

'As long as they're more than just that.' She looked at the dark shadow of his face. 'We are, aren't we?'

He laughed. 'What a stupid question, of course we are. We're married, aren't we?'

It had been a long day at the salon, and Hannah was treating Maxine to a back and neck massage.

'Sometimes,' she confided, kneading the knotted muscles between Maxine's shoulders, 'I wish he was gay.'

Maxine, who was draped forwards across Hannah's massage chair, screwed her head round to stare at her in disbelief. '*Gay?* You're saying you wish Nick was *gay?*'

When Maxine put it like that, it did sound a bit crazy; but Hannah knew what she felt, and if that was crazy, there was nothing she could do about it. 'Well, gay or ... or impotent or something. Then it wouldn't be an issue. Don't twist your neck like that, you'll pull something.'

Maxine pressed her face back against the hole in the chair. 'I don't get it.' She chuckled dirtily. 'And neither would you if Nick was gay.'

'That's the whole point.'

'You're having me on.'

It was obvious Hannah wasn't getting through. 'This isn't a joke you know,' she insisted, her fingers working on Maxine's overstretched tendons. 'I'm deadly serious. The other night

48

when we ... you know ... it was all I could do not to push him off me.'

'Ow!' Hannah's fingers probed a little too vigorously. 'All right, don't take it out on me.' Maxine winced and sat up straight. It was hard to have a meaningful conversation with your head stuffed into a hole. 'What's wrong, kid? Is it your hormones?'

That was the last thing Hannah wanted to hear. 'No, it is not my bloody hormones! Why does there have to be something wrong with me, just because I don't enjoy having sex with Nick any more?'

'Well ... he is your husband,' Maxine pointed out.

'So? Just because you and Jay are always at it like rabbits, that doesn't mean the rest of us have to be.'

'No,' agreed Maxine, 'but it helps if you don't feel like throwing up every time your bloke touches you.'

'Don't exaggerate. Anyway, just because I don't fancy doing it with Nick, that doesn't mean I've gone off the whole idea of doing it at all. I'm not some sort of dried-up vegetable, you know!'

'I never said you were.' A light dawned in Maxine's eyes. 'Don't tell me you've got a thing for somebody else! You have, haven't you!'

'No!' exclaimed Hannah, not quite sure whether to be appalled or exasperated, or both. 'I am not, repeat not, interested in another bloke. Got that?'

Maxine shook her head. 'Then I don't understand. Why would you suddenly go off Nick for no reason? I mean, I know people get used to each other over the years, but hey, with a bit of imagination and some kinky underwear from that shop in the Regent Arcade ...'

'Who said it was a sudden thing?' Her mouth took control and made her blurt out a lot more than she'd intended. 'Who said I ever fancied him in the first place? Maybe I've just got to the point where I can't bear pretending any more.'

'Aw, c'mon, you don't mean that.' Maxine stood up and put a sisterly hand on Hannah's shoulder. 'What's really up? All you seem to talk about at the moment is how much you and Nick aren't getting on. But everybody knows you two get on like a house on fire.'

Hannah grunted. 'Oh they do, do they?'

'This is all about him wanting a baby, isn't it? Why don't you two leave Lottie with your mum and dad, and go out for a nice romantic meal and talk about it properly? Give yourselves a bit of space and you'll sort it out in no time.'

Hannah sighed sadly. 'I wish it was that easy.'

At that moment, her mobile rang, and she had to drag herself back to practicalities.

'The Beauty Room, Hannah speaking.'

'Hannah, it's Mum. Can you come round on your way home from work? I'm afraid we've got a family crisis.'

The Maddrells lived in a tidy semi-detached bungalow in Bishops Cleeve, with a nice view of the hills. On clear days you could sit in the neat little garden and watch the hot air balloons taking off from a nearby field.

On this particular autumn day, however, most of the hot air was coming out of Mr Maddrell's ears, while his wife flapped around in a fluster, making cups of tea and dropping things.

'I don't care if he is your father,' Derek fumed, 'I am not having him in this house. He'll have to go to your cousin Maureen's.'

'He can't, love, she won't have anything to do with Dad since he called Timothy a smug-faced ponce when they let him out for Mum's funeral.'

Hannah couldn't help smirking behind her cup of terrifyingly strong PG Tips. If anybody deserved to be called a smug-faced ponce it was Uncle Tim; and if Grandad Herbie was such a good judge of character, maybe he wasn't all bad after all. Not that Hannah remembered much about him; he'd spent most of his life – and hers – behind bars. Her one abiding memory was of an amazingly agile character who could shin up drainpipes faster than she could, and she seriously doubted he could manage that these days, not at seventy-six.

'If they're thinking of letting Grandad out of prison,' she said, 'surely it must be because they think he's harmless now?'

Her mother and father stared at her as though she had just announced that Genghis Khan liked fluffy kittens.

'Stay out of this, dear,' advised Erica. 'You don't know what you're talking about.'

'Then why did you drag me all the way here, like there's some earth-shattering family crisis or something? Don't I get to have my say?'

'I can't see there's much to add.' Derek bit grimly into a slice of sticky treacle tea-bread. 'Not unless you're offering to take him in yourself.' He took in the look on Hannah's face. 'No, thought not.'

'You said the probation people wouldn't let him live with us because of Lottie,' she reminded him, deep down rather ashamed at being so pleased to have a cast-iron excuse. 'In case he was a bad influence and all that. And besides, you've got a bungalow,' she added. 'It'd be perfect.'

'Perfect,' replied Erica firmly, 'is not how I'd describe it.'

The news that the authorities were seriously considering releasing Herbie on parole had hit the Maddrells smack in the face, like a very large and smelly cowpat. For more years than anybody cared to remember, Herbie Flowers had been the coal-black sheep in a family of little white woolly lambs. The fact that he was also Erica's dad had been an endless source of mortification over the years, culminating in his being arrested right in the middle of his daughter's wedding. Nobody had ever quite forgiven him for that – particularly former Police Constable Derek Maddrell.

Consequently, the announcement that Herbie could be released if 'a suitable responsible person or persons' could be found to take him in had prompted a flurry of excuses from every single member of the Flowers' extended family.

'What about Auntie Jane?' asked Hannah.

'Three-month holiday in South Africa.'

'Archie in Arbroath?'

'Double hip-replacement.'

'Great Uncle Matt?'

'Dead.'

Hannah threw her hands up, her mental address book exhausted. 'That's it, then,' she declared. 'You can't just leave Grandad to rot in jail, can you? You'll *have* to take him in.'

Derek Maddrell scowled into his moustache. 'Over my dead body.'

'I ought to be home by now really,' remarked Nick as Mark went up to the bar at the Two Tuns and got in another round. 'I'm supposed to be making a start on the upstairs skirting boards.'

Mark slammed a half down in front of him. 'Come on, mate, don't let me down. Tell you what, I'll be your excuse for being late home if you'll be mine.'

Nick raised an eyebrow. 'I thought you couldn't wait to get back to your new family.'

'I can't. Well, I can . . . Actually baby Liam has got an attack of really smelly diarrhoea. To be honest, I can't face his bottom without a couple of pints inside me. Anyway,' he slurped his Guinness, 'one look at your long face and I knew it was my sacred duty to take you down the pub.'

'Very public-spirited of you.'

'Oh, I know. It's hell sitting here by the fire with a pint of ale and a bag of crisps, you know. So, what's got into you anyway? And don't say "nothing", 'cause that's boring.'

Nick directed a half-hearted kick at the leg of the table – and missed. 'All right then, nothing much.'

'Still boring. Come on, out with it. Not still having trouble with the missus, are you?'

Nick squirmed uncomfortably on his chair. He was starting to regret having let slip that all was not rosy at Château Steadman, even if only to good old reliable Mark. 'Oh, you know. Actually it's not just that.'

'What then? Don't tell me – work?'

'What else? Wall-to-wall external exams and assessments, hysterical kids, manipulative parents . . . and if there's any time left over the Government still expects us to actually teach the kids something.' He took a gulp of beer. 'Teaching.' He shuddered. 'Do you know what's worst of all?'

'Go on.'

'I'm good at it. And it's the only thing I'm good at. How bloody depressing is that?' A jaw-cracking yawn escaped from his mouth, reminding him how little sleep he'd managed the night before, thanks to Hannah and this whole new crop of hang-ups she'd developed. 'Then there's all the other stuff.'

Mark sat forward in his chair, masticating a mouthful of cheese and onion crisps. 'What other stuff?'

The awfulness of remembering exactly what made Nick sink an inch in his chair. 'My sister,' he said gruffly. 'Janine.'

Mark's face registered interest. 'The good-looking older one with the boring husband?'

'The good-looking older one with the boring *estranged* husband.'

'Oh, right. I had no idea.'

'Neither had anybody else, until she started gallivanting round town with her twenty-four year-old toy-boy.'

If Mark noticed the mortified expression on Nick's face he certainly didn't acknowledge it. In fact he gave an impressed whistle. 'Way to go!'

'No, way *not* to go!' snapped Nick, beetroot-red with embarrassment. 'Have you any idea how humiliating it is when one of your Year Nine pupils announces to the whole class that he's seen your sister out clubbing in a see-through top and hot pants?'

'Not really,' admitted Mark. 'But then I've only got a brother, and he's a trainee vicar.'

'Lucky you. I ask you, how can anybody let their whole family down like that? How can anybody have such a complete lack of responsibility?'

Mark scratched his ear sympathetically. 'OK mate, so it's a bit embarrassing.'

'A bit!'

'But she's not *your* responsibility, is she? She's an adult, it's up to her if she wants to make an exhibition of herself. And it's not like she's got any kids to complicate matters. 'Besides,' he winked, 'as I recall she's got plenty to make an exhibition of.'

That definitely pressed all the wrong buttons. 'Oh, thanks. I might have guessed you'd think it was funny as well.'

'As well as who?'

'My mum and dad. According to them, it's "just a phase" and it'll "burn itself out".'

'Perhaps they're right?' ventured Mark.

Nick ignored the suggestion. 'And then there's Hannah of course – who thinks I'm "overreacting as usual". Fine lot of moral support I'm getting. Not that that's anything new.' He pushed away the rest of his half of lager; he'd suddenly lost the taste for it. 'Everything's turning to shit.'

There was a short silence.

'This isn't about your sister, is it?' said Mark, who wasn't normally given to flashes of insight. 'It's about you and Hannah.'

'Don't be stupid,' growled Nick, getting to his feet and picking up his bulging briefcase. 'Look, why don't you stick to changing nappies, and leave the cod psychology to people who know what they're talking about?'

He turned round, pushed his way through the happy-hour crowd like a gargoyle at a beauty pageant, and vanished, leaving Mark staring open-mouthed at Nick's discarded glass, a crisp poised halfway to his mouth.

Comfortably sprawled on the bunk in his cell, Herbie reread Hannah's letter and laughed out loud when he got to the bit about her sister-in-law Janine. Good for her. It was the funniest thing he'd heard since Big Eddie's teeth turned up in the macaroni cheese. He could just imagine the looks on Erica and Derek's faces when they heard about it – they were probably worried sick in case behaving like an oversexed thirteen-year-old was contagious or something.

Strange he should get a letter from his granddaughter after such a long time, but obviously she'd heard about all this parole board nonsense.

And nonsense it was. Herbie wasn't really a betting man, but if he had been he'd have put his shirt on his latest parole application being turned down. In fact it was a racing certainty. Not that this made him in the least unhappy: it was exactly the way he'd planned it. In the last few weeks he'd made himself as objectionable as possible, even going to the lengths of staging a small fracas in the kitchens where he worked, involving several hand-picked stooges and a pan of custard.

He stretched out an arm for his mug of tea, and dunked a biscuit in it. Yes, over the years, he'd grown to like it here. And nobody was going to evict Herbie Flowers before he was good and ready.

The next morning, the staffroom at Alderman Braithwaite Comprehensive was buzzing – and not just with gossip about the deputy head girl and the groundsman.

'I'm telling you, it's true,' insisted Graham. 'The head went to check something in the filing cabinet, and as he was looking for what he wanted he noticed that the envelopes with the exam papers in were in the wrong order.'

'Maybe zay were wrongly filed in zee first place,' suggested Claudette, deftly twirling the luxuriant black fleece of her hair into a more practical chignon.

'That's a point,' agreed Colin. 'Maybe somebody was in a hurry and made a mistake?'

'Not a chance; I was there at the time, I checked them myself.'

'All zee same . . .' said Claudette with a shrug.

'Besides,' Graham went on, 'whoever did it didn't stick the envelope back down properly.'

At that moment Nick walked into the staffroom. Conversation stalled and all eyes turned on him. 'What's up?' he demanded. 'Somebody die?'

'Worse,' said Harry. 'Somebody's been tampering with the physics exam papers. And the head's calling in the police.'

Chapter 7

'I don't believe it,' declared Claire, putting down the salon phone. 'That makes three already today and we've only been open half an hour.'

Maxine looked up from filling in an order form for perming lotion. 'What – not another one for the "lucky chair"?'

'Yup. Since the *Courant* ran that piece about the big bingo win, everybody's desperate to sit in the same chair Miss Fabian always uses. Talk about pathetic – they must be really stupid or something.'

Maxine wagged her biro at her. 'Don't knock it, business is up twenty per cent this week. If people want to believe a load of superstitious nonsense, that's fine by me as long as they spend lots of money in the salon.'

The day's rush had yet to begin, and Hannah was busy working on reshaping Gloria's eyebrows while she sat waiting for her latest hair colour to take. 'You're quiet today,' Gloria commented, scrutinising Hannah's reflection in the mirror. 'Something wrong?'

'Why would there be anything wrong?' she replied flatly.

'Well, let's just say if you had a tail, it'd be between your legs. Don't you agree, Phil?'

Philomena tittered in the nervous way she had when she wasn't quite sure what she was supposed to say. 'Ooh, well, I suppose . . .'

'Look, I'm fine, really – I've just got a bit of a headache,' protested Hannah as Claire and Maxine turned to give her the once-over as well. If she'd ever wondered what it was like to be a goldfish in a bowl, she needn't wonder any more.

Gloria smiled knowingly. 'I bet it's a man,' she declared.

Philomena looked impressed. 'How can you tell?'

'Because it's always a man, and believe me I should know.' One of Gloria's half-plucked eyebrows rose up her forehead, making Hannah's job virtually impossible. 'Go on, love, you can tell me,' she said, in the tones of a sympathetic auntie. 'I'm right, aren't I?'

'What you are,' replied Hannah, 'is very lucky.' She waved her tweezers in front of Gloria's nose. 'Any more sudden moves like that, and you'll have a big bald patch where your eyebrow used to be.'

'Don't change the subject,' Gloria scolded playfully. 'You're not answering my question.'

Hannah sighed. 'Not that it's any of your business, *madame*, but no, it isn't a man; in fact it isn't anything at all. Sorry to disappoint you, but there it is. I'm absolutely fine.'

'Except for the headache?'

'Well, yes. Except for the headache.'

Hannah hoped she was doing a better job of convincing Gloria than she was of convincing herself, because frankly she hadn't felt this morose in a long time. Gloria was right, of course: it was a man . . . but it was more than that. More than just the fact that she and Nick had taken to tiptoeing around each other, or just plain avoiding each other's personal space, as if each of them was surrounded by a big invisible bubble that might shatter on impact.

She had started dreading going home. There was an atmosphere not of hostility but of muted fear in the house: fear that if they sat down together for more than a couple of minutes, they might fight or – worse – accidentally say something meaningful. When you thought about it, it was a bit pathetic really. More pathetic even than people who turned up at the salon wanting to sit in Miss Fabian's 'lucky' chair.

Gloria patted Hannah's hand. 'If you want to talk about it, love,' she began hopefully.

The doorbell jangled and everybody glanced round instinctively.

Talk of the devil, thought Hannah, literally saved by the bell. As the door opened, it revealed a small figure in a big check coat and a fluffy pink beret, clutching an oversized, bucket-shaped pink handbag. Hannah fully expected the other two musketeers to follow her into the shop, but for the first time in recorded history Miss Fabian was on her own.

'Hello, dears!' trilled Clarice Fabian, beaming at Jason as he held the door open for her. She fluttered her eyelashes at him girlishly, and he duly squirmed with embarrassment. 'I don't suppose you could squeeze me in for a teensy-weensy shampoo and set tomorrow afternoon?'

Jason looked at Claire. Claire looked at Maxine. Maxine didn't need to look at the appointments book: it was fuller than a pub on Christmas Eve. 'Well, it is Friday tomorrow,' she reminded Miss Fabian, 'and you know how hectic we are on Fridays. I could do you now though, if you like. Ten per cent senior citizen discount.'

'No, no, dear, today's no good at all. Besides, I don't need the discount now, do I? No, it has to be tomorrow.'

'Oh. Weeeell ...' Maxine picked up a rubber and erased a small boy's pudding-basin cut from the schedule; she'd square it with his mum later. After all, you couldn't turn away a bingo jackpot winner, could you? 'Seeing as it's you, I'm sure we can find a way of fitting you in. How about two thirty with Claire?'

Claire looked positively enthusiastic, thought Hannah – no doubt sensing the prospect of a decent-sized tip after those endless cut-price pensioners' perms.

'Ooh lovely, you girls are good to me.' Miss Fabian's pug stuck his round, pop-eyed head out of the handbag, sniffed the hairspray-imbued air and promptly sneezed. 'Got to look my best for Reginald, haven't I?'

'Reginald?' Maxine left off adding up.

Miss Fabian giggled, and pink dimples appeared in the middle of her cheeks. 'Mr Gosling, from the over-sixties' luncheon club. He's taking me to a tea-dance at the Town Hall, you know.'

'That's nice,' remarked Hannah. 'How about Mrs Lorrimer and Mrs De'Ath? Are they going too?'

Miss Fabian's demeanour changed faster than a whippet with diarrhoea. 'I wouldn't know, I'm sure,' she sniffed.

Always on the alert for good gossip, Gloria was in like lightning. 'Dear me, you three haven't fallen out, have you?' she coaxed with a smile. 'Can't they agree what to spend their share of the money on?'

If it were possible, Clarice Fabian's expression grew even frostier. 'What share of the money?' she sniffed.

This time everybody's eyebrows soared skyward.

'But I thought you were sharing ... well, we all did,' said Claire. 'Like you always do,' she added lamely.

'Then you thought wrong, dear. It's my money, I won it fair and square and I don't care what anybody says.' After that brief diatribe, the little-old-lady smile returned to the apple cheeks. 'Now, two thirty tomorrow, wasn't it? See you then, toodle-pip.'

The door closed sharply behind Miss Fabian, leaving an array of dumbfounded expressions.

'Fucking hell,' whistled Claire.

'Language,' reproved Philomena.

Jason left off refilling the big pump-bottles of conditioner. 'Did she really say she's keeping all the money for herself?'

'Steady on lad,' winked Gloria. 'Hark at him,' she nudged Hannah in the ribs. 'Can't wait to apply for the job of Miss Fabian's kept boy.'

Jason's face screwed up in horror. 'Ugh! Don't *say* things like that!'

With a chuckle, Gloria sat back and sipped her coffee. 'Of course, you could always be my toy-boy, but I don't think my new gentleman friend would like that very much.'

Philomena leaned closer, hanging on every word. Here we go again, thought Hannah, with a pang of something that might have been indigestion – or envy.

'You've got a new man then?' Philomena breathed excitedly, fumbling with Gloria's foil highlights. 'What happened to Giorgio?'

Gloria dismissed the memory of her Italian deli-owner with a wave of the hand. 'Oh, he was just too possessive, you know those Latin types. Couldn't bear to have me out of his sight for two seconds. Whereas Alexander ...' She smiled to herself. 'Let's just say *I* can hardly bear to be away from *him*.'

'What's he like? Is he really gorgeous?'

'Tall, natural blond, broad shoulders – sort of Scandinavian-looking. And the dreamiest blue-grey eyes. Works in import-export. You know something?' she giggled.

'What?'

'I really think it's true love this time.'

You always think it's love, thought Hannah irritably, as 'Love Is in the Air' came on the radio, right on cue. It wouldn't have been quite so bad if Claire hadn't started humming along to it and doing a little dance around the reception desk.

Love. Ugh. Who needs it? she thought, wiping her tweezers on her uniform top.

And the woebegone answer came back: I do.

'Oh for God's sake,' snapped Nick, marching into the front room, striding over to the CD player and switching it off, 'do we have to listen to this crap?'

Annoyance stirred in the pit of Hannah's stomach. She'd worked a long day, dealt with an abusive client, listened to Gloria going on about luuurve, helped Lottie with her homework, cooked the evening meal, washed all the dishes, put Lottie to bed, read her another chapter of Harry Potter, listened to Nick moaning about work like he was the only one who ever had any problems . . . and now she was completely worn out. All she'd wanted was a half-hour's relaxation with her favourite chill-out album. Was that so much to ask?

'I was listening to that,' she said quietly. 'And you were in the other room.'

'So? The walls aren't that thick.'

'It wasn't loud. And you said you liked it last time I put it on.'

'Well that was last time. This time it's crap. Can't we ever just have a bit of peace and quiet?'

He made as if to leave the room, then changed his mind and came and sat down bad-temperedly in the armchair next to the sofa where Hannah had been lying. She swung her legs down and sat up. 'What's the matter?'

'Why does something have to be the matter?'

'Why do you have to be in such a foul mood all the time?'

'I'm not, you're imagining it.'

'Yeah, right. Like I imagined the way you threw that bowl at the kitchen wall and broke it.'

'That was . . . an accident.' His eyes narrowed. 'Anyway, you'd be less than sunny if you had to contend with what I've got on my plate right now.'

'What – like that business with the exam papers you mean?'

To her amazement he sneered, in a most un-Nick-like way. 'Well well, so you're not *completely* insensitive then?'

She could hardly believe she was hearing him talk like this. Not her even-tempered, fair-minded Nick. 'What!'

He didn't relent. 'I mean, so you've actually noticed things aren't exactly plain sailing at school at the moment? Well bloody done.'

Keeping her own temper in check was a tough call – which was ridiculous really, seeing as she and Nick never, ever rowed. This whole silly, escalating thing had something dreamlike about it. 'I could hardly have failed to notice, could I? You've been moaning on about it non-stop for days.'

'Oh, so when I want to talk to you about my problems it's moaning, is it? But when you want to talk to me—'

'You don't give me the chance!' she cut in. 'Do you realise you've hardly said one sentence to me lately that hasn't had the word "me" in it?'

That must have hit home, because Nick fell silent and just glared at the gas fire for a while, watching the flames lick greedily but pointlessly around the artificial coals.

'Look,' said Hannah after a few minutes, 'I know it's a stressful time for you at the school, what with the police asking questions and everybody being under suspicion.' She waited for Nick to say something, but he just kept staring ahead of him, so she went on. 'But they can't possibly think it was you who tampered with those papers.'

His head snapped round to look at her. 'Oh no? Why's that then? Have I got "whiter than white" tattooed across my forehead, or do you just think I'm too bloody boring to do anything that risky?'

'Anybody who knows anything about you knows you're straight as a die.'

'Tell that to the local paper.'

'The *Courant*? Who told them?'

'Who knows? Who cares? The fact is, my head of department's on long-term sick leave with his so-called stress problem, which leaves muggins here fending off every damn' local hack who wants to rake up a load of dirt about the school and everybody in it. Oh – and trying to keep the science staff sane and teach the kids at the same time.'

'I'm . . . sorry,' said Hannah, who couldn't think what else to say. If she'd thought it would placate Nick, she was wrong.

'Sorry for what?'

'Sorry for annoying you when I didn't mean to, I suppose. I'm not really sure.'

'What the hell's the point of being sorry if you don't know what for?' He threw up his hands and flopped back into the chair. 'What's the point of anything?'

'You sound really depressed.'

'I'm angry.' He turned to look at her. 'And fed-up.' Something in his eyes told her what he really meant.

'Fed-up with me?'

'I didn't say that.'

You didn't need to, thought Hannah. But this was getting them nowhere, so she decided to change tack. 'It's busy at the salon at the moment,' she said brightly.

'Oh really. How fascinating.'

'I take an interest in your work,' she said, unable to keep the note of accusation out of her voice.

'Yes, well, there's a bit more of mine to take an interest in.'

'Meaning?'

'Meaning, I do a bit more than pamper fat old ladies and their overfed egos. Talk about a waste of a good biology degree.'

Her jaw dropped. 'I can't believe you just said that! You've always been so supportive. You've always told me I should keep my work going, no matter what. And you know how much satisfaction I get from making people feel better about themselves.'

Nick let out a groan and rubbed his eyes. His head sagged. 'Oh . . . take no notice of me,' he said softly.

'Take no notice!' Her eyes prickled with angry tears. 'You've just told me I'm insensitive and my job's moronic. What is this – let's-pick-a-fight-with-Hannah-day? Let's put her down and make her feel inadequate?' He didn't answer. 'You do realise all of this is starting to affect Lottie, don't you?'

'All of what? Just because we have the occasional disagreement.'

'Oh come on Nick, it's more than that and you know it. Things have been bad for a while now. We're both on edge all the time, the poor kid's bound to notice.'

'What's she said to you?' demanded Nick.

'Nothing specific – yet,' admitted Hannah. 'But I'm her mum, I can sense these things.'

He took that badly. 'Oh, and I can't, is that it? I can't because I'm not her real father?'

'Don't be silly.'

'No, don't back off; say what you mean. Lottie's *your* child, is that what you're trying to say?'

She opened her mouth to tell him that that wasn't it, nothing of the kind; but at that moment she heard a little sound behind her, and turned round.

Lottie was standing in the doorway, a wan little figure in her pink pyjamas, eyes very large in her small white face.

'Sweetheart—' began Hannah. But Lottie didn't give her a chance to explain.

'I can't sleep, Mummy,' she said. 'Can I have a drink of water?'

Herbie was in love.

Deeply, contentedly in love with the lovely round social worker who visited him every week, unfailingly bringing him digestive biscuits and enquiring after the state of his angina. It was the perfect romance as far as he was concerned: no strings, and while they were having a nice cosy chat he could fantasise about the likely configuration of her massive underwear.

Alas, on this particular Friday afternoon his reverie was abruptly shattered by one of the warders, bringing him a summons to the governor's office.

'But I haven't done anything!' he protested.

'Well somebody obviously thinks different,' retorted the warder. 'Come on, Grandad, get your skates on, I haven't got all day.'

Getting to the governor's office involved unlocking and relocking countless steel gates, giving the other inmates plenty of opportunity to speculate on Herbie's likely crimes.

'Who's bin a naughty boy then?'

'Been diggin' another tunnel 'ave we?'

'Should've given the screws bigger bribes, mate.'

Herbie contented himself with throwing out a few black looks while racking his brains to remember what horrible offences he might have committed. True, he had provoked that little disturbance in the canteen, but he'd been punished for that already. Had he overdone the uncooperativeness? He hoped they weren't transferring him to another wing; he was nice and settled where he was.

The governor greeted him with a nod from the other side of her big black desk. She was one of those thirty-something career women who could run a home and a family, keep several hundred prisoners in order, and still manage to look like a bloke in drag.

'Herbie Flowers, ma'am,' announced the warder, poking him forward with a jab in the back.

'Mr Flowers,' she said; which caught him off-balance right away. He was more accustomed to 'Oi you', or 'Prisoner C837586'.

'Er . . . ma'am.'

'And how are you today?'

He swallowed. If this was a trick it was a dastardly one. 'Fine, thanks. Ma'am,' he added hastily.

'Well, I think you'll be feeling even better when you've heard what I have to tell you,' declared the governor. 'The result of your parole board's just come through, and you're going to be released on licence, to live with your daughter. Isn't that excellent news?'

Excellent news? thought Herbie, his heart plummeting seventeen storeys. Who for? This is a bloody disaster.

That night, when Hannah shooed Lottie off to bed, she could sense that something wasn't quite right. The way she held herself stiffly under the duvet, and refused her nightly chapter of Harry Potter, was enough to sound all the alarm bells in her head.

How much had Lottie overheard the other night? She hadn't said anything, but then again maybe Hannah was imagining it and there wasn't anything to say. Maybe Nick was right and she couldn't claim some special ability to read Lottie's mind, solely because she was her mother.

All the same . . .

She gave Lottie a goodnight kiss on the cheek, and got up to switch off the light. Just as her hand reached for the door handle, a small voice came from the bed, half-muffled by the duvet.

'Mum.'

She halted in her tracks. 'Yes, sweetheart?'

'Are you and Daddy going to keep on fighting?'

Hannah caught her breath. She fumbled her way back to the bed in the semi-darkness. 'We're not fighting, sweetheart. Whatever gave you that idea?'

'Yes you are,' Lottie insisted, her voice stronger now. 'You never used to, but now you do it all the time, it's just you do it without shouting.'

Out of the mouths of babes, thought Hannah, suddenly and profoundly ashamed. She wanted to be honest with Lottie, but in a way that wouldn't upset her. Was that an impossible goal? 'I guess Mummy and Daddy are just having a difficult time at the moment, that's all,' she said, sitting down on the edge of the bed and taking her daughter's hand. 'Sometimes grown-ups get tired and then they start being a bit bad-tempered with each other. Everything's going to be all right though, don't worry.'

'Why are you so angry?'

'We're not angry.'

'You are!' Lottie's voice quietened to a fearful whisper. 'Is it me?'

'You?' Hannah wasn't sure whether to laugh or cry. 'Oh Lottie, don't be silly, how on earth could it be you?'

'It must be *something*,' replied Lottie, 'and you always go all quiet when I come in the room.'

Hannah ran a hand over her daughter's silky hair. 'Listen to me, this isn't about anything you've done. I won't have you filling your head with silly ideas like that, do you hear? And neither will Daddy.'

Lottie said a reluctant 'OK' and turned over to go to sleep. But as Hannah crept back out onto the landing, closing the door behind her, she knew that wasn't the end of it.

Something had to be done.

It was Saturday night, and the rest of the world was out on the town, doing exciting things. Hannah had just worked her way through a basket full of ironing. It wasn't until she got to Lottie's gym shorts that she realised she hadn't seen Nick for hours.

She wandered into the kitchen and found the back door standing open.

'Oh bloody hell, bloody *hell*, this is all I need.'

Hannah followed the sound of Nick's voice out into the back

garden, where she found him sitting on the wooden bench by the picnic table, glaring at the evening paper by the light of the old street lamp they'd bought at an architectural salvage sale.

'What on earth are you doing out here?' she asked, hugging her cardigan to her. 'It's freezing.'

Nick brandished page five of the *Courant* at her. 'Have you seen this?'

'No, what is it – more about the school?'

'Worse. My delightful elder sister has been making an exhibition of herself all over town.'

Hannah took a look at the page and was confronted by a quarter-page colour photo of the contestants in a Miss Wet T-shirt competition. Five of the six were perky eighteen year-olds. The sixth was Janine.

'Oh,' she said.

'Is that all you can say, "oh"?'

What Hannah really wanted to say was, 'I hope I look that good at her age,' but she sensed that would go down like a lead balloon, so she settled for: 'I can see why you might be embarrassed.'

Nick let out a sigh, screwed up the paper into a ball and threw it half-heartedly into the bushes. 'No you can't,' he said flatly. 'You think it's all a bit of a laugh and stuffy old Nick is overreacting, like he always does.' She opened her mouth to protest, but he put up his hand to stop her. 'And maybe you're right. But whether I am or whether I'm not, I can't be anything but what I am.'

She sat down beside him on the bench. 'And neither can I,' she said softly.

His hand reached for hers in the soft glow from the old street lamp. 'I know.'

There was a strange hush in the air, a calm stillness, almost an expectancy. Something was going to happen; something was going to be said – something that could never be taken back.

'Lottie's really upset, you know,' said Hannah. 'She thinks we're angry with her and we're fighting because of something she's done.'

Nick's face screwed up in anguish. 'Oh God, no. You told her that it's not her fault?'

'Of course I did. But she's nine years old, Nick. She can't

understand why Mum and Daddy aren't getting on any more.' She leaned her head against Nick's shoulder and sighed. 'How the hell did we get here?'

'Maybe we started out from the wrong place,' he replied, gently stroking the side of her face. 'Sometimes it's not that things break down . . . it's more that they were never quite right to begin with.'

She turned her face towards his. 'But . . . but we love each other. Don't we?'

'Of course we do. But can you honestly tell me you've ever felt real passion for me? Can you?'

She hung her head. She could have lied and said yes, but what would be the point? 'Does that really matter so very much?'

'You know it does. And you know, all this time we've been married and talking about having a big family, I've been getting more and more worried about actually having to do it.'

'So what about all this talk of having a baby?'

'I know, I know. I think I wanted us to do it before I chickened out. I've been scared, Han. Scared that when it came to it, I'd be the worst father in the world.'

She stared at him. 'But you adore Lottie, you're a wonderful father to her.'

'Stepfather. You made that pretty clear the other night.'

'I didn't mean—'

'Shh, it doesn't matter. Not any more.' He put an arm round her shoulders and, ironically, she felt closer to him than she had done in years. 'What matters is, we're talking at last. And if we're honest I think we both know there's only one place we can go from here.'

'I don't want to lose you,' she whispered.

'And you won't. But be honest with me, Han: you don't want to stay married to me either – any more than I want to stay married to you.

'Let's stop punishing ourselves and each other, and admit it. We'd both be a whole lot happier if we got a divorce.'

Chapter 8

'Please tell me it isn't true!' exclaimed Erica Maddrell, her voice cracking as she sat down heavily on the wicker sofa. 'Not that! Oh Hannah, what will people say?'

Hannah sat down next to her. Her mother was clearly shocked to the core, but ever since the previous evening, Hannah had felt peculiarly calm; no, positively relieved. It was as though she had been suffocating in the darkness, and had finally clawed her way towards the fresh air and the sunlight.

She gave her mum a reassuring hug. 'I expect they'll say, "Oh look, another couple getting divorced," and then go off and talk about something more interesting. In any case, Mum, who cares what they say? What matters is, it's the right thing for us.'

Erica looked from Hannah to Nick and back again. 'I can't believe this, I just can't,' she repeated. 'It doesn't make sense . . . I mean, look at the pair of you – he had his arm round your shoulders when you walked in, for goodness' sake!'

'Just because we don't want to be married any more, that doesn't mean we have to hate each other as well,' said Nick gently. 'Hannah's my best friend and she always will be.'

Erica struggled to come to grips with a concept so alien to her generation. 'But that's what marriage is all about,' she protested. 'You surely don't think all that passion nonsense really lasts?'

'Every woman needs to feel desired,' pointed out Hannah. 'And so do I. And it's just not right with us any more. In fact, we're pretty sure it never was. That's why we've decided to do the brave thing and call it a day.'

The skin beneath Erica's blusher was completely white. 'That Anne Summers has got a lot to answer for.'

Nick and Hannah looked at her and blinked. 'Sorry?'

'Sexy underwear, sex toys, sex on the TV, aphrodisiac recipes – you can't move for sex these days.' There was real anger in Erica's voice. 'Doesn't anyone care about companionship any more? And what about poor little Charlotte? What's going to happen to her?'

'Nothing's going to happen to her, Mum. She's going to be fine, we'll make sure of that.'

'Fine? Without a father?'

'She won't be,' said Nick. 'She'll be able to see me as much as she wants to.'

'Oh, so you'll be there every night to tuck her in and read her a story, will you? And there whenever she needs a shoulder to cry on?'

'Maybe not all the time, but—'

'She's got me, Mum,' pointed out Hannah.

'And besides, I won't go far away. She'll be able to come and spend weekends and holidays with me.'

Hannah looked at him sharply. 'Hey, not every holiday.'

'Well, no, maybe not *every* one. But some, yeah?"

'Yeah, sure; I guess.'

'I mean, we're not going to fall out over it, are we? You did say you wanted me to go on being an important part of Lottie's life.'

'Of course I do. But she needs to spend time with her mum, too.'

Erica looked on and despaired. 'So what does Charlotte have to say about all this?' she enquired quietly.

Hannah and Nick fell silent. It was the question neither of them wanted to answer.

'We . . . haven't actually . . .' admitted Nick eventually.

'You haven't *told* her?'

'But we will,' pleaded Hannah. 'Really we will. And soon. It's just a question of finding the right words.'

Nick's friend Mark was so flabbergasted that all the chutney from his lunchtime baguette shot out and landed on his Simpsons tie.

'Nick . . . mate . . . You're having me on.'

Nick shook his head. ''Fraid not. But keep it to yourself for now, yeah? We haven't even told Lottie yet.'

'Oh my God.' Mark scrubbed ineffectively at his tie. 'But you and Hannah, you're so ...' He gesticulated with the baguette, unable to articulate what he felt.

'Perfect for each other?' suggested Nick.

'Exactly! Perfect for each other. You look great together, you're on the same wavelength, the kid adores you both. What the hell went wrong?'

There was international rugby on the big-screen TV in the corner of the bar, but as far as Nick was concerned he could have been sitting on top of Everest for all the impact it had on him. He'd been like that all day: on autopilot, shutting out virtually everything but the one overwhelming issue in his life right now – his dying marriage.

'I know, I know. And we really care about each other. But it hasn't been right for a long time, Mark, you know that. Yeah, we have a lot in common, but you can't keep a marriage going on the basis that you both like the same flavour of Pot Noodle, can you? I think we both woke up one morning and realised we weren't like – well – you and Caroline, for example.'

'What – sleep-deprived, bad-tempered and covered in baby puke?'

'I'm serious, Mark. I mean, we love each other, sure we do – in a you're-my-best-mate kind of way – but we've never been *in love*. Not like you and Caroline, not even like Harry and Jane.'

'Or Colin and – what's her name?'

'Dunno, never met Colin's missus. Don't know anything about her really. I heard she was something special though, bit of a looker.'

'No wonder he's always going on about her.'

'Yeah.' Nick turned his pint of orange juice and lemonade round in his fingers, watching the light playing through the cloudy liquid. There was probably some interesting chemical reaction going on in there, but right now he couldn't have figured it out to save his life. 'The thing is, Mark, we've sorted the thing out in our own minds, and we feel better for it – but how do you tell a nine-year-old girl her mum and dad are splitting up?'

Mark fell silent and stared down at the table. 'I don't know, mate,' he replied. 'But I hope I never have to find out.'

Nick raised his glass to take a swig and almost poured the whole lot down his front as a large, authoritative hand landed heavily on his shoulder.

'Mr Steadman?'

'Er . . . yes.' Glass still in hand, he swung round. A man who looked like a travelling salesman in a badly fitting suit flashed him something shiny in a wallet.

'Sergeant Rickworth, Cheltenham CID. Maybe we'd better go somewhere quieter. I think we need to have a private word.'

'Oh Han,' sighed Maxine, moving a face-steamer out of the way and sitting down on the bench under the window in Hannah's treatment room. 'I was afraid you were going to come out with something like this.'

'You guessed?'

'Love, you've been going on for weeks about how things weren't the way you wanted them to be. Almost like you were trying to talk yourself into doing something radical.'

'Something stupid, you mean?'

'Hey, I didn't say that.'

'No, but you were thinking it. And now I have.'

'Haven't you just. The question is, is it the right thing?'

'Yes, it is.' Hannah nodded emphatically, joining Maxine on the bench. 'That's the one thing we're both sure about. You wouldn't believe what a relief it was, Max, finally getting everything out into the open. It turns out we've both been as miserable as each other, only we couldn't bring ourselves to say so. I didn't want to hurt him, he didn't want to hurt me . . .'

'That's a whole lot of caring, sharing stuff for two people who've just announced to the world that they're getting a divorce,' commented Maxine drily.

'Not a divorce,' corrected Hannah: 'Well, not for a long time yet anyway.' She wasn't exactly sure why it mattered to be precise about that. 'Just a separation to start off with, then we'll take things gradually from there. And by the way, we haven't announced anything officially,' she added, lowering her voice even though the door was closed and there was nobody within earshot. 'Apart from Mum and Dad, you're the first person I've told, so you will keep it to yourself for now, won't you?'

Maxine frowned. 'The first person after your mum and dad and Lottie, yeah?'

Hannah glanced down, avoiding her gaze.

'You *have* told Lottie, haven't you? Oh Hannah!'

Hannah's heart contracted with utter shame. 'I know, I know. But it's so difficult.'

'Maybe,' replied Maxine grimly. 'But it'll be a hell of a lot more difficult if the news gets out and somebody else tells her first.'

Nick was in total shock. Sitting there in the head's office, flanked by a couple of CID officers, he felt like he'd just been arrested for the crime of the century. Merely looking at their grim faces made him feel guilty. But then he'd always felt guilty even in the presence of his own father-in-law, and he was only a retired traffic cop. He supposed that must be the penalty for having an overactive conscience.

'Colin?' he repeated slowly, certain that he had misheard. 'Colin *Rooney*?'

'That's right, sir.' Sergeant Rickworth nodded. 'Quite new here I understand.'

'Yes, he's not been here long. He transferred here mid-term from another school. What's this all about, officer?'

'The matter of some examination papers being tampered with.' The other detective paused. 'Do you know much about Mr Rooney's wife, sir?'

Nick scratched his nose. 'Nothing really. Why? Look – surely you're not suggesting *Colin* tampered with those papers?' He visualised Colin's face in his mind's eye: bright, fresh, innocent; the very image of his own at the same age. It was unthinkable.

'I'm afraid all the evidence does point that way, Mr Steadman. At first, I must admit, we thought it might have been you.'

The blood drained from Nick's face. 'Me!'

'Irritability, irrational behaviour, increased drinking ...' That's a bit steep, thought Nick. All I've had is a couple of pints down the pub with Mark. 'Then we heard about your domestic troubles. Sorry to hear about the break-up with your wife, Mr Steadman. Still, these things happen.'

His jaw dropped. 'How did you know?'

'We are the CID, sir. Now, about Mr Rooney,' the sergeant went on. 'Were you aware that he had had trouble at his last school? Trouble involving his wife?'

'No. No, he never said. What kind of trouble?'

Sergeant Rickworth sat down on the corner of the head's desk.

'The sort of trouble that leaves a man open to blackmail, Mr Steadman.'

You couldn't keep anything quiet for long. By the time Nick left for home that afternoon, everybody at Alderman Braithwaite either knew the truth or had invented something even more lurid.

As he drove out of the car park, Nick felt the last droplets of his faith in human nature oozing out of his battered soul. Teaching had become an increasingly disillusioning experience lately – until Colin Rooney turned up, with his puppyish enthusiasm and endless devotion to the job. It had been like an injection of teenage vitality.

Now Colin was facing a lonely night in the cells, and Nick had been forced to accept that his own judgement of character left a good deal to be desired. But who could have guessed that Colin had married a former prostitute? Or that he loved her so intensely that he would do anything to protect, not his own reputation, but hers?

And who would have thought that the same people who had tried to exert pressure on him at his first school would simply move across town and do the same thing all over again here, in a clumsy attempt to get their thick sister through her exams? If only you'd said something to me, thought Nick. If only you'd been less proud. If only the two of you had moved further away and made a completely fresh start. Or if you'd just been a bit less cack-handed, added a small voice in his head, then nobody would have noticed the papers had been tampered with and we'd all still be going along in blissful ignorance.

When he arrived home, he found Hannah's car already parked outside and the lights on. He sat there for a few minutes in the dusk, just watching her silhouette move back and forth across the windows.

Already he was beginning to feel like an outsider.

Alone in the kitchen, Hannah peeled potatoes at the sink as she watched Lottie out in the garden, feeding the animals.

There was a chill in the air. 'Don't stay out too long,' she called through the window. Lottie grinned and waved, and went back to stuffing carrots into a fat brindled rabbit.

The initial feeling of relief had evaporated, and now Hannah felt a kind of faint, dull ache where the excitement had been. Not the ache of having done something wrong, just the ache of regret. That was the funny thing about hindsight. With the benefit of it, you could feel nostalgia even about things that had been horrible – like lacrosse in the snow, or Great-Aunt Betsy's bristly kisses. And whatever the shortcomings of her marriage to Nick might have been, you could never say it had been *bad*. Just . . . misguided, maybe. A close friendship taken one step too far.

I do love him, though, she thought soberly as she dug the eyes out of the potatoes. And I can't imagine him ever not being part of my life. It's just that we've been playing parts for so long, and they aren't the ones we should be playing.

Am I being impossibly selfish? she wondered, watching Lottie scampering around the garden. She's so happy. Is it wrong for me to want to be happy too?

The kitchen door opened and Nick came in, looking utterly exhausted. She waited, still half-expecting the customary peck on the cheek, but he flung his briefcase into a corner and sat down on one of the kitchen stools.

'Bad day?' she asked.

'You could say.' He unbuttoned his coat. 'The police marched Colin Rooney down the station to be charged.'

'Colin! It was him all the time? But why?'

'It's a long story. It doesn't matter, not now.' He gazed over Hannah's shoulder into the garden, golden in the centre from the patio lights, and fading into deep-blue twilight at the edges. 'Not a care in the world,' he murmured.

'Lottie, you mean?' She turned back to look at her husband. 'We have to tell her, you know.'

'Now?'

'We've left it too long already. What if she was to hear it from somebody else?'

She tapped on the window and mouthed 'Come in'. Lottie giggled and pulled a silly face. But she picked up the bag of guinea-pig food and carried it back towards the house.

'Hello, Daddy. Tea's not ready yet, is it, Mum?'

'No, not yet.'

'So can I go back out and play with Doom?'

'In a little while maybe. Take your coat off and sit down, we've got something to tell you.'

Lottie looked from Hannah's face to Nick's, searching for clues. 'Are we going to Disneyland?' she asked, more out of hope than expectation.

In spite of everything, a slight smile twitched the corners of Nick's mouth. 'Maybe next year. Just sit down and listen.'

Reluctantly, Lottie sat down on a stool next to Nick. Hannah wiped her hands on a tea towel and leaned back against the sink. 'The thing is,' she began, and they were the hardest words she had ever had to get out, 'Mummy and Daddy have been having some . . . problems.'

'You mean all the being angry with each other and stuff?'

'All that stuff, yes.'

'It *is* me, isn't it? That's why you're talking to me now, to tell me it's my fault.'

Nick shook his head emphatically. 'Nothing is your fault, do you hear? You see, mums and dads sometimes get things wrong all on their own, without any help from their kids.'

Lottie looked puzzled. 'And you've got things wrong?'

Hannah nodded. 'You know Mummy and Daddy love you very much, don't you?' Lottie nodded slowly. 'And Mummy and Daddy love each other too. Only they don't love each other quite in the way that mummies and daddies should – you know, like boyfriend and girlfriend.'

Lottie's eyes started to narrow. Hannah knew that sign. She was a bright child, sometimes frighteningly so. You couldn't wrap truths up in candyfloss – she just tore it off and went straight for the heart.

'You mean you and Daddy don't fancy each other?'

Hannah's face burned scarlet. Nick coughed embarrassedly. 'Well . . . sort of,' he conceded. 'Mummy and Daddy love each other like friends do.'

The bright eyes were virtual slits now. 'Sometimes I fall out with my friends,' said Lottie quietly. 'Have you and Mum fallen out?'

'Not exactly,' said Hannah. 'Like I said, we love each other very much. We just . . .' It was as if a mighty weight was crushing her chest. 'Just don't want to live together any more.'

There was a horrible, sickening silence. It seemed to Hannah as if the whole world swayed on its axis for a second, before righting itself and rolling on, oblivious again to the troubles of three small people.

Lottie said not a word. There were red patches in the middle of her white cheeks. 'Everything's all right,' said Nick reassuringly. 'You'll be staying right here and Daddy won't be far away, I promise.'

'I don't understand. How can you be my mummy and daddy if you don't live in the same place any more? Are you getting a divorce?'

He went to put his arm round her shoulders, but the child leapt away from him as though he had given her an electric shock. 'No!' she said, her eyes aflame.

'Sweetheart,' began Hannah.

'No, you can't! I won't let you!'

'We're sorry, darling, really we are,' said Nick.

'No you're not!' Lottie snarled at him, 'you don't care at all. I hate you, do you hear? I hate you both.'

Then she ran out of the room and thundered away up the stairs, slamming her bedroom door behind her.

Chapter 9

'She'll come round, Han,' said Maxine, setting a cup of coffee in front of her.

Hannah stared down at the floor, heavy with misery. 'Will she?'

Maxine perched on the arm of Hannah's chair and gave her a hug. 'Hang in there, kid, you know she will. Just give her time and don't push her.'

They were sitting in Hannah's living room, Maxine stealing an hour off work and Hannah cancelling a whole day's treatments because she simply couldn't face the salon. Not today. And no, it wasn't because everybody was talking about her split from Nick. It was because of Lottie.

Hannah glanced up at the ceiling. 'Oh Maxine, she spent practically the whole weekend up there on her own!'

'I know.'

'It wasn't as if she was even crying, just sitting up there doing nothing. I had to practically drag her downstairs for her meals. And when she went off to school this morning, she barely said a word.' She swallowed hard. 'She wouldn't let poor Nick come near her.'

'It's a terrible shock for her,' pointed out Maxine. 'She's bound to take it hard. But why take it out on Nick? I thought she adored him.'

'She does . . . did. I don't know, Max, it's just such a mess. And I feel as if it's all my own fault.'

'For wanting a life of your own you mean?'

'For wanting . . . well, more I guess.' She looked around her, taking in the indecently pleasant surroundings: the nice new kitchen, the freshly painted walls, the neat row of potted herbs growing on the windowsill, the conservatory beyond, with its wicker armchairs and potted palms. 'Oh God, Max, how can anyone say they want more than this?'

'Hey, stop this.' Maxine shoved a packet of custard creams under her nose. 'Biscuit. Eat.'

'But I don't—'

'Yes you do.' Maxine fed a biscuit between Hannah's protesting jaws. 'It won't make the bad stuff go away, but at least it gives you something else to think about.' She dragged up another chair and sat down opposite. 'Now, are you going to talk to me properly about all this, or do I have to take you out and get you drunk first?'

The ghost of a smile flickered on Hannah's lips. 'Don't tempt me.' She swallowed a mouthful of biscuit, forcing it down her dust-dry throat. 'Oh Max, I know in my heart of hearts that what I'm doing is right – for me. But is it right for Lottie?'

Maxine took a sip of coffee, pulled a face and added another sugar-lump. 'Hey, I'm not one of those life coach people, I can't tell you what you should or shouldn't do. And I'm not Lottie's mum. But if you and Nick are unhappy being together, surely that can't be good for Lottie?'

Hannah nodded, profoundly grateful that Maxine could see things that way, that she wasn't convinced that Hannah was just making it up to excuse her own selfishness. 'That's what we thought. It's not that we don't care about each other, Max, but when we're together like this, well, the atmosphere's all wrong. And I know Lottie's sensed it – she even asked me the other day why Mummy and Daddy were always fighting. What kind of environment is that for a kid to grow up in?'

'All the same, you can see why she's worried. All she's ever known is you and Nick being together, and suddenly her whole world is breaking apart.'

'Not breaking apart, don't say that.' Hannah couldn't bear that thought. In all this talk of splitting up, she had clung doggedly to the absolute belief that whatever else they did, she and Nick would never drift far apart. As lovers they might be a failure, but as friends they would always be a part of each other's lives. 'Nick and I won't let that happen.'

'How are you going to manage that?'

'By staying close, making sure Lottie knows her Daddy's there for her whenever she needs him. Making sure she can see him as often as she wants to.'

'Nick won't be moving far away then?'

'Oh no! We're going to find him somewhere as close to here as we can, with a spare room so he can have Lottie to stay. And I'm sure he'll be round here a lot anyway – he knows he'll always be welcome.' She noticed the look on her friend's face. 'Why are you smiling at me like that?'

'Oh, just thinking it's not exactly the bust-up of the century. It sounds as if you'll be seeing almost as much of Nick as you are at the moment.'

Hannah shrugged. 'Is that so wrong?'

'Not at all. Actually, it sounds a bit like marriage but without the sex.'

'Good.' Hannah fiddled with the handle on her coffee mug. 'Because that's the bit that could never have worked. Why I didn't realise that from the start, I'll never know.' She gave Maxine a sidelong glance. 'I think I took one look at you and Jay one day, and thought: hang on, what am I doing here? That's how it's supposed to be.'

Maxine looked surprised. 'Me and Jay?'

'You and Jay. You've always had that . . . spark. Even when you fight you fancy the pants off each other. You're lucky, you know.'

'I know.' Maxine looked suddenly awkward. 'Han . . .'

'Hmm?'

'I wasn't going to tell you this now, 'cause it's really crap timing, but. . .'

Hannah's mind instantly conjured up all kinds of bizarre possibilities. 'But what? Oh God Maxine, there's nothing wrong with you and Jay is there?'

'Not exactly.' Maxine gave a little laugh. 'The thing is, you're my best mate and I wanted you to be the first to know. I think I might be pregnant.'

'And she ate her breakfast?'

'Yes, all of it.'

'And she went off to school OK?'

'Yes love, she was a bit quiet but we didn't have any tears or tantrums.'

'Thank goodness for that. Maybe she's coming round then.'

'Maybe.'

'See you later anyway.'

'Yeah. Later. Bye.'

Nick put down the phone in the science department office and let out a long, relieved breath. At least things didn't seem to be as bad with Lottie as they had been the night before. He'd seriously considered not coming in to work today, and bugger his responsibilities for once.

But that was easier said than done.

He turned back to the middle-aged man in the tweed jacket, sitting on the other side of an enormous pile of textbooks. A man who had the look of one who had been thumped more times than he could remember, but still got up every time convinced it wasn't going to happen again.

'So,' sighed Nick.

'I'm sure it was only high spirits,' said Harry. The worst thing was that he probably believed it.

'Harry, they watered all the lab plants with hydrochloric acid! That's a whole term's GCSE experiments ruined.'

Harry Turnbull shrugged ineffectually. 'I'm sure they didn't mean any real harm. It might have been a mistake. And anyway,' he added lamely, 'we don't actually know it was them, do we?'

Nick knew. There was a hard core of troublemakers in 3C and whenever anything bad happened, you could be sure they were involved in some way. Proving it, though, was rather more difficult. 'Whatever am I going to do with you, Harry?' he asked. It was a genuine question.

Chapter 10

As flats went it was more *FHM* than *Ideal Home*, but then again maybe that was just what Nick needed now he was a cool young man about town again. Well, a man about town anyway.

Hannah walked across to the window and pushed aside the trendy slatted blind. 'Nice view,' she remarked, 'and you've even got your own bit of garden to sunbathe in.'

'Dig up and grow veg in, more likely,' laughed Nick. 'You ought to know by now I'm not one for neat little patios.' His gaze met hers. 'But then you never were the *Good Life* type, were you?'

It could have sounded confrontational, but they both knew there was no hostility in it, just a simple statement of fact. Hannah liked flowers; Nick preferred parsnips. God knows how we ever got it together, Hannah mused for the hundredth time. Not that it was something to regret: they'd had some good times together, but now it was time for them both to move on.

'What do you think about this corner?' Arms folded, Nick surveyed the alcove beside the curiously futuristic glass-brick fireplace. 'Bookcase?'

'Maybe. Or TV.'

'Wouldn't there be too much reflection from the windows?'

'Yeah, you're right. Bookcase. Besides, you've already got a focal point with that fireplace.'

Nick scratched his head. 'Focal point, is that what you call it? I was just wondering how to cover it up.'

Now that the owner's furniture had been shipped overseas and the flat was virtually empty, it held all the exciting promise of a blank canvas and a box of oil paints. Hannah couldn't help thinking back to the day she and Nick had first viewed the house in Foley Road, the way they'd promised themselves they'd be sensible but found themselves falling over each other to devise ever-more-ambitious plans for it. A new conservatory here, take away that wall and extend the kitchen, open up the roof space and make room for a nursery . . .

Funny how this was the same and yet completely different. They were making plans, sure, but this time it was like talking interior design with a brother who'd just bought his first place. It was oh so weird – all civilised and chatty. And she had to remind herself that this wasn't for them as a family; it was just for Nick. The first, defining step in his brand-new life; and hers for that matter.

The thought gave her shivers, half of excitement and half of fear. This could feel like being reborn, if she got it right. And if she didn't, well, there'd be no one to blame but herself, and no one to run to, to kiss it all better. Well . . . good. It was about time she learned to stand on her own two feet.

They wandered through the kitchen – all brushed steel and concealed halogen lights – across the hallway, and into the smaller of the two bedrooms. It had been used as a home office and was nothing very spectacular: magnolia walls, plain laminated flooring and a few shelves. But that could be remedied.

'Where's Lottie?' asked Hannah, suddenly realising that the little girl had drifted from her side.

'Probably still gawping at that amazing see-through bidet thing in the en-suite. I reckon I'll be keeping goldfish in it.' He called out to her. 'Lottie? Lotpot, come and see this.'

A voice answered reluctantly from somewhere in the next room. 'Why?'

Nick rolled his eyes. 'Never mind why, just come and have a look.'

A few moments later, Lottie trailed in. 'What?' she demanded with a toss of her lustrous hair, looking, thought Hannah, for all the world like the moody teenager she oughtn't to be for several more years yet.

'What do you reckon to this room?' asked Nick.

'It's boring.'

'It won't be boring soon,' said Nick, 'because you and I are going to change it into whatever we want it to be.'

Lottie frowned. 'Why?'

'Because,' Hannah explained patiently, 'this is going to be your room.'

'I've got a room at home.'

'Yes, yes, I know you have. I mean, this is going to be your room when you come here to stay with Daddy.'

Lottie eyed her mother suspiciously. 'When?'

'Whenever you like,' Nick assured her. 'Weekends, holiday times, the odd night in the week if Mum says it's OK. And I want you to help me change this room so it feels like yours. You know, choose decorations, furniture, help me pick the colours you like, all that stuff.'

'Oh,' said Lottie. 'OK.'

It wasn't exactly an expression of boundless enthusiasm, reflected Hannah, but at least it was a start. 'You'll have fun. And I bet there aren't many girls in your class with two bedrooms,' she pointed out.

Lottie shrugged. 'Can I have pink fur cushions?'

'If you like.'

'And one of those mini-fridges to keep drinks in?'

'Well . . . maybe. If Daddy can afford it.'

Nick clapped a hand on Lottie's head and tousled her hair. 'Daddy'll afford it.'

For a moment Hannah wanted to warn Nick that simply giving Lottie everything she demanded wasn't necessarily going to make her happy or mend her broken heart. On the other hand, when you were afraid of losing your little girl's love, who could blame you for clutching at any way of winning it back?

Besides, Lottie was looking almost relaxed for the first time in days. She was even starting to talk to Nick again, so things really were looking up.

Weren't they?

While Hannah and Nick were standing in the kitchen, talking in that funny way that wasn't like Mum and Daddy at all, Lottie mooched about the little patch of back garden, a wet mulch of mud and dead leaves after the late autumn rains.

The ground squished mournfully under the soles of her new red boots. She'd been told not to get them all wet and muddy, but it didn't seem to matter any more. Mum probably wouldn't even notice. And as for Da—.

She stopped herself short. Not Daddy, it was Nick now, or Uncle Nick, or anything, but not Daddy. Never Daddy again.

In her short life she'd had two daddies. The first one, she'd never even known. Mum had explained about him. He was called Rhys and he wasn't a very nice person. In fact he must have been horrible, because the minute he'd known Mum was having a baby he'd gone away and left her. Her and me, thought Lottie. But me mostly, because if I hadn't been going to happen he wouldn't have gone away and left Mum, would he?

And then there was Daddy the Second. Her only ever real Daddy, or so she'd thought. Until the day he'd turned round and said that he was going away too. It didn't matter that he was only going a few streets: leaving was leaving. She'd told him if he loved her he would stay, and he was still going, so what did that prove?

That he didn't love her, that's what.

Everybody leaves, she thought, watching a sparrow take flight from the bird table as she took a step forward. And everybody leaves because of me.

Gloria was positively glowing.

'He's the one,' she purred, taking a sip from the cup of coffee Jason had just made her. 'I just know he is.'

Philomena hung on her every word as she mixed up the honey-brown root tint in a plastic bowl. 'Didn't you say that about the last one?' she ventured.

Gloria's serenity barely faltered. 'Everybody makes the odd mistake,' she pointed out.

'So how do you know you're not making a mistake this time?' enquired Hannah, who was manicuring Gloria's nails while Philomena touched up her roots.

Gloria pursed her full lips, glossy with Rouge Noir. 'I just do,' she replied. 'He's . . . he's *different*.'

Yeah, yeah, of course he is, thought Hannah. She felt curiously detached as she listened to Gloria drivelling on about her latest amour; almost self-righteous in fact. She, after all, had got the measure of so-called love. She'd loved Rhys right enough, all those years ago, and where had that got her? Pregnant and alone, that's what, and ready to fall into the arms of the first kindly man who took an interest in her. Instead of which, she was now building herself a new, independent life bursting with possibilities and freedom. Heck, she almost felt sorry for Gloria, even if she was glowing like loved-up plutonium.

'What's he like anyway, this Damien?' asked Philomena, her brush dabbing at the barely emergent roots.

'Damon,' Gloria corrected her. 'Gorgeous, that's what. Tall, broad-shouldered, a smile that makes you go weak at the knees . . . All that and a deluxe town house in Prestbury.'

'That's nice.' Hannah felt the envy quivering through Philomena's matter-of-fact observation. Poor Phil: with the kind of crappy existence she led, it was small wonder she resented Gloria's tales of amorous adventure almost as much as she was addicted to them.

'He's even single, would you believe!' Gloria laughed. 'Never been married, so no bunny-boiling ex-wives prowling around or anything.'

'How about ex-boyfriends?' ventured Hannah, unable to resist the bait.

'Boyfriends? I hope you're not suggesting my lovely Damon bats for the other side!'

'Well you never can tell,' Hannah pointed out. 'It happens to the best of us.'

'It doesn't happen to me!' declared Gloria, oblivious to the irony of her own words. 'Damon's a national treasure, and I'm making sure I keep myself nice for him; don't want him straying, do we?'

Philomena looked as if she might quite like Damon to stray in her direction, but maybe Hannah was just imagining it. 'What a load of trouble to go to, just for a man,' she observed, rubbing cream into Gloria's cuticles. 'He should like you just the way you are, don't you think so, Phil?'

Philomena shrugged. 'But they're not like that, are they, men? They say they like you the way you are but they never mean it. Course, some of them wouldn't notice if you ran around stark naked with a carnation up your nose,' she added sharply.

'Besides,' added Gloria with a half-smile, 'if men like Damon didn't want women like me to take good care of themselves, there wouldn't be any work for women like you. Isn't that right, Hannah?'

'One at a time, I said ONE AT A TIME!' bellowed Nick, raising his voice from merely menacing to full-on Prince of Darkness.

That usually worked wonders, even on the likes of 3C, but this time round it had scarcely any effect. The kids poured off the coach like a pent-up horde of soldier ants, one or two of them taking the opportunity to settle old scores with clipboards and book-filled rucksacks.

The last few weeks of the winter term were always a bit of a shambles, with staff and pupils rivalling each other in eagerness to stop doing any work and break up for Christmas. This year things were worse than usual, what with the school being several members of staff down and the science department more devoid than most.

That was how Nick had found himself having to return a favour for Miss Grable, the Food Technology teacher who had got him out of a hole with a couple of level-one chemistry classes. He was now wondering if the favour had been worth the price. No one in their right mind would volunteer to partner Harry Turnbull in escorting a Year Seven food technology group on a field trip to the farmers' market. Not a Year Seven group that included some of the most adept truants and kleptomaniacs at the school.

'Keven Delderfield, I've got my eye on you ... Cassie, give that back. Now, has anybody *not* got a worksheet and a clipboard?'

'I have sir, I've got a worksheet.'

'So have I.'

'I said who *hasn't* got one. Put your hands up if you *haven't* got a worksheet.'

Eventually everybody had one and even Harry could just about marshal a couple of dozen eleven- and twelve-year-olds sufficiently to get them across the Promenade without anyone being lost or run over.

'Everybody knows what to do, yes?' Heads nodded. 'You go round all the stallholders and you ask your list of questions *politely*, do you hear?' More nods, accompanied by stifled giggles. 'Mr Turnbull or I will help you if you have any problems.

And remember: any trouble and you'll wish you'd never been born.'

The kids scattered like buckshot from a cannon.

'God, I wish I had that much energy,' commented Harry, screwing up the 'kick me' Post-it note some juvenile Oscar Wilde had stuck on his back. 'Or that they didn't have so much.'

'Most of it's misdirected, that's the problem. Now, are you all right watching that lot over by the organic meat stalls? I'll take the fruit and veg end.'

'Yeah, fine.'

'And give me a shout if—'

'If there's a problem, I know.'

As it happened, once the problem came it had nothing to do with Harry. Nick was casting a watchful eye over a tempting display of local organic cider, when there was a shout from a neighbouring stall.

'What the – hey, you, put that back, you little scumbag!'

Nick swivelled round, just in time to catch Cassie Morrison by the hood of her parka as she tried to lose herself in the milling crowd. 'What is it this time?'

'Oi, get off, sir, you'll tear it.'

'Hand it over then.'

'What?'

'Don't give me that, hand it over.'

A hand appeared from within the folds of Cassie's coat, revealing a large jar of honey.

At that moment a tall young woman appeared at Nick's side, tousled black hair escaping from a tweed cap, fetchingly rustic in apron and jodhpurs. Nigella Lawson plays Barbara Good, thought Nick appreciatively. With just a hint of Margo.

'I'll have that, thank you.' She prised the jar out of Cassie's hands, ignoring the girl's sullen expression, and turned to Nick. 'Honestly, can't you control them better? I'm an apiarist, not a policewoman.'

'I'm sure Cassie's very sorry, aren't you, Cassie?' Nick's narrowed eyes burned fire into her very soul. Cassie grunted. 'What was that?'

'Sorry. S'pose.'

'Not good enough. Apologise to the lady properly.'

Cassie weighed up the situation with a practised eye. It wasn't worth the candle. 'OK, OK, I'm sorry I took it. Miss —.'

'Moss,' added the young woman. 'Miranda Moss. Hmm, not much of an apology but I guess it'll have to do. Why did you take it anyway?'

Cassie stared at the tips of her shoes. ''cause.'

''cause what?'

''cause my mum likes it and it's Christmas.'

'And you think you can just take stuff because you want it?'

This elicited another shrug and a grunt, so Nick took her across to Harry and told him he wasn't to take his eyes off her for the rest of the morning. Then, for some reason he couldn't quite put his finger on, he wandered back in the direction of Miranda Moss's stall.

She was still there, selling her pretty jars of honey and her beeswax candles with a smile and just a hint of the poshness Nick had always found slightly erotic. Erotic? What was he thinking of? He'd only come to apologise.

'Hi,' she said, raising a slender, arching eyebrow.

'Hi. I've ... er ...' Unexpectedly tongue-tied, he picked up a jar of honey. 'This looks nice.'

'It should be, it comes from my own bees and they only collect pollen from the purest organic flowers.'

'Oh. So you've got your own bees then.'

'Yes, I just said so. I run a smallholding near Cirencester. Look, can I help you with something? Only I'm busy.'

'I'll take this.' He pulled a note from his wallet and paid. 'My mum and dad have a smallholding,' he said suddenly. 'In France. They've got vines.'

'Really.' Was that interest he detected in her eyes, or pity for his appalling gaucheness?

'Yes, it's always been my dream to have my own place in the country too.'

This time she actually smiled at him. Handing him his jar of honey, she slipped a card into the bag. 'Well, here's my card. Give me a call if you want to talk about it.'

He could hardly believe she'd given him her number; in fact he was so dumbfounded that he didn't even notice Cassie making off with a bottle of scrumpy. Come to that, it wasn't until he was back on the coach and counting heads that he remembered.

He didn't even like honey.

It was only late afternoon, but the year was old and it was already dark outside. Rain was pattering on the window-panes like tiny running feet.

Hannah sat on the double bed she no longer shared with Nick, taking a few moments just to take stock of who and where she was. This was a big change. A good change, no doubt about that, but big all the same. She felt like some kind of insect, crawling out of its chrysalis into blinding light, not yet sure quite what it was or what it was supposed to do with itself.

There were gaps everywhere in the room. Some big, like the square imprint where the upstairs telly had stood; others small, so insignificant that nobody else would have noticed them at all. A three-inch absence on the dressing table where his electric shaver had lain while it was charging. An incongruous emptiness around the alarm clock on the top of his bedside locker. Nothing much; and everything.

Despite all this, she didn't regret what they'd done. Nor did she feel afraid of this big new world. On the contrary, she had felt strangely calm and in control ever since she and Nick had agreed to separate. And they were brave enough not to have called it a 'trial' separation, either – this was the real McCoy.

Funny, though. Just like everything you ever longed for and then suddenly got, all this freedom was one hell of a big thing to get your head round. Give someone a blank canvas, or a white-walled, empty room, and tell them to fill it however they like. That's my life, she thought to herself.

'Mum.'

Hannah looked up. 'Hello there, finished your homework already?'

Lottie nodded. 'It was easy.'

It was often easy. Lottie, a bright kid, was always near the top of her class. Maybe that was why she was finding it so hard to cope with all these changes; being bright gave her too much imagination, too much power to dream up all the bad things that might happen.

'Want some hot chocolate?'

Lottie shook her head. The albino ferret in her arms wiggled its nose appealingly. 'Can I . . . can Gnasher and me sit with you for a bit?'

Surprised, Hannah slid a little way across the bed. 'Of course you can. What's up?'

'Nothing. Gnasher just wants a cuddle, that's all.'

You and me too, thought Hannah; it was the very first time she'd missed Nick since he moved out.

Chapter 11

'It's a bit chilly in here,' remarked Erica, rubbing her hands.

'Mum broke the central heating again,' announced Lottie, who was standing on the dining-room table in a pink vest and pants, surrounded by metres of white net curtain. 'Well, one of the radiators anyway.'

'I did not!' protested Hannah.

'Yes you did, you went to turn it on and the valve thingy came off in your hand. And now the heating's not working downstairs.'

Erica frowned, in that unbearably concerned-mother way she had. 'I hope you've phoned the heating engineer. Didn't you sign up for that emergency repair service your dad recommended?'

Hannah squirmed slightly. 'I'll do it in the morning – if I can't get it working.' She didn't add that Nick would probably have been able to fix it in five minutes, but suspected that that was what her mother and her daughter were both thinking. When it came to elderly plumbing, Nick had always had the golden touch.

'Well make sure you do, dear. Can't have you and Charlotte freezing to death, can we? And what if you get a burst pipe or something? I do worry about you being here all on your own . . .'

'Can I put my jumper on now?' demanded Lottie, dancing from one foot to the other in an effort to get warm.

'No, love, not quite yet. We've still got some pinning-up to do. But Mummy will turn up the fan heater, won't you, dear?'

Mummy obediently did so, and a sort of hot mini-mistral blew through the dining room, ruffling up the net curtain so that Lottie looked as though she was emerging from a big white cloud. Quite appropriate really, seeing as they were trying to put together her angel costume for the school Christmas play.

91

'Can I have real wings?' asked Lottie.

Hannah rummaged around in the mess for a missing sequin. 'What do you mean, real wings?'

'Real ones. With feathers.'

Not unless you grow them yourself, thought Hannah.

'Oh, I expect so dear,' murmured Erica, calmly pinning away and patently not listening.

'And they have to be really big. Like, from the top of my head right down to the ground.'

'Er . . . I don't know about that,' cautioned Hannah, who had been wondering if they could make do with the £3.99 pair of fairy wings she'd seen in Woolworth's. Proud though she was of her daughter's starring role, the thought of gluing on five million white chicken-feathers was stretching motherly affection just a little too far. 'Little gauzy ones would look nice. Wouldn't they, Grandma?'

But Grandma was humming away to herself and measuring Lottie's arms for long, medieval-style sleeves.

'Miss Grimshaw at school says that some of the really top important angels in the Bible have three pairs of wings. That's six wings! Can I have six wings? 'Cause if I'm the Angel of the Lord I'm important, aren't I?'

'Of course you are, dear,' agreed Erica.

Hannah decided that indulgence had its limits, even for budding divas who had to sing a whole verse of 'While Shepherds Watched' on their own, *a cappella*. 'Hang on,' she said, 'this is Farmington Lane Juniors, not Covent Garden. You'll have a tinsel halo and like it.'

But Lottie wasn't quite done. 'All right then, how about pretty shoes? I'll need pretty sparkly shoes with heels so I look taller than the ordinary people, won't I?' she reasoned.

'Angels don't wear high heels dear,' said Grandma, smiling, much to Hannah's relief. 'In fact, if I remember what they taught us at Sunday School, the Bible doesn't even say if angels are male or female. And Gabriel is rather a boy's name, you know.'

'I'm not a boy angel!' protested Lottie.

'No dear, and with this lovely dress nobody will think you are. Now, hand me that needle and thread will you, Hannah? I need to tack this up before we take it off.'

'Do I look all right?' asked Lottie anxiously, trying to look down at herself without snagging herself on all the pins.

'Gorgeous,' declared Hannah. 'You've got a very clever Grandma.'

Hannah could only marvel at her mother's handiwork. If she'd tried to knock up an angel costume out of some old Christmas decorations, net curtains and a duvet cover, the result would certainly have moved the audience to tears – of hysterical laughter. Instead, Lottie was going to be the best-dressed Angel of the Lord Farmington Lane had ever seen.

Erica blushed appreciatively. 'Ah well, time was when all little girls were taught to sew and cook – and quite right too. Much more useful than all that stuff about oxbow lakes. You were never that interested so I didn't force you to learn.'

'Well, it's very good of you to make Lottie's costume for her,' said Hannah.

'It's a pleasure, dear. You know how I missed out on all this prettifying when you were a child; all you ever seemed to be cast as were shepherds, kings and Christmas puddings.'

It wasn't unkindly meant but, not for the first time, Hannah felt like an immense disappointment to her parents. 'I did play an earwig once,' she reminded her mother. 'That must've been a challenge.'

'Yes dear, but not quite in the same league as an angel.' Erica stood back to admire her handiwork. 'There. Don't you look nice? Jump down and have a look at yourself in the mirror, then you can take it off – *carefully,* mind!'

'I bet Melanie-Anne's costume's not nearly as good as yours,' remarked Hannah, only too aware of the friendly rivalry between the two girls. Melanie-Anne's family might be dripping with spare cash, but they didn't have their very own Coco Chanel. 'How's her mum getting on?'

Lottie didn't turn round from admiring herself in the mirror, but Hannah saw her back stiffen. 'Dunno.'

'I expect she'll hire something from that place in the High Street,' said Erica sadly. 'So many of them do these days. As if it's not perfectly easy to do something with a tea towel and an old blanket. What does Melanie-Anne think about playing a shepherd, dear?'

'Dunno,' repeated Lottie. The words 'and I don't care' hung silently on the air.

'You two haven't fallen out, have you?' enquired Hannah. Lottie's silence was as good as a yes. 'I don't know, you girls! What's it about this time?'

'Oh, I wouldn't worry, Hannah, whatever it is they'll have forgotten all about it by tomorrow,' Erica assured her. 'Now, let's fold this up carefully; we don't want anything happening to it before the big night.'

'Yes,' enthused Hannah. 'And Daddy can't wait to see you up on that stage; he told me today how much he's looking forward to it. Bet you're looking forward to seeing him at the weekend, too,' she added hopefully.

There was a silent, empty moment before Lottie stepped out of the costume, leaving a crumpled O of net on the carpet, turned to her mother and replied: 'I told you, I haven't got a Daddy.'

Then she walked off up the stairs and closed her bedroom door behind her with a short, dry click.

*

What with the tensions at home, the awkwardness of empty evenings, and a series of impossible clients at the salon, Hannah was grateful for the invitation to have a midweek dinner with Maxine and Jay.

Not that it was anything particularly out of the ordinary. They'd been eating dinners at each other's houses for years now, and Hannah knew the layout of Maxine's kitchen almost better than she knew her own. There was just one new element tonight though: this was the first time she'd come along without Nick.

Even the time he'd had viral pneumonia, they'd simply relocated the meal to Hannah's house and eaten it sitting round his bed. But this time she was flying solo – and it felt very strange indeed.

Almost before she'd got her finger to the doorbell of the neat semi-detached, the door swung open and Maxine dragged her inside. 'You're late, we've been waiting ages!'

'But it's only ten past—'

'Don't just stand there,' Maxine giggled, 'come in, take your coat off, there's someone Jay wants to introduce you to.'

Somewhat bewildered, Hannah allowed herself to be half led, half dragged into the living room. There, on the orange sofa in the middle of a minimalist sea of birchwood laminate flooring, sat a very tall man who looked even more bewildered than she felt.

'Hannah, hiya darlin'.' Jay smooched her on the cheek and presented her with the fullest glass of red wine she'd ever set eyes on. 'This here is Justin. Justin, this is our mate Hannah.'

Justin got to his feet and immediately seemed to grow about ten feet in height as his oversized legs took over. He looked, thought Hannah, rather like an embarrassed spaniel crossed with a very big stick insect.

'Er . . . hello, Hannah. Pleased to meet you.' The voice was melodious and rather public-school, the smile a disturbing expanse of very large, very white teeth.

'Likewise,' said Hannah, though frankly she wasn't especially. She mouthed a silent protest at Maxine, who simply giggled again.

'We just *had* to invite the two of you so you could meet,' she said, fussing around them with a bowl of nibbles. 'You've got so much in common! You've just split up with Nick, and Justin and his wife split up a year ago, so he's on his own with the triplets now . . .'

'And don't forget that Indian thing,' cut in Jay.

'Oh yes, the Ayur—what's it called again?'

'Ayurvedic chakra realignment, it's a really new technique,' enthused Justin, still a little nervous but rapidly warming to his subject. 'It's what I'm specialising in right now – when I'm not focusing on the tantric sex workshops.'

'You see?' went on Maxine. 'He's into personal growth and therapies and stuff too, you two could even go into business together!' She shoved a dish under Hannah's nose. 'Cocktail blini?'

Hannah was just about to try and extricate herself from this terrible descent into the blind date from hell, when a sudden change of expression crossed Maxine's face. Within the space of a millisecond, her all-year-round-tan had turned to ashen grey.

'Ooh dear, I'm off again.'

'What's wrong?' demanded Hannah.

Without a word, Jay emptied a bowl of crisps onto the table and stuck it under his wife at the precise moment she threw up. Completely unfazed by this unscheduled command performance, he turned a dazzling smile on his guests, while Maxine quickly excused herself.

95

'Pregnancy, eh? That's the tenth time today. Best thing that's ever happened to us, though,'

'You bet it is,' agreed Maxine, as she returned. 'Now, anybody for more blinis?'

In a corner of the classroom, Lottie was painting something with a lot of black in it. She felt black, all in all, and if there had been a colour even blacker than black she'd have used that too.

'What's *that* supposed to be?' demanded Melanie-Anne, demure as ever in a fluffy white jumper with not a speck of paint on it.

Lottie felt like saying: 'Your stupid face,' but instead she just shrugged and said: 'Whatever.'

'Your painting's stupid, it's all black. Mine's a cow.'

Lottie glanced at it. 'It's got five legs.'

'No it hasn't! That's its tail.'

'What's a cow got to do with Christmas?'

'More than your black thing has.' She glanced over her shoulder at Miss Grimshaw, who was absorbed in explaining to Jason Allsopp that the Wise Men weren't generally thought to have toted AK-47s. 'Going round to see your *daddy* at the weekend, are you?'

Lottie's face darkened. 'Shut up.'

'Told you he wouldn't stay just 'cause you wanted him to.'

'Shut *up*.'

'First they leave your mum, then they leave you, and you never see them again. Just you wait and see.'

A fraction of a second later there was a squeal, and Miss Grimshaw turned round to see Melanie-Anne spattered from head to feet in black paint.

'What on earth is going on?'

Melanie-Anne pointed furiously at Lottie. 'She . . . she—'

'Sorry miss, it was an accident miss,' said Lottie contritely, and went back to her painting.

By Thursday, Hannah was beginning to think that maybe the downstairs heating wasn't going to stage another of its Lazarus-like revivals. Sooner or later she was going to have to admit defeat and phone the heating engineer . . . or Nick. No, not Nick, she told herself for the umpteenth time. Snap out of it, Hannah, you're an independent woman. You can plaster a ceiling, you can leap tall buildings in a single bound.

Yes, she pointed out to herself; but you can't mend sodding plumbing, can you?

She was musing on the general malevolence of all things mechanical as she walked out of the salon at lunchtime – and smack bang into Nick.

'Hi.'

'Er . . . hi.' She looked him up and down. 'What are you doing here?'

He looked a little crestfallen. 'I can go away again if you like.'

'No, no, you don't have to do that.' She didn't add that actually she was quite pleased to see him. 'Is something wrong?'

'No. Nothing. Quite the reverse. In fact I . . . fancy lunch in that little caff over the road?'

'The one we used to eat in when my student loan was running out?'

'Yeah, why not? For old times' sake.'

She shrugged. 'Why not.' And they walked across the road together, very nearly the same way they had walked everywhere when she was a beauty-therapy student and they had no money because every penny went into the house or taking care of Lottie.

They squeezed into a corner, ordered egg and chips, and Hannah looked at Nick expectantly. 'Well?'

'Well what?'

'I'm assuming there's some reason for you turning up out of nowhere and inviting me out for a slap-up feed?'

He sighed. 'You know me too well.'

'Maybe.' She smiled at him with genuine warmth. 'Or not enough. Anyway, tell me.'

Nick drummed his fingers on the wipe-clean check tablecloth. 'I thought we ought to talk.'

'OK. We're talking.'

'The thing is, I've . . . you know, and I thought you ought to know about it before anybody else.'

She frowned, utterly perplexed. It was only a few days since she'd last seen Nick, but already their lives were taking distinctively different turnings. It was weird, not knowing everything about what he was doing, and knowing that he was probably thinking the same thing about her. 'You've what?' she demanded.

He swallowed very, very hard, like there was an enormous pebble stuck in his throat and if he didn't get it down he would die. 'I've met someone.'

A tiny electric shock tingled up Hannah's spine. Covering up her confusion, she took a swig of hot, sweet, obscenely strong tea. 'Someone?'

'Someone . . . special.' Now that he'd finally got the first words out, it was as if the dam had collapsed and all the other ones were tumbling out in their wake. 'She's called Miranda, and she runs a smallholding near Cirencester, with her own bees and everything, and she's really nice, you'd like her.'

The electric tingle had gone away, leaving in its wake a kind of cold, numbing paralysis. 'Yeah,' said Hannah quietly. 'Yeah, I'm sure I would. She sounds . . . like you say. Nice.'

Nick looked into her face, a trace of concern in his eyes. 'You are all right about it, aren't you?'

She forced a smile onto her face. Goodness knows why she had to force it there; after all they weren't an item any more and this was exactly what she'd been hoping for him. She decided it was just the suddenness of it all. 'Of course I am, Nick.' She leaned across the table and planted a very chaste, very sisterly kiss on his cheek. 'I'm really happy for you, sweetheart, you know that.'

And she was. Truly. It was just going to take a little while to make herself understand the fact.

Hannah was sitting watching TV, wrapped up in her biggest jumper, when a shrill cry came from the downstairs loo.

'Aaaagh! Mum!'

Hannah got up and went out into the hall. 'Lottie? Are you OK?'

She was halfway through the kitchen when the door at the far end opened and a bedraggled figure appeared, towel in hand. 'Mum, I'm all wet!'

It was the understatement of the year. Lottie was soaked through from her knees down to the soles of her school shoes. 'Good grief, what on earth happened?'

'I was sitting on the loo, Mum, and all of a sudden there was this sort of . . . gurgling sound from the radiator and then there was all this cold water sloshing round my legs!'

Hannah put an arm round her soggy child's shoulders. 'Better get you towelled down and into some nice dry socks,' she said. She stuck her head round the cloakroom door. It wasn't quite as bad in there as she'd feared, but it was bad enough. There was a half-inch of water all over the floor and the radiator was still leaking rapidly. With a silent prayer to the god of plumbing, Hannah went and fetched the mop and a couple of buckets.

'Mum,' said Lottie.

'Go and get yourself dry.'

'In a minute. Mum, you will phone the man to come and mend the heating, won't you? It's so cold even Doom's getting fed up, and the vet said he ought to keep warm 'cause of his arthritis.' The three-legged Rottweiler contributed a mournful look of agreement.

'Yes, yes, tomorrow. I expect.'

'Now, Mum. Please?'

It was no good. She'd tried everything in her armoury and it just hadn't worked. Half an hour on her belly on the utility room floor, trying to re-fire the boiler, had produced nothing more useful than grazed elbows and a cricked neck. 'Oh, all right.'

Face it, she thought, you're not quite as independent as you thought you were. You've got three choices: Nick, your dad, or that super-expensive heating engineer who makes you feel mentally subnormal.

With a groan she picked up the telephone and dialled. 'Hi. Is that the twenty-four-hour heating repairs service?'

It was Saturday morning, and the house was blissfully warm for the first time in nearly a week. Hannah almost purred with contentment as she eased herself out of the bath into a fuzzy warm bath towel and padded out onto the landing in her fluffy mules.

'Lottie.'

No reply.

'Lottie, I hope you're up, 'cause Daddy's coming to pick you up in half an hour and you haven't had your breakfast yet.'

She continued along the landing to the door with the sign on it that read 'Parent-Free Zone', knocked, and went in.

Lottie was lying on her belly on the duvet, still in her pyjamas, an empty holdall on the floor beside her and clothes scattered all over the place.

Hannah frowned. 'Are you OK, love? Better get a move on, Daddy'll be here soon and he's got all sorts of exciting things planned for you this weekend.'

Her daughter didn't answer.

'Lottie?' Hannah sat down beside her and instinctively placed a hand on her forehead, but she wasn't burning up or cold and clammy. 'Is something the matter?'

The little head with the red mane lifted off the folded hands, and the pointed chin seemed to acquire a defiant tilt. 'I'm not going.'

'What? Don't be silly, of course you are. And you're going to have a great time.'

Lottie's eyes flashed a warning, and she shrugged off her mother's reassuring hand. 'I'm not going, Mum. And he's not my daddy. And you can't make me.'

Chapter 12

Hannah laid a hand on Lottie's shoulder. This time, thankfully, it wasn't shrugged off. 'I know this is hard for you, sweetheart,' she said gently, 'and I'm truly sorry, but taking it out on Daddy isn't the way to make things better.'

Lottie's eyes still held a spark of fury as she said, very slowly and distinctly, 'He's *not* my daddy.'

Hannah's heart was breaking with guilt, but she couldn't let it show. Not only would it make Lottie think she could win this battle of wills, it might also sow the seeds of doubt in her own mind. And that, above all things, could not be allowed to happen. The rightness of what she and Nick had decided, like sensible adults who cared about each other, could not be called into question. Not if they were all going to get through this emotionally unscarred.

'We've already talked about this lots, you know,' she went on. 'You don't have to call him Daddy if you don't want, but you know it hurts him very much when you say things like that.'

The look in Lottie's eyes said: 'And maybe that's precisely why I'm doing it.' She lay on her tummy on the bed and kicked her legs. 'So what am I supposed to call him, then?'

'What would you like to call him?'

'What's the point? He'll be gone soon anyway.'

That shocked Hannah to the core. 'Gone? What are you talking about? Daddy's not going anywhere, he loves you!'

'He said he'd never leave us, but he did.'

The depth of Lottie's hurt left Hannah feeling helpless. How could she get through to her daughter, make her see that just because two grown-ups didn't want to be tied together any more, that didn't mean they would ever dream of letting her down?

She took a deep breath. 'Look sweetheart, I can't make you believe this, but it's the truth. Daddy and I both love you just as much as we've ever done, and the only reason Daddy's not living here any more is because we realised that being married was making us both unhappy. He hasn't left you, he'd never leave you. Why on earth do you think he wants to spend this weekend with you?'

Lottie rolled over and sat up. 'Dunno.'

'Can't you give him a chance? Let him prove to you that he's still the same Daddy he's always been?'

There was a long silence. Then Lottie picked up a T-shirt from the floor and threw it into the holdall. 'All right,' she said finally, 'I'll go. But you can't make me enjoy it and you can't make me call him Daddy.'

It was the weirdest weekend Hannah had ever spent. Weirder even than the one when Cheltenham was snowed in and she'd had to find room for fourteen Vietnamese exchange students on her floor.

The house was utterly silent, an echoing shell. It didn't matter how loud she turned up the radio, she could still hear that eerie silence – as if the house's soul had left it, along with Lottie.

There was an abandoned rollerblade halfway up the stairs, but she didn't tidy it away. Its very presence was a kind of insurance policy, a reassurance that come Sunday evening, Lottie would be back and demanding hot chocolate with extra marshmallows.

Saturday morning wasn't so bad, as she had a wedding party coming to the salon for facials and Indian head-massage; but the rest of the day seemed to lie in front of her like a blank sheet of A4 paper in a maths exam, waiting expectantly for her to fill it with something meaningful, and probably in for a big disappointment. It was all she could do not to ring Lottie's new mobile, ostensibly to check that she was OK, but really just to hear the sound of her voice.

As if she could possibly *not* be OK. She was with Nick, and they were at that new theme park, having a brilliant time. Stop moping, she told herself; this isn't a bad thing, it's an opportunity. How long is it since you had the freedom to do exactly what you want?

Blimey, she thought as she opened a box of chocolates and ate every single orange cream, just because she could; I could walk round the house naked if I wanted. Or spend all day in the pub. Or eat orange creams till I throw up all over the carpet.

Spoilt for choice, she went shopping, bought a new doormat and then cleaned out the kitchen cupboards. Not exactly rock 'n' roll perhaps, but everybody had to start somewhere. Then she microwaved herself something out of the freezer, fed the menagerie and settled down in front of the telly with a ferret on her lap.

As luck would have it, they were screening *Twenty-Four-Hour Party People*. She'd seen it before, but there was something fascinating about watching other people screwing their lives up. Really she ought to feel superior – after all, she had a nice home, a beautiful daughter, and even if she and her husband weren't together any more, they were still the best of friends, and that was more than these losers had ever achieved.

But she found herself feeling quite wistful. There was no avoiding the truth: living irresponsibly might be stupid but it didn't half look fun. Besides, you could party without going over the top, couldn't you? Go out and have fun while you were still young and able to enjoy it. After all, she reminded herself, Nick wasn't exactly letting his life stand still, was he?

Yeah, thought Hannah. Fun, that's all the therapy I need. The question is, how does a semi-detached thirty-one year-old go about finding it?

Hannah was tentatively exploring chat rooms on the Net when the doorbell rang on Sunday evening. Feeling slightly guilty and not knowing quite why, she disconnected and ran downstairs to open the door.

Lottie and Nick were standing on the doorstep, Nick wearing an absurd cowboy hat and Lottie carrying an enormous pink stuffed elephant.

'Hi Hannah,' said Nick with a grin, taking off the hat and sticking it on her head. 'There you go, it looks much better on you.'

'Lottie, sweetheart!' Hannah gave her a huge hug. 'Did you have a good time?'

'Fantastic,' enthused Nick. 'Didn't we, Lotpot?'

Lottie opened her mouth, closed it, opened it again and at last said in a very small voice: 'Great.'

'We won this on the rifle range, didn't we?'

'*You* won it, I just watched.'

'Yes, but you were my lucky mascot.'

'I'm going in now, are there any biscuits? I'm starving.' Lottie pushed past Nick and her mother, and headed for the kitchen.

'Aren't you going to say thank you to Daddy?' Hannah called after her. But the kitchen door had already closed behind Lottie's back.

'You win some, you lose some, I guess,' said Nick, his grin fading.

'I'm sorry, Nick, I'm sure she had a good time though.'

'Maybe. It was hard to tell. Just when she looked like she was enjoying herself, she'd clam up on me and I'd start to think she really does hate me.' He looked at Hannah with a puppy-dog need for reassurance. 'You don't think she does, do you?'

'Of course she doesn't, she's just a hurt little girl. But we both know it's going to take time for things to settle down into a routine she can accept.'

'I guess all we can do is give her plenty of love and stability.' He grimaced. 'God, I sound just like a social worker.' He glanced at his watch. 'Oh well, better be on my way, I suppose.'

'You don't fancy coming in for a coffee then?' Hannah suggested. 'Before Lottie eats all the custard creams?'

'I'd love to, but I'm off to ... er ...'

'Going somewhere special?'

Nick coloured slightly. 'Actually I'm going round to Miranda's.'

'Ah. Right.'

'Sort of said I might take a few of my things round there this evening. We're um ... getting on really well, you know.'

Hannah raised an eyebrow. 'Sounds like it.'

'I mean, it's early days and all that, but yes, we really are getting on great. So when Miranda suggested I might like to move in—'

Hannah's head spun. 'Move in!'

'Only on a sort of trial basis, you know, see how things go. But I'm pretty confident it's going to work out for us.'

'That's ... amazing.' Hannah's mouth was dry as dust, her heart pounding like a steam hammer.

Nick smiled broadly, put his arms round Hannah and gave her

104

the most fraternal of hugs. 'I knew you'd be pleased for me. I can't wait for you to meet her – and Lottie too. She's incredible. She's got this—'

'Hang on a minute,' cut in Hannah, at last finding her voice. 'You're moving in?'

'That's right.'

'And you've known this woman how long?'

'I dunno, a few weeks.'

'What if it all goes wrong?'

Nick patted her arm reassuringly. 'Don't worry, love, I'm keeping the flat on for the time being, just as a back-up, you know.'

'Good.' Hannah's eyes narrowed. 'Because I have to tell you, I'm not happy about Lottie spending her weekends with you round at this Miranda woman's house.'

'But why?'

'Stability, Nick. Haven't we just been saying that's what Lottie needs?'

'Yes of course, but—'

'Do you really think she needs to be hauled off to some strange house to see her daddy smooching his new lover?'

Nick looked frankly bewildered. 'It's not like that. Anyway, I wasn't planning to have her to stay there, not yet anyway.'

'I'm glad to hear it,' replied Hannah. 'Because if you care about Lottie as much as you say you do, you're going to have to make some decisions about what really matters to you.'

'Lottie matters to me more than anything, you know that! I'd never do anything to hurt her.'

'Then you'll have her to stay in the flat and spend time with just the two of you together?'

'Of course I will.'

'OK then. No problem.' Forcing her face into some semblance of a relaxed smile, Hannah reached up to push the hair off her face and realised she was still wearing Nick's stupid cowboy hat. Snatching it off, she stuck it back on his head. 'You can have this back, though, I don't think it's quite me.'

It was only after Nick had gone, whistling his way back to the car as if he hadn't a care in the world, that the full force of Hannah's resentment hit home. I didn't say all of that just for Lottie's sake, she thought to herself, I did it to make him feel bad.

If there was one thing worse than not lusting after your husband, it was knowing that some other woman did. And that he thought the sun shone out of her perfect backside.

How could he get over me so easily? she seethed. How dare he get over me at all?

On Tuesday afternoon, while she was giving Miss Fabian a warm-wax treatment for her arthritic hands, Hannah got an unexpected telephone call.

'The Beauty Room, can I help you?'

'Mrs Steadman? Miss Grimshaw here, Lottie's teacher. I was wondering if we could have a little chat.'

Hannah wiped a hand on her crisp white tunic. 'Well, it's a bit difficult just at the moment, I've got a client with me.'

'Oh, I didn't mean this minute. To be honest, I think it would be much better if we met up and talked face to face. I'm a little bit concerned about Lottie.'

'Concerned?' A stab of alarm tightened Hannah's chest. 'Why? What's happened?'

'Are you free this afternoon after school? Say, four thirty in my classroom?'

Hannah cast a glance at her crammed appointments book. Free she was definitely not, but if this was something to do with Lottie then she'd make the time. 'I . . . yes, I guess I can free up some time then?'

'That's wonderful. Will Mr Steadman be coming along too?'

Hannah made a lightning decision. In the past, she'd have been straight on the phone to Nick, but now things were somewhat different. The balance had shifted and, when all was said and done, she was Lottie's flesh and blood mother. This was her responsibility and nobody else's. 'No, I don't think he'll be able to make it.'

'Ah well, never mind. I'll see you then, Mrs Steadman. 'Bye.'

Miss Fabian had been hanging onto Hannah's end of the conversation with great interest, while her pop-eyed pug, Bertie, squatted under the treatment table in a malodorous cloud of his own farts. 'Problems at home, dear? Nothing serious, I hope?'

'Nothing I can't handle,' Hannah promised her; but inside she wasn't quite so sure.

*

She arrived at the school five minutes early, as the last of the teachers' Minis and Fiestas were rolling through the gates onto Farmington Lane. Miss Grimshaw's little silver Vespa sat girlishly beside the bike-racks; and Hannah wondered how she could possibly feel nervous about meeting someone who looked about sixteen and rode a scooter with L-plates.

Sadie Grimshaw was waiting for her in her Year Four classroom, busily tacking up displays of project work about Hadrian's Wall, each one neatly framed in brightly coloured card.

'Ah, Mrs Steadman! It's good of you to come at such short notice.' Miss Grimshaw put down her staple gun on top of a pile of cut-out Roman legionaries. 'Do take a seat.'

Feeling quite uneasy, Hannah perched on a chair that even Lottie would have found a bit small, while the teacher cleared a small space and sat on the corner of the desk. Talk about being looked down upon from a great height, thought Hannah, beginning to wish she had brought Nick along, if only so that he could feel humiliated too.

'So, what's this all about?' she asked. 'Why are you worried about Lottie?'

Sadie Grimshaw slid open the drawer behind her and took out sheet of paper. 'What do you make of this?' she asked.

Hannah turned it this way and that, but without a great deal of success. 'Not much,' she admitted. 'It's just a mess of black paint.'

'And what would you say if I told you that was what Lottie came up with when I asked the class to paint a picture entitled "Christmas"?'

Hannah's eyes widened. 'Christmas? You're not serious?'

'I'm afraid I am, Mrs Steadman. And it's not the first time Lottie's pictures have been . . . let's say . . . a little disturbing lately. Then there's the fall in the standard of her work.'

Hannah listened through a kind of fog of disbelief. Her Lottie? Falling behind in class? 'But surely . . . Lottie's really bright, you said so at the last parent-teacher evening. Right up there at the top of her class, you told us.'

Sadie Grimshaw nodded. 'And she is bright, that's why I'm so concerned. These last few weeks she's been like a completely different child in class – uninterested, lazy, moody, sometimes even disruptive.'

'You can't mean that! Lottie's never been any trouble at all. Mrs Williams in Year Three always said she was a joy to teach.'

The young teacher sighed. 'It's never easy to say these things about a child,' she said. 'Especially one with as much potential as Lottie. But please believe me, after the incident with Melanie-Anne I just couldn't let it go on any longer without speaking to you.'

'What incident?' demanded Hannah.

'The one I told you about in the note I sent home with Lottie.'

'What note?'

'Ah. So she didn't deliver it to you? I was wondering why you hadn't been in touch. The thing is, Lottie threw her school lunch all over Melanie-Anne in the dining room last week. And there was an incident where I'm almost sure Lottie deliberately threw black paint at her. None of us could get any sense out of her as to why she did it, and I thought maybe you might be able to shed some light on it.'

'I don't believe this, I just don't believe this,' Hannah kept repeating, rubbing her hand across her temples as if the action might force acceptance in through her thick skull. 'Why on earth would she do a thing like that? I thought they might have had a bit of a falling-out, but Melanie-Anne's her best friend.'

Miss Grimshaw got up and walked across the classroom to the window. Outside, thin sleet had started to fall, turning to golden spears in the glow from the street lamp on the other side of the road. 'I can't help wondering if there's something worrying Lottie,' she said quietly. 'Perhaps something at home?'

This is all my fault, thought Hannah glumly. My fault and Nick's. She took a deep breath. 'My husband and I . . . we split up recently.'

'Ah. I see.'

'Lottie's having some problems coming to terms with Nick leaving, but we're still on good terms and it's not as if he's gone far. And she sees him every few days.' She looked up. 'We're doing our best,' she said, almost begging to be believed.

'I'm sure you are.'

'And I don't see what it has to do with Melanie-Anne.'

'No. But perhaps Lottie will tell you if you ask her.' Miss Grimshaw rubbed her chin, leaving behind a faint smudge of blue marker pen. 'In the meantime though, I think I may have to make a few changes to the Christmas play.'

Hannah's heart was in her mouth. She cast her mind back to happy, laughing Lottie, parading around the dining room in net curtains and home-made wings. 'You're not going to write her out, are you? Please don't do that, she'll be heartbroken.'

Miss Grimshaw smiled. 'Oh, I don't think it'll come to that. But it might be best to ensure the two girls aren't in any scenes together. It's challenging enough dealing with a live donkey in the school hall, without two of the stars fighting on stage as well.'

'I've got a tummy ache,' insisted Lottie when Hannah tried to quiz her about the incident with Melanie-Anne. 'I don't feel like talking.'

'I don't feel much like having an argument with you,' replied Hannah, 'but if you behave badly at school and throw away notes from your teacher, what am I supposed to do?'

Lottie fell silent. 'I'm sorry,' she said. 'About the note. I knew you'd be angry so I threw it away.'

'But why did you throw your lunch – and paint – all over Melanie-Anne in the first place?' repeated Hannah, trying her utmost to be patient and understanding. 'Did she do something to provoke you?'

Lottie turned her head away, but not before Hannah had caught a glimpse of unshed tears in the corner of her eye. 'Hey, ratbag, what's up? You can tell me, you know; I only want to help.'

'I told you, I've got a tummy ache.'

Hannah laid a hand on Lottie's forehead. It did seem a little hot and dry, but that could just be because she was upset. Either way though, there didn't seem much point in pressing on, not tonight. 'All right love, let's get you into bed with a nice hottie.'

'It hurts, Mum, it really does,' insisted Lottie as Hannah tucked her into bed.

'I know, sweetheart; but it'll be all better in the morning, just you wait and see.'

She kissed her on the forehead, put out the light, and wished everything else could be cured so easily.

Nick sat down heavily on Hannah's sofa. 'Why on earth didn't you tell me her teacher wanted to see us? I could have got there by half-past.'

Hannah slid a mug of coffee towards him and sat down beside

him, one leg tucked underneath her. 'I know, I'm sorry. I just thought, on the spur of the moment . . .' She didn't add "that I'd punish you for not being here and not being Lottie's dad and being too bloody happy by half", because she knew she'd been childish and vindictive and that really had to stop. 'It just seemed easier,' she ended lamely.

Nick flopped back, arms stretched out along the back of the sofa. 'I can't believe it,' he said. 'Any other kid, maybe. But not Lottie.'

'That's what I said. But you didn't see that painting she did.'

'No.'

'Nick, I'm really, really worried about her. I never thought us splitting up would have this bad an effect on her – was I just being naïve?'

He reached out, took her hand and gave it a squeeze. It wasn't much but right now she really needed it. Needed to know that they were united in this, if not in their marriage then at least in their love for their daughter. And she *is* your daughter, thought Hannah, no matter what the DNA might say. She's your daughter as much as she is mine.

'Maybe we both were. But that doesn't mean we did the wrong thing. I mean, staying together for the sake of the kids – that's the classic bad news cliché, isn't it? The thing you shouldn't ever do. Look at that couple in Gloucester, the ones in the paper. They stuck it out for twenty-two years and then she stabbed him with the bread knife the day the last one left for university.'

Hannah couldn't suppress a smile. 'I wouldn't do that.'

'No?'

'Definitely not. Much too messy. Give me poison any day.'

They sat in companionable silence, sharing something of the way things had been before, the quiet togetherness of an evening doing not very much at all, while Lottie slept safe and sound in her bed upstairs.

'What are we going to do?' asked Hannah after a while.

'I'm not sure. Just go on giving her as much support as we can, I guess. What did Miss Grimshaw suggest?'

'Pretty much that. Plus maybe a referral to a child psychologist if things get any worse.'

'A child psychologist!' Nick looked stunned. 'My God, I think of the kids I've labelled "difficult" and "disruptive", and then I think of Lottie, and it's like, this isn't really happening, it can't be.' His arm curled round Hannah's shoulders. 'Look, whatever else is happening to us, I want you to know I'm here for Lottie. Always. Nothing's ever going to come before that, not ever.'

Hannah wanted to ask, 'Not even Miranda?' but she was feeling warm and fuzzy and comforted, and couldn't bring herself to be quite that mean.

'There is just one thing I've been thinking about, though,' Nick went on. 'And it's getting nearer all the time.'

'What's that then?'

'Christmas. You talking about Lottie and her angel costume made me wonder what we're going to do over the holidays.'

The thought dropped into Hannah's brain like a very large and unexpected stone. 'I haven't a clue. To be honest I haven't really thought about it.'

'We'll have to though, won't we? I mean, do we do the two-separate-Christmases thing, with one of us having Lottie on Christmas Day and the other on Boxing Day, or do we get together for the big family do like we always have done? Or do we do something different?'

Hannah looked at him quizzically. 'What sort of different?'

'We-ell . . . I was talking to Miranda the other day.' Hannah felt her blood pressure climb just the merest fraction. 'And she was saying that if you wanted – and only if you were happy about it of course – everybody could come round to the cottage and we could all spend Christmas Day there. I know it's a bit sudden, but hey, we've all got to meet up sometime. So what do you reckon to that then?'

111

Chapter 13

It was the worst day of Herbie's life.

Even worse than the day he'd been arrested bang in the middle of Erica and Derek's wedding. And it wasn't a lot of fun being rugby-tackled by your own future son-in-law, in front of two hundred and fifty gawping relatives.

That was bad. But this was definitely worse.

Clutching the small suitcase that contained all his worldly goods and his faithful budgie, he bid a final farewell to Bomber, Charlie, Kev and all the other lads and wended his miserable way towards freedom. His twenty-year-old suit smelled funny and pinched under the arms, and he was already missing his nice comfortable prison blues.

'So, looking forward to getting out?' enquired the prison officer who signed him out.

'No.'

'Course you are.' The officer slapped him on the back. 'Just make sure we don't see you again here, OK? You're far too old for this lark.'

Too old to be thrown out into the big wide world, that's for sure, brooded Herbie as the gates were unlocked and he took his first reluctant steps into life outside. He shivered as the wind hit him. Even the weather was unfriendly – not like his nice warm cell, where the social worker had fixed him up with his own fan heater and hot-water bottle.

To make matters worse, it was Thursday. And Thursday afternoons meant an illicit poker game in Charlie's cell. Herbie was good at poker. He didn't suppose there'd be many opportunities to play at Erica's though, illicit or otherwise.

Exactly as he feared, there was a car waiting for him across the road – just far enough from the prison gates to look as if it might not have anything to do with them, or the elderly man in the brown suit. Herbie had never seen Erica and Derek's car, but he knew it was theirs even before the passenger door opened and Erica got out. It looked just like a panda car without the stripes. Once a cop, always a cop, he thought morosely.

For a moment, he had a mad impulse to leg it. Then he remembered he had arthritis in his knees and only ten quid to his name. With a last regretful glance back at his home from home, he shuffled across the road towards the waiting car.

'Hello Dad,' said Erica, without much enthusiasm.

He grunted. Derek barely acknowledged his presence. Some family reunion.

Even as the car was pulling away, Herbie was wondering what kind of a crime he'd need to commit to get sent right back.

'Anyway, he hardly said a word all the way home,' Erica went on, 'but that's probably for the best. Your grandfather's language isn't exactly public school.'

'How's he settling in?' enquired Hannah, trying not to get butter on the cordless phone as she prepared sandwiches for her and Lottie's packed lunches.

'He's not. He spends all day sitting in a corner glaring at everybody and complaining about everything. And when he's not doing that he's trying to shock me with his obscene jokes.'

Hannah strained to remember this paragon of grumpiness, but could only recall someone who'd pulled silly faces and made her laugh. Still, you always saw people differently when you were a kid, didn't you? Most probably she'd liked Grandad because he was every bit as childish as she was.

In the intervening years there hadn't been much opportunity to keep in touch, exept via the occasional letter and Christmas card. Gradually, Herbie had refused all family visits, quite understandably since Erica spent the whole time looking terrified that someone she knew would see her talking to a convict, and Derek just plain glowered. Nobody asked Hannah if she wanted to go anyway: in fact she was twenty-three before she got her parents to admit that Gramps wasn't working abroad on an oil rig after all.

I should've tried harder, she told herself, feeling suddenly guilty. We all should.

'We'll pop over and see him in a day or two,' she promised. 'Maybe a visitor or two will cheer him up.'

'Hannah love, I don't think *anything* would cheer your grandfather up.'

'Give him time,' she advised. 'He's only been with you a day or two. It must feel strange, after being in prison for so long.'

'Yes, I suppose you're right,' conceded Erica. 'But it would help if he was even the tiniest bit grateful. You'd think he'd be pleased that we've put ourselves out to take him in, but to listen to him ...' She tutted softly. 'It's like having a teenager in the house again. Do you remember when you went through that phase of saying everything we said or did was complete nonsense? And I told you not to try and bleach your hair with Domestos but you did it anyway and it all fell out?'

Hannah did. She winced at the memory. 'Oh Mum, don't! I've still got that to look forward to with Lottie.' Though actually, she thought to herself, the poor kid's doing a fair impression of a troubled teenager already.

'How is Lottie? Has she got over that tummy upset she had?'

'More or less, I think. Just the odd twinge.'

'Ah well, you know what kids are like – they bounce back before you know it.'

Hannah glanced at the clock and was horrified to see that it was almost eight thirty. 'Anyway, I'd better go now and drag her out of bed, or she's going to be late for school.'

'Lottie, late for school?' Erica laughed. 'That'd be a first. I've never met a kid who loves school like she does!'

'Actually, she's not quite so keen on it at the moment,' confessed Hannah. 'You know that falling-out she had with Melanie-Anne? Well, I think some of the other kids may be getting at her a bit because of, you know, me and Nick.'

There was a short silence on the other end of the line. 'I won't say anything dear, because I know you'll think I'm an interfering old busybody.'

'No I don't,' Hannah protested.

'Of course you do, I'm your mother. But you know, sometimes it does help to think about the consequences of something before you ahead and do it.'

Erica's words were still ringing in her ears as Hannah rang off and headed for the foot of the stairs. 'Lottie! Are you up and dressed yet?'

No answer.

'Lottie, get out of that bed *right now*! I won't tell you again.'

Still nothing, save what might have been a faint grunt or even – heaven forbid – a snore. Exasperated, Hannah stomped up the stairs, across the landing, and straight in through the door of her daughter's bedroom. Nothing of Lottie was visible, save a big lump under the middle of the duvet.

'It's no good Lottie, you're getting out of that bed even if I have to —' She whisked back the duvet and the threat dried in her throat. 'Lottie? Lottie, sweetheart, whatever's the matter?'

Lottie lay like a little ball of misery on the rumpled sheet, her knees drawn up to her chin, her eyes screwed tight shut and tears trickling down her cheeks. She was shaking all over, her arms wrapped tight around her belly.

'Mum,' she whimpered, opening her eyes and fixing Hannah with a look of helpless pleading. 'Do something, Mum, it really, really hurts.'

Lately, Nick had got out of the habit of coming to school early, and it was starting to show. Lesson plans had gone out of the window, and as for organising the day-to-day running of the science department, he was pretty much doing that on a wing and a prayer.

Waking up next to Miranda was just so addictive, that was the problem. He kept telling himself, just another five minutes and then I'll get up and, before he knew it, it was eight thirty already and he was throwing on his jacket and tie almost as he drove in through the school gates.

Anyhow, he'd decided to get a grip on himself. Starting tomorrow. Or maybe next Monday. But soon, really soon.

It was increasingly hard to get worked up about school these days though. He yawned and kept eyeing the clock on the lab wall as his first-year GCSE group revised the periodic table for next week's mock exam. He'd half intended to make it interesting with a quiz or something, but the motivation just wasn't there. It seldom was any more, not since that demoralising business with Colin ... and now the cut in government funds that meant losing yet another member of staff.

How are we supposed to teach these kids? he demanded in silent fury. Stick them all in one big room and show them a video?

Five minutes before the end of the lesson, there was a knock at the lab door and a tiny Asian girl entered timidly. 'Please sir, excuse me, sir.'

'Yes, what is it?'

'Mrs Reynolds in the office said to give you this, sir.' She handed him a sealed envelope.

'Thank you.' The girl hovered nervously. 'It's OK, you can go back to class now.'

The door closed behind her retreating back. What now? he wondered, tearing open the envelope. Another staff meeting about the cuts? Another stern warning about smoking in the girls' toilets?

Whatever he'd expected, it was nothing like this. His face turned ashen as he read the note – so much so that Chantelle in the front row asked, 'Is everything all right, Mr Steadman?'

No, it isn't all right, he thought, as the end-of-lesson bell went and the lab erupted into grateful chaos. It couldn't be less all right if it tried.

Hannah was waiting in A&E, sitting beside the examination couch where Lottie lay, her face flushed and her eyes swollen from crying.

'It's OK, sweetheart.' She stroked the hair out of Lottie's eyes. 'You'll start to feel better now they've given you that injection.'

'Mum, I'm scared.'

So am I, thought Hannah, but she smiled. 'There's nothing to be scared about. You heard what the doctor said, lots of people have to have their appendix out.'

'But she said they're going to cut a hole in my tummy.'

'Only a little one. And it's not everyone who has a scar to show off, is it?'

'Mum.'

'What, sweetheart?'

'Where's Daddy?'

Daddy, thought Hannah, with a rush of emotion. That's the first time she's called him that since we told her we were splitting up. 'Daddy's at work, but he's coming soon.'

'Promise?'

Hannah crossed her fingers where Lottie couldn't see them. 'Promise.'

She needn't have worried. Even as she was speaking, Nick was punching his way through the door of A&E.

He swung round, trying to work out where to go, and spotted a middle-aged bloke on reception. 'My daughter,' he panted. 'Lottie. Charlotte Steadman. She's been brought in here.'

'Hey,' objected a woman at his shoulder. 'Get in the queue like everybody else.'

'Yeah, wait your turn,' chimed in a squat man with a bandage on his finger.

The receptionist had seen it all before. He swiftly weighed up the chances of another punch-up. 'If you'd like to take a seat over there, sir, I'll get a nurse to come and speak to you.'

'But —' The look on the receptionist's face said 'don't argue', so reluctantly Nick went and sat at the end of a row of plastic chairs.

His mind was still reeling. What was wrong with Lottie? Why had she been brought in as an emergency? He'd tried phoning Hannah's mobile, but of course you couldn't use them in hospitals so it was switched off. Maybe if he'd still been living at home, he'd have noticed there was something seriously wrong with Lottie and she could have been treated sooner? That was probably rubbish, but all of a sudden he felt so cut off, so out of touch.

The wait was unbearable. Just as he was contemplating taking matters into his own hands, a young student nurse came through the double doors that led to the examination cubicles. 'Mr Steadman?'

He stood up, knocking a dozen copies of *The People's Friend* to the floor. 'That's me.'

'If you'd like to come with me, I'll take you to your daughter.'

He was so hot on her heels there were practically flames around his ankles. 'What happened to her? Is she going to be all right?'

The nurse smiled reassuringly. 'She'll be fine when she's been operated on.'

'Operated on!' What little colour remained in his cheeks drained instantly away.

'Don't worry, it's one of the commonest operations we per-form. You'd be amazed how many cases of appendicitis we get here. She'll be up and about again in a couple of days, just you see.'

Nick didn't know whether to be relieved or upset. Operated on? His little girl? The thought of her being ill and in pain was bad enough, without that as well.

'Here we are, Mr Steadman.' The nurse whisked aside a flow-ery curtain. 'Charlotte may be a little drowsy though, we've just given her her premed.'

Two faces turned towards Nick as he stood frozen in the entrance to the cubicle. Hannah's was pale as raw putty, and dominated by eyes that looked more like dark holes. She looked pretty bad. But it was Lottie's face that drew him: a flushed circle lying on the pillow, surrounded by a tangle of uncombed hair.

'Nick!' There was a world of relief in Hannah's voice. 'Thank God you're here, I thought you might not make it through the traffic before they took Lottie down to theatre.'

'Come on, you know I wouldn't let anything keep me from my little Lotpot.'

Lottie's and Nick's eyes met. For a split second, he saw the familiar flash of anger, obstinacy and resentment, and then it was gone. Tears spilled out of the round blue eyes. 'Daddy,' she sobbed, reaching out her arms for him; and no word in the world had ever sounded sweeter.

A strange mixture of emotions churned inside Hannah. Gratitude and relief, of course, that Lottie was going to be OK; anxiety just in case she wasn't – and the merest twinge of pain and resent-ment that when the chips were down, it was Nick whose timely arrival had made Lottie's eyes light up.

Not that Nick didn't deserve a break after the way Lottie had been punishing him, but when she looked at the two of them together, it brought such a flood of conflicting feelings she could hardly bear it. So much for emotional maturity, she thought.

'Like a coffee?' she asked Nick as she stood up. 'There's a machine down the corridor.'

He glanced up. 'What? Oh, yeah, that'd be great, thanks.'

'Can I have a drink too?' piped up Lottie.

'Sorry, Lotpot.' Nick ruffled her already mussed-up hair.

'Nothing for you till you come back from theatre. Never mind though, we'll give you the best Christmas you've ever had, won't we, Mum?'

'Of course we will.' Hannah smiled. 'Now, don't you go anywhere, I'll only be a minute.'

Christmas. She winced at the prospect as she set off in search of the vending machine. She still had to explain to Nick why his 'brilliantly practical' idea of staging Christmas at Miranda's place was a complete non-starter. Am I being immature and jealous? she wondered. Or is Nick just being naïve?

She never actually got as far as the coffee machine, because as she rounded the corner into the A&E waiting room a voice called out: 'Sprout? Is that you, Sprout?'

Hannah started, pivoted slowly round and gaped. '*Grandad?*'

It might be years since they'd last set eyes on each other, but she knew it was him the minute she saw him: somehow smaller and more wizened than she remembered, but still with that self-same, irreverent twinkle in his crinkly grey eyes.

'It *is* you, I knew it was.' He slapped his thigh with his right hand. The other one was dangling in a makeshift tea towel sling. 'Blimey, Erica, you never said my little Sprout had grown up into such a looker!'

The other patients in the waiting room tuned in with interest. Hannah's cheeks flushed.

'Shush, Dad,' urged Erica. 'Keep your voice down, it's embarrassing enough being here at all.' She looked questioningly at Hannah. 'What are you doing here anyway, dear? Who told you about Grandad's accident?'

'Nobody did. What accident? I'm here with Lottie.'

Erica's expression turned to one of alarm. 'Lottie? Oh no, dear, whatever's happened?'

'Appendicitis. She gave me such a fright, Mum, she really did. I've never seen her looking so poorly. But the doctors say she'll be fine once she's had the operation.'

Erica was on her feet. 'Oh Hannah love, you've not left her on her own?'

'Of course not, Nick's with her. If you come now, you can see her before they take her to theatre.'

'What about me?' demanded Herbie, getting to his feet.

Erica pushed him back down onto his seat. 'You've caused

119

enough trouble for one day. You're staying right here and waiting your turn for X-ray.' She turned to her daughter. 'Honestly love, trying to shin up a drainpipe – you'd think at his age he'd have more sense.'

Herbie winked at Hannah. 'Not me. If you ask me, there's plenty of time to be sensible once you're dead. Now then.' Firmly pushing Erica's hand out of the way, he got to his feet again. 'Are you going to take me to see this great-granddaughter of mine?' he asked in a loud voice, glancing across at the uniformed man on Reception. 'Or do I have to bribe that SS guard over there?'

Hannah and Nick gazed down at the sleeping child in the hospital bed and exchanged looks of profound relief.

'The surgeon said it was really badly infected,' said Hannah softly. 'A few more hours and it could have burst. And then, goodness knows what might have happened.'

Nick gave her a squeeze. 'Yes, I know, but the operation went really well. It's all over now, she'll be bouncing around again before we know it.'

'All this worry, you know, about us . . . you don't think that could've brought it on, do you?'

'Stop trying to find things to feel guilty about, Han.'

'Only if you do too.'

They sat and watched Lottie sleep for a while, just grateful that the three of them were all there, and safe, and that things were going to be OK. It felt, thought Hannah, almost like the old days, when they were still a boring, uncomplicated nuclear family.

'About Christmas,' she said out of the blue.

'What about it?'

'What you said, about us all going to Miranda's house. I'm sorry, Nick, but it's not on.'

To her surprise, he didn't argue. 'No,' he sighed, 'I guess not.'

'It wouldn't be fair on Lottie.' Or on me, thought Hannah; but if Nick had had any sensitivity he'd have seen that for himself.

'No. It was stupid of me to suggest it when you haven't even met her yet. Look, we'll do whatever you want for Christmas, I don't mind. Really I don't.'

'No,' Hannah corrected him, 'we'll do whatever Lottie wants. The poor kid's been through the mill; the least we can do is make Christmas really special for her.'

They sat and talked about nothing in particular for a while, both quietly relieved that they were grown-up enough to sort things out in such a civilised way.

'How's work?' asked Hannah.

He grimaced. 'Unbearable. No money, no staff, no motivation.'

'But you love teaching.'

'Correction: I used to love teaching. It's not the same job it used to be, Han. I can't get excited about it any more. In fact . . .'

His voice tailed off and Hannah looked at him expectantly. 'In fact what?'

'I've come to a decision. It was Lottie who made up my mind in the end, but I've been thinking about it for a while. I'm going to jack in teaching and do something completely different.' He saw her face and added, 'Yes, I know it's sudden, and yes, I know I've done it before; but I just don't feel the same way about teaching as I did.'

Hannah couldn't have been more stunned. Was this really the same Nick who'd slogged through five years of dental training, then realised his true vocation lay in teaching and hadn't wanted to do anything else since that day? 'You're kidding! What sort of thing?'

'I'm taking an unpaid one-year sabbatical, and setting up an online business, selling healthy foods and supplements for kids. You know, tooth-friendly sweets, snack foods, minerals, that sort of thing. It's a gamble, but it won't cost much in initial outlay, and Miranda's got a spare room I can use as an office. Bless her, she's being really supportive.'

'Well of course she is.'

Miranda. The blessed, sainted, ethereally perfect Miranda. It was stupid and childish and unreasonable, but each time she heard that name Hannah felt a little more inclined to dislike its owner.

Nick must have detected the note of sarcasm in her voice, because he looked at her earnestly. 'You will like her, you know.'

Hannah shrugged. 'Does it really matter whether I do or not?'

'Yes, it does,' he replied, to her surprise. 'Because you and Lottie are a part of my life, and now she is too. The sooner you can accept that the better, because believe me it's not something that's going to change.'

*

121

When Lottie woke up, her head felt all fuzzy and her tummy hurt, but not nearly so much as before and in a different way.

She opened her eyes sleepily and her heart leapt, because they were both there: Mum and Daddy, one on either side of the bed, holding her hands. They looked tired, but when they saw that she was awake they smiled and Mum asked 'How are you, sweetheart?'

'Hungry,' she whispered, and they laughed and Daddy gave her a sip of water to moisten her lips.

As she drifted back to sleep, Lottie's last thought was that that she was happy again, for the first time in ages. She didn't care about her sore tummy, only about the fact that the three of them were together again: Mum, Daddy and Lottie, the way it always had been and the way it ought to be.

The way it *would* be. From now on, Lottie told herself, everything was going to be just fine.

Chapter 14

The doctors were right. Even Hannah was surprised at how quickly Lottie bounced back from the operation. One minute flat on her back, sucking ice cubes; the next, asking about her space-hopper, and whether she could have riding lessons for Christmas.

In fact, she'd made such a swift recovery that her stand-in for the Christmas play hadn't so much as tried on the wings before Lottie was back in full force, word-perfect and demanding to know where her halo was.

And all this time, Nick was there to watch her getting strong again: a nightly presence on the sofa bed in the spare room, and a smiling face at the breakfast table. It was only temporary of course, all three of them knew that; but it proved surprisingly easy to function as a kind of unit again.

One morning, Nick watched her scamper down the path and into Hannah's car. 'She's back to her normal self all right,' he commented. 'I found a plastic spider in my cornflakes this morning. In fact . . .'

Hannah grabbed her lunch and her handbag off the worktop. 'I know what you're going to say. You're moving back to Miranda's, right?'

He hesitated just the smallest fraction of a second, then nodded. 'We did say it was only until Lottie was back on her feet again, and – well, just look at her. Besides, it's not very fair on Miranda.'

'Lottie'll be upset,' pointed out Hannah. 'You do realise that?' She didn't add, 'And so might I,' because that would have been silly. Why should she be troubled by the ending of a purely practical arrangement? If she hadn't been upset by

123

Nick's announcement that he was jacking in his career and shacking up with a woman he'd only known for five minutes, why should she be by this? 'Don't you think you should explain to her?'

Nick waved to Lottie and she squashed her face against the car window, stuck her thumbs in her ears and wiggled her fingers. 'I'll do it tonight,' he promised. 'But I'm sure she'll understand. Things have been so much better between us since she was in hospital. I really feel we've got close again.'

Maybe, thought Hannah; but something told her things might not be quite that simple. They seldom were with Lottie.

'Don't you think you should take a break?' asked Maxine, standing in the door of the Beauty Room with an armful of clean towels.

'In a bit,' replied Hannah distractedly, rearranging the bottles of essential oil in their cabinet. 'Do you think if we renovated the storage room next door I could manage to do two clients at once?'

Maxine screwed her face up. 'What?'

'You know, one could be relaxing with a face treatment on while the other one was having a massage. Of course, it'd mean I'd have to be really careful not to get behind with the appointments . . .'

After placing the towels on the painted wooden table by the door, Maxine towed Hannah to her own treatment chair and sat her down. 'Have you lost your mind? You're wiped out by the end of the day as it is!'

'It wouldn't be *that* much more work,' said Hannah doubtfully.

'Oh come off it! Can you imagine, two Councillor Plowrights at the same time? Or Gloria in one room, having her eyebrows done, while there's a mother-to-be in the other one, trying to decide whether or not she's having contractions?'

'But think of the extra money,' pointed out Hannah, indicating some scribbled figures on a Post-it note.

Maxine shrugged. 'Extra money in return for an early grave? No thanks.'

'Not even if it meant we could start thinking about opening up another salon?'

This produced a look of surprise. 'You're not still thinking about that, are you? I thought we gave up on that idea ages ago.'

'No, Jay gave up on it, and I just sort of went along with him because I couldn't think of a way round the cash problem. But you know how oversubscribed I am here, and with all that extra business flooding in we'd be sure to stand a better chance of getting finance from somewhere.'

Maxine scratched her head. 'I don't get you, Hannah. One minute you're talking about having a baby with Nick, the next you're getting a divorce, and then you want to be a business tycoon again.'

Hannah had to admit it sounded inconsistent. But life was like that – just when you thought you had things worked out and the future nicely mapped, it tossed in a variable and you had to start doing the sums all over again. 'Things have changed,' she said, rather lamely. 'I'm just changing with them.'

'Meaning?'

'Meaning, it was different when Nick and I were together,' replied Hannah, rather wishing Maxine would stop probing. 'Now it's just me and Lottie, and I want to give her the best. Plus, I want to show her what I can do.'

'Aha. I get it. Nick's got his new life and his new business, and you want to prove you can do it too. Without him.'

'No I don't,' lied Hannah, who in truth had only just realised that Maxine had hit the nail on the head. 'I want to do this for me.'

'Fair enough. But remember, there's more to life than being successful in business,' said Maxine, patting her barely rounded stomach. 'I should know.'

'Not when business is all that's left in your life,' said Hannah quietly.

Maxine's eyes widened with concern. 'You don't think that – you can't! Oh Hannah, what about your friends, what about Lottie, your mum and dad . . . everything?'

'Everything but a bloke, but hey – what do I want with one of those?' Hannah laughed humourlessly. 'I mean, I've only ever had two serious boyfriends. The first left me pregnant, and the second turned into my brother. Maybe I should lay off romance for good.'

'Now you're just feeling sorry for yourself.'

Hannah pouted. 'Can if I want.'

'Can't.'

'Can.'

'Can't to the power of infinity plus one.'

Their eyes met and they both burst out laughing. 'I win,' declared Maxine. 'Which means you take a break for ten minutes—'

'But I've got Mrs Dawkins at quarter-past.'

'And it's only five to, so you've got plenty of time for a coffee. Why don't you pop downstairs? Gloria's telling us all about this club she went to with Damon last night.'

'Great,' groaned Hannah with mock-seriousness. 'I've got no sex life of my own, so you're going to make me listen to somebody else's. You just want me to turn into Philomena, don't you?'

'Oh shut up, Eeyore. Listen carefully and we might both learn a few tips.'

Gloria was holding court around her chair while Philomena did spiky things with her new asymmetric cut. Phil was the only hairstylist Hannah had ever met who could cut hair without even looking at it, which was just as well, seeing as she was fully occupied drinking in Gloria's every word as avidly as a tramp with a fresh bottle of meths.

'- multiple orgasm,' said Gloria as Maxine and Hannah came down the stairs from the Beauty Room; and a chorus of titters ran round the salon. A woman in curlers and perm lotion giggled, 'No, don't!' and nearly choked on her Rich Tea biscuit. Mrs Lorrimer leaned towards Mrs De'Ath, sitting beside her in the waiting area, cupped a hand to her ear and demanded loudly, 'What did she say?'

Claire wagged a reproving finger in Gloria's face. 'I don't know, you'll get yourself arrested one of these days, behaving like that.'

Gloria winked. 'Bet you want to hear the rest of it though, don't you?'

'Oh, go on then.'

Jason was hovering around the reception desk, looking embarrassed as only a seventeen-year-old youth could. Even his spots were blushing.

'Fancy putting the kettle on?' suggested Maxine, and he fled into the kitchen with a look of undying gratitude.

'And I said Damon darling, if you keep doing that to me you'll get us thrown out, but he kept on doing it anyway, and thank God it was a dark corner, that's all I can say, because I ended up going home with my knickers in my handbag.' At Hannah's approach, Gloria swung round and almost forced Philomena to snip off the wrong bit of hair. 'Hello, Hannah love, how's the single life treating you? Got yourself fixed up with a gorgeous stud yet?'

'Not quite,' Hannah admitted. 'Why, are you offering to share Damon with me?'

Gloria chortled. 'Not bloody likely, darling, get your own.'

'She wants to get out and about more,' opined Claire. 'Isn't that right, Max?'

Hannah felt a bit like a specimen in a jar as all eyes turned towards her. 'Hey, I'm not exactly in purdah you know!'

'No,' conceded Claire, 'but when's the last time you went clubbing?'

'I can't remember,' lied Hannah, who wasn't about to admit that it was when she was nineteen.

'There you are then!' Claire made it sound as if that were the answer to everything.

In the waiting area, Mrs Lorrimer was reading out chunks of the local paper to Mrs De'Ath. 'They're putting up some new bollards in the High Street, dear.'

'Some what?' Mrs De'Ath strained to hear about the drone of the hairdryers.

'Bollards.'

'Well honestly, there's no need to be rude.'

'And I see You Know Who's been throwing her money around again.' Mrs Lorrimer pointed to a photograph of Clarice Fabian and her dog, handing over a cheque to the local animal shelter.

'Not that it *is* her money,' sniffed Mrs De'Ath.

'Quite so.' She turned the page. 'Oh look, "Nature Notes with Petunia", my favourite. "Christmas is almost here, the bees are slumbering in their hives, and the little woodland birds are flocking to my bird table for their special seed cake. Inside the cottage, logs are drying out beside a roaring fire, and warm, spicy cooking smells are wafting from the Aga while chestnuts roast on the hearth . . ." Ooh, lovely,' she sighed. 'Just like when I was a little girl in the country.'

'Sentimental rubbish,' declared Philomena. 'As if anybody really lives like that. I bet it's nothing like that at all.'

'Yeah,' laughed Claire. 'This Petunia woman's probably twenty-five stone and lives in a squat in Whaddon. And her real name's Gladys Shufflebottom.'

'Either that or she's one of those scary horsey types who won't eat anything unless they've just killed it themselves,' suggested Maxine, accepting a cup of coffee from Jason.

'Ugh.' Mrs Lorrimer shuddered. 'Do you really think so, dear?'

'Either way,' Claire went on, 'I bet she's not half as toothsome as our Hannah here. Or as shaggable.'

'Don't!' Hannah squirmed.

'So I reckon we should all put our heads together and think of a way to get Hannah fixed up with a nice bloke. What do you say?'

'Don't look at me, love,' said Philomena. 'I'm a married woman, what would I know about shagging?'

'To be honest,' said Gloria apologetically, 'I'd gladly help but I don't think any of the men I know would be Hannah's type.'

'I've already tried setting up a blind date for her,' said Maxine. 'And she took one look at the bloke and legged it. So, do we know any other single men who might be up for it?'

Everybody looked at Jason, who quailed and ran off to put the kettle on again.

'Oh well,' said Claire, folding her arms across her ample chest, 'looks like it's down to me then.'

Hannah hoped she was joking. 'What do you mean "down to you"?'

'I mean, you'd better be ready with your party pants 'cos on your next free weekend, you and me are going clubbing!'

*

That night, true to his word, Nick sat Lottie down in Hannah's sitting room, and had a quiet little chat with her. To say that she didn't take it well was an understatement.

'Sweetheart . . . Lotpot.'

She turned on him, her eyes full of hurt. 'Don't call me that! Don't you dare call me that!'

'Lottie sweetheart, I know you're sad that I'm going, but we

128

did tell you I was only moving back here until you were better. And I'm not going far, am I?'

The deep blue eyes sparkled with unshed tears, whether of pain or rage it was difficult to tell. 'First you said you'd never go away, but you did anyway. Then you came back, and now you're going away again. To be with *her*.'

'Her name's Miranda,' Nick said softly. 'And she's really nice. You'll like her a lot once you get to know her.'

Nick's eyes invited Hannah to say something supportive, but what was there to say? For one thing she'd never met the woman, and for another she had no particular inclination to. Deep down, she could understand only too well how Lottie felt. In the end, she settled for: 'Daddy's not going very far, sweetheart. And you'll still see him every weekend and sometimes in the week as well.'

'That's right,' agreed Nick. 'We'll have some really great times together. Just like while you've been poorly, only better.'

Lottie was silent for a few moments, clearly weighing things up. Then she turned to her mother. 'Do I have to?'

'Do you have to what?'

'Go with *him*.'

'With Daddy? No, of course you don't, but—'

Lottie sprang to her feet. 'Then I *won't*.'

And without so much as a backward glance, she stalked out of the room.

The following morning, before it was light, Nick packed his things back into his overnight bag and drove away. To wait until Lottie was awake would only have prolonged the agony.

Hannah wasn't quite sure how she felt about his going, not any more. The first time, she'd thought she was glad, and then the more she was on her own, the more she'd missed him ... if not Nick himself so much as his presence. This time, she'd thought at first she was sad, but after he'd gone and the house was quiet, she began to think that maybe she was glad after all. Glad of the stability of knowing she was on her own again, not playing 'let's pretend' with a man whose heart was somewhere else and would never return.

She was a little bit sad for Lottie, of course. Maybe if Nick hadn't moved back in while she was ill, giving her false hope, they'd have been building bridges again by now. Well, that was a lesson learned for the future. She still wanted Nick to be closely involved with Lottie's life, of course she did; but she also reminded herself that she and Lottie were the family unit now, not she and Lottie and Nick.

There wasn't much time to dwell on any of it anyway, not with it being Lottie's last week of term before the Christmas holidays. Even Lottie herself was too excited at the prospect of global mega-stardom to sulk or make dark pronouncements about Nick's 'betrayal'.

All the same, when Hannah and Nick talked about it on the phone, it seemed better if he didn't come to the play. The previous year there had been an incident where one of the Three Kings caught sight of his father and stepmother having a row in the audience, and had run off-stage in tears. For Lottie's sake, they decided, Nick would keep his distance this year.

'Hey,' announced Hannah when Maxine stopped by the Beauty Room. 'I've got two tickets for the hottest show in town. Fancy coming with me?'

Maxine's ears pricked up. 'What's this then, the all-star panto at the Everyman?'

'Much better than that. Lottie's end-of-term play. What do you say?'

Maxine laughed. 'You're on.' She prodded her stomach. 'After all, I need the practice – in a few years' time I'll be doing it for real.'

If there was one thing you could always guarantee at Farmington Lane Juniors, it was a full house. In fact, by the time every star, supporting actor, chorus member, dancer, and backstage helper had dragged along a couple of family members, it was standing room only.

Maxine and Hannah squeezed in about halfway down the hall, at the front of the tiered seating. 'This way, we'll get a good view of the stage without putting Lottie off,' explained Hannah.

'Does she put off easily then?'

Hannah chuckled. 'Don't they all? I'll never forget when she was dancing in the Infants' summer show, dressed up as a sunbeam. She spotted me and Nick in the audience, waved, and tripped over one of the pixies so they all fell down in a big heap. Needless to say, Nick caught the whole thing on his camcorder . . .'

'So when she's sixteen and she brings her latest boyfriend home, and she's trying to look all sophisticated, you'll drag the video out to embarrass her?'

'Something like that. Mind you, I still can't imagine her ever being grown-up. It doesn't seem five minutes since I was holding her in my arms and thinking, "How did I ever manage to create something so tiny and so lovely?"'

'Make the most of it, chum,' Maxine advised. 'From what I hear, one minute they're a gleam in Daddy's eye, and the next they're putting you into an old folks' home.'

'Hmm, well, the way things are going with Nick, she's more likely to chain him up in the dog kennel with Doom.'

'Still not forgiven him then?'

'I'm not sure what hurt her more – the fact that he left the first time, or the fact that he came back and then went away again. Mind you, that was my fault – it seemed like a good idea at the time.'

'You weren't to know.'

'But I should have. I'm her mum, I'm supposed to be able to read her like a book, but these days she's more like *The Times* crossword puzzle.' Hannah watched Miss Grimshaw determinedly marshalling stray members of the cast, and chasing a boy dressed as a Christmas pudding across the front of the stage and into the wings. 'All in all, I think it'd have been better if he'd just moved in with this precious Miranda woman and flipping well stayed there.'

At the mention of Miranda's name, Maxine grabbed Hannah's arm. 'Oh, did I forget to tell you?'

'Tell me what?'

'I met her, you know. Miranda what's-her-name. Moss, wasn't it?'

'Moss,' repeated Hannah, shell-shocked and finding herself caught between needing to know, and really not wanting to. 'Where?'

'At some Chamber of Commerce do Jay took me to. God, it was boring. You know, old farts in suits and women with faces you could cut yourself on, droning on about business opportunities. I know I ought to be interested, for Jay's sake, but honestly—'

'But Miranda. You said she was there?'

'What? Oh, yes. Apparently she's a member too. Sells stuff from her smallholding or something. Anyhow, I heard somebody mention her name and next thing I knew we were being introduced. Quite pretty, isn't she?'

Of course she bloody well is, thought Hannah. 'I don't know,' she replied. 'I've never met her.'

'Oh. Haven't you? I didn't know. Anyhow, we talked for a few minutes about this and that, and I must say I was quite surprised. She seemed really . . . well, sweet. You know, genuinely nice. Between you and me, I think Jay was a bit besotted with her.'

Hannah knew Maxine would never be malicious towards her, but it still felt as though each word was another nail hammered into the coffin of her self-esteem. 'Oh,' she said quietly. 'Well, I always said Nick had good taste.'

'No, Han,' objected Maxine, looking Hannah straight in the eye. 'Nick's got terrible taste. He must have: he left you.'

OK, so maybe the West End version would've had bigger sets and glitzier costumes; and the piano wouldn't have had middle C missing; and the songs would have been written by Andrew Lloyd-Webber rather than Mr Lake the deputy head. But would it have had a live donkey that bared its teeth every time Joseph went anywhere near it; or a woolly sheep on wheels; or an Angel of the Lord who looked like she'd just drifted straight down from Heaven on a tide of net curtain?

Hannah's eyes were misty with pride. 'Oh Max, she's so good! Isn't she *good*!'

'Brilliant,' agreed Maxine. 'And she's not letting Melanie-Anne put her off, either.'

Melanie-Anne, second shepherd and stand-in Mary, had been scowling at Lottie throughout the performance, but Lottie – little trouper that she was – had sailed through the whole first half, not even turning a hair when one of her wings slipped its moorings and slid halfway down her back.

'I wonder what it is between those two,' mused Hannah.

'Search me. You know what little girls are like. When I was Lottie's age I had a feud with this other girl for a whole term, just because she told the teacher I'd kissed Billy Pearson behind the bike racks.'

'And had you?'

'Are you kidding? He had zits and a squint.'

Hannah giggled, and a fat woman in a hat swung round and shushed her into embarrassed silence.

This is wonderful, thought Hannah as Lottie sang her song and held the whole hall spellbound; but she couldn't help feeling just the tiniest bit guilty. If only Nick could have been here to see his little girl's moment of triumph.

The second half consisted mainly of songs and dances on a festive theme, including a chorus line of Christmas puddings, an extract from *The Wind in the Willows*, and a resounding version of 'We wish you a merry Christmas', with a noisy descant provided by the donkey.

With a camera full of digital snaps and the whole thing captured on Jay's camcorder for the benefit of Nick and the assorted grandparents, Hannah and Maxine made their way through the crowd to the exit.

Maxine hopped from one foot to the other. 'Got to have another wee,' she hissed. 'Is being pregnant like this all the time?'

Hannah grinned. 'Oh no, you've still got the varicose veins and the stretch marks to look forward to. And the swollen ankles, and the—'

'Thanks a bunch, Han, you could've warned me *before* I got myself up the duff. Look, I'll see you and Lottie back here, OK? Only if I don't run there's going to be a puddle.'

Hannah hummed to herself as she waited in the corridor outside the hall, nodding occasionally to the odd parent or child she knew. She was feeling quite festive, even without the mug of rather strange-tasting mulled wine the grown-ups had been served in the interval.When Lottie came back from getting changed, she was going to get the biggest Christmas hug ever.

She was leaning against the wall, idly watching people come and go, when she caught sight of a flash of lime-green and orange among the crowd. Normally it wouldn't have rung any particular bells, but it just so happened that Nick had bought himself a cut-price ski jacket in exactly that colour combination. And Hannah was pretty sure that nobody else in Cheltenham had fashion sense as bad as Nick Steadman's.

She called after the retreating figure: 'Nick?' But there was no response and it disappeared into the throng heading out towards the car park.

Maybe it wasn't him. After all, they had agreed that it was better he didn't come tonight, and Nick wasn't one to go back on his word. But if it *was* Nick ... Hannah found herself not annoyed but pleased, because in all fairness he didn't deserve to be shut out of such a magical event.

On impulse, she decided to go after him and thank him for coming. His presence there hadn't done any harm, had it? And Hannah was sure that in years to come Lottie would be glad he'd been here, too.

She trotted down the corridor, excuse-me'd her way through the crowd and squeezed out through the double doors into the crisp evening air.

There he was just a few yards ahead of her, heading diagonally across the car park. She set off after him, expecting to intercept him when he got to his car. But she was in for a shock.

The car he was making for wasn't his own little blue hatchback. It was a great big, glossy 4x4: a silver giant of a thing, its engine purring and the passenger door standing invitingly open.

Hannah stopped in her tracks as the realisation hit her. And as she watched, Nick climbed up into the car, exchanged a passionate kiss with a pretty, dark-haired woman, and then drove away into the night.

Hannah didn't feel much like going to a party on Friday night, even if it was only a pre-Christmas drinks do with Maxine and Jay. Try as she might to deny it, her reserves of festive cheer had been distinctly sapped by the sight of Nick and Miranda snogging like teenagers in the school car park.

Worse, she was certain that Nick would have been invited to the party as well – after all, he was Maxine and Jay's friend too. And if Nick was there, what were the chances that *she* would be too?

But there was no chickening out of it. Her mum had arrived to babysit Lottie, there was a gift-wrapped bottle of half-decent wine on the kitchen counter, and Hannah had put on her best shimmery-blue designer dress. The backless one that made the best of all the good bits and skimmed over the rest.

She said goodnight to Lottie and Erica, promised not to catch her death in that flimsy little outfit, and took a final look at herself in the hall mirror. 'Well, Han,' she told herself, 'Nicole Kidman you ain't, but you don't scrub up too badly.' She thought of Miranda and her country smallholding and allowed herself a fierce smile. 'And at least you don't smell of manure.'

It might be the depths of December, but that didn't stop Maxine and Jay living the outdoor life. Huge patio heaters were arranged all round the paved area outside the French doors, creating a comforting fuzz of warmth.

As usual, Jay had gone mad with the Christmas decorations. There were skeins of tiny multicoloured lights hanging in the trees, a life-size illuminated reindeer on the lawn, and one whole side of the house looked like leftovers from Blackpool Illuminations.

Hannah had never met anyone who loved Christmas as much as Jay did. If he could have made it last all year round, she was quite sure he would. He never looked happier than when he was wearing a flashing Santa hat and playing charades – unlike Nick, who moaned about rampant commercialism from the time the first cards appeared in the shops in September until the last desiccated tree had been dragged down to the municipal tip.

'Han, baby!' Jay's bricklayer friend Norris gathered her up in his hairy arms. 'You're looking great, as ever.'

'So are you. Is that a new tattoo?' It was hard to tell, among the plethora of hearts and daggers, dragons, large-breasted biker chicks and flags of St George.

'What, the British bulldog? Well spotted, took him hours that did, and then it went septic on me. Worth it in the end though.' He gave Hannah's bottom a squeeze. 'Hey, I heard you're single again, does that mean I'm in with a chance?'

If she'd thought he was serious she'd have run a mile, but Norris had been married for twenty years and Ramona was a formidable woman who'd once thrown a traffic warden through a plate-glass window.

'Course you are, Norris. I'll add you to the list.'

He saw her gazing across the patio, eyes nervously searching for the two people she least wanted to see. 'You OK?'

'Hmm? Oh, yes, fine.'

Norris might be five foot eight of lard and muscle, but thick he wasn't. 'They're over there,' he said, pointing past the barbecue, where Jay was grilling marinated turkey legs, to a little huddle around the ornamental fountain. 'But don't you worry yourself about her. I wouldn't kick her out of bed like, but she's not a patch on you.'

Bless you, thought Hannah; bless you, even if it's not true. As the chattering figures moved she caught glimpses of Nick, laughing with a glass of wine in his hand, and of someone tall and willowy, tossing back a mane of jet-black, wavy hair. Thoroughbred, thought Hannah, feeling like a pit pony.

At that moment, Maxine came along and scooped her up like so much flotsam. 'Come on,' she said, thrusting a plate and a glass into her hand.

'Where?'

'Over there.' She pointed right in the direction of Nick and Miranda.

Hannah shook her head. 'Uh-uh.'

'Don't be a coward, you know you've got to meet her sooner or later. Besides, I told you, she's OK.'

Before she knew it Hannah was being skilfully steered across the patio, into the circle of warmth and light that enclosed Nick and Miranda. She was hanging on his arm, noted Hannah; gazing up at him all dewy-eyed. And Nick was punctuating everything he said with kisses on her upturned lips.

Hannah's stomach churned. But there was no time to run away, because Miranda had already spotted her.

'Look who I've brought to talk to you,' announced Maxine, giving Hannah such a poke in the back that she nearly fell headfirst into the fountain.

'Hello, Nick,' said Hannah, her mouth desperately dry. 'And you must be—'

'Miranda,' gushed the dark-maned thoroughbred, enviably sleek in denim-blue velvet jeans and a white long-sleeved T-shirt tight enough to show that she didn't need a bra. She dotted kisses on both Hannah's cheeks. 'I've been wanting to meet you for ages. Nick's told me such a lot about you.'

'Really?'

'Really,' Miranda assured her. 'He *respects* you so much, you know.' Somehow she managed to make it sound like a criticism.

Hannah looked at Nick. He gave a sort of cheesy but embarrassed grin. 'That's . . . nice,' she said flatly.

'Oh yes.' Miranda beamed. 'You two must be so relieved now you can both let your hearts fly free.' She gazed into Nick's eyes. 'I know Nick's never been happier, isn't that right, Nick?'

'Of course it is, darling.' Their fingers interlaced and tightened into a loving clasp. Hannah felt vaguely nauseous.

'But of course, we're all going to be great friends, aren't we?' Miranda went on. 'You, me, Nick . . . and Charlotte.'

'Lottie,' Hannah corrected her. 'She hates being called Charlotte.'

Miranda waved aside this trifling problem. 'Does she? I'll have to remember that. Anyhow, we'll all have a chance to get to know each other better over Christmas, won't we?'

Hannah's mouth fell open. 'Christmas?' She stared at Nick. 'Didn't you tell her what we decided?'

Nick flushed. 'Yes, I . . . er . . . had this idea.'

'Oh you did, did you?'

'Yes, I thought . . . well, of course I'm spending Christmas morning with you and Lottie and your mum and dad.'

'But?'

'The thing is, I thought, why don't I leave after lunch and go back to Miranda's? After all, it's hardly fair if I don't spend part of Christmas Day with her, is it?'

'And Cha—I mean *Lottie* can come back with him,' declared Miranda, as if that was the logical solution and therefore the only possible one. 'Then everyone's happy. You can come too, if you like,' she added, in a voice that made Hannah think 'over my dead body'.

Hannah looked Nick straight in the eyes. 'You said you'd spend Christmas Day with us,' she said.

'Well, I will be, most of it. And if Lottie comes back to Miranda's with me in the afternoon . . .'

'So Lottie thinks this is OK, does she? I mean, you have actually asked her?'

'I sort of mentioned it to her, yes.'

'And what did she say?' Hannah had a fairly good idea.

'I'm sure she'll come round to the idea,' cut in Miranda. 'You know what little girls are like.'

That was just too much. 'As a matter of fact I do, yes,' she said

137

between clenched teeth, 'seeing as I've lived with one for the last nine years. But what makes you such an authority?'

'Hannah,' urged Nick. But she wasn't listening. Even if Miranda had been the loveliest person in the world Hannah would have wanted to smack her face and, as it was, there was definitely something about the woman that got right up Hannah's nose.

So she went for it. 'I mean, you haven't actually got any kids of your own, have you?'

It was intended to be wounding, but instead of being offended Miranda just turned to Nick with the coyest of smiles, and walked her fingers up his arm. 'Not yet,' she giggled.

A horrible cold shiver ran down Hannah's spine. 'Not . . . yet,' she repeated mechanically.

'Yes,' Miranda purred. 'Go on Nick, tell her.'

Nick swallowed hard, and looked as if he would rather be anywhere else on earth at that precise moment 'We were going to keep it under wraps for a little bit longer but hey, what the heck?' He smiled feebly. 'I'd like you to be the first to hear – after all, I know you'll be pleased for us.' He seized Miranda's hand and pressed it to his lips. 'We're thinking of starting a family. The sooner the better.'

Chapter 15

Life was good.

Miranda sat at her little Victorian desk, by the window in the attic bedroom she used as an office, and gazed out over the Gloucestershire countryside. Below, in the yard, Old Tom was raking up muck and attending to the thousand and one tasks that had to be taken care of every day on a smallholding.

She thanked her lucky stars for Old Tom. When you were fresh from ten years in the City, and your agricultural knowledge didn't extend much beyond watching a few episodes of *River Cottage*, a proper countryman like Tom was beyond price. Not that his price was high anyway; he'd been happy to stick around after he'd retired and sold up, glad to be able to give the city girl a hand.

And if it had turned out to be rather more than just a hand, well, where was the harm in that? It was, she liked to think, a successful working relationship. She liked riding horses, and Tom didn't mind cleaning up after them. She liked honey, and he was used to getting stung. He was good at wading around in mud, and she liked putting on a crisp white pinny and fluttering her eyelashes at the farmers' market.

Presentation was, after all, one of her main strengths. She'd started off in marketing, moved on to writing advertising copy, and had finally hit the jackpot with a couple of really successful ad campaigns and an investment in a chic little restaurant that went global. At that point, three years ago, Miranda could have done pretty much anything she wanted; she had the ability and the capital. Only trouble was, she'd lost interest.

That was the trouble with a mind like hers: it moved so fast from one idea to the next, so that today's brilliant, ground-breaking notion became yesterday's been-there-bought-the-T-shirt. She'd taken a long, detached look at London, and her so-called friends with their six-figure bonuses, and thought about all those idyllic childhood holidays in the Lake District, and suddenly realised what she wanted.

Within six weeks she'd sold up, bought Far Acre Cottage and constructed herself a whole new way of living.

Idly she pressed one of the keys on her laptop and watched a row of Xs appear; then erased them. Thinking up ideas for a weekly column about country life wasn't as easy as she'd thought it would be, but lately she'd been getting lots more inspiration.

In fact these last few weeks her whole life had been infused with a new excitement. Ever since she met Nick, in fact. The first time she'd set eyes on him, she'd sensed that here was the missing jigsaw piece, the little nagging omission that had kept her awake at nights, wondering what it was she still lacked. It's you, she'd thought with some surprise, as she gazed at that rather serious but not un-handsome face, that fashionless mop of hair, those appallingly nondescript clothes. You: my Tom Good, my Gabriel Oak, my big strong, no-nonsense man; the future father of my dozen rosy-cheeked children.

And Nick was everything she'd known he'd be: reliable, faithful, totally committed to making a new life in the country with her. All the homespun qualities that in the old days she'd have dismissed as hideously boring now glittered like virtuous diamonds. She smiled at his photo, framed on the corner of her desk. It was just like a fairy tale.

Now all she had to do was persuade Lottie to write herself into it.

The stone crashed through old Mrs Waverley's greenhouse window with a sound like an explosion.

'Get out of it, you little gits!' roared Herbie, his lungs straining as he came flying down Erica's garden path and out into the road. 'I'll have you, I swear I'll have you!'

The trio of eleven-year-old boys sniggered and pulled faces at him as he gasped for breath.

'Come an' get us then, old man.'

'What's stopping you?'

Herbie swore under his breath – not so much at the little hooligans as at himself, for being so old and out of shape. Even ten years ago, he'd have kicked their ignorant backsides halfway across town. 'She's a defenceless old lady, what's she ever done to you?'

The boys shrugged. 'Old woman your girlfriend, is she?' They laughed unpleasantly. 'You want to back off, mister, we might do you next.'

That was too much for Herbie. Out on licence or not, he couldn't just let them walk all over him. And once he got going, he discovered he still had a surprising turn of speed for a man of seventy-six.

'Ow, gerroff!' howled the boy with the ginger hair as Herbie's fingers grabbed his ear and twisted it so hard that he saw stars. 'You can't touch me, I . . . I'll have you!'

'Yeah, he'll have the police on you,' agreed the two other boys, from the safety of several yards away. 'For assault.'

'Fine,' replied Herbie, perfectly calm now. The lad deserved it, and besides, frankly he couldn't care less. Nothing could be worse than life as Erica's neutered lodger. Already he could see the doors of his nice cosy cell opening up to let him back in.

'What?'

Hannah chose that moment to come round the corner into the Avenue. 'If you go to the police,' she told the boys, 'so will I.'

'I'll tell them he hit me.'

'And I'll tell them you hit him first. A frail old man with a bad leg and bronchitis, how will that look? Not to mention vandalising that poor old lady's greenhouse.' She narrowed her eyes and took a closer look at the ginger-haired boy. 'Don't I recognise you? You were in Mr Steadman's class at Alderman Braithwaite . . .'

It was more of a guess than a statement of fact, but she must have struck it lucky, because within seconds the boys had legged it, leaving Herbie fuming on the pavement.

'What did you want to go interfering for?' he demanded. 'I had him right where I wanted him.'

'Don't talk daft, you silly old fool! You can't go round attacking little boys, even if they do deserve it.'

Herbie's bushy grey eyebrows knitted in displeasure. 'Who are you calling a silly old fool?'

Hannah grabbed him by the arm. 'Do you *want* to go straight back to prison?'

'Well, now as you mention it . . .'

She stared at him. 'That's not funny, Grandad.'

'It's not meant to be.' Herbie freed his arm from Hannah's grasp and smoothed the wrinkles out of his jumper. 'It's all right, Mrs Waverley,' he shouted to the worried face pressed up against next-door's front window. 'They've gone now.'

The face withdrew and the curtain whisked across. 'Between you and me, I think she's more afraid of me than those little hooligans,' lamented Herbie. 'I say so much as "hello" to her, and she runs off like I've got horns and a forked tail. And don't tell me I'm imagining it,' he added as Hannah opened her mouth to protest. 'Everyone round here knows where old Herbie Flowers spent the best part of the last twenty years.'

'Then I guess we'll just have to show them they're wrong about you.' She shivered and pulled her jacket tighter around her. 'Shall we go in? You'll catch your death in your shirtsleeves.'

Herbie threw her a black look, but allowed himself to be nudged back into the house. 'And what's all this about me being a frail old man with a bad leg and bronchitis?' he demanded as Hannah hung her coat up in the hall. 'I've never had bronchitis in my life! Fit as a flea, I am.'

Hannah tapped the side of her nose. 'Yes, but they didn't know that, did they? How's your wrist, by the way?'

'Fine.' Herbie flapped it around to demonstrate. 'I only twisted it a bit, but you know what your mother's like – overreacts to everything.'

'Like climbing drainpipes?' enquired Hannah.

Herbie shrugged. 'Got to check you've still got what it takes, haven't you? Never know when you might need to make a quick getaway.'

Hannah smiled and shook her head. 'Don't let Mum hear you say that, she'll go mental. You're supposed to be a reformed character, remember?'

'Huh.'

'Where is she, anyway? I've brought her the video of Lottie's show.' She laid it down on the kitchen counter.

'I dunno, down town buying tinsel or something. God knows why, it's like Santa's bleedin' workshop in here already.'

Hannah smiled to herself, wondering what Herbie would make of Jay's seven-foot inflatable Santa. Reaching up to one of her mum's top cupboards, she took out the really strong tea bags and the tin of chocolate fingers. Herbie looked like he needed someone to moan at, and she didn't feel much like going home to an empty house.

As they sat drinking tea and watching Lottie's video, Hannah realised this was the first time she'd spent any length of time with her grandfather since she was a kid. At first he'd seemed almost like a stranger, but as they talked all the old resonances started to come back.

'You used to love Christmas,' she commented, dunking the end of a chocolate finger in her tea. 'You were a bigger kid than I was.'

'Yeah, well.' Herbie looked embarrassed. 'Your grandma was still around then, it was different.' He hung his head. 'After she passed away Christmas was never the same.'

Poor Gramps, thought Hannah, suddenly realising just how much Herbie missed his wife, a shadowy figure she could scarcely remember. 'We'll still have a nice time though, won't we?' She patted his hand and his face crumpled into something approaching a grudging smile.

'S'pose you're going to make me, are you?'

'Oh definitely. And Lottie won't let you get away without a couple of games of Mousetrap.' She chuckled. 'And Twister, of course. There's no escape from Twister when our Lottie's around.'

Herbie's eyebrows knitted. 'Twister? With my leg?'

'Give over, Gramps, there's nothing wrong with you, you just said so.'

'Hrrmph. Well, you can't make me enjoy myself,' he declared, defiantly snapping a chocolate finger in half.

'Oh dear,' sighed Hannah, 'you sound just like Lottie.'

'Ah,' said Herbie. 'Still not a happy bunny, then?'

'It's all this business with me and Nick.' She rubbed at her aching temples. 'It's really hit her hard, and to be honest I'm a bit worried about her health. It's weeks since the operation, but she's still getting tummy aches. The doctor said it might be adhesions.'

'Or fretting,' said Herbie reflectively. 'I always used to get a bellyache whenever I saw a police car.'

'Yes, well, that's hardly surprising, is it?' Hannah gazed into the depths of her cup of tea, as though the answers might lie there. 'The thing is, Gramps, I can't help thinking that she'd still be a happy little girl if it wasn't for me and Nick.'

'And this new woman of his,' Herbie pointed out. 'Sounds to me like half the problem is, Lottie's jealous of her.'

She's not the only one, thought Hannah, surprising herself with the strength of her own resentment at the saintly Miranda. 'Yes, I'm sure she is. But what do we do about it?'

Grandad Flowers munched contemplatively, took out his top set, and sucked out a bit of chocolate from between the molars, provoking a shudder from Hannah. When he'd quite finished, he continued: 'You're not happy with the way things are?'

'No, of course not.'

'Well, do you want things to go back to the way they were before?'

The idea horrified Hannah. 'No, definitely not!'

'Then it's going to take time. Like when I was a kid – it took me a long time to get over losing my ma.'

This was all new to Hannah. Grandad was so ancient, she'd never really thought of him as a child, complete with parents. 'Your mother died when you were little?'

'I was six and my brother Alfie was two,' Herbie recalled. 'When the TB took Ma, our dad couldn't cope on his own. That's when they came and carted us off to the orphanage. He used to come and see us the odd time, but after he married again he never bothered much with us any more.'

'That's terrible!' gasped Hannah.

Herbie shrugged. 'You get used to things,' he said. 'You adapt. You think you'll never get through stuff but you always do.' He winked. 'Besides, I learned how to pick locks off a lad at the orphanage, so I was never short of a bob or two.'

'You're an old villain, Herbie Flowers.'

'And you worry too much.' Herbie drained his cup and set it down. 'Know something, Sprout?'

'What?'

'You make a terrible cup of tea.'

Christmas morning dawned with a crash and a thud as one of Lottie's tribe of ferrets got into the living room and knocked over the tree. By the time Hannah and Lottie had calmed down the ferret and retrieved all the baubles from under the furniture, it wasn't worth going back to bed.

'Happy Christmas, sweetheart.' Hannah wrapped her arms tightly round Lottie and kissed the top of her head.

'Happy Christmas, Mum. Mum . . .' Lottie's voice was muffled by the folds of Hannah's dressing gown.

'What, sweetheart?'

'I can't breathe.' Her face reappeared, pink and bright-eyed. 'Can we open our presents now, Mum?'

'Of course we can. But we mustn't forget to feed the animals afterwards. It's their Christmas too.'

Lottie bounded off, reached the doorway and then turned round. 'Mum.'

'Hmm?'

'You know what you said, about us going round to Granny and Grandad's for the day?'

'Yes, what about it?'

'Do we have to?' Lottie wheedled. But to no avail.

'Of course we do! We always go to Granny's on Christmas Day. Besides,' Hannah pointed out, 'Daddy's going to be there.'

Nick awoke in the perfumed softness of Miranda's arms, dimly aware that it was Christmas morning and that he was quite possibly the luckiest bastard he knew.

Miranda stirred and whimpered in protest as he rolled sideways to look at the clock. 'Darling . . . where are you going?'

'Nowhere.' He rolled back and her arms and legs enfolded him again like some divinely tailor-made suit. 'Just wondered what time it was.' He returned her passionate kiss. 'Hmm, shouldn't we be getting up and feeding the goat or something?'

Miranda gave a sexy chuckle. 'Don't worry, Old Tom'll take care of all that.' Her fingers walked up his thigh, making him shiver all over. 'Why don't you come here and let me give you your Christmas present?'

'Oh. Yours is downstairs, should I go and fetch it?'

'Not that kind of Christmas present, silly. The sort that doesn't need wrapping.' Her kisses came thick and fast on his willing skin.

A nagging doubt lingered at the back of Nick's mind. 'The only thing is . . .'

145

Miranda's eyes opened in exasperation. 'What now?'

'I said I'd be at Hannah's mum and dad's for twelve.'

'Oh Nick . . .' Her fingers gently kneaded the aches out of his back as her tongue explored uncharted lands. 'It's Christmas Day. Can't you stay here with me? Do you really have to go?'

'Of course I do,' replied Nick, surprised that she needed to ask. 'Lottie's going to be there.'

There were limits to a man's patience, and Herbie had very nearly reached his. Putting him in an apron and making him peel carrots lay several light years beyond the call of duty; not even National Service had been this humiliating.

The trouble was, Erica didn't even realise it *was* humiliating. She probably thought he was loving every minute of it, making himself useful, finding something constructive to do instead of moping in his room on his own. Then again, she wasn't to know that his plans for doing over the jeweller's in the High Street had reached a delicate stage. These things required a lot of thought; and you couldn't do much of that while trying not to cut your own fingers off with a vegetable knife.

At least being more or less confined to the kitchen had shielded him from the worst of the relatives and friends who'd been dropping in all morning. Most of them had only stayed long enough for a sherry and a mince pie, but Derek's Uncle George was still audibly enjoying himself in the living room, alternately farting and singing rude words to Erica's *Carols from King's* CD.

Herbie smiled to himself. It was nice to know he wasn't the only embarrassment in the family.

He glanced at the clock above the bread bin. Ah well, not long till lunchtime, and then maybe everybody would be so full they'd all go to sleep and leave him alone. Right about now, his old prison cronies would be sitting down to turkey and two veg, prior to a small scuffle breaking out in the recreation room and then everyone being locked up for the rest of the day. Herbie liked a nice regular routine. This freedom thing was horribly overrated.

However, maybe the rest of today wouldn't be all bad. After all, Hannah and Lottie would be there.

*

Erica took a long, despairing look at Derek's Uncle George and marvelled at how such a decent family could have produced something so gross. However, she reflected, every family had its cross to bear and hers was Dad, though even in his worst moments Dad would never have sunk to the level of George's 'alternative' Christmas carols.

Never mind, she thought; Uncle George was a small price to pay for a nice family Christmas, and in any case he generally behaved himself once he was full of turkey and Derek's single malt. One thing was for sure: it was going to be lovely having Hannah and Lottie here. Christmas wasn't Christmas without a child to spoil rotten.

On the subject of spoiling, though, there was just a small hint of worry at the back of Erica's mind. Things hadn't been plain sailing for Hannah and Lottie lately, and she so wanted the day to be a good one for their sake. It wasn't that she had any problem with Nick himself – in fact he'd always seemed like a very decent sort of chap to Erica – but what if he and Hannah didn't hit it off? What if an argument broke out over some silly thing and Erica didn't manage to defuse it in time?

Yes, the only problem with today was that Nick was going to be here too.

I needn't have worried, thought Erica, beaming all over her face as she doled out second helpings of home-made Christmas pudding. Everybody's getting along just fine.

Uncle George was too busy stuffing his face to annoy anybody; Hannah and Nick seemed to be getting along perfectly amicably; and even Lottie was almost back to her normal self, challenging Herbie to games of Twister and telling anyone who would listen that Daddy had bought her a real electric scooter for Christmas.

All they needed now was for Dad to cheer up a bit, and they could mark today down as a real success.

Hannah's face was starting to ache from smiling continuously, all through lunch. She and Nick had promised each other that they'd make today special for Lottie's sake, but even so it wasn't the easiest thing in the world to pretend that this Christmas was just the same as all the other ones they'd spent together. It wasn't helped by the perceptible distance that crept into Erica and Derek's voices whenever they spoke to Nick, almost as if they were already subconsciously sawing off his particular branch of the family tree.

They're punishing him, thought Hannah; punishing him for not being 'real' family. They probably don't mean to, but they're doing it anyway. And unfair as that was, it made up a little for having to look at Nick and imagine the kind of Christmas celebrations he'd been having with Miranda. Why can't I be going home to a drop-dead-gorgeous hunk? she lamented into her pudding. Why does it have to be just me, Lottie and the cast of *Animal Hospital*?

'Any more for any more?' invited Derek, serving spoon poised invitingly over the mangled corpse of the plum pudding. He was answered by a chorus of groans.

'In that case, let's all go into the lounge and watch the Queen's speech,' suggested Erica.

'Can't we play games?' protested Lottie. 'I want Daddy and Grandad Herbie to play Twister with me.'

There was a short, expectant silence. Nick's mouth opened, then he swallowed, then tried again. 'Actually, Lotpot,' he reminded her softly, 'I did say I had to go after lunch, don't you remember?'

Lottie's dancing eyes turned to frozen pebbles. 'You said you'd spend Christmas Day with me.'

Nick's smile was only a little strained at the edges. 'And I am, sweetheart. I'm here, aren't I?'

'But now you're going away again. To be with *her*.'

All eyes were now firmly fixed on Nick. His cheeks flushed crimson. 'Miranda's on her own, sweetheart, she'll be lonely if I don't spend some of Christmas Day with her.'

'Honestly man,' muttered Derek. 'You're surely not going to run off back to your fancy-woman and leave your daughter?'

Nick flashed him an angry scowl. 'No Derek, I'm not. I'm taking Lottie back to Far Acre with me, so she can have her tea there and play on her scooter where it's nice and safe and there's no traffic.' He turned back to Lottie. 'Isn't that right, Lotpot?'

Lottie turned away. 'I've got a tummy ache,' she said dully.

Erica shook her head in dismay. 'I did say not to eat quite so much, you know.'

'Why on earth didn't you say you were poorly before?'

Hannah laid a hand on her daughter's forehead. 'You're not hot,' she said with relief, 'but you are a bit pale. Is it a bad tummy ache?'

Lottie nodded. 'Want to go and lie down.'

'That's OK, the spare bed's all made up,' said Erica, slipping easily into mother-hen mode. 'I'll pop on the kettle for a hot water bottle.'

'But . . .' began Nick. Everybody seemed to be glaring at him, even Herbie, though he'd been glaring at everybody all day.

Hannah stood up. 'You go if you like, Nick. But she's not going anywhere, not if she's poorly.'

Nick thought fondly of Miranda; of the warm scents of the little country cottage; the crackle of logs on the fire. And then he looked into Lottie's sad, accusing eyes and took out his mobile phone.

'It's OK,' he said, 'I'll phone Miranda and tell her I'm staying here.'

When Hannah went to check up on Lottie a couple of hours later, the room was in darkness and at first she thought she was asleep. Then a little voice said: 'Mum, is he still here?'

'Daddy? Yes, he's downstairs. He's very worried about you, you know.'

'No he isn't. He doesn't care about me, he only stayed because you made him feel guilty.'

Hannah wondered if that was partly true, but decided to give him the benefit of the doubt. 'Don't be silly, he's your daddy and he wanted to be with you.'

There was a short silence, then: 'Why doesn't he just go away and leave us alone, Mum?'

Shocked, Hannah hardly knew how to respond. 'What are you talking about, Lottie? He wouldn't ever do that.'

'Yes he would. He will. So he might as well do it now, mightn't he? Then we can pretend he never existed.'

Hannah sat down on the bed and reached for her daughter's hand. 'Who's been telling you Daddy's going to go away and leave us? Who's been filling your head with all this nonsense?'

'Nobody.'

Hannah knew her daughter well enough to recognise a lie, even in the dark. 'Lottie. Who says Daddy's going to leave you?'

There was another silence, longer this time, then Lottie's voice, smaller and sadder than ever: 'Melanie-Anne. Melanie-Anne says he's going away and he's never coming back.'

And then came the sound of Lottie sobbing softly under the bedclothes.

Chapter 16

What are you worried about, you big girl's blouse? Hannah asked herself a few days later as the metal barrier rose and she drove into Charlton Hills. So it's an exclusive private housing estate, so what? Chances are, you've waxed half the bikini-lines in this road, just think of *that* if she comes over all superior.

Not that Melanie-Anne's mother would be anything other than perfectly nice, Hannah was quite sure of that. While they'd only ever met fleetingly, on the odd occasion she'd dropped Melanie-Anne off to play with Lottie, Carolyn Carpenter had never looked askance at the pile of unwashed laundry by the washing machine, or a ferret with its head in a bag of Bovril flavoured crisps. Now Hannah was finally getting to see the inside of Château Carpenter.

Ah, Hannah reminded herself as she drove down the vast, tree-lined avenue, but those times you weren't turning up on her doorstep to complain about her precious daughter, were you?

Fairholme was a vast, mildly unattractive brick pile, discreetly screened by tall trees and the sort of drive that would have served the average Third-World country as a motorway. The wheels of Hannah's car scrunched on immaculate white stone chippings as she turned in, drove up to the house and parked.

A child's bike stood propped up against one of the mock-Georgian columns, a discarded rollerblade keeping it company on the doorstep; but there was no sign of Melanie-Anne, which was probably just as well.

Hannah rang and waited. She half expected a seven-foot butler with a bolt through his neck to answer the door, but when at last it opened she was greeted by Carolyn herself, looking quirkily chic in green silk combats and a fluffy white cashmere sweater.

'Hannah, hi, come in. Sorry the place is a bit of a mess, we're having a new kitchen put in. Nightmare, eh? How's all your building work coming along, by the way?'

'Oh, it's more or less finished now.' Hannah followed Carolyn past one well-scrubbed workman and a few neatly stacked aluminium cupboard doors. Evidently Carolyn's idea of mess wasn't quite the same as hers. 'Actually, I haven't really thought much about it since Nick and I split up.'

They entered a sitting room the size of a TV studio, and Hannah sank gratefully into the depths of one of the four matching sofas. At the mention of Nick, Carolyn's discreetly made-up face registered concern. 'Gosh, yes, I was forgetting. It must have been quite traumatic. Still, I'm sure you'll find you're much better off on your own.'

'Well, I—'

'Oh absolutely. Take it from one who knows. Men are far more trouble than they're worth. Now, would you like tea or coffee? Or a glass of something stronger?'

Hannah was about to decline politely when the door opened and in came Mr Carpenter. Hannah recognised him straight away as the man who trailed around behind Carolyn at parents' evenings. Tall, grey-haired, distinguished-looking, he was clearly a fair few years older than Carolyn, but wearing well. Hannah wondered what he thought of her views on men.

'Have you seen my reading glasses?' he asked.

'Same place you always leave them, on the mantelpiece.' Carolyn shook her head indulgently, as though humouring a child. 'We'll have to get you one of those chains, so you can wear them round your neck.'

He looked at her doubtfully. 'I'm not quite that bad, am I?'

She laughed. 'Worse. Oh, if you're going near the kitchen, put the kettle on. Hannah wants a coffee.'

'No, really, I'm fine,' stammered Hannah in embarrassment, but nobody was listening. And Mr Carpenter padded off in his slippers, faithful as an ageing Labrador.

'It, er . . . must be nice having your husband home with you all day,' ventured Hannah, breaking the awkward silence.

Carolyn stared at her. 'Sorry? My what?' Then her expression cleared and she burst out laughing. 'My husband? You thought Dad was my *husband*? That's priceless!'

Hannah was too busy trying to extract her foot from her mouth to do any more than smile weakly.

'No, it's just Dad and me,' went on Carolyn. 'Has been ever since my mother walked out on us when I was a kid. He looks after his business, and I look after him and Melanie-Anne.' She leaned forward. 'I wouldn't do it for any other man, mind you. Waste of space, the whole species.'

At least this gave Hannah an opportunity to steer the conversation in the right direction. 'You and Melanie-Anne's father aren't together any more then?'

'We never were, darling! Not unless you count an arrangement with a turkey-baster as together.'

Hannah coughed to cover her embarrassment. 'You mean ... you and he ...?'

Carolyn shrugged, in the sort of matter-of-fact way one might expect from someone who was more at home with foals than babies. 'It was all quite straightforward. I wanted a baby and I didn't want a man, so I put an advert in the *Telegraph*; you'd be amazed how many replies I got.'

'Really?' said Hannah, who couldn't think of anything else to say. 'That's fascinating.'

'Anyway, once I'd chosen the right one I handed over the cash and we agreed he wouldn't be involved in the child's upbringing – I was very strict about that. Melanie-Anne's my daughter; she doesn't need some guy calling himself her father just because he contributed a bit of goo in a yoghurt pot.'

Suddenly things were starting to become clearer in Hannah's mind. 'Doesn't Melanie-Anne miss having a daddy?' she ventured.

Carolyn swept aside the idea as though it were hardly worth considering. 'Melanie-Anne has everything she needs, I make sure of that.'

The sitting-room door opened and Mr Carpenter came in, carrying a tray. 'I couldn't work the machine, so I used instant,' he announced. 'Sorry.'

'No problem at all,' Hannah assured him, and Carolyn's reprimand died in her throat. 'Aren't you joining us?' she enquired, noticing that there were only two cups on the tray.

'Oh, you know. Things to do, workmen to supervise. Nice to meet you anyway.'

He left, and Hannah felt rather like leaving with him. Carolyn tasted her coffee and grimaced. 'So, what exactly was it that you wanted to talk to me about, anyway?' she asked. 'I've been intrigued ever since you phoned me.'

Hannah took a deep breath. 'Actually, it's about Melanie-Anne,' she said. 'I don't know if you're aware of it, but she's been saying some very strange things to Lottie lately . . .'

Hannah told Nick all about it that night, over a mug of hot chocolate. 'And she still reckons the kid doesn't miss having a father?' Nick shook his head in disbelief. 'Some people really don't have a clue.'

'The thing is, Carolyn really seems to think she's doing the best for her,' said Hannah.

'God knows how.'

'Yeah, I know. I think she must've had some unfortunate experiences with men and now she thinks they're all bad news. She just doesn't seem to accept that sometimes two parents can be better than one. '

Nick rubbed his head and sat down at the antique pine table they'd bought for the kitchen all those years ago; had bought even though it cost far too much, simply because they'd loved it on sight and, after all, it would be an investment for the future. Their family's future.

'Do you think Carolyn really will talk to her about the things she's been saying to Lottie?' he asked. 'Because if she doesn't, I will.'

Hannah laid a calming hand over his. 'Steady on, tiger, this is one unhappy little girl we're talking about here. We don't want to make it two, do we?'

'I don't care if she's only doing it because she's jealous of Lottie having a dad, I'm still not having her upset her any more.'

Hannah smiled at the passion in his voice. 'It's a pity Lottie's asleep,' she mused. 'It'd mean a lot for her to hear you talk about her like that. How could she ever doubt then how much she means to you?'

'By the time I've finished telling her,' promised Nick, 'she'll never doubt again. And if it doesn't work the first time, I'll just keep on telling her until she finally gets the message that I'm never going to leave her.'

'I can't go to school today,' insisted Lottie, as Hannah snapped the lid onto the plastic sandwich box and handed it to her. 'My tummy hurts.'

'I know,' said Hannah quietly. Then: 'I went over and had a chat with Melanie-Anne's mum yesterday.'

A faint glint of panic appeared in Lottie's eyes. 'Why did you do that?'

At that moment Nick emerged from the hallway, where he'd been hanging up his coat. 'Why do you think? Because she was worried about you. We both are. That's why we decided we were going to talk to you this morning.'

'I'm all right,' said Lottie, her lower lip jutting stubbornly. 'Except for my tummy. It really does hurt,' she added. 'Can't I stay off today?'

Hannah gently sat her down at the kitchen table. 'I think Melanie-Anne's a very sad little girl inside,' she said. 'She doesn't have a daddy like you, and she gets jealous. So when she heard that Daddy and I had split up, she thought she'd hurt you by saying nasty things.'

'But that doesn't mean those things were true,' cut in Nick. 'You've got to understand, sweetheart, just because your mum and I don't live in the same house any more, that doesn't mean I'm any less your daddy.'

'And running away from Melanie-Anne won't help,' added Hannah. 'It'll just make her think she's won.'

'I'm not running away!' protested Lottie. 'I've got a tummy ache.'

'I know darling,' agreed Nick. 'But I bet it wouldn't hurt half so much if Melanie-Anne wasn't at school today. Am I right?'

Lottie was silent for a long time. Then nodded slowly.

'Well, if it helps, I don't think Melanie-Anne's going to be saying any more nasty things to you, not after I spoke to her mum,' said Hannah. She looked into Lottie's big, round, worried eyes, peering out from underneath a Shetland pony fringe. 'You know, you don't have to have a tummy ache every time you're worried or unhappy about something,' she added. 'You could talk to us, and I bet we could sort it out.'

'No you couldn't!' Lottie cried, surprising Hannah and Nick with a sudden outburst of anger. 'It was you that messed everything up in the first place!'

'Hey, but we're trying to put it right,' pointed out Nick. 'We'd do anything to make you happy.'

'Liar!' Lottie spat the word in his face. 'How can you say that when all you think about is being with that woman? How can you say you're trying to put it right, when everything you do just makes it wronger and wronger?'

Nick's face was white with shock. 'I wouldn't lie to you, sweetheart. Not ever.'

But Lottie was trembling and tearful with rage. 'It's not true! All you ever do is tell lies. First you and Mum said you loved each other, and that was a lie. And then you said you were my daddy and you loved me more than anything, and that was a lie as well. And then you said you'd always be here, and—'

'Lottie, love,' pleaded Hannah, 'all of it was true. All of it. And it always will be.'

'No it won't.' Lottie rubbed a mess of tears and snot off her face with the sleeve of her school sweatshirt. 'And it'll never be all right again. Melanie-Anne was right; you're just going to keep going away until one day you don't bother coming back.

'So why don't you go now and do me and Mum a favour?'

'Thanks for popping over, dear,' said Erica, wiping floury hands on a tea towel as Hannah came in through the back door. 'I wouldn't have asked, only you seem to be the only one who can handle him.'

Harassed and fed up though she was, Hannah couldn't suppress a small smile at the image of Herbie as some kind of dangerous wild animal, who could only be kept in his place by means of a whip and a chair.

'I'm sure you're exaggerating,' she yawned, clapping a hand over her mouth to spare her mother the sight of her tonsils. 'He's just a lonely old man with no friends and nothing to do.'

Erica cleared her throat sceptically and went back to rolling out suet crust for the steak and kidney pudding. 'He's an old villain, dear, and I wouldn't trust him as far as I can throw him. But on the other hand,' she sighed, 'I don't want him being miserable either. And I'm really starting to worry about the amount of time he spends on his own in his room. Can't you persuade him to go out and . . . and *do* something?'

'Preferably something legal, I assume?' Hannah swiped a finger-full of butter-cream from her mum's Victoria sponge.

'Well, one can but hope,' replied Erica drily. She cut out a large circle of pastry, using the pudding basin as a guide. 'Was that another yawn? You're working yourself too hard.'

'No, no, I'm fine,' Hannah assured her.

'That's not what your friend Maxine said when I spoke to her the other day. She said you've been working all hours, and that when you get home at night you're too exhausted to go out or even read a book.' Erica peered sternly over her varifocals. 'All work and no play makes Jill a dull girl, you know.'

And not enough work gives Jill far too much time to brood, mused Hannah, but she just smiled and said, 'Don't worry, I'm just enjoying building up the business, that's all.' Then she added, not quite knowing why: 'and Nick's being really supportive, especially with Lottie.'

'Hmm.' Erica emptied seasoned steak and kidney into the lined basin. 'I know he's a nice man, dear, and we've always got along well; but remember, he's gone and got himself other responsibilities now. And when all's said and done, he's not actually Lottie's real father, is he?'

'As far as I'm concerned he is,' replied Hannah, silencing her mother's protest with a look. 'And that's the end of it. Now, where's the old reprobate? I hope he's not in one of his funny moods.'

Herbie's mood was not remotely funny. If anything it was downright morose. He sat by the window in his room and gazed out into the gathering dusk, watching the starlings huddling together in the copper beech, chattering and trying to push each other off the end of the branches. At least they've got someone to roost with, he thought gloomily. Not like me, stuck here all on my own. Who's going to notice if I have a funny turn and drop off my perch?

He turned to ask Reggie Kray what he thought, but the budgie was asleep with its head under its wing. Bloody typical.

All right, Herbie conceded, Erica would probably notice eventually; but only in an 'oh how typical of Dad' kind of way. And

Derek would probably go straight out and celebrate. Consequently, Herbie was not planning on sticking around. Just as soon as he could wangle it, he was going back to the one place he could be sure of getting a bit of respect: prison.

A knock at his bedroom door caught him unawares, right in the middle of working on his master plan. Before he'd had a chance to slide it under the duvet, Hannah was standing over him, reading it over his shoulder.

'Is that what I think it is?'

'No.' Herbie put his hand over it, but she calmly peeled his fingers away.

'Well it's definitely not a shopping list or a love letter.' Hannah folded her arms and gave him an old-fashioned look. 'If that's really a plan for robbing Lawson's in the High Street, I'd forget it right now. Crime doesn't pay, Gramps: if anybody should know that, it's you.'

Herbie scowled at the insult. 'I'll have you know you're looking at one of the South-West's finest.'

'So good that you once blew a hole in a police station wall instead of the bank vault? And wasn't it you who tried to fool a fingerprint scanner with half a grilled sausage?'

'Did you come here specially to insult me, or is it just a sideline?'

Hannah sat down on the bed, put her elbows on her knees and rested her chin on her hands. 'Mum says you're down in the dumps.'

'So would you be if you had an annoying granddaughter who kept pointing out your shortcomings.'

'Don't worry, you can't feel anywhere near as inadequate as I do.'

'Want to bet?'

Hannah unearthed the half-bottle of scotch Herbie kept behind Dad's old bowling trophy, and helped herself to a swig. 'Thanks, I needed that.'

'Oi, get your own.'

'How's about I take you down the pub and buy you a double?'

'Not in the mood.'

'Neither am I; we can be miserable together.'

Herbie grunted. 'What've you got to be miserable about? Least you've got all your teeth. And I thought the world was suposed to be your oyster since you gave miladdo his marching rders.'

'Hey, it wasn't like that, you know it wasn't. Nick and I just . . . ecided we weren't right as a married couple, that's all.'

'Your grandma and I decided that about half an hour into the vedding reception. Didn't stop us putting up with each other for he best part of thirty years though.'

Hannah wrinkled her nose. 'Sounds miserable if you ask me.'

'Oh, it was.' Herbie jabbed a finger at Hannah's middle. Which is why I'm telling you, young lady, that you've got no usiness mooching around and wasting your evenings with old odgers like me. You should be out there, living it up.'

'What if I like spending time with one particular old codger?'

'Then you're an even sadder case than I am. For gawd's sake et out and . . . what is it the youngsters say? Wide it?'

Hannah giggled. 'Large it, Gramps.' She got up and slapped im on the back. 'Tell you what, I'll do you a deal. You come out or a drink with me now, and I'll take up Claire's invitation to go lubbing with her on Friday night.'

'Hmm.' Herbie plucked out an annoying nostril hair. 'Sounds ike a plan. And maybe I can give you the benefit of a bit more of ne worldly wisdom, eh?'

'Maybe.' Hannah gently reached round him, picked up the heet of paper with his jottings on and crumpled it into a ball. But only if I can give you some of mine. Face it, somebody's got o keep an eye on you or you'll be back behind bars faster than ou can say Alcatraz.'

There was no point in denying it; Herbie's words had made her hink. He might be a hopeless old felon who thought he was Ron-ie Biggs, but whichever way you looked at it he was right about er. The time for moping around listening to the first album she nd Nick had ever bought together was well and truly past. It was ime to ditch the long faces and the comfy old clothes, smarten up nd hit Cheltenham's social scene so hard its eyes wouldn't ncross for days.

And Mum was right too. She couldn't go on living as if the nly thing that had changed was the fact that Nick wasn't living n the house any more. She had to stop deliberately not moving hings from where he'd left them, so that if she felt a bit lonely

159

she could pretend he'd only nipped out to the garden shed for half an hour.

Nick might still be part of her and Lottie's lives – an important one, even – but not the same part he had been before. And it was up to her to fill in the potholes that had opened up, not just sit around waiting for something to come along and fill them for her.

For weeks she'd been avoiding Claire and her exhortations to 'pull on her party pants' and enjoy a night on the town. The thought of sampling Cheltenham's club scene with Stroud's chunkier answer to Jordan filled her with dread. It wasn't so much that Hannah was afraid Claire would embarrass her; more that she'd turn out to be so far over the hill that she couldn't stand the pace.

At any rate, Claire had just asked yet again and she'd half made her mind up to chicken out for the umpteenth time, despite her promise to Herbie. Then the disturbance started outside the front of the salon, and she sort of forgot that she hadn't actually said no.

'Whatever's going on out there?' demanded Philomena. 'Sounds like a bunch of old fishwives.'

In the street outside, three old ladies were squaring up to each other like gunfighters in a spaghetti western.

'It's you who did it, I know it was you!' blazed Clarice Fabian, brandishing a sheaf of paper in Mrs De'Ath's face.

'What're you on about?' demanded Mrs Lorrimer.

'I know it was you, it's no good denying it! You stole my little Bertie, and I want him back right now!'

Hannah pushed open the door and went outside. Quite a crowd was gathering, but this wasn't really the sort of publicity Split Ends was after. Besides, the way she was shaping up, Miss Fabian might deck one of her rivals at any moment with a deadly swing of her handbag. Somebody ought to intervene, and it might as well be me, thought Hannah.

'What's the matter, ladies?' she enquired. 'Anything I can help with?'

'Clarice has gone potty,' declared Mrs De'Ath. 'Thinks we've done away with that mangy dog of hers.'

'They have! They couldn't have my money, so they took my little Bertie instead.' There was a brightness of tears welling up in old Miss Fabian's eyes, and Hannah couldn't help feeling sorry for her, even if she had got the wrong end of the stick. And surely she must have done. Mrs D and Mrs L wouldn't steal her beloved dog . . . would they?

'You've lost your dog?'

'No, they stole it!'

Mrs Lorrimer rolled her eyes. 'Not just mean with her money . . . mad as a spoon as well.'

'I'm not mad! I want my Bertie back and I want him back now!'

Miss Fabian was shaking with emotion, and the sheaf of papers in her hand started to flutter down to the pavement like oversized snowflakes. Maxine came out to join Hannah and they started rounding up as many as they could before they blew away. They were handwritten posters, bearing the words:

LOST DOG. PUG, ANSWERS TO NAME OF BERTIE. REWARD.

And underneath, a phone number and a dreadfully photo-copied photo of Bertie that made him look like Bernard Manning.

'Are you sure he hasn't just wandered off?' asked Maxine. 'He's only small, he could have slipped through the fence or something.'

'Small but fat,' Mrs Lorrimer pointed out caustically.

'*They* took him,' insisted Miss Fabian, with such venom that Mrs De'Ath and Mrs Lorrimer both instinctively took a step back. 'And they've only come here this morning to taunt me.'

'Don't talk daft,' said Mrs De'Ath. 'It's Friday. We're on our way to the Edwardian Tea Rooms for two small cappuccinos and a Viennese fancy. Come on dear,' she said, taking Mrs Lorrimer's arm, 'no point in staying where we're not wanted.'

They went off in their tweedy coats and identical mohair berets, leaving Clarice Fabian standing outside the salon. 'They *did* take him,' she said. 'I know they did. Who'd have thought they could be so horrible?'

'Come on,' said Hannah, putting an arm round the old lady's shoulders. 'Let's get you a nice cup of sweet tea, and then we'll put one of these posters up in the window. I bet you'll have your Bertie back in no time.'

That evening, after Lottie had gone off scowling to spend the weekend with Nick, Hannah was just about to microwave herself a pizza when the doorbell rang.

The figure on the doorstep was large as life and twice as scary, in a black leather miniskirt and beaded pink extensions that clashed unashamedly with the rest of her wild ginger mane.

'Claire?'

Claire's face fell. 'You're not ready! We said half-past, remember?'

Oh shit, thought Hannah as the penny dropped. I never got round to telling her I wasn't coming out tonight. So she must still think . . .

'Actually, I . . . um . . . meant to tell you, I'm not really in the mood tonight and well, you know,' she mumbled incoherently, standing there with a pizza in one hand and a tea towel in the other.

But Claire wasn't the sort of girl to be put off so easily. She stepped into the house, her large bulk more or less forcing Hannah to back away down the hall. 'Not good enough, missy!' she declared. 'I'm not letting you bottle out this time.'

'I'm sure you'd have a lot more fun without me.'

'Bollocks. We're going to have a great night, you and me.' She delivered a matey punch to Hannah's shoulder, almost knocking her over. 'Girlies behaving badly, eh?'

'But—'

'Your little girl with her daddy, is she?'

'Yes, but—'

'And you've fed all the animals?'

'Well . . . yes.'

Claire rubbed her hands together, cracked her knuckles and adjusted her push-up bra. 'Sorted! Come on then, get up them stairs and let's get you into your clubbing gear.'

'I haven't got any clubbing gear,' protested Hannah, who realised to her shame that she was so out of touch she wasn't even sure what clubbing gear was any more.

'Course you have.' Claire strode across the master bedroom. 'This your wardrobe, is it?' She flung open the double doors. 'Good God, *how* many pairs of tracksuit bottoms?'

'They're comfy!' protested Hannah, squirming. 'Look, why don't I come as I am and we can just go out for a drink or something?'

Claire ignored her completely, and went on rummaging among the hanging garments. 'Aha! This'll do.' With a flourish, she whipped out a black devoré bustier that Hannah had once impulse-bought in a sale and never dared wear.

Hannah was aghast. 'But that's . . . underwear!'

'Rubbish, it's meant to be seen. You've got nice boobs, you ought to show 'em off. Come on, put it on. Now, have you got a nice sexy little jacket and some tight trousers?'

Hannah would have said 'no', but there seemed little point. Claire was already pouncing on the red trouser suit that Nick said made her look like a tart. 'Can't we just go to the pictures or something?' she asked weakly.

But she could tell from the look in Claire's eyes that it was the Casbah Club or bust.

In point of fact, by the time they reached the Casbah Club, the night was not so much young any more as middle-aged and balding.

Hannah had lost count of the number of town-centre bars they'd visited; in fact she was beginning to lose track generally, after all those funny-coloured cocktails and alcopops; but hey, she was really starting to feel quite relaxed. Maybe she could even get to like this going-out thing if she practised hard, though walking around with your underwear on view took some getting used to. It's not as weird as not wearing my wedding band though, she mused, surreptitiously feeling the indentation on her left ring finger where it had been until a few hours ago. Not nearly as weird.

'I always come to the Casbah on Fridays,' Claire shouted above the din of hard house mingled with general chatter. 'Ladies get two free drinks for the price of one on Fridays, see.' She hauled Hannah through the swarm to the bar. 'What you having?'

'Actually, I don't really want anything.'

Claire threw her a despairing look. 'Two Sand Dances and two Strawberry Sheikhs,' she said, pushing the money across the bar top. 'That should keep us going for half an hour.'

Hannah had to admit the cocktails were very moreish. And she was getting quite thirsty after all this dancing and charging around. Besides, they were so sweet and sticky that they couldn't really be all that alcoholic, could they?

Mind you, her head was starting to spin a bit.

'Anybody you fancy?' enquired Claire with a wink. With her

back to the bar, she surveyed the talent, very much as a tipster might survey a procession of racehorses in the paddock.

'Well, I don't fancy yours much,' giggled Hannah, pointing to a nerdy-looking youth with terrible acne.

'Hmm, not much talent in tonight, is there?' agreed Claire. 'Mind you . . .' She nudged Hannah in the ribs, so suddenly that she nearly spilled her Strawberry Sheikh all down the front of her bustier. 'Hey, look at him, he's all right. Wouldn't mind a bit of that.'

It wasn't hard to work out whom Claire was pointing at, because he was the best-looking guy in the club by a mile. Tall, broad-shouldered, dark-eyed, with golden-blond hair and a tan that didn't look like it came out of a bottle, he was Adonis in a pack of cavemen.

'Go for it,' said Hannah. 'I'll be fine here.'

Claire looked at her as if she was crazy. 'Not me, dumbo, you!'

Hannah stared at her in utter panic. 'Me?'

'You came here to pull, didn't you?' Before Hannah could reply, Claire gave her a hefty shove in the back. 'So get out there and pull him.'

'But he's so—'

'Drop-dead gorgeous?'

'Young.'

'Good. In that case he'll be able to keep going all night long, know what I mean? Go on, go for it. He can't take his eyes off you.' Claire spotted someone on the other side of the dance floor. 'Oh look, there's Sharon and Dizzy. Hiya Shaz! Wait there, I'm coming over.'

'Don't leave me!' squeaked Hannah. But Claire was already disappearing into the throng.

She swallowed hard. Maybe if she just stayed here and didn't do anything, nobody would notice her. But she could feel eyes upon her, and when she looked up again the blond Adonis wasn't just looking at her, he was heading in her direction.

In fact, both of him were . . .

She blinked, but everything was getting really fuzzy, and the more she shook her head to clear it the more fuddled it felt. What's more, she was starting to feel really hot and just a little bit nauseous. Maybe she'd had just a teensy bit too much to drink after all.

'Hi there.' The blond Adonis gave her a crinkly smile. 'My name's Danny, what's yours?'

'H-hannah.'

'Someone as lovely as you shouldn't be all on her own.' His expression suddenly changed. 'Hey, are you OK? Only you look a bit flushed.'

'I'm fine,' Hannah assured him.

Then she passed out.

Chapter 17

The sun was shining down on Far Acre Farm, but all was not quite sweetness and light.

'It's only a few boxes,' said Nick as he stood in the kitchen, trying to figure out how to make toast on an Aga.

Miranda folded her arms in that combative way she had when things were starting to displease her. 'A few? Nick darling, the entire stable block is full of your unsold stock!'

'Don't worry, it won't be for long. Just till the orders start coming in.'

This provoked little more than a sniff of disbelief.

'What?' demanded Nick.

'Oh, nothing. Just that you're not likely to get many orders if nobody knows your business exists.'

'I'm a chemistry teacher, not a tycoon. You said you'd help me with the marketing, remember?'

'And I am doing.'

'Yeah, when it suits you.' He saw the look on her face and added hastily, 'I'm sorry, I didn't mean it to sound like that, but you always seem to be too busy these days.'

'Yes, well, running this place is a full-time job you know.'

Nick was tempted to point out that it couldn't be all that onerous, seeing as Old Tom did virtually all the work. He and Miranda had been having one or two minor disagreements lately, and he didn't want to spark off another row now, especially with Lottie in the house.

Turning round in search of the marmalade, he caught his hand on the spout of the whistling kettle and swore under his breath. 'Why can't you have an electric one like normal people?' he lamented.

'Oh, so I'm abnormal now, am I?'

'I didn't say that.'

'No, but you were thinking it. If you want to live in the country, darling, you've got to get used to country ways.'

And your horses, thought Nick, mentally reminding himself to take another antihistamine tablet. After living for years in Cheltenham's answer to Bristol Zoo, who'd have thought he'd turn out to be allergic to horses? Not a happy state of affairs when your beloved ate, slept and dreamed the blasted things.

All the same, she did look awfully good in that old shirt of his and not much else, her long legs all bare and inviting.

'Well, there are some country ways I just can't get enough of,' he breathed, abandoning the quest for the marmalade and turning his attentions to Miranda's cleavage instead.

She tilted back her head and gave him a teasing smile. 'Oh yes?'

'Don't suppose you've got a convenient haystack just begging for somebody to roll in it?'

'Wrong time of year, darling,' she replied with a throaty chuckle. 'Unless you want frostbite. Of course, we could always go back to bed and *pretend* it's a haystack.'

'Sounds good to me.' He enfolded her in his arms and sank into the softly scented paradise of her bosom.

At which moment a small voice piped up from the doorway. 'I'm hungry.'

Nick froze in the act of nibbling Miranda's neck, straightened up, blushed crimson, and coughed. 'We were, er, just getting the breakfast. Weren't we, Miranda?'

Miranda smiled, but it was a rather thin, tense kind of smile. 'Why don't you go back to bed and have a nice lie-in, Lottie?' she suggested.

'Don't want a lie-in, I'm bored,' replied Lottie, fixing Nick with a hard stare. 'And I'm hungry. And you said we were going out for the day and having pizza.'

'What?' said Miranda, to whom this was clearly news.

'Not you,' cut in Lottie before Nick could explain. 'Just me and him. Isn't that right, *Daddy*?'

'Oh God.'

Hannah opened one eye just the merest fraction, and a stiletto of daylight instantly stabbed right through it. The tiniest head movement was like sticking her skull in a vice. And that was nothing to the waves of nausea that engulfed her the minute she tried to sit up.

On reflection, she decided, she wouldn't do anything at all. She'd just lie here quietly, and wait for merciful death to come and take her.

'Are you OK?' asked a dark-brown voice a couple of feet from her ear. 'Only you were in a bit of a state last night.'

Hannah shot upright as though she had just sat on a red-hot spike, suddenly just about as painfully conscious as anyone could be. 'Who ... the hell ... are *you*?' she demanded, instinctively clutching the duvet to her bosom.

'I'm Danny.' The Adonis with the crinkly smile extended a tanned paw. 'Danny Richmond. We met last night at the Casbah, but I don't suppose you remember much about that.'

He was right there. All she could recall was having too much too drink, being abandoned by Claire, and then this young blond god walking over and introducing himself. After that ... zilch.

A horrible thought insinuated itself into her brain and, very very gingerly, she lifted up the edge of the duvet and peered underneath. To her surprise and relief, she was still wearing the same clothes she'd gone out in the night before. All of them.

'What are you doing here?' she demanded, shuffling away to the other side of the bed. Danny remained sitting in the wicker armchair. He didn't look very threatening, but then you couldn't always tell, could you?

'I brought you home,' he replied. 'Somebody had to, and your mate seemed to have disappeared. So I looked in your handbag and found an envelope with your address on.'

'You went in my handbag!' That rated pretty high up the scale of unforgivable violations, almost as bad as waking up with no knickers on.

He shrugged apologetically. 'Sorry, I didn't know what else to do. And of course I needed your keys to open the door when we got here.'

'You mean you've been here all night?' Hannah didn't know whether to be impressed or creeped-out. Not that there was any thing outwardly creepy about this guy. And if he was an axe murderer, wouldn't he have chopped her into little pieces by now?

'Uh-huh. Thought I'd better stick around in case you threw up and choked or something. Anyhow, now I know you're OK I guess I'd better be going.'

'Hang on a minute.' Hannah scrabbled back across the bed and grabbed his arm. 'You can't just go!'

'Why not?'

'Because . . .' She flailed her arms, trying to pick a good reason out of mid-air. 'Because we haven't been properly introduced.' Throwing back the duvet, she wriggled her crumpled self to the edge of the bed, stood up, thought better of it and sat down again. 'Hannah Steadman, I mean Hannah Maddrell.'

He raised an eyebrow. 'Aren't you sure? Or have you got a split personality?'

'Kind of. I used to be married, and now I'm not, only I keep forgetting.'

'Ah, right. Never been there myself – not yet, anyway. Danny Richmond, bachelor of some parish or other, at your service, madame.' He executed a daft little bow and Hannah giggled.

'Not local then?'

'Are you kidding? I'll have you know this tan is one hundred per cent genuine. Actually I've been crewing a yacht in the Med for few years; got bored with it and thought I'd come back to Blighty for a bit. Try my luck. That kind of thing.'

'And instead of getting lucky, you ran into me?' Good grief, I'm flirting, Hannah realised and instantly coloured up. But then again, like Claire said, he *is* drop-dead gorgeous.

'You're the best bit of luck I've had in days, I'll have you know.' Danny crossed his long legs and sat back in the wicker chair. 'Between you and me it's been a pretty bad week, one way and another. First the business opportunity I'd set my sights on fell through, and then my landlord had a heart attack and I've got to move out of my digs. Nightmare.'

'Nightmare,' Hannah echoed, trying to ignore the stupid idea that had just germinated in her mind.

Danny consulted his watch. 'If I go now, I can get round the letting agencies before they shut at lunchtime.'

'Wouldn't you like a coffee? And maybe a bit of breakfast?'

He cocked his head on one side. 'You wouldn't be propositioning me would you, Ms Maddrell?'

'No! I mean, well, maybe. That is, if you're interested I might just have a sort of proposition for you . . .'

'You did *what*?' Maxine's jaw dropped so hard that her lower molars came out in Australia.

'I only sort of suggested it to him. In principle.'

She and Hannah were in the tiny kitchenette at the salon, snatching a quick coffee between clients. A coffee that Hannah for one sorely needed; it was a long, long time since she'd felt as rough as this, and she suspected caffeine was the only cure.

'But Han, you just asked a complete stranger to be your lodger!'

'No I didn't! The thing is, he kind of mentioned that he needed somewhere to live, and I kind of told him I might be looking for someone to rent the spare bedroom, that's all. Subject to references and everything, of course.'

Maxine rolled her eyes. 'Well of course!'

'Nothing definite. We just said we'd meet up and go for a meal tomorrow, and then talk about it some more.'

'What if he's a nutter?'

'I told you, I'll get references. Besides, if he was going to murder me in my bed or something, would he have brought me home last night and stayed all that time to make sure I was OK?'

'Maybe he's the kind of nutter who worms his way into your affections and *then* murders you in your bed,' replied Maxine drily. 'And what about Lottie? You can't just invite strange young men into your house when you've got a nine-year-old daughter.'

'No, I realise that,' agreed Hannah. 'And what I said about references, well, I'm taking it very seriously. If I can't talk to at least a couple of responsible people who can vouch for him, then the deal's off. Plus, if Lottie's not happy with him being in the house, he goes. But I really do think he's a decent bloke,' she added.

'You thought Rhys was a decent bloke,' Maxine pointed out, 'and look how that turned out.'

'Yes, OK, but I knew Nick was a decent bloke the moment I set eyes on him, so I'm not always wrong, am I?'

'Just don't come running to me when it all ends in tears,' Maxine sighed as she stirred a teaspoonful of Marmite into her coffee.

Hannah grimaced in disgust. 'How can you drink that?'

Maxine grinned and patted her bump. 'Ask Thing here. It works in a mysterious way, but it stops me throwing up every ten minutes. Speaking of which, have you seen Claire?'

'Not since she disappeared into the staff loo with a face the colour of Astroturf.'

'Bugger, I'll have to cancel the rest of her morning appointments if she doesn't get her backside out here.' Maxine wagged a reproving finger. 'I'll have you know you're leading my staff into bad ways, Hannah Steadman.'

Claire did eventually emerge from the toilet, her face no longer green but the violent puce hue of a burst boil. Maxine took one look at her, sent her home with her ears burning, and rang up her friend Jade who helped out in emergencies.

'She can do the easy ones,' she told Philomena. 'You take her restyles and colours, and Jason –'

'Yes, Maxine?' He quivered eagerly; this could be his big moment.

'You can sweep the floor and make the tea.'

'Oh.'

'And this time when you're shampooing, make sure the water's *warm*. It's supposed to be a pleasant experience, not the Chinese water torture.'

'Yes, Maxine.'

Hannah had a busy morning too. Saturdays were always booked solid, with stressed office-workers desperate to have their knotted muscles ironed out, and affluent forty-somethings treating themselves to expensive facials. But the gods were definitely smiling down on Hannah: at the last moment Councillor Plowright phoned to say he couldn't make it because his car had broken down on the A40. Plus, her hangover was definitely on the way out. All in all, today was looking up.

She came downstairs around twelve thirty, leaving Gloria marinating in a seaweed wrap, and noticed a big, solid hunk of a man hovering around the reception desk where Philomena was writing something in the appointments book.

'Hmm, whoever's that?' she asked Maxine as she popped back into the kitchenette to fetch her sandwiches from the fridge.

'Hands off, you've already got one admirer,' hissed Maxine.

'Besides, he's taken. That's Gloria's latest, come to pick her up.'

'Wow, really?' Hannah was impressed. The guy oozed quality from his head to his Cartier brogues. 'I'd better go and tell her he's here.'

Maxine nudged her and stifled a giggle. 'Hey, just look at Phil. Is it me, or is she flirting with him?'

Hannah peered round the door frame. Phil looked like she'd seldom seen her before – all pink-cheeked and smiling and well, very nearly ... pleasant. And curiously, Gloria's bloke didn't look like he wanted to turn tail and leg it. So either he was exceptionally polite, or he actually *liked* her.

'Blimey,' she commented, 'that's a first. Last time I saw Phil smile was when old Plowright ripped his trousers on the L'Oreal display. Mind you,' she reflected, 'I had a good laugh myself.'

'Do you think she fancies him?' wondered Maxine.

'Don't be daft. The only thing Phil thinks men are any use for is getting the tops off jars. Between you and me, I don't think Gloria's got anything to worry about.'

Hannah didn't break the news to her mum and dad straight away, although she wasn't sure why. Instead she waited until the following Sunday, when she and Lottie were invited round for lunch.

'You know I said I might get someone for the spare room – you know, a lodger?' she said, spooning roast parsnips onto her plate.

'Yes dear, you said it'd be company for you,' said her father. 'Mind you, you'd have to be very careful who you took in.'

'Absolutely,' agreed Erica, handing round the gravy. 'Elbows off the table, Charlotte dear, there's a good girl. There are some very strange people out there, you read the most dreadful stories.'

'Some of these crooks,' Derek went on, 'will even try to steal your identity. They take your passport, your bank account details, everything – next thing you know, you're propping up a bridge on the motorway and some psychopath's living your life.'

'Thanks, Dad! That's really cheered me up.'

'Well, you do need to be aware of these things.' Derek cut himself a piece of Yorkshire pudding so perfectly square that Hannah yearned to bite the corner off it, just to make it a bit more lop-sided. 'The world's a dangerous place, you know.'

Herbie had been listening to all of this in silence, punctuated only by the rattle of his false teeth as he chewed on a resilient piece of gristle. 'Trouble with you,' he said, 'is you always see the worst in people.'

'Sometimes,' observed Derek darkly, 'there isn't anything else to see.'

'Oh I get it, this is have-a-go-at-Herbie day is it?'

'I wasn't talking about you.'

'Like hell you weren't.'

Erica laser-beamed the pair of them with one of her special hard stares. 'Please! This is supposed to be a nice, peaceful family Sunday lunch. More gravy, Hannah?'

'Thanks, just a little.'

'So you're actually thinking of going ahead then?' Erica went on. 'With the lodger?'

'Actually,' announced Lottie matter-of-factly, 'Mummy's already got a man in the spare room.'

Erica choked on a mouthful of dauphinoise potatoes, Derek dropped his fork and Herbie gave a dirty chuckle.

'What?' demanded Erica. 'What's Lottie talking about?'

'Mummy met a man at a nightclub, and she got drunk and he brought her home, and now he's living in our spare room.' She met the stares of horror with a look of total innocence. 'That's what she told Auntie Maxine on the phone.'

This was not how Hannah had planned it at all. Four pairs of eyes were all focused on her, waiting to hear how she was going to explain her way out of this.

'It's not quite like that, sweetheart,' she told Lottie, making a mental note to have stern words when they got home. 'Danny's a very nice man who looked after me when I was feeling ... unwell. He's been working abroad for a couple of years and has come back here to set up in business.'

'What sort of business?' demanded Derek.

'He hasn't quite decided yet.'

'Hrrmph. Doesn't sound like much of a businessman to me. And how old is this Danny anyway?'

'Er . . . a couple of years younger than I am.'

Erica's face registered frank dismay. 'Hannah darling, are you telling us you've just opened your home to some young man you met in a club, who hasn't even got a job, and whom you don't know from Adam?'

This was not going well, but Hannah wasn't about to be defeated by her parents' prejudices.

'Look, I know what you're thinking and I wasn't sure at first either. But there are people round here who knew him before he moved away, and they all say he's a decent chap. And his references are impeccable.'

'References can be forged,' scowled Derek.

'Yes, and I could be a Martian, but I'm not!' cried Hannah in exasperation. 'It's only like having a flatmate, Dad. And it's only on a one-month trial basis. If it doesn't work out, he'll leave.'

'I hope so,' remarked Herbie. 'Squatters can be a bloody nightmare to get rid of if they refuse to sling their hook.'

'Gramps! I thought you at least would be on my side.'

'I'm not *not* on your side,' protested Herbie, looking uncomfortable. 'I just think you ought to be careful, that's all. Derek doesn't *always* talk out of his arse.'

'Am I supposed to take that as a compliment?' demanded Derek.

'I'll be fine!' insisted Hannah.

Erica turned her attentions to Lottie. 'It's not you I'm worried about, Hannah, it's Charlotte. How on earth does she feel about having a strange young man in the house?'

Hannah threw Lottie a reassuring smile. 'Oh, Lottie likes Danny. She's fine about it, aren't you, sweetheart?'

But the look on Lottie's face said different.

Nick threw the last of the boxes into the back of the car and slammed down the hatchback.

'Right, that's everything.' Opening up his arms, he wrapped them round Miranda and slid one hand down over her perfect bottom, all warm and smooth and inviting underneath her jodphurs. 'Guess I'd better get on the road.'

'Good luck, darling. Sell lots of stuff.'

He threw her a boyish smile. 'I'll do my best. There are no guarantees of course. But if one of these parent-teacher groups really takes a fancy to my range of products, I could be looking at a breakthrough.'

'Let's hope so.'

'I'll make you proud of me, Miranda.'

'Of course you will. I'd better get on and do some work myself now. See you tonight then, darling.'

She was back inside the cottage before Nick's car had reached the bottom of the muddy, winding drive. Thank God she had the place to herself today, after another ghastly weekend with the child from hell. Two minutes later she was in the bedroom, stepping out of her jumper and jodhpurs and pulling open her lingerie drawer, the one with the pretty lace things she only ever wore on special occasions.

Selecting a gold satin bra and matching string, she slipped them on and modelled them in front of the full-length mirror. A shiver of anticipation ran down her spine as she saw how good she looked. Oh yes, they'd do very nicely.

A few strategic dabs of her favourite perfume, and she'd be just about perfect.

Chapter 18

'I mean, why shouldn't I have a lodger anyway?' complained Hannah as she and Maxine queued up in the coffee bar at Seuss & Goldman.

Maxine's hand hovered over the fresh fruit salad, then did a U-turn and went for the mulled-wine cheesecake instead. 'No reason,' she agreed. 'But he's not just any lodger though, is he? Don't look at me like that, I'm eating for two,' she added as she picked up a pot of clotted cream to go with the cheesecake.

'I take it the morning sickness has worn off then?'

'Yeah, I'm really lucky, only being a few months gone. Some people throw up for months. Now I just pee a lot and crave marmalade sandwiches at two in the morning.'

'What do you mean, Danny's not just any lodger?' demanded Hannah, sliding her tray towards the till.

Maxine laughed. 'C'mon, don't act the innocent with me! The man's a hunk – and he's younger than you.'

'What's that got to do with anything? I'm renting the guy my spare room, not setting up home with him!'

'Are you quite sure about that?' Maxine winked. 'Two large lattes please,' she said, reaching for her purse. 'And a banana milkshake. With croutons.'

'With what?' The girl behind the counter looked perplexed. 'Sorry, I thought you said croutons.'

'Yes, croutons! Look, I'm pregnant, OK?' Maxine poked her stomach. 'If the bump wants croutons, that's what the bump gets.'

'Yes madam, croutons, right away.'

They paid and made their way to their favourite table,

tucked away in a corner by the picture window that overlooked the street. Hannah had lost count of the times they'd sat there, speculating about the people who passed and dreaming up ever-more-ambitious plans for a worldwide hair and beauty empire. So far they might have only made it as far as the Cheltenham inner ring-road, but everybody had to start somewhere.

'Danny's just a lodger!' protested Hannah, queasily watching Maxine stir garlic croutons into her banana milkshake. 'How many times do I have to tell you?'

'It doesn't matter how many times you tell me,' retorted Maxine. 'I can tell just by looking at you that you fancy the pants off him.'

Hannah knew there wasn't much point in trying to deny it. Maxine had such a nose for bullshit that she could have hired herself out as a muck-spreader. 'Well OK, I guess he *is* quite good-looking,' she conceded, 'if you like that sort of thing.'

'And you're telling me you don't?'

'No, but just because I like him a bit, that doesn't mean he likes me, does it?'

Maxine snorted. 'You'll be telling me you're just good friends next.'

Hannah stuck out her tongue. 'Look, he's a really nice guy but we hardly know each other. It's just pleasant having another adult around the place, that's all. He's good company. What's wrong with that?'

'Nothing – in theory.'

'What's that supposed to mean?'

'Well, I can see why your parents are a bit less than thrilled. I think they were expecting you to take in some nice middle-aged spinster, not a Mr Universe contestant.'

This was all getting rather tedious and annoying. Hannah stabbed at a sugar lump with her spoon and the two halves shot off in opposite directions. 'Why shouldn't I have a sexy male lodger if I want?' she demanded, returning to her original gripe. 'After all, Nick's got a mistress.'

'Oh, I get it. This is about getting your own back on Nick.'

'No it's not!' She could see from Maxine's expression that she wasn't convinced. 'Well . . . maybe just a bit.'

'Now that I can understand,' said Maxine. 'Letting him know

you can pull just as easily as he can – it's natural. Besides, it can't be easy seeing him swan around with that Miranda woman draping herself all over him and talking about making babies.'

'Even if I don't fancy him myself,' cut in Hannah.

'Well, yeah.'

Hannah stirred her coffee tetchily. 'The thing is, how would you feel about your impressionable nine-year-old daughter spending nights in that cottage with your ex and his lover?'

'I don't know. And I'm not that keen on finding out.'

'I'm beginning to wish I'd not given in and said he could take her there,' admitted Hannah. 'She's only a little kid, she's not ready to see her daddy snogging other women.'

'Hmm,' Maxine replied through a mouthful of cheesecake.

'Hmm?'

'Just remember that when Danny tries to get into your pants.'

Hannah swatted her with her paper napkin. 'I told you, Danny's just a lodger!'

Maxine eyed her over the rim of her coffee cup. 'Hmm,' she repeated.

Miranda sat back in her chair and chewed the end of her pen. Inspiration was refusing to strike today. Then again, she had been woken up at an ungodly hour by Old Tom insisting on telling her something about one of the chickens having a bad leg. Not to mention Nick droning on over breakfast about whether he ought to buy his ex-mother-in-law a birthday present and, if so, how much he ought to spend on it.

If Miranda had had her way, he'd have forgotten about his old life completely, the way she'd forgotten about hers: slam the door on it, cut it off, clear the whole damn closet out, people and all. He wouldn't, of course. Nick was a sweet boy, and that was part of what had attracted her to him; but he just couldn't stop worrying about other people all the time. If it wasn't that precious stepdaughter of his, it was dopey Hannah, or some benighted stick insect the soppy pair had rescued from certain death.

The only thing you don't worry about half enough is me, she thought ruefully. You spend so much time on everybody else, I seem to come way down the bottom of the list.

If only life could be fairy-tale simple, like it was in her weekly newspaper column. Petunia never had any problems with men. Her 'Nature Notes' were one long hymn to sunny days and organic manure. A world in which her strapping farmer husband Rick was sexily dependable, and their delightful foster-daughter Lettie could charm the birds out of the trees.

So much for happy families, thought Miranda, drawing a line through her notes. I need a drink.

When Hannah got home that evening, she was amazed to find a wonderful smell of cooking pervading the house. Either Lottie had been having cookery lessons at school, or they'd been invaded by a crack team of Ninja chefs.

'Hello?' Hanging her coat on a peg in the hall, she wandered towards the kitchen just as Danny emerged, resplendent in a chef's hat and a PVC apron designed to make him look like he was wearing a French maid's uniform.

'Hannah, hi! Hope you don't mind, I thought I'd cook us a nice meal.'

'Mind?' Hannah gazed enraptured at the row of sizzling pans, not to mention the washed-up breakfast dishes and the neat pile of folded laundry on the table. 'Are you crazy?'

'You're not vegetarian, are you? Please tell me you're not vegetarian.'

She laughed at the look on his face. 'I'm not vegetarian! And even if I was, I think I'd make an exception for this.' Hannah raised the lid of a pan and took a sniff. 'This smells amazing – whatever is it?'

'My own secret recipe. Mediterranean-style tuna with olives and ratatouille, a goat's cheese pithivier – oh, and something a bit special for dessert. You see, I didn't completely waste all that time in the Med.'

Hannah sat down before she fell down. 'What on earth is all this for? You're my lodger, not the au pair.'

Danny looked crestfallen. 'I thought you'd be pleased.'

'Of course I am. I'm just not used to it, that's all.'

'Well, it's about time you were. You've been so good to me, letting me move in here, and I wanted to say thank you. Besides,' he added with that crinkly smile that made her legs go all wobbly, 'I thought it'd be nice to spend some time getting to know each other a bit better.'

Hannah had to admit the idea was more than tempting; then a thought struck her. 'Where's Lottie? Up in her room playing computer games?'

Danny shook his head, turned in a circle as though looking for something, then remembered and produced a folded sheet of paper from his jeans pocket. 'Nick called round, and left this for you. He said he didn't think you'd mind.'

'Mind what?' Hannah unfolded the paper. A scribbled note in Nick's hand read: 'Just been given three free tickets for that kids' show in Tewkesbury Lottie wanted to see. Starts 6.30, back before she turns into a pumpkin, love Nick.' 'Thanks for nothing, Nick,' she said in exasperation, 'you could have phoned to let me know!'

'Apparently he did, but your mobile was off and he couldn't get through to the salon.'

'How very convenient.'

Danny went back to stirring his pans. 'He seemed quite surprised when he saw me,' he remarked.

Hannah fought down a smirk. 'I bet.'

'Still, he seemed like a decent guy. Bit ... straight though, if you know what I mean.'

Yes, thought Hannah, I know exactly what you mean. And she imagined the look on Nick's face as he tried to work out whether she'd just acquired a lodger or a lover, or both.

'So it looks like we've got the whole evening on our own,' commented Danny, placing a dish of plump green olives and some crusty bread on the table.

'Just as well. Lottie hates olives.'

She reached out to take one, and their hands touched; very briefly, but just enough to send an electric thrill through Hannah's body.

'I wonder what we'll do after we've eaten,' she was shocked to hear herself say.

And he didn't disappoint her. 'Don't worry,' he assured her, 'I'll think of something.'

'Didn't I tell you? Didn't I?' Gloria was cock-a-hoop at her own cleverness. 'Didn't I say she'd end up in bed with him?'

'Shh,' reproved Maxine with a giggle, 'she'll hear.'

'What – from upstairs?'

'Besides, we don't know that she and Danny have actually . . . you know.'

Gloria swatted the air dismissively. 'Don't be silly, of course they have. Did you see the look on her face when she came in this morning? Happy as a blocked drain after Dyno-Rod's been round.'

'I'm not sure I'd put it quite like that,' said Maxine, 'but I get where you're coming from. Now, do you think that's about the right length for you?' She held out strands of Gloria's hair to show her in the mirror.

'Perfect, love.'

'OK then, I'll just fetch Philomena to put you a new colour on.'

It was Philomena's break-time, so Maxine headed out back to the staff restroom. Knowing Phil, she'd be flopped out in there with a copy of *Heat*, a packet of high-tar fags and the strongest coffee in all creation.

Oddly though, Phil wasn't there. In fact nobody was. But the back door was ajar and a wickedly chill breeze was whipping in through the gap, no doubt discharging hundreds of pounds' worth of central heating into the yard. Typical. People never thought about waste when they didn't have to pay the bills themselves.

Maxine was just about to shut the door when she heard Philomena's voice coming from the other side.

'Really? No, you don't mean that do you? Really?' Giggle.

Giggle? thought Maxine. But Phil never giggles. She barely ever smiles.

Intrigued, she crept a couple of steps closer.

'Oh Damon . . . that's what I want, too.'

Damon! That was a bit of a coincidence. Too much of a coincidence, perhaps. Maxine wished she could hear the other end of the phone conversation.

'Damon, you're so naughty! What would Gloria say if she heard? No! You're not serious! Really?'

Gloria . . . so, not a coincidence then!

Maxine was so close to the door that she almost got knocked flat when Philomena suddenly announced, 'Oh God, I'm five minutes' over my break time, got to go,' and came rushing back in through the door.

'Oh,' she said as Maxine scraped herself off the opposite wall. 'I . . . er . . .'

'Just came to fetch you to do Gloria's colour,' said Maxine breezily. 'Or would you like me to tell her you're busy?'

After the salon closed, Hannah, Maxine and Jay got together in Hannah's treatment room for an ad hoc business meeting. At least, it was *supposed* to be about business.

'You're kidding,' gasped Hannah. 'Phil and Gloria's bloke? No, you must have got the wrong end of the stick.'

'Well if I have it's a funny-looking stick,' retorted Maxine. 'You should've heard her – it was all "ooh Damon" this, and "Damon, you're so naughty". I tell you, I didn't know where to look when she came back in and found me standing there.'

Hannah shook her head in disbelief. 'No, it's no good, I still can't get my head round it.'

'As the actress said to the bishop.'

They fell about laughing while Jay glanced at his watch. 'Sorry to butt in, ladies, but I thought you got me here to talk business. I've got to be over the other side of town in half an hour to do an estimate.'

'Sorry, Jay.' Hannah coughed, sat up straight and tried very hard to be serious. It wasn't easy; ever since yesterday evening she'd been feeling light-headed and absurdly girlish. Even Lottie had been giving her funny looks over the Weetabix. 'It's about my . . . er . . . lodger.' Maxine sniggered. 'Danny Richmond.'

'What about him?'

'Well, he's just sold his share in a business sailing posh types round the Med, and he's looking for something to invest in round here.'

Maxine chipped in. 'So we thought . . . why not the salon?'

Jay didn't look as impressed as Hannah had hoped. 'It's a bit of a leap from sailing in the Med to cutting women's hair.'

'Yes, but he wouldn't be doing any of that, would he?' pointed out Hannah. 'He'd just be—'

Maxine fell about laughing. 'A sleeping partner!'

Jay was getting seriously unamused. 'Look, are you two going to act sensibly or shall we just forget this?'

'Sorry,' they chorused, and Maxine motioned a zipped-up mouth.

'I really think it would be a good idea,' insisted Hannah. 'I mean, we've been looking for new investment for ages, haven't we? If we're going to expand and maybe get another salon . . .'

Jay ran a hand over his brow. 'Not that again.'

Hannah was dismayed. 'What do you mean, "not that again"? I thought you wanted it too!'

He sat back wearily in his chair. 'I did. Kind of. But that was before, wasn't it? Things have changed a bit lately.' He patted his wife's stomach. 'New priorities and all that.'

Maxine looked at him quizzically. 'How does my having a baby affect Danny investing in the salon?'

'Look.' Jay took his wife's hand as though explaining something very simple to a very senile old granny. 'You're going to pop in a few months' time, and even now you're having to slow down a bit, aren't you?'

'Not much,' protested Maxine. 'And I'll be back at work inside a couple of months – you know me, can't stand being on my own at home.'

'Yes, but you won't be on your own, will you?' said Hannah. 'You'll have the baby.'

'Exactly!' declared Jay. 'You'll have the baby, and the baby'll need you. We'll both need you. Twenty-four seven. So it's hardly the right time to be talking about opening up another salon, is it?'

'Hang on a minute,' said Hannah slowly. 'Are you saying Maxine's not coming back to work after the baby's born?'

'Yes, Jay,' echoed Maxine, turning a stony gaze on her husband. 'Is that what you're saying?'

Jay became suddenly aware that two pairs of hostile eyes were boring into his head. 'Oh come on, love, you know it makes sense! Hairdressers are two a penny, and—'

'What!' snapped Maxine. 'Are you saying I'm worthless?'

'Calm down, you know what I mean. What I'm saying is, we can easily get another stylist in to manage the place, and you can come in on the odd day if you like, just to keep your hand in. Wouldn't that be nice for you?'

'No it bloody wouldn't,' replied Maxine. 'Because it's not going to happen! If you think I'm going to sit at home, up to my neck in dirty nappies all day, you can forget it.'

'Maxine, be reasonable. It's your hormones doing this to you, getting you all het-up.'

Cool as a cucumber, Maxine turned back to Hannah. 'You know something?' she said. 'I'm really starting to like this idea of yours. Let's get Danny in and have a chat to him. If he's interested in investing, why the hell shouldn't we think about expanding the business?'

Chapter 19

'You know, I've always been fascinated by hairdressers,' commented Danny as he and Hannah sat in the kitchen eating breakfast.

'I'm not a hairdresser,' pointed out Hannah.

'So? I can still be fascinated by you, can't I?' He picked a fresh strawberry out of his muesli and popped it between Hannah's lips.

Lottie entered the kitchen, glanced at Danny and went over to the kitchen cupboard by the cooker. 'Mum, can I have a chocolate biscuit in my lunch box?'

'I'd rather you didn't, sweetheart, not today. It's not good for your teeth to have too much chocolate.'

'Oh go on,' urged Danny. 'Let her have one, a packed lunch is no fun without a choccy biccy, is it, Lottie?'

Hannah sighed. 'Well, I suppose so.'

'There you go!' smiled Danny. 'Sorted. Can I get round your mum or what?'

But Lottie closed the cupboard door, picked up her lunchbox and walked away empty-handed. 'It's not up to you. Mum doesn't want me to have one so I'm not going to.'

The kitchen door slammed shut. A few seconds later, so did the front door.

'I don't think she likes me much,' said Danny ruefully. 'Am I trying too hard?'

'Of course she likes you,' Hannah reassured him. Truth was, she couldn't bear to contemplate the absurd possibility that Lottie might be less than thrilled with her brand-new boyfriend. 'She's just a bit touchy about men in general since Nick and I split up. I don't think she quite knows how to relate to you yet.'

Danny ran a hand lightly down the side of her face. 'Ah, but the question is, do you?'

'Actually,' admitted Hannah, 'I'm not too sure either. It's such a long time since I did this sort of thing, I can't quite remember what the rules are.'

Danny threw his head back and laughed. 'The rules are ... there are no rules! Relax, let things happen, enjoy the day and stop worrying about tomorrow.'

Hannah looked at him dubiously. 'That's easy for you to say – young, free, single and all that.'

'So what are you then?' retorted Danny. 'You're young, you're practically single, and you're as free as you want to be.'

It's a nice idea, thought Hannah, but obviously Danny still had a few things to learn about the real world. 'Free?' she smiled. 'With a daughter, and an ex, and a private zoo, not to mention a house and a salon to run?'

He leaned across the table and kissed her on the end of her nose. 'Freedom's all in the mind,' he told her. 'You could be a billionaire on your own private island in the middle of the ocean, and still feel trapped.'

'Chance would be a fine thing,' muttered Hannah.

'Or you could just be you, and realise that there's nothing holding you back but the limits of your own imagination.'

It was so inspiring, so mesmerising listening to Danny that she almost began to believe him. What it must be to have had a life without failures, she thought. Not like me. 'Yeah, well, I started screwing my life up early and never quite got into the habit of success,' she half-laughed, burying her face in her coffee mug. 'It's probably a bit late to start again now.'

He stuck a finger under her chin and tilted it up, forcing her to look him in the eyes. 'That is utter bollocks, Hannah, and you know it. You're a far bigger success than I am, for a start-off!'

'How do you work that one out?'

'To begin with I've never even had a proper job – I mean, you can't count bumming around the Med on a yacht as real work, can you? OK, so I made a bit of cash out of it, but I'm a long way off being a big success. And look at you: you've got a lovely daughter – doesn't she make you feel you've achieved something?'

'Yes,' conceded Hannah with a smile. 'She drives me spare half the time, she worries me sick, but she makes me prouder than anything else I've ever done, that's for sure.'

'Well then! Plus, you've got your own salon.'

'A share in a salon,' Hannah corrected him. 'And if it wasn't for Jay I wouldn't even have that.'

'All right, a share in a salon. That's more than I've got.'

Suddenly the moment fell right into Hannah's lap. 'Actually, Maxine and Jay and I were talking about that the other night. About you wanting to invest in something, that is.'

Danny's eyebrows lifted a fraction. 'Oh yes? Plotting behind my back were we?'

Hannah's cheeks burned. 'Oh God, it does sound a bit like that, doesn't it? Look, forget I mentioned it.'

He laid a hand on hers. 'No, go on. I'm listening.'

'OK. Well, I happened to mention that you'd said you had a bit of money you wanted to invest, and we wondered if you might consider putting it into the salon. It was only a thought,' she went on, aware that she was starting to babble. 'You probably wouldn't be in the least bit interested, I mean, a women's hair salon and a beauty parlour, it's hardly—'

'Shh.' He placed a finger on her lips. 'Who says I wouldn't be interested?'

'You would?'

'I don't know. Maybe.'

'Interested enough to come down to the salon and take a look around?'

Danny's smile broadened. 'Now you're talking. Any excuse to spend more time with you ... and a load of other gorgeous women. Sounds like heaven to me.'

Erica and Derek were locked in a Scrabble death-match with Lottie and Nick.

'Hope you didn't mind us coming round this evening,' said Nick, wondering what to do with a Q, an X and three Is, 'only there's a burst pipe at the cottage, and Miranda's away until tomorrow, and there's not much to do round at the flat.' He gave Lottie's ear a friendly tweak, seemingly oblivious to the glare she gave him in return. 'I said she could stay home with her mum tonight if she wanted, but she said she'd still rather spend the time with me.'

Erica and Derek exchanged meaningful looks.

'Family or not, you're always welcome round here,' said Derek.

'How *is* your mum, darling?' Erica asked Lottie, managing to put down EARWIG without taking her eyes off her granddaughter. 'She must be very busy, I haven't heard from her in days.'

Lottie shuffled her feet under the table. 'She's all right. I s'pose.'

Erica's radar homed in on the blip. 'Is something wrong at home? She's not ill?'

'No.'

'It's not something to do with that Danny fellow, is it?' asked Derek. 'He's not been making any trouble?'

'No. He's fine too.' She wriggled in her chair. 'Can I go and get some juice from the fridge?'

'Yes, but it's your turn next.'

Lottie's eyes registered desperation. 'I'm really thirsty, Grandma.'

'Yes, of course. You go.'

When Lottie had left the room, an uncomfortable silence descended.

'She never told me about Danny, you know,' said Nick. 'I had to turn up on the doorstep and find out that way.'

'You didn't tell her about Miranda,' pointed out Erica.

'Yes I did!'

'Not until you were a lot more than friends.' Erica sighed. 'I think we've all had a little readjusting to do lately.'

'And I daresay there's a whole lot more to come,' grunted Derek, never the most optimistic of men.

There was another short silence.

'I don't like it,' said Nick.

'Don't like what?' asked Erica.

'My Lottie being in the house with ... him.' Nick couldn't quite bring himself to utter Danny's name again. 'I'm not saying there's anything wrong with him exactly, I'm sure he's a decent enough bloke, but it just doesn't seem right somehow.'

'What does Lottie think about it, that's the question surely,' cut in Derek. 'Maybe you should ask her again.'

'What does Lottie think about what?' asked Herbie, shuffling into the room to warm his feet by the gas fire. 'Oh I get it, you're on about that Danny bloke again, aren't you?' He shook his head. 'Don't you think you should lay off that child a bit?'

Three pairs of critical eyes turned on him. 'We've got her best interests at heart, you know,' said Erica. 'Somebody's got to make sure she's all right.'

'Yes, sure, but do you really think pestering the life out of the poor kid's going to make her any happier? She must feel like you're trying to make her take sides or something.'

Erica tutted something to the effect that Herbie should confine himself to things he understood, and he went and sat by the fire and shut up, more convinced than ever that life was a whole lot simpler inside. Maybe he really ought to keep his head down and his nose out.

All the same, he had to admit that whenever the question of her mum's relationship with Danny came up, Lottie looked less than thrilled. Almost as fed up, in fact, as she looked whenever her stepfather mentioned Miranda.

Danny couldn't have been happier if he'd been presented with a giant train set to play with.

Far from being bored to death by the salon, he spent all morning ooh-ing and aah-ing over Hannah's non-surgical facelift machine, and watching in complete fascination as Philomena worked her spiky magic on a woman with a terrible poodle perm.

'It's great, I love it!' he declared in the post-lunchtime lull, sitting down in Maxine's styling chair and spinning himself round. 'Who'd have thought hair could be so interesting?'

'It isn't *that* interesting,' cautioned Jay, who clearly didn't quite know what to make of this young man and his boundless enthusiasm.

'Yeah,' agreed Maxine, 'try saying that when you've just done six shampoo-and-sets in succession.'

'Still, it's not just the work, is it?' he countered. 'It's the *people*.' He sat up straight. 'And that's what I'm into, you see, people. That's why I loved working on the yacht so much. You got different characters every week of the year – some of them were great, some were total shits, but they were all different. You could never get bored. And I can feel it's the same here.'

Hannah perched on the arm of Danny's chair. 'He's right, isn't he, Max? No two days are ever the same.'

Maxine shrugged a kind of agreement. 'I guess. But it's no good coming into this kind of business with your eyes closed. It's hard work, long hours and some of the clients make you want to spit.'

'You do get a laugh though,' said Claire. 'Remember the guy you had in that time you had a terrible cold? The one with the black hair?'

'Yes thanks, Claire, I don't need reminding.'

But Claire was going to remind her anyway.

'Maxine was doing the back of his head with the electric clippers, and she had this really bad sneezing attack,' she explained with a grin. 'It was OK though, he had no idea about the bald patch 'cause we covered it up with a bit of black hair dye.'

Maxine coloured up. Danny laughed. 'Remind me not to get my hair cut here unless I want a Number One.'

Everybody looked at everybody else. Nobody said anything.

'So – what do you think?' asked Hannah, desperate to break the ice. 'About Danny maybe investing in the salon?'

Jay stood up and pointed towards the staff restroom. 'I think we need to talk,' he replied. 'In private.'

'I know it's not a lot of money,' said Danny, 'but it could make a difference. Couldn't it?'

Jay had to admit that it could. 'The question is, do we want it to? I mean, does Split Ends need another investor right now?'

'Of course it does!' exclaimed Hannah. 'If we're going to expand—'

'Which is something we haven't decided upon,' Jay reminded her.

'You mean, something you've closed your mind against,' retorted Maxine. ''Cause you think I should be barefoot and pregnant all the time.'

'Don't exaggerate.'

'Only if you stop patronising me.'

Hannah handed round cups of coffee, rather wishing it were something stronger. 'Even if we didn't expand into another salon – I mean, not right away – it would help just to have a bit more capital though, wouldn't it?'

'Well . . . yes,' conceded Jay. 'Some of the equipment's getting a bit long in the tooth, and the salon's about due for redecoration.'

'You see?'

'Hang on a minute. The redecoration needn't cost much, 'cause I can use the painters from my shopfitting business, but it'd mean closing the salon for a week or so and that means lost trade.'

'All the more reason for having a bit more capital behind you,' suggested Danny.

'Maybe.'

'And we're not going to be getting a lot of trade if people think the salon looks dingy and old-fashioned,' added Maxine.

Jay looked from one eager face to another. 'I get the feeling I'm being outnumbered here,' he observed. 'I mean, does it really matter what I think?'

For once Danny dropped the floppy-haired schoolboy routine, and looked genuinely serious. 'Please don't get that impression. Of course it matters what you think. You're the main investor here, what I can offer is only pin-money by comparison. But I'm genuinely interested, and if you're willing to have my money I'll do my best to make a practical contribution as well.'

'A practical contribution?' puzzled Hannah. 'Like what?'

'Well, I'm sure if Jason can manage to shampoo old ladies without drowning them, I can too.'

Maxine fell about. 'What, you? Work in the salon?'

'Why not? After all, you said it yourself – Maxine's going to have to ease off the heavy work soon. I'm sure I could make myself useful about the place – why don't you give me a go?'

It was late on Sunday evening when Nick bumped his way up the winding path to Far Acre Cottage. It was also dark and cold, and he was knackered. But he was happy.

In spite of everything – burst pipes, a power cut at the flat, Miranda being away, the mere existence of Danny Richmond – Nick had just enjoyed a really good weekend with Lottie. He was starting to feel her relax with him again now, he was sure he wasn't imagining it. And it must be a good sign that she'd chosen to spend the time with him rather than stay at home with Hannah and her new love-interest.

He tried not to think too much about Hannah as he drove up to the cottage, because whenever he did Danny's grinning, irritatingly handsome face hove into view, provoking thoughts he really didn't want to have. Not that he was jealous; that would have been just plain silly. He was just concerned, for Hannah as well as Lottie. He hated to think that they might be taken in by some smarmy git, let alone one who just happened to be considerably younger and better-looking than himself.

Funny, he thought as he slid out of the car and noticed a light on downstairs. There really oughtn't to be anyone at home. Miranda was supposed to be at her organic producers' conference until tomorrow, and he'd said he wouldn't be back till Monday either. Maybe Old Tom was making late-night improvements to the plumbing; after all, he spent practically his entire life round here anyway.

Humming to himself, Nick retrieved his overnight bag, walked up to the door and stuck his key into the lock. Not that he needed to: the door swung open at his touch. Now that really was odd. Despite the cottage being in the middle of nowhere, Old Tom was comically paranoid about security. Even the hen-house had four mortise locks on it.

He stepped inside. 'Hello?'

The hall light was on but there was no reply. Maybe Tom had popped out to get something and would be back in a minute. Ah well, high time he got himself into a nice warm bath, fixed himself some hot chocolate and got a good night's sleep.

He slung his jacket over the back of the sofa, then strode up the stairs. It wasn't until he got to the landing that he heard it. At first he thought maybe someone had left the radio on, but then he realised the voices were for real.

For a moment, he hesitated. If he were to turn round now, go back down the stairs and drive away, this would never have happened. He would simply go back to the flat, erase it from his mind, and write something else in its place.

Only he couldn't. Not this time. This time he couldn't turn his back on it any more.

'Miranda? Are you in bed?'

He took a deep breath, pushed open the bedroom door and clicked on the light. Miranda was in bed all right.

But she wasn't alone.

Chapter 20

'I don't understand,' repeated Miranda. 'I just don't understand why you're making such a big thing of this!'

Nick looked at her, and saw that she wasn't lying: she really didn't. The realisation filled him with a huge, empty, sickening ache. How could you hope to make someone see what she'd done to you when that person's life revolved so completely, so hermetically around herself?

'Oh Miranda. How did we come to this?' Suddenly exhausted, he sat down heavily on the bed beside her. She hadn't even bothered to cover up the oyster silk basque she'd claimed she bought just for him. At least she'd had the good grace to send the blokes packing. Both of them.

She let out a little irritated sigh. 'So I fancied a little extra-curricular entertainment, so what?'

Nick had promised himself he wouldn't lose his cool, but if he'd ever in his life come close to slapping a woman, it was now. 'If you were so sure it wasn't a big deal,' he pointed out, 'why all the secrecy? Why wait till I was out of the way before inviting your lover-boys round for the night?'

'Because you always turn everything into some big drama! I mean, look at yourself!'

That was precisely what he didn't want to do. He knew if he caught sight of himself in the mirror he would see a white-faced, sweating, angry middle-aged man who was close to losing control. And losing control was the one thing that frightened Nick more than anything.

'No,' he said coldly. 'Why don't you take a good look at yourself?' He got to his feet and threw her dressing gown at her. 'For God's sake cover yourself up, you look like a cheap tart.'

That at least pierced Miranda's armour of serene self-absorption. 'How dare you call me a tart!'

'If the cap fits . . .'

Her pretty, red-smeared lip curled with sudden venom. 'At least I'm not clapped-out and incapable.'

He could have risen to the bait, but all at once he really couldn't be bothered. 'Yeah, whatever,' he said, walking across to the wardrobe and grabbing an armful of shirts.

Miranda scrabbled across the bed. 'What are you doing?'

'What does it look like?'

She caught his arm. 'You're not going!'

Coolly he detached her fingers. 'If I'd had any self-respect I'd have gone weeks ago.' He saw her eyes widen in surprise. 'Yes, that's right, I guessed what you were up to a while back but, pathetic romantic that I am, I just couldn't bring myself to believe it was over.' He half grunted, half laughed. 'Or maybe I just don't handle failure very well. God knows why, I've had enough practice.'

Grabbing a holdall, he stuffed in a few days' worth of clothes and a spare pair of shoes, then picked up his car keys from the floor where he'd dropped them. 'I'll be back in a couple of days to get the rest of my stuff.'

Miranda sat on the end of the bed, hugging her robe around her bare shoulders as though a sudden chill had just swept through the room. 'You don't have to go, Nick. We can sort this out. It was only a game.'

'Yeah, well, maybe that's the problem. Everything's a game to you, but like you keep saying, I'm just a serious-minded old fart. See you around, Miranda.'

And before she had time to find the words that might have held him back, he was gone.

Danny waltzed into the salon like Fred Astaire onto the set of a Hollywood spectacular.

'Morning, ladies! Not a very nice one out there, is it? But don't you worry, we'll soon brighten it up for you.' With a flourish worthy of Zorro, he produced a bunch of red carnations and presented one to each of the customers sitting waiting for a trim. 'Pour vous, madame.'

Philomena and Claire exchanged looks, and Jason coughed into his sleeve to cover his mirth at the sight of Danny's ultra-camp pink and orange shirt.

'I think somebody's seen too many soap operas,' commented Maxine as Hannah watched Danny's big entrance. 'Have you told him not all male hairdressers are gay?'

Hannah smiled indulgently. 'I know it's a bit over the top, but he wanted to make a big impression and seeing as it's Valentine's I thought, why not? Anyway, look – the ladies are loving it.'

What's more, it was true. Mrs De'Ath was blushing scarlet beneath half an inch of face powder, and giggling into her carnation, and even the younger, less easily impressed clients seemed to welcome a bit of harmless fun on a wet February morning.

'Talking of Valentine's,' Maxine went on, jotting down an appointment in the book, 'I trust yours was a big one?'

Hannah winked. 'Immense. And the card was quite sizeable too.'

'I don't know! Who'd think you used to be a respectable old married woman, eh?'

'You reckon I've changed then?'

Maxine eyed her expertly. 'Let's just say there's a wiggle in your walk that wasn't there before. Ah, Danny.' He snapped to attention in front of her and clicked his heels.

'Ma'am?'

'Jason's going to show you how to sweep up, aren't you, Jason?'

Jason smirked. 'You bet.' Showing somebody else how to sweep up was the closest he'd come to a promotion in a long while. He was going to enjoy this.

Danny's face registered dismay. 'Sweep up? I thought I was doing some shampooing and stuff.'

'First things first.' Maxine handed him a broom. 'You said you wanted to start at the bottom and Jason swept up for weeks before we let him anywhere near a backwasher, didn't you, Jase?'

'But—'

Hannah kissed him on the cheek. 'Go on darling, be a good boy and let Jason show you the ropes.'

'Ropes, eh? If there's any ropes involved I'd rather it was you showing me them.'

Hannah tittered, and he took the opportunity to move in and

squeeze her bottom underneath her white uniform tunic – much
to the fascinated amusement of the watching clients.

'Oi, that's quite enough of that,' ruled Maxine, breaking up the
impending clinch like a Madison Square Garden referee. 'Or I'll
have to turn the cold hose on the pair of you. Go on Danny, time's
a-wasting and there's half a ton of hair wants sweeping up over
there.'

Reluctantly, Danny trailed off behind Jason.

'You'll have to watch that, you know,' Maxine said reprov-
ingly.

Hannah felt uncomfortably like a small girl being scolded for
showing her knickers to the boy next door. 'Don't be like that, we
were only—'

'Yes dear, I know exactly what you were *only* doing, and if I
hadn't put a stop to it right then I reckon you'd be *only* at it like
knives under the dryers by now.'

'Don't exaggerate!' laughed Hannah. 'Besides, you're just
jealous.'

'Probably,' admitted Maxine ruefully. 'Jay seems to think now
I'm pregnant I'm so fragile he can't come anywhere near me.'

'Really?'

'Really. As if anything the size of a blue whale could be fragile.
But that's beside the point. I know you two are all loved-up, but
this is a salon, not a knocking shop. If you feel a desperate urge to
rip each other's clothes off, love, at least do it in the restroom.'

Hannah was having difficulty concentrating . . . on anything.

It was weird – like being a teenager all over again, frighteningly oversensitive and packed dangerously full of hormones, but
though the experience was weird and scary, she found it exhilarating too. Maybe Danny would turn out to be The One, maybe
not; but there was no denying that he was good for her. How
could anything that made her feel so alive not be good?

All the same, she knew Maxine had a point. A bit of fun in the
salon was fine, but when all was said and done they were supposed to be professionals; and Danny was going to have to learn
that too. Not that he was having any trouble getting on with the
clients, far from it. The old ladies in particular seemed to have
adopted him as a sort of mascot, and he was clearly loving every
minute of it.

She was clearing up after a bikini wax, and preparing for a warming seaweed body wrap, when her mobile rang. Usually she remembered to turn it off at work, but since Danny had erupted into her life nothing had been quite the same; good job she wasn't in the middle of a consultation. She fished it out of her coat pocket, flipped it open, and clocked the caller's number.

'Nick?'

'Hi. Sorry to bother you at work, but something's come up.'

'What kind of something? I'm really busy here.'

'Just ... um ...' She'd never heard Nick sound so hesitant before. 'I'd rather not talk about it on the phone if it's all the same to you. Can you come for a drink after work?'

'I guess so. Lottie's being picked up from gym class, so there's no tearing hurry to get home.' Though I'd rather be at home with Danny than having a drink with you, thought Hannah, slightly guilty at her lack of interest in Nick's problem – whatever it was.

'Right.'

'I finish around six. You can pick me up from here if you like.'

'OK, see you then.'

''Bye.'

I wonder what all that was about, thought Hannah, dropping the phone back into her coat pocket. But there was no time to ponder, because at that moment Jason phoned from downstairs to let her know that her one thirty appointment had just arrived.

Still, given Nick's neurotic concern about everybody and everything, whatever he wanted to talk to her about was bound to be something and nothing.

Danny had style, and he knew it.

If you had to push a broom round the salon, you might as well do it as if you were really enjoying it. It worked for him, for example, to imagine that the broom was Angelina Jolie in pink satin underwear and sky-high heels.

All the same, a whole morning of sweeping up other people's scummy bits of hair wasn't exactly rocket science, he was hungry, and it was altogether too long since he'd had his hands on Hannah's delectable bum.

Time to break for lunch.

He headed on up the stairs to the beauty room, two at a time, gave a brief knock on the door and burst straight in.

The awful green slimy thing on the couch took one look at him, and screamed so hard that its rock-hard facemask cracked into crazy paving.

'Aaah! A man!'

'I'm so terribly sorry, Mrs Quentin,' gasped Hannah, grabbing the nearest towel and enveloping her client's seaweed-slathered modesty. She fixed Danny with a glare that would dissolve concrete. 'I can't imagine who let him in.'

'What?' said Danny, snapping out of his slack-jawed trance.

'Out!' snapped Hannah, marching towards him with slimy green hands, shoving him out of the beauty room and slamming the door behind her.

'What was that for?' demanded Danny. 'I've got green slime all over me now.'

'You can't just barge in like that!' hissed Hannah. 'My poor lady was half-naked!'

'Oh, it's female, is it?'

'Danny!'

'Well you've got to admit it's a bit hard to tell.' He reached out and dragged Hannah towards him. 'Anyway, it's lunchtime. Aren't you hungry?'

'I'm working, Danny! I haven't got time for food.'

He wiggled a provocative eyebrow. 'Who's talking about food?'

For a split second, Hannah was almost tempted to leave her slimy green client sprawled out on the treatment couch and run off to play hookey with Danny; then reason kicked in again.

'Go away, Danny. I'm busy.'

'But you've got to take a break sometime.'

'Later. Maybe.'

'But—'

'And don't you dare do that ever again. Got that?'

He grinned. 'Got it, Herr Obergruppenfuehrer.'

She swiped at his head with a slimy green paw, but he was already halfway down the stairs.

It comes to something, thought Danny, when the lady in your life can't even spare half an hour to share a sandwich and a snog.

Nobody else seemed to have much time for him at the moment either. Apparently they were 'rushed off their feet', but he was sure that if they organised themselves a bit better they could have a bit more fun and still get through the work. Once he'd persuaded them to let him reorganise their appointments system, there'd be some dynamic changes around Split Ends. Maybe he'd even persuade them to trade in the name for something less suburban and a bit more, well . . . dangerous.

In the end, he gave up trying to explain his ideas to Maxine, who was showing Jason how to cut a fringe, and losing her temper in the process.

'Oh well,' he announced to nobody in particular, 'I guess I'll take a lunch break then.'

'If you're going out the back, you can take the rubbish with you,' said Claire, handing him a couple of overflowing bin bags.

You'd never think I was a valued investor, mused Danny, trudging through the salon and down the short corridor to the staff restroom. Still, just wait till I've got the hang of the business and I'm running this show.

He nudged open the door with his knee, and dragged the bin bags through. If he hadn't fumbled with the catch on the back door, he might never have noticed the sounds coming from the staff toilet.

'Oooooh . . .'

He stopped and turned round. That was Philomena's voice: there was no mistaking her hard-edged Dublin drawl. Had she got herself locked in? Was she ill? He almost shouted out, 'Are you OK in there?', then was rather glad he hadn't.

'Oh . . . Oh yes . . . Oh yeeeeess!'

Now that was definitely not Philomena's voice, not unless Philomena had suddenly grown a beard and a whole new set of hormones to go with it.

'Damon . . . Oh Damon, touch me there; do it again . . .'

Damon? Danny was stunned. Damon was not the name of Philomena's husband, he knew that much. On the other hand, he happened to know that Damon *was* the name of Gloria's latest *amour*. The love of her life, apparently. The only one for her; her one true soulmate.

And here Philomena was, right under her nose, sneaking the cherry off Gloria's fairy cake without so much as a by-your-leave.

Oh dear, he thought, tiptoeing out of the back door and closing it quietly behind him. I wonder what Gloria will think if she ever finds out what's been going on . . .

Nick turned up right on time, just like Hannah knew he would.

He shuffled from one foot to the other, hands in pockets like an embarrassed schoolboy. 'Hi.'

'Hi.'

'Anywhere special you fancy going?'

'Not bothered. You choose.'

As they walked round to the Jolly Foresters, where they'd downed many a happy-hour lager, Hannah tried to get to the bottom of what was bugging Nick.

'I was surprised when you rang me at work,' she said.

'Yeah. I'm sorry about that. I felt I needed to contact you right away, and I didn't really want to phone you at home. I wasn't sure you'd answer.'

'Danny's a human being, you know. He doesn't bite.'

She felt the hostility radiating out of Nick at the mention of Danny's name, and almost regretted mentioning him; but when all was said and done, they were grown-ups and they had to face realities. After all, she'd had to face the reality of Miranda bloody Moss.

'Yes, well, anyway, I needed to talk to you.' He pushed open the door of the lounge bar and they tramped inside, shaking the drizzle out of their hair.

'Hello, strangers!' Just their luck, Pete the head barman was on tonight, and Pete had known them on and off ever since they'd moved to Foley Road. 'Haven't seen you two in here for ages.'

'Er . . . no,' agreed Nick, fumbling in his habitually overloaded pocket for a handful of pound coins.

'I was beginning to think something had happened to you!' Pete grinned, delivering a mock-punch to Nick's shoulder. 'Now, what can I get you and your lovely lady?'

Hannah coloured. Nick paled.

'Just a small white wine thanks,' said Hannah, hastily turning and walking off to the most secluded table she could find, right in the dingiest corner underneath the one-eyed deer's head.

'She OK, your missus?' enquired Pete solicitously. 'Looking a bit of a funny colour. Come to think of it, you're not looking too well yourself. Touch of this South American flu, is it?'

'Something like that,' said Nick, shoving far too much money across the bar top. 'Keep the change.'

He joined Hannah at the table. 'Sorry, I picked the wrong place didn't I?'

She shrugged. 'Whatever. It doesn't really matter, does it? Wherever we go we're going to run into people who don't know what's happened.'

'I guess. I just don't want things to be uncomfortable for you, that's all.'

'Stop worrying about me, Nick. I'll be fine. I *am* fine.'

She squeezed his hand briefly, and then they were apart again; two very separate entities that had once been one, and hadn't yet quite worked out how to relate to each other in a new way.

'What was this thing you wanted to talk to me about?' she asked, sipping her wine. 'Because if it's Lottie, don't worry – I'll make sure you know about all the parents' evenings and school reports and everything.'

He shook his head. 'Actually it's not Lottie. It's me – and Miranda.'

Hannah's stomach seemed to plummet to the bottom of a deep, dank pit. This was it then: the happy-ever-after, I'm-getting-married-in-the-morning speech. Oh and by the way, can you just sign these divorce papers to make it all legal?

'Right,' she said. I'm not going to make it easy for you by asking you all the right questions, she thought; I ought to, but I'm not.

'We're. . .' Nick downed a very large swig of beer, closed his eyes, took a deep breath. 'We're splitting up.'

'What?' I'm hearing things, thought Hannah; I'm definitely hearing things.

'Miranda and I . . . Well, the upshot is, I've moved out of the cottage and back into the flat.'

'But when? More to the point, why?'

Nick slumped back onto the itchy moquette bench-seat. 'Lots of reasons,' he said. 'Let's just say that living in the country wasn't all I'd thought it would be, and . . .'

'And neither was living with Miranda?' ventured Hannah, with a hint of bitchiness.

'Yes. I guess you could say so. But it's nobody's fault,' he added, avoiding Hannah's gaze. 'We just woke up one day and realised we weren't really seeing life the same way.'

'It's really over then?'

He nodded. 'Really over.'

There was a short, painful silence. In the background, Mariah Carey was wailing 'can't live ... if living is without you', and a young couple at the bar were sucking each other's faces off like a pair of ravenous leeches.

Hannah reached for Nick's hand, and laid her own gently on top of it. 'I'm sorry, Nick. Really I am.'

And in a funny way she was.

But it was still all she could do not to jump up, punch the air and shout: 'Yes!'

Chapter 21

Days passed, and life settled into a kind of mad routine. Then the days turned to weeks, and suddenly it was well and truly spring.

'Mum,' said Lottie, as she, Danny and Hannah were watching TV one evening.

'Yes, sweetheart?'

'You know that summer adventure camp in Devon? The one they sent a letter home about from school?'

'Summer camp?' Danny wrinkled his nose. 'What – all tents and singing round the campfire, like in America? Sounds gross.'

'Sh,' said Hannah. 'Yes, sweetheart. What about it?'

Lottie took a sudden interest in her toes. 'I think I might want to go.'

This really was news to Hannah. 'But Lottie, the last time you mentioned it you said it sounded worse than the Brownies. And you only lasted a fortnight there!'

'Maybe I changed my mind.'

'Maybe you did,' replied Hannah, 'but what interests me is why.'

Lottie scowled. 'Can't I just change my mind 'cause I want to? You do, all the time.'

'Grown-ups are allowed to,' said Danny, trying to keep things light-hearted. 'Privilege of being old and wrinkly, eh darling?'

She poked him in the ribs. 'Who are you calling old and wrinkly?'

'Well, you are a whole four years older than me!'

They play-fought on the sofa, and then Hannah remembered she was supposed to be a responsible parent, not a teenager high on hormones. She coughed embarrassedly. 'Go on. What were you saying?'

'I'm going to my room,' said Lottie sulkily.

'No, don't go, we're sorry, aren't we, Danny?' Hannah pushed Danny away and sat down on the arm of Lottie's chair. 'Tell me about this camp. When is it?'

'First two weeks of August.'

'But sweetheart, don't you remember? That's when I've arranged to take leave from the salon so you, me and Danny can all go on holiday together.'

The look on Lottie's face suggested that this might be the very reason why the camp seemed so attractive. The realisation was horribly wounding. Not for the first time, Hannah felt her heart torn between her uncompromising love for her daughter and the desperate need to make choices about her own life.

'Don't you want to come on holiday with us?' she asked.

Lottie said nothing.

'Talk to me, Lottie. Please. Tell me what's wrong.'

'It's me, isn't it?' said Danny wearily. 'She doesn't want to come on holiday because of me.'

Lottie glared at him. 'Don't talk like I'm not here.'

'I'm not, I just—' He threw up his hands. 'Oh Lottie, I don't know what to say. Why don't you like me? I do try, you know.'

'I don't not like you,' Lottie replied. 'You're OK – most of the time.'

'Then what's the matter?'

She looked him straight in the eyes. 'You can be Mum's special friend if you like. But I want you to stop pretending you're my dad.'

Jay was unmoved. 'I still say this is a bad idea,' he said, arms folded defensively across his chest.

Maxine shifted position on her chair to try and ease Junior off her bladder. Having a bump might be nice when people gave up their seats for you on the bus, but that hardly made up for the hours you had to spend on the loo. 'You think everything's a bad idea these days,' she retorted.

'Now you're just being childish.'

'Hark who's talking.'

'Hey, break it up you two, OK?' Hannah flopped onto one of Maxine and Jay's stylish but incredibly uncomfortable designer sofas.

'Yeah,' agreed Danny, looking increasingly ill at ease. 'I don't want to cause a load of trouble or anything.'

Jay grunted. 'Look mate, nothing personal.'

'No?' enquired Danny wryly.

'No. But I'm thinking about the business here. And Max.'

'So are we!' insisted Hannah. 'Surely if Danny takes on a bit more responsibility at the salon, it'll give Max more of a chance to rest up?'

'You did say you wanted me to take things easier,' pointed out Maxine. 'And you're far too busy with the shopfitting business to get involved in running Split Ends.'

'But he doesn't *know* anything!' protested Jay in exasperation. Danny looked wounded. 'I'm learning.'

Jay rounded on him. 'Yeah, learning. Learning how to sweep up and make tea. How much managerial experience have you got?'

'I worked on the yacht all that time.'

'Doing what, precisely? Pouring Martinis for your rich clients?'

Danny flailed. 'Well . . . whatever needed doing really. I used to order in all the food supplies, for a start-off.'

'There you are then,' Hannah declared triumphantly. 'He can take over ordering supplies for the salon. It's quite straightforward, isn't it, Max?'

'A trained chimp could do it,' agreed Maxine.

Jay sniffed. 'Then Danny should be right at home.'

Gloria was not her usual self. It was taking all of Danny's charm to get the smallest of smiles out of her.

'The hair's looking fab today, darling,' he said, camping it up for all he was worth as he arrived with tea and a selection of biscuits on a little silver tray.

'Thanks, love.' Gloria sighed. 'Pity I'm not feeling that way.'

He sat down in the empty styling chair next to hers. 'Bad day?'

She gazed despondently at her freshly-manicured nails. 'Bad life.'

Danny frowned. 'That's not like you. Don't tell me – man trouble?'

'What else?' She swivelled round in her chair, so as to look directly at him. 'You're a man, Danny.'

'Well, I was last time I looked.'

'Shush, listen, I'm serious. Like I said, you're a man – so tell me where I'm going wrong. Why is it when I find someone I'm sure is The One, and it's all wonderful for a while ... why is it that all of a sudden he starts going cold on me?'

'Damon, you mean?'

She nodded glumly. 'It's nothing I can put my finger on, not really. He just doesn't seem so ... intense about me any more. Like there's something else on his mind. Or somebody,' she added gloomily.

Danny chewed his bottom lip. 'Maybe you're imagining it?' he ventured.

Gloria gave a humourless laugh. 'Come on, credit me with a bit of sense. I've been around long enough to know when the gilt's coming off the gingerbread.'

'Have a biscuit,' said Danny, selecting the nicest one and offering it to her.

'I'm not hungry.'

'It's a chocolate one. I saved it specially for you.'

He wafted it under her nose, and with a rueful smile she gave in and took a bite. 'You'll make me all fat and spotty, and then Damon really won't love me any more,' she scolded.

'If he doesn't, he's just plain stupid. Come on, have another bite. And then some of this coffee I made for you, it'll make you feel better.'

'Promise?'

'Promise. I'll even put a dash of medicinal brandy in it if you're very good.'

At that moment, Philomena returned from the stockroom. 'Where's all the extra-body conditioner gone?' she demanded. 'There's only three bottles left, and you know Gloria always takes one home with her.'

'Ah,' said Danny, his matinée-idol smile wilting. 'I thought the order would have arrived by now, they said Tuesday at the latest.'

Philomena gave a hiss of disapproval. 'I'd better give Bracewell's a ring then. They've never let us down before.'

'Actually I'd better do it,' Danny said as she prepared to march off and do battle.

'No, don't you worry, I'll put the fear of God into them.'

'The thing is,' explained Danny, 'there's not much point in phoning Bracewell's. I sort of . . . changed our supplier.'

Philomena froze. 'You did what?'

'Well, there's this other supplier I found in Coventry, and they were offering this really amazing half-price deal, so I thought—'

Philomena groaned and mimed hitting her head on the wall. 'Not . . . Godiva Hairdressing Supplies? Tell me it wasn't Godiva Hairdressing Supplies.'

Danny blinked in puzzlement. 'Why? What's wrong with them?'

'Apart from the fact that the owner's a crook and all their products are substandard? Oh, nothing. Nothing at all.'

'Oh shit,' said Danny. 'I didn't realise.'

'Obviously not. But surely you checked with Maxine first? Or Hannah?'

He shrugged helplessly. 'I thought I'd show a bit of initiative.'

'Holy Mother of God.' Philomena flashed him a look of irate despair, and stalked off to make an emergency phone call to Bracewell's.

Gloria gazed fondly after her. 'Quite passionate when she's roused, our Philomena.'

'You could say that,' agreed Danny, not entirely thinking about the Bracewell's fiasco.

'And what a talented hairdresser.' Gloria patted her new style and admired it in the mirror. 'She's an absolute treasure, that girl. Whatever would I do without her, Danny?'

*

Nick was buried in a mountain of business correspondence when the entryphone buzzed. He wasn't expecting any visitors, but frankly he was grateful for the interruption. If his entry into the world of commerce had taught him anything, it was that he really, *really* hated keeping accounts. Even more than he'd hated doing all that pointless admin at school – and that was saying something.

He yawned, stretched and pressed the button on the intercom. 'Hi.'

There was a short silence, then: 'It's me.'

'Miranda?' After the best part of three months with scarcely a word, the sound of her voice knocked the wind right out of his sails.

'Can I come in?'

Nick hesitated for a moment, then buzzed her in. 'I guess so. You know your way up.'

In the time it took Miranda to climb the stairs to his flat, Nick went through a thousand scenarios in his mind. She'd come to taunt him; she'd come to coax him back; to seduce him and then reject him again, just for the hell of it. He'd read about women like that in Hannah's magazines. Scheming temptresses with a screw loose. Maybe Miranda was one. Face it, he told himself, she could be anything; it's pretty obvious you never really knew her at all.

He heard her knock on the door and went to open it, prepared – or so he thought – for all eventualities.

The one thing he wasn't prepared for hit him square between the eyes. Even without the tight T-shirt it would have been pretty obvious. Miranda was usually pencil-thin but now Nick couldn't take his eyes off her tummy.

'Hello, Nick.'

He swallowed. 'Oh my God. You're—'

'Pregnant, yes.' She smiled weakly. 'I had noticed.'

He stood aside, feeling numb from his head right down to the tips of his toes. 'You'd better come in . . . sit down.'

She walked meekly into the living room and perched on the edge of the sofa. 'Long time no see,' she remarked. 'You're looking well.'

Nick rubbed a hand over his eyes, as though that might clear the mist that had descended over his brain. 'How much . . . I mean, how long?'

'Four months, maybe a bit more.'

Without consciously doing so, he instantly made the mental calculation. Mine, he thought; it has to be mine. Unless . . .

'Do you want something – some tea? Or a glass of wine? Oh no, you can't have alcohol, can you? Not if you're pregnant.'

'Nothing, thanks.' Miranda shuffled her feet on the laminated wood floor. She looks pale, thought Nick – but he didn't think it in the warm, concerned way he would have done before; now it was as though he was looking at her down the wrong end of a telescope: he felt detached, curiously disconnected. 'Funny isn't it? There we were, talking about starting a family, and then it all went wrong. And now it looks like I'm starting one all by myself.'

'Not necessarily,' replied Nick.

A glimmer of hope lit up Miranda's beautiful eyes. 'You mean you might come back?'

'No. No, I don't mean that.' He watched the glimmer fade. 'But I could help. In fact, I want to.'

'But you don't even know if the baby's y—'

Nick cut her off short. 'I don't want to know, Miranda.'

'Just as well,' she admitted. 'To tell you the truth, I'm not sure myself.'

Questions were milling around in Nick's head like wasps trapped in a jam jar. 'Why now?' he asked. 'Why wait until now to tell me?'

Miranda fiddled with the strap on her handbag. 'At first I wasn't sure,' she said. 'Before you left I thought I might be pregnant, but I didn't get round to telling you and then you were gone. And besides, I was angry with you. So I thought, maybe I'll get rid of it just to spite him, and then tell him about it afterwards.'

'Nice touch,' observed Nick sarcastically.

'But I didn't, did I? I couldn't do that.' She laid a hand piously on her belly. 'Not to *our* baby.'

'You said you didn't know whose it was,' Nick reminded her.

'Yes, well, I was almost sure, wasn't I? Anyway, then I thought, maybe I won't tell him at all. I'll just manage on my own like lots of other women do.'

'So what changed?'

She looked up at him with beseeching eyes. 'I miss you, Nick. Won't you come back home?'

'This is my home.'

'A rented flat you've borrowed from some guy who could come back from Spain any time he wants? Come on, Nick, with me you can have a proper home and now we can have a proper family too. You can forget Hannah, Lottie, everything – you can start all over again.'

Nick sank slowly into the chair opposite the sofa. 'You just don't get it, do you?'

'Get what?'

'I don't *want* to forget Hannah, and I definitely don't want to forget Lottie! They're a part of my life; the fact I don't live with them now doesn't change that, and it never will.'

Miranda's expression changed to one of resentful pleading. 'But aren't we a part of your life now too? Me and this baby?'

He looked at her and knew what she was doing, the game she was playing. This baby could be anybody's; maybe it was his, maybe it wasn't, but either way she was playing it for all she was worth.

'Yes,' he admitted reluctantly. 'I guess you are. But that doesn't mean you and I are going to have any kind of relationship beyond being the baby's parents. You hurt me too much, Miranda. This time, whatever I do I'm doing it with my eyes wide open.'

With hindsight, leaving Danny in charge of Split Ends while Maxine and Hannah attended a health and beauty fair might not have been the ideal choice. But sometimes beggars couldn't be choosers, and with Philomena off sick it was a question of either closing the salon completely on a Friday afternoon, or everybody pitching in.

It had the potential to work out perfectly well. Despite the Bracewell's debacle, Danny seemed to be getting the hang of the paperwork, and even Jay had to admit grudgingly that his revamped appointments system was an improvement on the old one. Hannah was confident he'd get through – after all, it was only half a day and all he had to do was be nice to people, wash their hair and answer the telephone. How could he possibly mess that up?

But of course, love was blind.

It started to go wrong about five minutes after Hannah and Maxine had driven away from the salon, when Claire turned the page to see how many clients she had for the afternoon session.

'What the *hell?*'

Several pairs of eyes turned in her direction, and she lowered her voice to a horrified whisper.

'What's up?' enquired Jason.

Claire glared at Danny, who was whistling to himself as he salsa-ed round the salon with his broom. 'Ask the boy genius over there.'

Danny pirouetted back to the reception desk. 'Somebody call?'

Claire jabbed a finger at the appointments book. 'What does it say at the top of that page?'

'"Maxine",' replied Danny.

'And where is Maxine?'

'On her way to Birmingham ... Ah.' He scratched his head. 'Oops. I seem to have booked her an afternoon's worth of appointments and she's not actually here.' He looked up hopefully. 'But we can handle it, can't we?'

'*We?* What's "we" got to do with it?' seethed Claire. 'You can barely do a dandruff treatment, and Jason's still getting the hang of walking on two legs. Which leaves me. And I am *not* doing all Maxine's appointments as well as my own. You'll just have to phone round and grovel.'

'But some of these are her best clients,' commented Jason, scanning the page. 'Mrs Carthy ... and that girl from the Ladies' College. They'll go spare if they don't get their restyles today.'

'Oh for God's sake!' Claire resisted the urge to bang everyone's heads together and go home. 'OK, I'll fit the really important ones in somehow, but the rest Danny'll have to cancel. And if anybody wanders in off the street, they can bloody well forget it.'

Half an hour and a dozen phone calls later, Danny came up smelling of roses. 'Sorted,' he announced. 'Just call me Mister Fix-It.'

'Mister Fuck-It-Up more like,' growled Claire, brandishing her styling comb like a stiletto.

What with too many appointments and the non-appearance of the conditioner delivery, things were already looking a bit rocky. But it could still all have worked out OK in the end – if it hadn't been for Claire's coffee break.

'It's no good,' she announced after her fourth client of the afternoon, 'if I don't get a sit down and a ciggie I'm going to die. I'll be back in fifteen minutes. Just don't *do* anything, either of you. Got that?'

Danny and Jason nodded like a pair of choirboys. Jason got on with blow-drying Claire's last restyle, and Danny fiddled about round the desk, looking important.

The door opened, and a girl with a trendy burgundy-coloured bob came in. 'Hi,' she smiled through an overgrown curtain of hair. 'My fringe is a bit out of control and I've got a hot date tonight – you couldn't just give it a quick trim for me, could you? It'd only take five minutes.'

Jason waved a warning arm and mimed 'No', so vigorously that he ricked his neck. Danny, however, was mesmerised by the brilliant idea forming in his own head.

'Well, we're rather booked up,' he admitted, and a look of relief appeared on Jason's face, 'but I think I can just squeeze you in.'

'What?' squeaked Jason.

'Is there a problem?' enquired the girl as Danny slipped off her coat and helped her into a gown.

'Not at all, our junior's just a little lacking in confidence. Don't worry, Jason, I'll do this one myself.'

Jason was by now turning whiter than his own T-shirt, but Danny was just getting into his stride. 'Just take a seat, Miss . . .'

'Karen, call me Karen.'

He smiled at her in the mirror, reached for a pair of scissors and felt the ultimate rush. This was what it was all about: creativity, power. By the time he'd finished, they'd all be proud of him. And hey, it wasn't as if he had anything to worry about; he'd watched Claire showing Jason how to cut fringes loads of times.

Besides, if Jason could get the hang of it, how hard could it be?

Chapter 22

Herbie wasn't making an awful lot of headway with Mrs Waverley from next door, but it wasn't for want of trying.

The trouble was, she just didn't seem to understand that he wasn't in league with the pack of vicious little guttersnipes who seemed hell-bent on making her life a misery – not to mention the lives of anybody else they thought they could victimise. Just like hyenas, thought Herbie. Put 'em together and they think they're invincible. They can sniff out vulnerability a mile off. But pick 'em off one by one and it shows them up for the pathetic little cowards they are.

Which was how, on this particular evening, Herbie came to be facing one of them off down a back alley with the nearest weapon to hand – the baguette he'd just bought for Erica from the corner shop.

'I'm not afraid of you,' sneered the brat, trying to look menacing under his Scooby-Doo hoodie.

'Well, you ought to be,' replied Herbie, his arthritic hip clicking loudly as he advanced a step. The boy backed up closer to the fence that marked the dead end of the alleyway. 'Where are your mates now, eh? Scarpered and left you to face the music.'

'What's it to you, Grandad?'

'I bet the police would love to hear about what you've been up to this time. Sneaking about in the dark, scaring old ladies. Bet it makes you feel really big, doesn't it?'

'You're just a sad old git. Nobody listens to you.'

'Oh really?'

'Yeah, really. And you can't touch me 'cause you're only out on parole, and if you get into trouble they'll put you back in jail.'

'Doesn't stop me getting a good look at your face though, does it, sonny?' pointed out Herbie. 'Or taking photos of you and your mates next time you're trying to cause trouble round here. Bet the police'd be really interested to see them.'

'You wouldn't do that.'

'Oh wouldn't I?'

In all honesty, when the kid suddenly turned round, sprang up the fence and dropped down on the other side, Herbie was almost relieved. He hadn't been quite sure what he was going to do next; the kid was stocky for an eleven-year-old, his bad hip was playing him up something chronic, and a baguette – even a crusty one – wasn't much of a weapon in a straight fight.

He listened to the sound of running footsteps fading into the distance. Little git. The kid was right about one thing though; he wouldn't tell the cops, not this time. Not because he was afraid of going back to jail, but because every time he'd reported the kids in the past he'd been told the police were very sorry but they couldn't do anything. Lack of manpower, apparently. Too busy issuing parking tickets to protect a terrified old lady, he thought grimly. It made him mad.

Herbie would have been tempted to take the law into his own hands if it wasn't for Sprout getting under his skin. Reconnecting with Hannah after all this time, and getting to know his great-granddaughter, had dented his cynicism in a way he'd never have anticipated. He might still be doodling plans for the crime of the century on the backs of old cigarette packets, but deep down something had started to change inside him.

For the first time since he'd been ejected into the cold, cruel world, he'd begun to wonder if there might not be one or two advantages to not being in prison. Maybe he didn't want to go back inside after all.

Well, not just yet anyway.

It was way past closing time, but the lights were still on at Split Ends. In fact the place was so full of electricity, the halogen spotlights in the salon were practically redundant.

Jay was incandescent, Maxine was only just coming down off the ceiling, and even Hannah had to admit that Danny wasn't her favourite person right now. And as for Danny himself, he wasn't helping matters by continuing to plead his good intentions.

'I was only trying to help,' he insisted, sorrier for himself than for the trouble he'd caused.

'Help!' Jay grabbed Danny by the shoulders and just about resisted the urge to head-butt him. 'Did you see what you did to that poor woman's hair? Did you?'

'OK, so it was a bit uneven . . .'

Jay dropped him like a sack of potatoes, turned round and punched the wall.

'Danny,' said Hannah as gently as she could, 'it was a disaster. If it hadn't been for Philomena being so nifty with the scissors, and Hannah arranging for that big bouquet, we'd probably have a lawsuit on our hands.'

At least Danny had the good grace to squirm a little. But he still wasn't about to lie down and take the rap. 'I was doing my best,' he protested. 'She wanted it doing straight away. What else could I do?'

Maxine exploded. 'You could stick to sweeping up and sorting out the appointments, like we told you to! You had no business even picking up a pair of scissors, let alone cutting hair.'

Danny put up his hands. 'OK, OK, I won't do it again.'

'Too right you won't,' snapped Jay, 'because nobody is going to leave you in charge of this salon ever again. Got that?'

'Oh come on, one little mistake and—'

'No, Danny, not one little mistake; about a dozen big fat ones. Who was it screwed up the stock control system and nearly lost us our regular supplier?'

Furious though she was with Danny, Hannah felt honour-bound to put in a word for him. 'He was only trying to save us money, Jay,' she pointed out. 'He wasn't to know.'

'My point exactly!' replied Jay. 'He doesn't *know* anything! He's a complete idiot, a walking disaster, a—'

'Valuable investor?' suggested Danny, with a look that said 'and don't you forget it'. 'Important source of capital for the business?'

All that did was infuriate Jay still further. 'You know what you can do with your capital? You can stick it up your—'

'Jay!' Maxine barked at him so suddenly that he shut up in surprise. 'Cool down and let's talk about this like grown-ups, shall we?' Her voice softened. 'Look, Danny, we all appreciate your . . . enthusiastic contribution to the business. It's just that everybody has to be aware of their own strengths and weaknesses.'

'And your strengths definitely don't include cutting hair,' said Hannah, noticing for the first time how extremely young Danny looked in spite of his size; how very much like a sulky schoolboy, with that jutting lower lip and that look of wronged innocence in his eyes. She couldn't figure out whether to kiss him better or give him a smacked bottom.

'So you will promise never to do anything like that ever again. Won't you?'

Danny was bright enough to see that Maxine was issuing an order, not asking a question, and he nodded. 'Yeah, whatever.'

'"Yeah, whatever". Is that it?' demanded Jay.

'What more do you want?'

'Sorry would be nice.'

'OK, I'm sorry. Now can we forget about this? It's late and I'm tired.'

'Oh, you're tired, are you? Well, I'm tired too. Tired of your interfering and your incompetence.'

The two men were practically nose to nose. Hannah had the distinct impression that one step further, one more incendiary exchange of words, and they'd be rolling around on the floor like scrapping schoolkids, trying to punch each other's lights out. And all at once it seemed impossibly childish.

'For pity's sake grow up,' she said wearily. 'And that means both of you,' she added with a meaningful stare at Jay.

She ought to have known better than to try and lay the law down to Jay. 'Listen Hannah,' he said, his voice quivering with barely restrained anger, 'you've been a friend of ours for a long time and it pains me say this. But so help me God, you'd better keep that cretin out of my sight from now on.

''Cause the way things are going, I'm not even sure I want to be involved with Split Ends any more.'

Hannah felt an icy trickle of fear down her back. 'But you can't think about pulling out . . . without you, there *is* no Split Ends!'

'I've said my piece,' he replied, purse-lipped.

Maxine grabbed him by the arm and handed him his jacket. 'Come on tiger,' she said. 'Let's go home before you do something we'll all regret.'

*

Nick wasn't naïve enough to think he'd seen the last of Miranda. After all, he had made it clear he was willing to support her in bringing up the baby – whether it was technically his or not.

All the same, it still took him by surprise when he answered his mobile in the public bar of the Royal Oak and found her on the other end of it. He supposed he must still be in shock about the whole thing; he hadn't even adjusted to it himself, let alone thought about how he was going to break the news to Hannah. The sound of Miranda's voice made him wish for something stronger than pale ale.

'Nick, it's me. Miranda.'

'Oh. Right.'

'I need you.'

'What do you mean? What's happened?' The obvious thought leapt into his mind. 'Is there something wrong with the baby?'

'No, no, not that.' She sounded faintly irritated that he should be thinking about the baby rather than about her. 'It's me, I'm all on my own. Old Tom's in hospital.'

Nick straightened up in his seat. 'Oh no! Poor Tom. What's the matter with him?'

The same hint of irritation, a little more pronounced now. 'He had an accident, he fell off a ladder. It was his own fault. The point is, I'm stuck here on my own and I can't manage without some help.'

'Is he going to be all right?'

'For God's sake!' snapped Miranda. 'He just fell off a ladder and broke his hip, that's all; he's going to be fine. But it's going to be weeks and weeks before he can do anything around the place again. Don't you care about me being pregnant and alone out here? How am I supposed to manage?'

At that moment, Nick had one of those epiphany moments when a man thinks, What the hell did I ever see in her? He was sorely tempted to tell her he couldn't care less whether she managed or not; only of course he did care, not about her but about the baby.

'Get somebody in from one of the farms,' he suggested.

'I don't know anybody well enough to ask them to do me a favour.'

'Then pay them. You can afford it.'

The petulant tone modulated to a kind of little-girl pleading. 'I don't want anybody else Nick, I want you.'

'You can't have me, I'm sorry.'

'You said you'd help me with the baby.'

'And I will.'

'Then move back in. Please Nick, I miss you.'

Nick slunk further into the corner to avoid interested eyes and ears. 'Look, Miranda, we've been over this already. It's over between us. Finito.'

'I know, but I need your help right now. I really, really do.'

He knew it was no good trying to sever the cord. If he did that it would mean cutting himself off from the child as well, and for the child's sake – and maybe his own too – he just couldn't do that.

'All right,' he said, 'I'll pop over in the morning and help you with some of the heavy work. But that's all, OK? Because there is no way in heaven and earth that I am moving back in with you, Miranda.'

As Nick was cursing the day he set eyes on Miranda Moss, Hannah was sitting in the garden shed at her mum and dad's house, drinking hot chocolate with Herbie.

'I can't believe what you've done with this place!' she exclaimed, taking in the neat square of fitted carpet, the portable TV, the two-bar electric fire, and the table football game salvaged from a pub skip.

'Well, a man needs his own space,' said Herbie sagely. 'And your mother will keep "popping in" to my room every five minutes to dust me whatnots or check to see if I've dropped dead.'

'I'm sure it's only because she cares,' advanced Hannah.

'Maybe, but I'm a lot happier when she's doing it up the other end of the garden.' Herbie snapped a Kit-Kat in half and handed two of the fingers to Hannah. 'Besides, nice little shed like this almost reminds me of home.'

'Home?' Hannah realised and laughed. 'You mean prison? Oh Gramps, what are we going to do with you? This is your home now.'

Herbie eased his bum more comfortably into his folding garden chair. 'Home's what you're used to,' he declared. 'And if I ever get used to your mother's crocheted toilet-roll covers, or your dad's collection of police badges through the ages, you've got my full permission to shoot me.'

They sat there in companionable silence for a little while, listening to the spring rain pattering lightly on the shed roof.

'You're not yourself tonight,' observed Herbie.

Hannah tried to make light of it. 'No? Who am I then?'

'It's no good, you can't fool me, Sprout. Something's got you down. What is it – man trouble?'

'Everything trouble,' she admitted glumly. 'But Danny's got a fair bit to do with it. I like him an awful lot, really I do, and we have such a lot of fun together. I mean, when was the last time I went quad-biking or white-water rafting?'

'That might be fun to you,' grunted Herbie, 'but it sounds more like punishment to me. Anyhow, if you're having so much fun what's the problem?'

Hannah didn't know where to begin. So she started with all the disasters at the salon, and Jay's threat to pull out his investment in Split Ends, and her suspicion that Lottie was trying to get sent to the summer adventure camp purely so she didn't have to go on a family holiday that included Danny.

'I just don't know what to do for the best. I mean, most of the time she seems to get on OK with him, and then all of a sudden he'll say something that touches a raw nerve, and she won't even be in the same room. What do I do? Do I have to sacrifice any hope of having a relationship myself for the sake of Lottie?'

'Buggered if I know,' replied Herbie flatly. 'Don't ask me how to run your life, I can't even keep track of my underpants. But she's a good kid, you know, just a bit shaken up. And it can't be easy watching some young buck taking up with her mum where her daddy left off.'

'I know. And she'll soon be coming up to that difficult age,' mused Hannah, more to herself than to Herbie.

'Huh. With girls, every age is a difficult age,' retorted Herbie. 'And just you wait till she hits thirteen. That's the age your mother started playing truant.'

For a moment Hannah thought she'd misheard. 'Truant! You're having me on.'

Herbie shook his head. 'As I live and breathe. I blame myself really, I was in prison most of the time see, and your grandma . . . well, she did her best but it can't have been easy. Luckily your mum saw sense and got herself back on the straight and narrow before it was too late, otherwise . . . who knows?' He leaned across and wagged a finger in Hannah's face. 'But don't you dare let on to her I told you, or my privileges won't the only thing she's cutting off.'

Hannah could hardly believe it anyway. Her mum, a teenage truant? If ultra-respectable Erica could have had her tearaway moments, goodness knows what might become of headstrong Lottie if she got things wrong.

'You see, that's why I want Lottie to have a man around the place,' she explained. 'Maybe I'm imagining it, but I always think the kids without dads are the ones who really go off the rails.'

'And you think Danny's the right father-figure for her?'

'We-ell . . . Maybe more of a big brother figure,' she admitted. 'Nick's her daddy, after all, whether she's happy to admit it or not. God, what a mess. Do you think it'll ever get sorted out?'

Herbie leaned back in his chair and closed his eyes. 'Oh, I shouldn't think so,' he replied serenely. 'But then where would the fun be in life if you knew what was going to happen next?'

If Hannah had known that, she would have taken the following morning off work, full appointments list or not.

As it was, she walked into the salon at the very moment the paramedics were helping Philomena out to the ambulance, a bloodstained white towel clasped to her nose.

'What on earth has happened?' she demanded. 'Phil, are you all right?'

Philomena just mumbled incoherently and flicked her eyes towards a slumped figure in the corner of the empty salon, weeping copiously into one of the backwashers, her shoulders shuddering with sobs.

'Gloria?' Hannah headed across. 'Gloria, what's wrong?'

The bedraggled head lifted a few inches off the sink, revealing a puffy red face and rivulets of mascara worthy of Marilyn Manson. 'He loves her,' she gasped between sobs. 'He loves *her*. And all the time I thought he was The One.'

Hannah laid a hand on her shoulder. 'Her? Who? What are you talking about?'

Maxine came back into the salon and led Hannah aside. 'They've taken Phil to the General. Looks like it's only a broken nose, thank goodness. No thanks to you-know-who.'

'What – Gloria? But why?'

'Because she found out Philomena's been practising the horizontal tango with her beloved Damon.'

'Really?' Hannah nearly choked. 'I thought you'd got the wrong end of the stick or something. . .'

'Nope, looks like I was right all along. Gloria just marched right in the minute we unlocked the door, took a swing at Phil's nose with a bottle of extra-body conditioner and said, "See if he still loves you looking like that."'

Now I've seen it all, thought Hannah. Now I really have seen it all.

Chapter 23

'Well, it could have been a lot worse,' observed Maxine later on that morning. 'At least Philomena doesn't want to press charges.'

'Would you?' pointed out Claire, 'if it meant you'd probably end up all over the local paper as the scarlet woman of Tivoli?' She shook her head in bewilderment. 'I still can't quite believe it,' she said. 'I mean – *Phil* of all people!'

'It could happen to any one of us, dear,' intoned Mrs De'Ath wisely. 'Believe you me, passion does funny things to people. You should have seen the look in my Sidney's eyes the day he thought he'd caught me out with the coalman.' Seeing the look on Maxine and Claire's faces, she added, 'Of course, it was all an innocent misunderstanding.'

Claire gave her a sceptical look. 'If you say so, love. You know, I reckon we've got a dark horse here, Max.'

As Maxine was fetching a bottle of 'Hint of Sapphire' hair tint from the stockroom, Hannah hove into view, wearing a look of grim resignation and with the top button of her tunic very firmly done up.

'Don't tell me,' said Maxine, 'it starts with Councillor and it ends with Plowright. Do I win a prize?'

'You do if you can come up with a way to make him keep his sweaty paws to himself.'

'I thought you laid down the law and told him if he didn't behave himself you wouldn't treat him any more.'

'I did. And if you recall, he said if I refused to treat him, he'd bad-mouth the salon all over town. Tell the whole world we're a knocking shop.'

'Nice man,' observed Maxine, pulling a face. 'And let's face it, he's got a lot of influence round here.'

'Tell me about it.' Hannah took down a bottle of sweet almond massage oil and another box of tea-lights for the essential oil burner. 'All the same, I don't see why I should put up with his threats and his insinuations.'

'Neither do I. What does Danny make of it all?' enquired Maxine.

'Well ... he says he sympathises, but I'm not sure he really understands. Between you and me I think he thinks it's a bit of a joke.'

Maxine grunted. 'Men. They just aren't on the same wavelength, are they? It's like when I tell Jay I want to get back to work as soon as possible after the baby, and he pats me on the head and says, "Don't you worry, princess, you won't need to work, you've got me to provide for you." Sometimes I just want to ... grrrr!'

'You're not giving up then?'

Maxine laughed. 'Me? Give up? I'm the girl who seduced the president of the Gay Society at college, remember? I *never* give up. Now get up those stairs and give Councillor Plowright the massage from hell.'

Councillor Plowright's red, sweaty face glistened with lustful anticipation as Hannah mixed up a blend of massage oils.

'What am I getting today then?' he enquired.

'Bergamot, black pepper and patchouli,' replied Hannah, ignoring his emphasis on the word 'getting'.

He caught hold of her wrist as she walked past the couch where he was lying face down, flaccid as a big stranded cod in green underpants. 'I wasn't talking about the oil, love. What've you got for me that's a bit ... special?'

Hannah peeled away his fingers with enough firmness to ensure that it hurt. 'I've got a special offer on peppermint foot balm,' she replied coolly. 'Two for the price of one.'

The smirk on the councillor's face hardened. 'Come on, Hannah, don't play games with me. Least, not those sort of games. You know what I'm talking about.'

For two pins, Hannah would have picked up the indoor fountain and emptied its contents over his head. But then, in a perverse kind of way, he would have won. 'Mr Plowright, I'm a qualified therapeutic masseuse, not a cheap tart. It's about time you remembered that and treated me with a little respect.'

He chuckled. 'Who's talking about cheap? I can be very generous you know, *very* generous. When I get what I want.'

'And if you don't?'

'Let's just say I've heard you're planning big things with this place. Building extensions, stuff you need planning permission for. I've got a lot of friends on the planning committee, Hannah, maybe you ought to think about that. After all,' he pointed out, running a fingertip up her thigh, 'all I'm after is a little therapy. Is that so much to ask?'

*

'Don't you worry about Plowright,' said Danny, serving up a late supper of pan-fried red snapper and Mediterranean roast vegetables. 'Old tossers like him are all talk.'

'I'm not so sure about that,' replied Hannah, slumped over the kitchen table with her chin resting on her folded arms. 'He's a really nasty piece of work. Maxine told me it was him that forced through the order making that family demolish their kids' playhouse because it was half an inch taller than it was supposed to be.'

Danny sat down opposite her and lit the candles. 'So he's petty-minded. So what?'

'If he doesn't get what he wants he might just decide to have a go at destroying me. And the salon while he's at it.'

'He's only a councillor, not God!'

Hannah poked a fork into her dinner. It looked and smelt delicious, but she had absolutely no appetite. 'You don't understand how these things work,' she said. 'Local government's all funny handshakes and who you know.'

Danny forked up a mouthful of fish and held it under her nose. 'I spent ages doing this,' he complained. 'You might at least taste it.'

'Oh Danny, I'm sorry.' Hannah dragged herself upright, opened her mouth and ate. 'It's lovely.'

'Now say it like you mean it.'

Hannah took in his woebegone expression and felt like the most miserable, ungrateful person on the planet. How many women would kill to have a golden-haired love-god romance them with his culinary skills?

'It *is* lovely, really it is,' she assured him. 'And I do appreciate your cooking this special meal for us. I'm just a bit upset, that's all, and you know I can never eat much when something's upset me.'

Danny chewed, swallowed, laid down his fork and sat back in his chair, arms folded. 'We're not going to get anywhere until we've sorted this out, are we?'

'Probably not,' she admitted.

'All right then, what are your options? You could tell him to go fuck himself.'

'If I was really stupid, yes.'

'So say it nicely. Tell him . . . tell him you're not treating male clients any more.'

'Some of my nicest clients are men!'

'Tell him you're a lesbian. No, second thoughts you'd better not, it'd probably turn him on.'

'Besides which it's not true!'

'Who says it has to be true?' Danny pointed out. 'You're not very good at this sort of thing, are you?'

'Not really,' Hannah admitted, not entirely sure she wanted to be good at lying. 'Anyhow, it doesn't matter whether it's true or not, if I say no to him one more time I really think he's going to do something nasty.'

'All the same, sometimes you have to tell people stuff for their own good. Like I had to tell Gloria about what Philomena was up to.'

Hannah's mouth fell open. '*You* told her?'

Danny looked pleased with himself. 'Yes, little old me. Aren't you proud of me, the Coiffured Crusader, righting wrongs and all that? I'll be leaping tall buildings in a single bound next.'

Hannah groaned. 'Have you any idea of the trouble you've caused? Gloria's a complete basket case, Phil's off work with her nose so we're a stylist down and I can't find anyone good to rent her chair.'

'Gloria had to be told,' Danny insisted.

'What if she'd brought charges? That would've looked great in the paper!'

'So what? She still had to be told! Wouldn't you want to know if your lover was shagging some other woman behind your back?'

And she was bound to find out sooner or later. I just speeded things up a bit.'

'I suppose so,' Hannah conceded grudgingly.

'There you are then!'

'But things aren't always black and white, you know. Sometimes they're really complicated.' A leering face imposed itself on her consciousness. 'Like Councillor bloody Plowright, for one.'

'Oh for God's sake!' Danny raked tanned fingers through his golden hair. 'Just . . . deal with it, yeah? Either tell him where he gets off, or . . . or . . .'

'Or what?'

'I dunno, give him what he wants!'

'What!' Hannah's fork clattered onto her plate. 'You're telling me to drop my knickers for that slimeball?'

Danny shifted uneasily on his chair. 'Not drop your knickers exactly . . . I mean, you needn't go quite that far.'

'Thank you very much, that's reassuring to know!'

'But couldn't you be nice to him, string him along a bit?'

'Nice?' Hannah couldn't believe she was hearing this. Not from the man she'd been sharing her bed with for months. 'Just how nice is nice, Danny? I mean, what exactly are you suggesting?'

'Oh . . . I don't know.' Weary of the entire subject, Danny tried to wave it away. 'Look, forget it. It was just a wild idea, OK? There's no need to get at me, I was only trying to help.'

'Yeah, well, if that's your idea of helping I can do without it, thanks.' She pushed her plate away.

'What's the matter now?'

She got up. 'I told you, I'm not hungry.' And then she walked out of the kitchen and left him sitting there, probably still wondering what he'd done to annoy her.

Herbie was so angry that he choked on his syrup sponge.

'He said you should do *what*?'

Hannah patted her grandfather on the back to dislodge the crumbs. She really didn't want to have to try out the Heimlich Manoeuvre in the middle of a greasy spoon café down the bottom of the High Street. There'd been quite enough drama for one week.

'I don't think he meant it,' she said, though she had a suspicion that at the moment he'd uttered the words, Danny had meant every one of them. 'He's just a bit impulsive sometimes.'

Herbie coughed unimpressedly. 'You won't like me saying this, Sprout, but this toy-boy of yours sounds like a right idiot.'

'He's not a toy-boy,' protested Hannah, 'he's only four years younger than I am.'

'Pity he doesn't act that way then,' muttered Herbie.

'And he's not an idiot either,' Hannah added. 'Whatever people might say.'

Herbie pounced. 'Aha, so it's not just me saying it then?'

'Well . . .'

'Oh, Hannah. I know you think the sun shines out of his backside, and I'm sure he's got his good points between the sheets – '

Hannah blushed. 'Gramps!'

'– but you've got enough on your plate without letting some empty-headed boy upset you with his stupid ideas.' He gave her downcast face a little tweak. 'Chin up, Sprout – somebody's got to tell you the stuff you don't want to hear.'

She knew he was right, up to a point. But she prided herself that she knew Danny really well – in fact better than anyone. He could be crass and annoying and irresponsible, that was true; but he could also be kind and funny and impetuous in a way that couldn't help but make you feel good.

'He makes me smile, Gramps.'

'You're not smiling now.'

'No. But it's not Danny I'm upset about, there's other stuff. Stuff I haven't told you about.'

Herbie put down his spoon and wiped a blob of custard off his cravat. 'Go on then, I'm waiting.'

'It's Nick. Well, not Nick exactly. Not on his own anyway, I mean, it takes two doesn't it?' Hannah was all too aware from Herbie's expression that she was babbling incoherently, and made a big effort to force the words out in some kind of order. 'Miranda's having a baby,' she said.

'Ah,' said Herbie. 'That'd be your Nick's baby then?'

'Er . . . possibly,' replied Hannah, feeling stupidly embarrassed on Nick's behalf. 'He's not sure.'

It was strange, really strange; she ought to be furious with her estranged husband, who'd been desperate to have a baby with her one minute, and busily impregnating his mistress the next. But all she'd felt when he told her was sadness, and a slight resentment that it was Miranda who was expecting, and not her. And that didn't make any sense at all, not bearing in mind the fact that she'd practically run off screaming the last time he'd tried to persuade her to have his child.

'Bit generous with her favours, is she?' ventured Herbie, reassuringly unshocked by the concept.

'Half of Gloucestershire's been under her duvet, from what I can gather,' Hannah replied gloomily. 'The odd thing is, though, Nick doesn't seem to care. In one way he does – I mean, he dropped Miranda like a red-hot brick – but as far as he's concerned he wants to be a father to the baby even if it isn't his.'

'And you'd rather he told Miranda where she gets off?'

'No. Well, not exactly.' Hannah wasn't quite so saintly that she didn't relish the thought of seeing the smug expression wiped right off Miranda Moss's face. 'Actually I think what he's doing is really something. It's just . . .'

'Just that you're jealous as hell?' enquired Herbie.

'Don't be silly,' protested Hannah. 'No, I just keep thinking and wondering . . . what if it had been me instead of Miranda?'

'Sounds like jealousy to me,' hrrumphed Herbie.

'And then there's Lottie. I made Nick tell her about the baby and I thought she'd be devastated, but all she said was, "Oh, right," and then went on playing computer games. At first I thought she was in denial, but now I think she's just plain not interested.'

Herbie retrieved his spoon and began eating again. 'You sound like you want her to be hysterical or something.'

'Of course not! I just can't help thinking that one of us at least ought to be outraged. Only we're not.'

'Good,' said Herbie, shrugging. 'Being outraged is a complete waste of energy. And it's not as if you can do anything about it, can you? Besides,' he added, 'I'm sure your mother will be outraged enough for six when she hears about it.'

Hannah wrinkled her nose in horrid anticipation. 'Oh God. Don't remind me.' She drummed her fingers on the table top. 'You're right though, I should be focusing on the stuff I can actually do something about, not Nick and the baby.'

'Like Plowright?'

'Maybe. If I could only think of something I could do.'

Herbie's roguish old face creased into a custard-rimmed grin. 'The thing is, Hannah, it's not what could you do, it's what we're *going* to do.'

She looked at him wonderingly. 'How on earth are you going to get involved with Plowright – challenge him to a duel? Nice idea, Gramps, but I think I'm on my own this time.'

He seized her hand and squeezed it tight. 'Oh no you're not. You've helped me a lot since they let me out – kept me on the straight and narrow, stopped me going crazy. Now it's time for me to do the same for you.'

'But how?'

He tapped the side of his nose knowingly. 'I always was the brains of the outfit on any job, you know.'

'I know, Gramps.' Lord help us, thought Hannah, recalling the number of times Herbie's 'foolproof' plans had gone disastrously wrong. We'll probably both end up getting arrested.

'So just you tell me everything you know about this Plowright,' Herbie instructed her. 'And then leave me to do some thinking.'

Over the next few days, a faintly ominous calm descended over Split Ends. Nothing bad happened, but then again nothing particularly good happened either. The three old ladies came and went, still refusing to make up their differences; Jay occasionally mooched through the salon with a look like thunder; a monosyllabic stylist called Raymond took over Philomena's chair for the week; and Maxine took to munching on Jaffa Cakes dipped in piccalilli.

Councillor Plowright stayed away. But to Hannah it still felt like the calm before the storm.

'Petunia's "Nature Notes" haven't half got depressing lately,' commented Claire, scanning the local paper in an idle moment.

'Ah well, things haven't been the same for her since her husband was fatally attacked by that swarm of bees,' said Mrs Lorrimer, sipping her PG Tips.

'Or since her foster-daughter got locked up in the secure psychiatric unit,' agreed Mrs De'Ath. 'Tragic I call it.'

Hannah wrinkled her nose. 'I thought it was supposed to be a nature column, not *EastEnders*. If you ask me, she's making it all up.'

Claire threw down the *Courant* and yawned. 'Who cares? It's boring anyway. Chuck us that *Daily Mirror,* will you? There's bound to be some juicy goss in there.'

She flicked through the first few pages in search of the celebrity stories, but only got as far as page seven. If it hadn't been for the 'Hunk of the Month' on page six, she might never have paused long enough to notice it.

'Hey, Han – look at this!'

'What?' Hannah left off clipping Mrs De'Ath's fingernails to glance over.

'This photo.' She jabbed a finger at a colour shot of a small, pop-eyed dog with a lolling pink tongue. The caption underneath read: 'A RIGHT DOG'S DINNER.'

'What about it?'

'Listen. A butcher was driving his delivery van round Northampton, right? He heard this funny noise and when he opened the back doors, he found this little pug dog had eaten half his stock. Now the local animal shelter is trying to find out who he belongs to.'

'Ah, how cute,' said Mrs Lorrimer, not really looking.

'But it's *him*!' exclaimed Claire. 'Look, Han – I'm sure it is! How many pugs do you know who've got half an ear missing and no front teeth?'

Hannah took a closer look. In point of fact she only knew one pug, though she had to admit it did look an awful lot like him. 'But ... in Northampton?'

'It's him, I'm telling you. Get Miss Fabian on the phone, Jason, and tell her it looks like we've found her Bertie.'

Chapter 24

When Councillor Plowright picked up the phone and realised it was Hannah on the other end of the line, he could hardly believe his luck.

'So . . . you've been thinking over my proposition then?'

'Yes,' she admitted. 'Quite a lot, actually.'

'Good, excellent.' He was practically drooling already. 'And you're sure you've, let's say, got my number?'

'Oh yes, completely.' Hannah's voice was husky, a little breathless, with just a hint of titillating fear; it made him go all moist in the hollows behind his knees. 'I know exactly where you're coming from . . . Clarence.'

The sound of his name in her honeyed tones made him whimper with anticipation. 'So when do I get to see you, then?'

'I thought I'd save you an appointment for next Friday afternoon, say five thirty? All the other clients will have gone by then, you'll be my last one of the day.'

'So it'll be just you and me? No chance of us being disturbed?'

'Exactly.'

'And you'll give me some special treatment?'

'Oh yes. I'm sure you'll find it a very . . . stimulating experience.'

At that moment, Mrs Plowright's voice thundered out of the kitchen. 'Who are you talking to out there, Clarence? Your steak and kidney pudding's going cold.'

He swore silently in her direction, then answered sweetly, 'Be right there. It's just someone from the Council about that blocked drain in Winchcombe Street.' He cupped his hand around the receiver. 'As long as we understand each other.'

'Oh we do, don't worry.'

'In that case I'll see you next Friday.' He grinned and added for his own benefit, 'with any luck, all of you.'

*

Hannah had stopped trying to understand human nature.

Considering the fact that Clarice Fabian had just got her beloved Bertie back after weeks of utter despair, you would have thought she'd be dancing on the rooftops. But no. She was telling anybody who would listen that Dastardly Deeds had been done, and that she for one knew exactly who the culprits were.

'It was them,' she insisted, as the lady photographer from the *Courant* tried to pose her and Bertie in front of the Split Ends sign in the salon window. 'And I want you to put that in your paper.'

'Yes dear, I'm sure. But could you just hold the dog still for me? Or he'll come out all blurred.'

The reporter, a nice young lad too junior to be given anything more challenging than giant marrows and human interest stories, nevertheless had enough sense to sniff a libel suit in the air, and tried to steer his interviewee onto safer ground. They didn't want a repetition of the Evesham Christmas Pudding affair – that had been five years ago, and they were still in litigation about it now.

'Why don't you tell me how you felt when you got that phone call?' he coaxed. 'I mean, you must have been surprised – Northampton's a long way from Cheltenham.'

'How did I feel?' Miss Fabian looked positively indignant. 'How would you feel if your best friend had been kidnapped? Furious of course!'

'But you must have been delighted to see Bertie again?'

Clarice contemplated the pop-eyed ball of lard in her arms and tears welled up in her eyes. 'Of course I was! Bertie's my only real friend in all the world. And to think of everything he's been through, because of *them*.'

'You don't really *know* that,' pointed out Maxine.

'And after all,' added Hannah, 'he doesn't seem to have suffered too much.'

Miss Fabian's expression turned to outrage. 'Not suffered? Just look at him – he's so thin! A shadow of his former self. And all because they were jealous of me and my money.'

Hannah drew Maxine aside. 'Let's leave them to it. I don't

think anything short of brainwashing's going to change her mind.'

'I suppose it's just possible she's right,' commented Maxine.

'What, about Mrs D and Mrs L kidnapping Bertie?'

Maxine shrugged embarrassedly. 'I know it sounds daft, but you never can tell. It's dog-eat-dog down that bingo hall, you know. Well, not literally.'

Hannah giggled. 'Yes, it could've been worse – they could have turned him into a big meat pie and then invited her round for dinner.'

'Now that's what I call revenge. Bet he'd be all lard and gristle though.' Maxine rubbed the small of her aching back and settled herself in an empty chair. 'Does my hair look greasy to you?'

Hannah gave it a good look. 'Nope.'

'No, don't be nice, be honest.'

'I am! It looks fine to me.'

Maxine plucked at it dissatisfiedly. 'Well it feels all lank and greasy to me. Must be my hormones. And look at all this flab on my arms!' She plucked at a couple of microns' worth of skin. 'I can't believe Jay still finds me attractive.'

Hannah perched on the arm of the chair. 'There you are, I told you he'd start fancying you again, didn't I?'

'Fancying me?' Maxine laughed, then lowered her voice. 'D'you know something? He says it's actually a turn-on, me being this size! Can you believe that? He can't keep his hands off me, it's all a bit kinky really.'

Hannah shook her head in amusement. 'I dunno, there's no pleasing some people.'

'What if he goes off me again after the baby's born? What if he doesn't fancy me any more unless I've got two sofa-cushions shoved up my jumper?'

'Now you're just being silly!'

Maxine hauled her feet up and rested them on the ledge beneath the mirror. 'I'm allowed to be silly, I'm pregnant. What's your excuse?'

Hannah frowned. 'Silly? Me? What've I done?'

'Don't give me that, I know Plowright's been hassling you again. And that you and your daft granddad have been trying to dream up schemes to get the better of him.'

'If we don't do something,' pointed out Hannah, 'he will.'

'So let him.'

'What – let him destroy Split Ends?'

Maxine took her hand and squeezed it. 'He can try. Maybe he'll succeed. But either way it's better than having you put yourself in a dangerous situation. Or compromising your principles.'

'I won't do anything silly,' promised Hannah, fingers firmly crossed behind her back. 'But I'm sorry Max, I can't let that repulsive old bastard get away scot-free.'

If you didn't count two black eyes and a faceful of sticking plaster, Philomena had emerged relatively unscathed from the Damon and Gloria affair, complete with an unexpected nose job and a new live-in lover. She knew how close she'd come to being sacked from the salon, and that a word from Gloria had probably swung things in her favour. Then again, maybe Gloria hadn't relished the thought of being dragged into court on an assault charge.

Then there was Bernard. A small, proud, self-destructive part of her had almost hoped he would demand the truth about her broken nose, so she could spit her infidelity right back in his face. But he'd swallowed her ridiculous story about being hit in the face by a cupboard door; soaked it all up as if he really believed it, and then she hadn't had the courage to tell him it was all a big fat lie.

In the end, she'd just ordered him to pack his bags and move out – and, to her surprise, he had. And Damon had moved in.

Now it was Friday afternoon, and she was standing on the doorstep of Gloria's smart town house. She desperately wanted to turn tail and run away. But she knew she couldn't contemplate going back to work until she'd confronted the object of her shame. She reminded herself of what Hannah had said when they'd talked it over: 'Take it from me, sometimes even bad things are better out in the open. Then at least you have a chance to get on with your life.'

She took a deep breath, shifted the bouquet to the other arm and pressed the doorbell.

The sound echoed far, far away. Time seemed to stand still. She was probably only waiting for a few seconds, but it seemed like a whole lifetime before the door clicked open and Gloria was standing in front of her, unnervingly calm and expressionless.

'Oh,' she said. 'I thought you'd turn up sooner or later. I guess you'd better come in.'

On Friday afternoons, Herbie liked to take a walk into town and browse around the shops, or not so much browse as window-shop. If he tended to concentrate mainly on the windows of the jewellers' shops that dotted the posher parts of the shopping centre, then that was pure coincidence.

Hannah might have highlighted the pitfalls of some of his more ambitious plans, but he still hadn't given up on the idea of the ultimate jewel heist. He happened to know that Sammy 'The Cat' Morris and Jimmy 'Fingers' Vicario, once the South Midlands' finest safe-blower, had both retired to the Cotswolds. If he could get in touch, talk them round, persuade them to join in with his own kind of personal pension scheme, the plan could really work. And what a day it would be for Grey Liberation, the day three old fogeys did over a high-class jeweller's and made off to the Riviera on the proceeds.

Assuming, of course, that they didn't get caught. But they wouldn't; this time, Herbie would make one hundred per cent certain he'd got everything worked out, down to the last detail. Nothing could go wrong.

He whistled to himself as he sauntered into Costbeaters' supermarket in the Strand, fumbling in his pocket for the shopping list Erica had given him. Half a dozen eggs, a couple of tins of beans, a cabbage . . . he'd be out of here inside ten minutes, and then it was back to Erica's, where he'd use Derek's computer to do a bit of furtive research on alarm systems. Not that Derek would know – but then Derek was a gullible idiot.

Not like me, thought Herbie with a smile. Not like me at all.

'Frankly,' said Gloria, 'you're welcome to him.'

Philomena shifted uncomfortably on her reproduction Georgian chair, the bouquet still lying across the library table where she'd left it. 'But I thought . . .' She swallowed. 'I thought you were in love with Damon.'

'So did I,' replied Gloria. 'But then again I thought he was in love with me, and thanks to you I found out he wasn't.'

Utterly mortified, Philomena wished Gloria's enormous double-fronted sideboard would obligingly fall over and squash her out of her misery. But it just stood there, looking superior in a burr walnut kind of way. 'I don't suppose saying I'm sorry is going to do much good, is it?' she ventured.

'Not a lot,' agreed Gloria. 'But there's no point because I'm not angry any more – well, not with you.'

'Not angry?'

'Only with myself,' Gloria explained. 'You see, I've always worn my heart on my sleeve, but you'd think by now I'd be old enough to have a bit of savvy in the love stakes. Well, wouldn't you?'

Philomena didn't answer. She half-wondered if it was a trick question.

'The fact is, I'm an idiot. A pushover. The average sixteen-year-old has more sense than I do when it comes to men. And if you ask me,' she added with a meaningful look at Philomena, 'you're not much better.'

Philomena hung her head. 'I don't have a lot of experience with men,' she confessed. 'Bernard was my first, and he's . . . well, you've seen him, you know what he's like.'

'Barely sentient, as far as I could see.'

'Damon seemed . . . you know . . . so different.'

Gloria sighed. 'Different from Bernard maybe, but believe me, Phil, the world's full of Damons. It must be, 'cause I seem to meet a new one every other month. And when I say you're welcome to him, I mean it. I just think you ought to be really sure he's what you want.'

'Yes,' murmured Philomena, recalling the soft warmth of Damon's kiss, the fervour of his lovemaking, the thrill of stolen passion. 'But it's got to be better than what I had before, surely.'

Gloria shook her head indulgently. 'The grass isn't always greener, Phil. Not really. In California they spray it so it looks green, but it's all dried-up and brown underneath. Some men are like that too.'

'Damon, you mean?'

'Maybe. That's for you to work out for yourself.' Gloria stood up. 'I have to go out in a few minutes,' she said, 'but I'm glad we've had this conversation.'

Philomena's head whirled. 'Me too,' she said, though in truth she was hardly sure.

236

At the door, Gloria touched her on the shoulder. 'Oh, before you go – can we make an appointment?'

Philomena turned back, puzzled. 'An appointment?'

'For you to do my hair.'

A grand piano falling out of the sky could not have stunned Philomena more effectively. She gaped. 'You still want me to do your hair?'

Gloria gave her a world-weary look. 'You may have done the dirty on me with Damon, but you're still the best stylist in town. Just keep your hands off the next one, OK? 'Cause at my age I really can't stand the competition.'

'And one twenty-seven change, thank you, sir.'

Herbie smiled at the checkout girl and pocketed the handful of coins. He still hadn't got used to being called 'sir', and it still didn't feel quite right, but nevertheless it gave him back a tiny bit of self-esteem in a world that seemed determined to rob him of every last drop.

Those kids from the estate, for instance. They wouldn't know respect if it jumped up and bit them. Every other day seemed to bring some new confrontation with them; but Herbie wasn't about to give up even if nobody else was interested. One way or another, he'd teach them a lesson and get them off the old folks' backs.

He'd just walked out through the automatic doors into the Strand, and was vaguely aware of a loud bleeping noise, when a hand touched him on the shoulder.

'Excuse me, sir.'

He turned round, about to say that no thank you, he didn't want to take part in any opinion polls or market research surveys; but the woman behind him didn't look like a market researcher. She was dressed in a forbidding navy-blue uniform with a badge that read 'Bulldog Security'.What's more, he realised that the noise he heard was actually the security alarm bleeping fit to bust.

An unpleasant sensation of déjà vu made all the hairs on the back of his neck stand on end. But that was silly; he hadn't done anything wrong, why should he feel uneasy?

'What is it?' he asked.

'Would you mind accompanying me back inside, sir? I have

reason to believe you have taken certain items from the store without paying for them.'

Friday afternoon. It had come round so quickly, and now Hannah wasn't at all certain she was doing the right thing.

She'd almost phoned Herbie, but she knew he'd only tell her not to chicken out. And besides, it was all arranged. There was nothing to do now but go through with it.

It was too much to hope for that Plowright might spontaneously combust on the way to the salon, or even have a flat tyre and have to cancel. Hannah had a feeling that this was one appointment he wouldn't miss even if he had to walk over red-hot coals to get to it.

She was just imagining him doing precisely that – hopping up and down with smoke rising up from his char-grilled feet – when the phone beside the treatment couch rang.

Oh shit.

With a trembling hand, she picked it up. 'The Beauty Room, Hannah speaking.'

'It's only me,' said Maxine. 'Just thought you'd want to know he's driving into the car park. Should be with you in two minutes.'

'Oh great.'

'And Hannah.'

'What?'

'Be careful, OK?'

The manager's office at Costbeaters was a horrible, dingy little cell of a room with a square of grubby orange nylon carpet and a desk with a wonky leg.

Herbie knew what everybody would say – especially Derek. Trust old Herbie to get himself arrested in a store selling cheap rubbish. How appropriate. Once a failure, always a failure. Go back to jail, do not pass go, do not collect two hundred pounds.

The supermarket manager, a frayed-looking man in his fifties with wispy grey hair, was rapidly tiring of this game. 'For goodness' sake,' he said, 'it's an open and shut case. Why don't you just own up that you did it and then the police can bail you and we can all go home?'

If only it were that simple, thought Herbie grimly. 'I'm not

238

confessing to something I didn't do,' he insisted for the umpteenth time.

The manager wiped a weary hand across his perspiring brow. 'Then what is this?' he demanded, prodding the object on the desk.

Herbie regarded it with distaste. 'A Michael Bolton CD.'

'Correction. A Michael Bolton CD that was in your pocket. A Michael Bolton CD you didn't pay for.'

'But I didn't put it there!'

'Then who did?' enquired the manager with none-too-subtle sarcasm. 'Your fairy godmother?'

Being patronised by a little creep in a shiny polyester suit was just too much for Herbie. It was bad enough being framed for something he hadn't done, but he couldn't even stand the sight of Michael Bolton, let alone the sound. In a rush of blood to the head, he leapt to his feet, grabbed the edge of the desk and bellowed into the supermarket manager's face.

'For the last time, man, I've got my pride! I'm a well-respected jewel thief, not a bloody shoplifter!'

The woman security guard laughed unkindly. The manager dropped his pen on the desk and raised his eyes to Heaven. 'Yes, and I'm James Bond. Now, sit down, Grandad, and be quiet till the police get here. I'm tired of listening to your stupid fantasies.'

Councillor Plowright had the look of a man who'd been waiting for a very long time to get what he wanted, and was at last within grasping distance of it.

'I knew you'd see sense,' he beamed, stripping off his tie so enthusiastically that it took the top button of his shirt with it. 'Clever girl like you, you know which side your bread's buttered.'

Hannah shuddered as he made a grab for her and gave her bottom a lecherous squeeze. Fortunately he took it as a quiver of lustful anticipation.

Deftly, she managed to ease out of his embrace. 'Steady on,' she breathed, 'I haven't even blended the massage oils yet.'

He chuckled unpleasantly. 'Trying to tease me are you, you cheeky little slut? Well, just as long as you're not trying to fob me off.'

'Would I do a thing like that?' Her skin crawled as she dripped essential oils into a little china bowl and blended them with the sweet almond carrier oil. 'Why don't you just make yourself comfortable and relax on the couch? I'll be ready for you in just a few moments.'

He was stripped down and ready for action within seconds. 'I'm still waiting,' he reminded her after a couple of minutes, his voice holding just the faintest hint of menace. 'And you know how Uncle Clarence hates being kept waiting.'

It took all Hannah's self-control not to throw up as she brought the massage oil across to the couch and perched on the corner of the table beside it, making sure to display a goodly amount of leg. 'Tell you what, Clarence,' she purred, 'why don't I massage your back and you can tell me exactly what it is that you're asking me to do to you?'

He rolled onto his back and made a grab for her wrist, so suddenly that the bowl of oil slipped out of her fingers and fell to the floor. 'No, I've got a better idea,' he said, his eyes as hard and black as two lumps of coal. 'Why don't you get your kit off right now and show me what colour panties you're wearing?'

'But—'

'I've been patient with you, Hannah. But I'm getting tired of all this messing about. If you've got any sense you'll cut the chat and give me what I came for.'

Right, thought Hannah, resisting a gargantuan urge to spit in his repulsive face. 'So,' she said, raising her voice, 'you're telling me if I don't have sex with you right now, you'll make things difficult for me?'

'Difficult?' He laughed so hard, the whole of his fleshy body rippled like an agitated airbed. 'Sweetheart, you don't know the meaning of the word till you've crossed Clarence Plowright.' His fingers tightened around Hannah's wrist. 'If you and your friend want to keep working in this town, you'd better be very, very nice to me. Starting now.'

Whatever Councillor Plowright was expecting next, it wasn't the sound of the door crashing open, or the booming female voice that shrivelled his ardour in his pants.

'Clarence Plowright, you disgusting, degenerate little worm! I might have guessed you hadn't changed your ways.'

Mrs Plowright strode into the room like a tweed-clad Valkyrie:

240

a six-foot woman mountain topped with an iron-grey perm that wouldn't have budged an inch in a hurricane.

Clarence sat bolt upright, grabbed the nearest towel and shielded his groin. 'M-mother?' he stammered.

'Yes, Clarence. Your long-suffering mother. Reduced to spying on your pathetic goings-on through a hole in the wall from the room next door.' She towered over him, lip curled in a sneer of utter disgust. 'So, still sneaking off to these sleazy little places, are we?'

'Excuse me,' Hannah cut in indignantly, 'this is a perfectly respectable beauty salon.'

Mrs Plowright fixed her with a withering stare. 'Sleazy little places and women who are no better than they ought to be,' she continued. 'And you wonder why no respectable woman will touch you with a bargepole. If your father was alive today, he'd have you horse-whipped.

'Now, get your clothes on and get out of this place, before you catch something off that slut.'

*

'I can't believe it,' said Maxine, as she sat with Hannah and Danny in the bar of the Jolly Foresters half an hour later. 'She actually blamed *you* for leading him astray?'

Hannah nodded. 'According to her, Clarence has a weakness for cheap tarts and that's apparently what I am.'

'Charming!'

'Mind you,' Hannah went on, 'the woman's no fool. And she could see what was going on. Underneath all that bluster I'm sure she knows perfectly well what he's been up to. After all, why would I have called her in the first place. . .'

'I guess it's not easy to admit that your only son's a nasty, manipulative sleazebag?' suggested Maxine.

'Exactly.'

'Still,' remarked Danny, draining his second bottle of Stella, 'at least Herbie had a good idea for once in his life. I mean, Plowright's finally off your back now, isn't he?'

'Hmm, maybe,' said Hannah. 'Unless he decides to do something out of spite.'

Danny chuckled. 'Or his mother takes it on herself to tell the whole of Cheltenham you're a cheap tart.'

Hannah looked at him sharply. 'That's not amusing, Danny.'

'Come on, you've got to see the funny side of it.'

'Oh do I? Well funnily enough, right now I don't.'

She glared at him, caught between hurt and anger, and he must have got the message because he looked away. 'I was only trying to keep things light-hearted,' he said defensively.

'Like when you told me I ought to give Plowright what he wanted?'

'Oh, not that again! I told you, Han, that was a joke!'

'You know what really bothers me?' she snapped back. 'I'm not so sure it was.'

'Oi, you two, pack it in.' Maxine's pregnant belly loomed up between them on the scratchy bench seat. 'Let's face it, we're all a bit on edge. Can't we just have a quiet drink and thank our lucky stars nothing went wrong?'

A jumbo-sized packet of honey-roasted cashews and another round of drinks went a long way towards calming everybody's nerves. Hannah glanced at her watch. She was about to say, 'We should go soon and pick up Lottie from Mum's,' when she got a burst of the *1812 Overture* on her mobile.

She answered. 'Hi Mum, how's things?'

Hannah listened; listened some more; then gasped, 'No! You're kidding, there must have been some mistake. Don't do anything – I'm coming straight round.'

She looked from Danny to Maxine and back again. 'It's Grandad,' she said in a small voice.

'Oh, Hannah love.' Maxine looked concerned. 'He's not been taken ill, has he?'

Hannah shook her head, slowly and dazedly. 'No; worse. He's been arrested – for shoplifting!'

Danny snorted and threw up his hands. 'Well done, Herbie! Give that man a prize. Still, I suppose it was bound to happen sooner or later – once a thief, always a thief.'

Hannah threw him a look of contempt. 'And once a prat, always a prat,' she replied, picking up her handbag and hurrying out to the car.

Chapter 25

'He still insists he didn't do it,' said Sadie Millbank, 'and I'd like to believe him; but the evidence isn't exactly in his favour.'

Hannah was sitting with her mother and the young duty solicitor in the corridor at the police station, waiting for someone to decide what to do with Herbie. 'If Gramps says he didn't do it, he didn't do it,' she said firmly.

Erica shook her head sadly. 'I know you're very fond of your grandad, darling, but when all's said and done he's got a criminal record as long as your arm.'

'Yes Mum, I know he has, but not for petty shoplifting. It's just not his style. Believe me,' she told Sadie, 'Grandad wouldn't lower himself to nicking a CD of music he doesn't even like. What would be the point?'

'Habit? Excitement?' suggested the solicitor. 'Or maybe it's just that he feels like a fish out of water and secretly wants to go back to prison? It does happen quite a lot with ex-prisoners who've become very institutionalised.'

Even Hannah had to admit that there might be a grain of truth in that. How many times had she heard Herbie bemoaning the lot of the old ex-con who'd been top of the heap in jail but was less than nothing in the big wide world? Even so, she didn't believe it; Herbie might have wanted to go back, but not like this. This wasn't him at all.

'No,' she said firmly. 'He wouldn't do it, I'm sure of that.'

Sadie Millbank doodled on her notepad. 'I did suggest to him that we might put forward his age and failing memory as mitigating factors.'

'Failing memory!' The sheer ridiculousness of the idea made

Hannah laugh in spite of herself. 'Grandad's not one of those vague, forgetful old age pensioners you know – his mind's like a steel trap.'

'Yes, well, he wasn't bright enough to avoid getting himself arrested,' Hannah's mother reminded her.

'And he might just have put the CD in his pocket and forgotten to pay for it' pointed out the solicitor.

'So what did Grandad say when you suggested that?' demanded Hannah. 'He told you it was a load of rubbish, didn't he?'

'Let's just say I'm still working on it,' admitted the solicitor. 'But I'm afraid he'll have to face facts eventually. And as regards his parole status . . .'

Hannah knew exactly what that meant. 'You're saying, he's going straight back to jail?'

'If he's convicted of any offence I'm afraid he will be, yes.'

Erica put an arm round her daughter's shoulders. 'It might be the best place for him, you know.'

'Oh Mum, how can you say that?'

'It was probably a mistake letting him out in the first place after all that time. He just can't adjust to normal life. And he's not exactly the best of influences on Charlotte, is he?'

Hannah leapt up. 'That's rubbish! Lottie loves him.'

'That's rather what I'm afraid of, darling,' said her mother. 'I mean, who knows what sorts of things she's learning from him.'

Hannah loved her mother dearly, and generally had a great deal of regard for her common sense; but this was a step over the edge into paranoia. 'Mum, that's utter nonsense and you know it. Herbie's constantly telling Lottie about all the mistakes he made when he was young, and trying to make sure she'll never fall into the same traps he did.'

'All the same,' insisted Erica, 'she's not exactly had the most stable start in life, has she? And what with all that trouble at school last term, your father and I have really been worrying about her lately.'

Sadie Millbank was starting to look decidedly uncomfortable, caught as she was in the middle of somebody else's heated family discussion. 'I think there's a new coffee shop just down the road,' she announced brightly. 'I might just go and get myself a macchiato while we're waiting. Can I get you anything?'

Hannah shook her head. 'Nothing thanks.'

'That's very kind of you, dear,' smiled Erica, 'but no.'

The double doors of the police station swung shut behind Sadie's back, leaving Hannah and her mother alone in the uninviting corridor, with not so much as an inebriated tramp or a lost piglet to divert their attention from one another.

'You know I'm right, dear,' said Erica, tenacious as a crab with lockjaw.

'About what?' demanded Hannah, refusing to make it easy for her mother.

'About Charlotte of course. She needs stability in her life, and most especially, she needs a stable male figure. A father.'

Hannah groaned inwardly. Oh no, not again. 'Mum, how many times do we have to go over this? Lottie's got a father – she's got Nick. Besides which, she has got two grandfathers who dote on her, as well as Herbie.'

Erica opened her mouth to object. 'Nick's not—'

'Her father? Oh Mum, I just don't understand how you can keep on saying that. He's been there for Lottie ever since she was a tiny baby.'

'But he's still not biologically her father, is he? Not even her adoptive father, come to that.'

'Only because we both wanted to wait until Lottie was old enough to make her own decisions about adoption. And why's it so important anyway?'

Erica was undeterred. 'Perhaps it wasn't so very important while you were a proper couple, but now that the two of you aren't together any more, there's really no permanent link between Nick and Charlotte at all. Is there?'

Hannah's chin jutted defiantly. 'Of course there is!' she declared. 'Nick's as much a father to Lottie as anyone could ever be. And deep down that's how Lottie feels about him too.'

Erica raised an eyebrow. 'Are you absolutely sure about that, Hannah love? Really sure? As I recall, this is the same little girl who said she hated Nick and never ever wanted to see him again. And the number of times you've had to bribe her to get her to spend time with him . . .'

'That was before. Things are getting better again now,' said Hannah. 'Especially since Nick split up from Miranda.' She didn't mention the slight complication in the form of Miranda's pregnancy – if Erica found out about that, it would only confirm her in her view of Nick as basically nice enough but not half as reliable as she'd once thought he was.

'Well, maybe they are at that,' conceded Erica. 'But all the same, your father and I are fully agreed.'

'About what?' Hannah didn't like the sound of this: it made her feel like she was being ganged-up on.

'About Lottie needing a father. Her *real* father.'

Hannah looked into her mother's face and suddenly realised what she'd been getting at all this time. A sickening lurch seemed to turn her stomach inside out. 'Not ... Rhys? You're not seriously suggesting I should get in touch with him?

'Yes, dear, that's exactly what we're suggesting.'

The idea would have been laughable if it hadn't been so repellent. 'Mum, you're crazy! Don't you remember what he was like? The minute he found out I was pregnant, he couldn't get out of town fast enough! He even tried to make out the baby wasn't his.'

'I know,' agreed Erica, 'but you have to remember, you were both very young at the time. People grow up.'

'Rhys never will.'

'People grow up,' repeated Erica firmly, 'and realise that things that once seemed like disasters are really blessings. How could Rhys not be proud of having a beautiful, clever daughter like Charlotte?'

'I'm sorry, Mum, but the answer is no,' said Hannah quietly.

'Listen to me, Hannah, the child deserves to have a father and she has one out there. A successful one too, from what I've heard. They tell me he's making quite a career for himself in cable television.'

'Bully for him.'

'Apparently he's even in line to front a new Sunday religious programme. Doesn't that tell you something about how he's changed?'

'No Mum, it just tells me he's as good at playing a part as he ever was.' She stood up. 'I think I will go and get that coffee after all.'

'Don't just turn your back on the idea,' pleaded Erica. 'Think about it.'

'I don't need to, Mum,' replied Hannah. 'Rhys could be the

emperor of the universe and it wouldn't make any difference. He's still the last person in the world I want anywhere near Lottie.'

As spring grew heavy and waddled into summer, Maxine had to admit that the pace of salon life was beginning to get her down. In fact life in general was taking some keeping up with.

'I'm not a woman any longer, I'm a whale,' she lamented, puffing and panting as she hauled her bulbous frame into the passenger seat of Hannah's car. She might only be eight months' pregnant, but she was so enormous that she'd long since given up trying to drive. Even with the seat right back it was like being squashed into a giant bulldog clip, and she was sure that couldn't be good for the baby. Not to mention Hannah's suspension.

'What's so bad about being a whale?' teased Hannah. 'Everybody likes whales. You could charge tourists to come and take photos of you swimming in Pittville Lake.'

'Oh ha ha, most amusing. Look, the sooner I can stop being Moby Maxine and go back to being human again, the happier I'll be. Even if Jay won't,' she added with a grimace.

'Still?'

'Oh yes. The bigger the better, apparently. Weird, I call it.'

'Well, that's men for you. Always obsessed with size.'

They set off through the school-run traffic for Maxine's checkup at the Regency Clinic. Maxine would've been quite happy to queue up with all the other whales at the Cotswold General, but Jay wouldn't hear of it. Nothing but the best would do for the mother of his perfect child; and as far as he was concerned, best meant private.

'Of course, I never had any of that when I had Lottie,' reflected Hannah as they drove along. 'You know, the father acting strangely and all that – unless you count buggering off as strange behaviour. It was just me and the bump, and my mum going on about how she'd tried to teach me about contraception but I obviously hadn't been listening.'

'Still, from the sound of it you were better off without the father,' commented Maxine, glaring at her stomach as a tiny foot kicked her in the ribs. 'And I'd have been better off keeping my legs crossed.'

Hannah smiled. 'You don't mean that.'

'Don't I? Say that again the next time you're up the duff.'

'Not much chance of that.'

It was funny, but as she said the words, Hannah felt just a faint twinge of sadness. So much had happened over the last six months that she hadn't given much more thought to the idea of having a baby: the idea that had kept her and Nick together for so long – until the bubble had finally burst and reality came flooding in.

Now she had opened up her mind a chink, and that idea had its foot in the door again, whether she wanted it to or not. There had been moments over the last few months when she'd felt a stupid urge to get herself pregnant, just to have someone else around who would love her unconditionally, forever. But that wasn't a good reason for having a baby. Besides, Hannah wasn't ready to face that ordeal all over again, not alone and unloved and struggling to cope, the way it had been with Lottie.

Maybe that was why she felt suddenly sad. Because with Danny she would always, in a way, be alone. He was fun, he was exhilarating, he was an injection of lost youth: but father material? Having a baby with him would be pretty much a solo experience.

She knew, deep down, that she never would.

Maxine looked at her sharply. 'Something wrong between you and Danny?'

'No, nothing. Not really.'

'What do you mean, "not really"?'

'Oh, I dunno, I just can't see us ever having kids together, that's all. Maybe I was only ever meant to have the one.' She shook off the last vestiges of self-pity. After all, she had an awful lot to be thankful for. 'Maybe you're going to have the other one point four for me!'

'Not bleeding likely,' replied Maxine, watching her mammoth belly undulate beneath her overstretched T-shirt. 'If Jay wants a bigger family, he'll have to make do with a dog.'

They drove into the car park at the Regency Clinic with a good ten minutes to spare, so Maxine was able to lumber across to the main entrance in leisurely fashion. 'Don't know why Jay insists on me coming here,' she sniffed. 'I mean, what do you get for your money? Free coffee and a few cushions in the waiting room.'

'Nice to think he cares enough to fork out all this money though,' pointed out Hannah as they signed in and looked for somewhere to sit. As she turned round, she clapped a hand to her mouth. 'Oh hell, look who it isn't!'

Maxine followed her line of sight and found herself looking right into a very familiar face. 'Miranda! My God, she's got fat.'

'Hark who's talking.'

'Yeah, but she can't be more than six months gone, and she's almost as big as me! Come on, I'm going to say hello.'

Hannah freaked. 'What!'

Pretty much the last thing she fancied was a cosy tête-à-tête with her husband's pregnant ex-mistress. But Maxine had her by the arm and when Maxine got an idea into her head there wasn't much point in resisting. Besides, she'd already attracted Miranda's attention.

'Miranda – coo-ee! Long time, no see!'

The eyes that met Hannah's were still annoyingly dark and beautiful; but the face that surrounded them had turned all pale and puffy, like uncooked bread dough. In fact the whole of her had the look of having been inflated with a bicycle pump and then kept in a sunless cellar for six months. Whereas Maxine was visibly blooming, Miranda looked like someone for whom pregnancy wasn't so much a blessing as an affliction.

'Oh,' she said, unenthusiastically. 'It's you. You're looking well,' she added with a glance at Maxine's bump. She made it sound like an accusation.

'So are you,' lied Maxine, digging Hannah in the ribs. 'Isn't she, Han?'

'Actually,' replied Hannah, inexplicably feeling rather sorry for Miranda, 'you're looking dreadful. Are you OK?'

Maxine rolled her eyes at Hannah's tactlessness; Miranda looked surprised but unoffended. 'I'm trying to run a smallholding practically single-handed, Old Tom says he's still not well enough to work full-time, the bees have caught some stupid parasite, and I'm developing varicose veins. Would you be OK?'

Hannah sat down in the chair next to Miranda's. 'Sounds like you're having a tough time.'

Before Hannah had time to stop her, Maxine cut in with, 'Aren't you getting any help off Nick?'

'Max!' hissed Hannah.

Miranda sniffed. 'If you can call the odd day here and there help. He's not exactly falling over himself.'

'I'm sure he's doing all he can,' said Hannah, instinctively defending her ex. Nick might have his faults, but ducking out on his responsibilities definitely wasn't one of them.

'Well it's not enough,' declared Miranda, flicking back a strand of rather lank black hair. 'That's why I've decided I'm not keeping it.'

Maxine and Hannah exchanged glances. 'Not keeping what?' asked Hannah, just to be absolutely sure she hadn't got the wrong end of the stick.

Miranda looked at her as though she was stupid. 'The baby, what else? Just as soon as I get this thing out of me, I'm putting it up for adoption.'

'But I thought . . .' Hannah's head reeled. 'At Maxine's Christmas party, you were saying how much you wanted to start a family. You couldn't wait to get pregnant.'

'That was then,' replied Miranda tartly. 'Things were different. Besides, everybody can make a mistake.'

'Pretty big mistake,' murmured Maxine, her hand moving protectively to her own bump, as though she wanted to shield it from Miranda's coldness.

Hannah wasn't thinking about Miranda any more; her thoughts had travelled to Nick, to how he must be feeling at the prospect of the child, *his* child, being given away to strangers like a pair of unwanted socks.

'H-how . . . I mean, what does Nick think about this?' she heard herself ask.

Miranda smiled thinly. 'Actually, I've been so busy I haven't got round to telling him yet.'

'You haven't *told* him!'

A crisp-uniformed nurse emerged through the door leading to the consulting rooms. 'Ms Moss? Ms Miranda Moss?'

She hauled herself to her feet. 'Maybe you'd like to tell him for me, save me the trouble, seeing as you two are such bosom pals?'

The look in Miranda's eyes was full of defiance; but behind it all, the pain of rejection glowered like a malevolent troll, its only pleasure the prospect of passing that pain on to someone else.

*

It was a beautiful June Saturday, but Herbie wasn't deriving much joy from the scampering squirrels in Sandford Park, or the dazzling floral displays, heavy with scent and buzzing with overexcited bees.

He sat down heavily on a bench by the fountain, and wondered how many more times he'd get to do this before they stuck him behind bars again. Funny; he hadn't thought he'd mind so much.

The waiting was the worst bit. If only they could just get on with his court appearance and get it all over with. But the wheels of justice were grinding exceedingly slowly, merely putting off the evil hour when he'd be carted away and Erica would have her spare room back again. It was his own fault of course; if he'd taken the solicitor's advice and pleaded guilty, it could all have been over and done with by now. But he just couldn't bring himself to do it. In all his years of crime, he'd never owned up to something he hadn't done – and he wasn't about to begin now.

'Hello, Great-Gramps,' said a little voice beside him.

He looked up. 'Lottie! What are you doing here?'

'Mum said I could walk back from drama club on my own as long as I was careful crossing the roads. I thought you might be here.'

'Yes, well, you don't want to waste your time hanging around with me,' said Herbie. 'You get back and have some fun with your friends.'

'Can't I have some fun with you?'

Herbie couldn't imagine anyone having fun with him right now, but he was touched that Lottie was willing to give it a go. 'What about Melanie-Anne? Don't you want to go and play with her?'

'You know I'm not friends with Melanie-Anne any more, not since she was so horrible to me,' Lottie reminded him. 'Anyway, her mum's sending her to that posh private school in Gloucester now, the one where they only take girls.'

'More fool her,' commented Herbie.

'She says I'm a bad influence.'

'Good for you.' He grinned. 'Won't Danny be waiting for you at home?'

Lottie pulled a face. 'I don't *have* to go back there just yet, do I?'

Herbie cocked his head on one side. 'You still not getting on with Danny then?'

Lottie twisted the bottom of her T-shirt in her fingers. 'He's OK, I s'pose.'

'But?'

'You won't tell Mum, will you?'

'Scouts' honour.'

'He's not like a grown-up, he's so . . . silly all the time. And he sits around the house all day and doesn't do anything to help. And he says nasty things about you and upsets Mum.'

Though he would quite like to have said exactly what he thought of Danny, Herbie just smiled and patted his great-granddaughter on the shoulder. 'You don't want to worry about that, everybody says nasty things about me. I probably deserve most of them.'

'No you don't!' protested Lottie. 'You're *not* a pathetic old loser, you're my lovely Great-Gramps.' She paused. 'Great-Gramps . . .'

'Hmm?'

'Are you going back to prison?'

He sighed. There wasn't much point in spinning her a line. 'Probably,' he admitted.

'But you didn't steal that CD, did you?'

'No. No, I didn't. And I don't care if they don't believe me – nobody's going to make me say I did.'

'I believe you,' said Lottie, slipping her hand in his.

'I know you do.'

'And so does Mum. That's why she keeps having arguments with Danny. Sometimes I wish he'd just go away,' she admitted. 'But then Mum would be sad all over again. And I still wouldn't have a daddy.'

'You've got Nick,' Herbie pointed out. 'Or is he still not your daddy?'

'I don't know,' she said glumly. 'I don't think I know what he is any more. And he tries too hard, and that makes me feel like I have to try as well, and then everything goes all wrong. Is it all my fault, Great-Gramps?'

'Of course it isn't. None of it's your fault. Your trouble is, you've got an awfully old head on those little shoulders of yours,' remarked Herbie. 'Too much thinking and worrying, that's your problem. One of these days you're going to tire your head out so much it'll fall off and roll away.'

252

Lottie giggled. 'No it won't!'

'Yes it will, and I'll probably glue it back on the wrong way round and then you'll have to walk everywhere backwards.'

She snuggled into the crook of his shoulder. 'I love you, Great-Gramps.'

'I love you too.'

'One of the ferrets has had babies.' She looked up at him hopefully. 'Do you want to come home with me and see?'

How could he refuse? It was the best invitation he'd had all year.

Chapter 26

It was two days before Herbie's case was scheduled to come to court, and he'd just about got all his affairs in order. After the verdict had been pronounced and they whisked him off in the prison van, things would swiftly get back to normal, and Erica and Derek could forget he'd ever darkened their door.

Then, halfway through his Rice Krispies, he got the telephone call.

'DS Marchant here, can you get down the station this morning, around eleven?'

'Why?' he demanded, instantly suspicious.

'There's something I'd like you to see.'

'What if I don't want to see it?'

'Oh, I think you will.'

Hannah couldn't help wishing, just now and then, that Danny could see things from her point of view.

'It's just not a good time, Danny,' she tried to explain as she cleared away the breakfast dishes. 'Lottie's got her dancing exams coming up, and poor old Grandad's in court the day after tomorrow.'

But Danny just looked mystified. 'What's that got to do with anything? How does Herbie's trial stop you coming out clubbing with me?'

Trying to talk to Danny about worries and responsibilities was like speaking Arabic to an Inuit. 'I just can't concentrate,' she said, 'don't you see? Lottie's getting herself all worked up about the exams, and she needs lots of support.'

'She'll be fine. She's always fine.'

'Only because she gets the support she needs. And goodness knows what Grandad's going through right now.'

'Whatever he's going through,' declared Danny, 'the old fool's only got himself to blame.'

That was just too much. Hannah rounded on him. 'You've judged him and convicted him ten times over!' she snapped. 'And you hardly know him.'

'You think you do?' retorted Danny. 'Open your eyes Hannah, he's just a sad old loser who can't shake off his old habits. Everybody else worked that one out ages ago – why can't you?'

'Maybe everybody else is wrong,' she said between clenched teeth, practically hurling the breakfast dishes into the sink with an infernal clatter.

'Or you just see what you want to see.'

She flushed with anger. 'Bit like you, you mean?'

'What are you on about?'

'Face it, Danny, you can't bear the thought that I might be right and he might be innocent, can you? You can't wait for him to get sent down.'

'Well, at least once he's out of the way you might stop mooning around with a long face and start having some fun with me again.'

Hannah gripped the edge of the sink to prevent herself gripping Danny by the throat. 'So that's what this is all about: you. It's always about you, isn't it? Have you ever considered thinking about other people for a change?'

'Have you ever considered growing up?'

She swung round to confront him with a furious glare. 'Me! Hark who's talking.'

The phone rang for a long time before Danny's nerve broke and he answered it. 'Guess what, it's for you,' he said with a sarcastic smile. 'Herbie. Says he wants you to go down the cop-shop with him.'

To be fair to DS Marchant, thought Hannah, he does at least look uncomfortable. And he has every reason to. This really does beggar belief.

She watched the grainy black and white footage play through again on the VCR in the interview room. 'You mean to say you've only just bothered to take a look at this CCTV footage from Costbeaters?'

255

'No. Not exactly,' replied the detective sergeant, avoiding looking her or Herbie in the face. 'There was a bit of . . . um . . . difficulty in tracking it down. At first, the manager thought there wasn't any film in the cameras that day, then it turned out one of the security staff had got the tapes mixed up and the footage had been sitting on his desk all the time.'

'Efficient,' commented Hannah drily.

Herbie just sat and stared at the sight of himself comparing the prices of soap powder while a small figure sneaked up behind him and deftly slipped something into his coat pocket. 'The little bastard,' he muttered. 'Just you wait till I get my hands on him.'

Hannah laid a hand on his arm. 'I don't think that would be a good idea, Gramps. I reckon we'd better let the police deal with him. If they're sure they're up to it,' she added pointedly, at once exultant that Herbie had been proved innocent and enraged that he had been so shabbily treated.

'I take it you recognise the lad then?' DS Marchant pointed at the boy on the screen, little weaselly face poking out from under his Scooby-Doo hoodie.

'Oh yes,' said Herbie. 'He's one of the ones who've been terrorising the old folk on the estate.'

'The ones he's been telling you about for months,' Hannah added. 'Only you said you were too busy to do anything about it.'

'Not too busy exactly, just chronically undermanned,' protested the sergeant, but he was definitely back-pedalling for all he was worth. 'Anything you can tell me about him – name, school, where we can find him?'

'Certainly,' replied Hannah. 'I don't know his name, but I do know he's in the first year at Alderman Braithwaite. He used to be in my hus—I mean ex-husband's chemistry class. Nick. Nick Steadman.'

'Then you'd best give me his name and contact details,' said the sergeant, grabbing a notebook and pen. 'I think we need to have a chat with Mr Steadman.'

You and me both, thought Hannah, guiltily recalling the conversation she'd been planning with Nick ever since her encounter with Miranda at the clinic. But surely by now Miranda would have told him anyway?

Wouldn't she?

*

'For God's sake, Hannah,' complained Danny, 'I've been kicking my heels all day, and now you want to go off into some cosy little huddle with your ex! I'm beginning to wonder if you enjoy his company more than mine.'

'It's not my fault you get bored in the daytime,' pointed out Hannah. 'If you hadn't made such a mess of things down at the salon, Jay wouldn't have barred you from working there.'

'It was boring anyway,' retorted Danny. 'I need a proper challenge.'

'Fine. So go out and find one. But don't blame everything on me just because I have to go out and have a discussion with Nick. He's an important part of Lottie's life, you know.'

'Yeah, yeah, so you keep telling me,' sighed Danny. 'Look, why don't I come along as well, and when you've finished talking about Lottie the two of us can go out for dinner and a club? Your mum won't mind having Lottie for the night – or we could take her to Nick's and leave her there.'

'She's not a parcel, Danny!'

'What did I say? I thought she liked sleepovers.'

Tired of wrangling, Hannah met him halfway. 'I really need to talk things over with Nick alone,' she insisted gently, 'but I tell you what. I'll call you when we've done and you can pick me up. And maybe we can go to the pub or something.'

'Whoopee, the pub again,' said Danny. 'I don't think I can stand the excitement.'

'Pity,' replied Hannah, ''cause I'm afraid you're going to have to.'

It's changed, thought Hannah as she stepped through the door into Nick's rented flat.

Now that he had moved back in properly, instead of dividing his time between there and Far Acre Cottage, it was clear to see that he was beginning to transform it from a place to sleep into a kind of home. The cardboard boxes had almost all been unpacked, and their contents redistributed all over the flat. The jumble of CDs and books on the shelves had been rearranged into Nick's compulsive alphabetical order. Favourite vintage movie posters hung on the bare walls, and in the hallway pride of place went to a framed poem Lottie had once written him for Father's Day.

Nick fetched an open bottle of wine from the fridge and a couple of glasses. 'You're still OK with dry white?'

She smiled. 'It's OK, Nick, I haven't suddenly changed out of all recognition just because we're not sharing a house any more.'

'You have changed, though,' he commented.

'Have I?' The thought rather surprised her. 'How?'

'I don't know, it's hard to pin down. But you seem ... I don't know ... more you, somehow. It's like before you were sort of muffled, and then someone took the lid off and suddenly there you are, loud and proud.'

'Loud!' she laughed.

'Oh, take no notice, you know I'm no good with words. Never was, never will be.' He sighed. 'Don't think I'm much good with women either. Reckon I'll give 'em up as a bad job and stick to minding Lottie's menagerie.'

'No, don't do that,' said Hannah softly. 'There's some incredibly lucky lady out there, just waiting for you to come along and carry her off on your white charger.' Oh hell, thought Hannah. Now's my chance to steer this conversation round to the one thing neither of us really wants to talk about. 'Just because things didn't work out with Miranda ...'

Nick shuddered. 'I know, I know; but I think it's going to be a while before I want to get myself in that situation again. If I ever do.'

'You will,' Hannah assured him. 'It's like really deep bruises. They go on hurting for a long time, but in the end they will go away. At least, that's what all the books say.' She shuffled her feet awkwardly. 'I ... er ... saw Miranda a few days ago.'

He looked up. 'Where?'

'At the Regency Clinic, when I took Maxine for her antenatal check-up. Miranda was there too. She didn't seem very happy.'

'No. No, she wouldn't.'

'Apparently she's having trouble coping on the smallholding, but you've been helping her out a bit.'

'Well, yeah. Off and on, when I can.' Nick was really starting to look uncomfortable. 'You're not drinking your wine.'

'What? Oh, sorry.' She took a sip. 'It's very nice. The thing is,' Hannah went on, twiddling the stem between her fingers, 'she said some things that really worried me, and I ... I felt I'd better tell you, in case you didn't know.'

Nick's whole body tensed. 'What things?'

Hannah took a deep breath. Was she dropping a bombshell, or telling him something he'd been mulling over for weeks? 'She told me she's going to give the baby up for adoption as soon as it's born.'

Nick seemed to deflate, every ounce of breath leaving his body. He sagged forward until his elbows were on his knees, his forehead resting on his hands. 'So I was right.'

'She hasn't told you?'

'Not in so many words, but she's been dropping heavy hints for a long time. At first I think it was just a way of punishing me for leaving, but now I'm pretty sure she genuinely can't cope. Or doesn't want to. It amounts to the same thing.'

Hannah stretched forward and stroked his hair. 'You're not just going to sit back and let her? Let her have your baby adopted?'

'No. No I'm not.' He looked up at her from under a tangle of hair; suddenly not nearly-forty Nick any more but Nick the hapless schoolboy. 'Whether it's actually my baby or not.'

Hannah caught her breath. 'You mean it might not be?'

'Let's just say the reason we split up had a lot to do with Miranda's ideas on fidelity.'

'Which were?'

'It's a quaint old-fashioned institution, but who wants to live in an institution?'

'Oh my God. That changes everything!'

Nick sat up. 'Actually, it doesn't,' he replied. 'I've thought about this a lot, and I made up my mind a long time ago: that baby's my son or my daughter, whether that's biologically true or not. Whatever it takes, I'm going to do my very best for it; and if that means being a full-time parent . . .'

'But what about your career? And what if you're making all these sacrifices just to bring up some other man's child?'

A smile played around Nick's lips. 'What about Lottie?' he reminded her. 'I've always loved her as much as any biological father could ever love his child; why not this little one too? And as for my career – what career? The online business is going belly-up anyway; I was an idiot to think I had what it takes. I should be able to get enough supply teaching to keep me going. Who knows?'

Hannah felt an overwhelming urge to hug him. For the first

259

time in a very long time, perhaps the first time ever, she saw the true depths of tenderness and selflessness within him and found them not irritating, but profoundly touching. In that same split second she thought of Danny, with his knee-jerk judgements and his 'if it's not fun it's not worth doing' philosophy. Perhaps it was an unjust comparison, but she couldn't help imagining how Danny would have reacted in Nick's situation. Or if he'd met her when she'd been at her lowest ebb and Lottie was just a fatherless babe in arms.

'You're a good man, Nick,' she said quietly.

He grimaced. 'You make me sound like I ought to be wearing a hair shirt and living in a cave.'

'Don't joke about it, I mean it.' She got up and sat down next to him on the sofa, leaning her head against his shoulder. 'I was right, you know, Miranda was bloody lucky to have you. And if she didn't realise that, more fool her.'

But what about you, Hannah? whispered a little voice inside her head. Does that make you a fool too?

Nick awoke with a fuzzy head and a mouth like a battered old carpet tile. That'd teach him to sit up late with Hannah, downing bottles of cheap white wine and reminiscing about times past.

He'd enjoyed it though. And not in a self-indulgent, miserable way; it had really been good to get close to her again, have a proper chat for the first time in who could say how long. For a few hours he'd even forgotten that Danny and Miranda had ever existed.

Back to reality again now. And the reality of the matter was that he'd run out of milk again. One thing was for sure: he was going to have to get his head round this housekeeping lark if he really was going to bring up Miranda's baby as his own, something he now knew with absolute certainty that he would do.

The doorbell rang before he'd had a chance to get washed and dressed; so it was an unshaven Nick in a tatty dressing gown who greeted Mark on the doorstep.

'Hiya mate, how's tricks?' Mark clapped him on the back and slipped inside. 'You're looking a bit rough – heavy night?'

Nick scratched his stubbly chin. 'Not really, just a few drinks with Hannah.'

Mark's face registered interest. 'Hannah, eh? You old dog.'

'Sorry to disappoint you, all we were doing was talking. We are still allowed to do that you know, even though we're separated.'

'Just joshing, Nick, you know me.' Mark scampered into the living room, clearly bursting to tell him something. He shifted from one foot to the other. 'It's no good, I can't wait, I've got to tell you.'

Nick lowered himself onto the sofa. 'Tell me what? Go on, you've finally blown up the chemistry block at school.'

'Nope. Guess again.'

'Harry Turnbull's been killed and eaten by 3C.'

'Close but no cigar. No, the school's so pathetically short of facilities that the government's giving us some extra money!'

'Christ, put the flags out. How much, two pound fifty?'

'Enough to restructure the whole science department.'

'You're having me on.'

'Oh no I'm not. And it means we're actually going to be able to advertise for a proper head of science at last. I know you probably won't be interested . . .'

'Says who?'

'I thought you were a hard-nosed businessman now.'

Nick laughed. 'More like a soft-headed one. Let's just say I won't be giving Richard Branson any sleepless nights.'

'Oh. OK. Well, the head was saying that seeing as officially you're only on an unpaid sabbatical until this July, technically it'd be an internal promotion and she'd look very favourably at an application from you. Assuming you wanted to apply, of course.' He looked at Nick like an eager little puppy-dog. 'What do you reckon?'

'I reckon you need to go to the corner shop for a pint of milk. And then we make ourselves the biggest pot of tea in the world and have a very, very long talk.'

Chapter 27

Maxine breathed in for all she was worth, but still only just managed to squeeze her impressive bulk behind the reception desk.

'Watch yourself,' cautioned Claire. 'We don't want to have to call the fire brigade to cut you free.'

A dreamy expression spread across Maxine's face. 'Oh I don't know,' she reflected. 'I could quite fancy being manhandled to safety by a load of hunks with big shiny helmets.'

The spots on Jason's neck all turned crimson. Philomena stifled a giggle. Claire wagged a reproving finger. 'I don't know, you should be ashamed of yourself having such thoughts, and you a mother-to-be.'

Maxine patted her bump. 'You know, I've been thinking,' she said.

'You want to watch that,' commented Hannah. 'Dangerous habit.'

'And I reckon it's not a baby in here, it's just the accumulated lard from all the food I've been scoffing over the last nine months. You mark my words, I'll go into hospital and give birth to an enormous chocolate cake. By the way,' she added, opening drawers in the reception desk and rummaging in them, 'has anybody seen those minty indigestion tablets I left lying around the other day?'

Hannah reached into the pocket of her uniform tunic. 'Here, have a Polo mint. What've you been eating this time? Not more Maltesers dipped in Branston Pickle?'

'No! Nothing weird, honest. Just one of Jay's super-hot vindaloos. I told him to go easy on the chillis, but you know what he's like. If it doesn't burn the roof off your mouth it's not a proper curry.'

'Hmm,' commented Philomena. 'He's been feeding you that many of his curries lately, when this baby finally does come out it'll probably burst into flames in the midwife's hands.'

'At least you've got somebody who likes cooking for you,' said Claire. 'When I go home it's just me, the cat and a microwave pizza.'

'Don't knock it, kid, it's a whole lot less trouble that way,' replied Hannah, gathering up a big stack of fluffy white towels.

'Oh dear, oh dear,' tutted Philomena, scenting juicy gossip. 'Don't tell me the lovebirds have fallen out again?'

Hannah didn't rise to the bait – or point out that Philomena and Damon had had more than a few arguments lately. 'Let's just say no relationship's hearts and flowers all the time – is it, Max?'

'Don't drag me into this!' protested Maxine, crunching on another Polo mint. 'I'm an old married woman, I don't do hearts and flowers. Mind you,' she admitted, 'I'll say one thing for husbands, they're useful around the house.'

'Poor Jay!' laughed Claire. 'You make him sound like a hostess trolley.'

Maxine grinned. 'Not quite *that* useful.'

Hannah had to admit that if you disregarded the petulance, the immaturity and the tendency to prolonged sulks, Danny had his uses too. This evening, for instance, he'd promised to pick up Lottie from her dance rehearsal. If he hadn't agreed to do it, Hannah would have had to turn down Nick's invitation to a pre-birthday drink with him and his mates.

Not that Danny hadn't moaned about it, though. Sometimes it seemed to Hannah that all he did these days was moan about one thing or another. But then again, all relationships went through bumpy patches. Maxine and Jay had been known to yell the place down, but they'd never been less than besotted with each other, had they?

Somewhere deep down, Hannah knew that she and Danny were different, but she couldn't think of any good reason why. Good sex, companionship ... hell, he could even cook! You expect too much, that's your trouble, Hannah told herself as she climbed the stairs to the beauty room. Maybe you always have.

And she thought of Nick. And wondered.

*

'To be honest,' admitted Miss Fabian, 'I'm not quite at my best today. A spot of acid indigestion, I think. It's been bothering me ever since last night.'

'You too, eh?' sympathised Maxine, producing the packet of indigestion tablets she'd finally tracked down in the staff biscuit tin – the legacy of a batch of Philomena's inedible cheese scones. 'My tummy's been playing me up all morning. Here you are, love, you'd better have a couple of these.'

She finished trimming Miss Fabian's rather sparse white locks, soaked the hair in perming lotion and started rolling it up onto curlers. 'You are looking a bit pale, I must say. Can Jason get you another cup of tea?'

'No thank you, dear, I'll be fine in a minute.' Clarice Fabian settled back in the chair and closed her eyes. 'If I could just get rid of this silly indigestion. It's spreading all down my left side, you know. Still, if I will go eating pickled onions late at night . . .'

Maxine was about to ask Clarice if she'd ever tried Maltesers dipped in Branston Pickle when the old lady let out a little cry and clasped her left shoulder. 'Oh! Oh, I—'

'Miss Fabian?' Rubber gloves dripping perming lotion, Maxine stared in helpless horror as her client crumpled forward in the chair. 'Miss Fabian, are you all right?'

A ripple of concern ran round the other clients. 'Perhaps she's fainted.'

'Has she choked on that biscuit she was eating?'

'Try slapping her on the back.'

Hannah was just heading down the stairs for her break when the hubbub broke out. 'What on earth's happening?'

'It's Miss Fabian!' gasped Maxine, suddenly snapping back to life. 'She's having some sort of funny turn.'

'Look,' said Claire, 'she's gone all grey and clammy.'

Hannah took one look and lunged for the phone. 'Jason, ring nine-nine-nine right now! I think Miss Fabian's having a heart attack.'

Erica and Derek had had a busy morning.

Important letters always took a lot of planning out, but this one had taken more than most. Four times they'd typed and retyped it, fiddling about with it again and again until at last they were satisfied.

They sat back and gazed at the letter, displayed in all its glory on Derek's computer screen. Derek's finger hovered over the mouse, ready to double-click and print it out.

'You're sure we're doing the right thing?'

'Of course we are. We agreed.'

'Yes, but it still seems a bit . . . sneaky.'

'I know it does, love.' Erica gave her husband's hand a reassuring squeeze. 'But in the circumstances I don't see what else we could do. We have to think of Charlotte, remember.'

Derek had to admit that his wife was right. He sat and watched the paper spool through the printer and shoot out into the tray, immaculately and irrevocably typed. 'Well, it's done now.'

'Yes.'

'Are you going to phone up, or am I?'

'Would you? I feel really nervous about it, I don't know why.'

Derek picked up the phone and dialled the number he'd got from the media yearbook. 'Hello. Is that Pendragon Productions? I wonder, could you give me a contact address for Mr Rhys Donoghue's agent? I'd like to send him a confidential letter.'

Despite the horrors of Cheltenham's one-way system the paramedics had arrived within five minutes. So swiftly, in fact, that Maxine had no time to neutralise Miss Fabian's perm, and had to trot behind the stretcher with the solution as it was trundled into the ambulance.

'Is she going to be OK?' asked Hannah anxiously as the paramedics strapped an oxygen mask over the old lady's face.

'We're doing all we can, love,' replied one of the paramedics with a professional smile. 'Are you coming with her to the hospital?'

'I'll have to,' declared Maxine, laboriously heaving herself up the step into the ambulance. 'If I don't neutralise that perm she'll have a burnt scalp as well as everything else. Bugger, Han, I'm stuck. Give us a shove, will you?'

Hannah applied maximum force to Maxine's buttocks and between them they just about managed to prevent her toppling backwards onto the pavement. 'Oh well,' said Hannah cheerfully, 'looks like I'm coming with you.'

'You? Why?'

'Because somebody's got to push you out again when we get to the other end.'

By the time they reached the Cotswold General, Maxine was towelling the excess neutraliser off Miss Fabian's head and the whole ambulance stank like a hairdressing salon.

'How's she doing?' asked Hannah anxiously. Miss Fabian lay so very still and doll-like on the stretcher, almost like a wax dummy. The only signs of life were the rhythmic bleep of the heart monitor and the hiss of oxygen from the mask.

'Don't you worry, love, she's in good hands,' replied the senior paramedic as the doors opened and they rolled the stretcher towards A&E. 'Perhaps you could go to Reception could you?' he called back over his shoulder. 'They'll need her details – next of kin and stuff.'

Maxine and Hannah stood in the entrance, looking at each other. 'Next of kin?' wondered Hannah. 'Has she got any?'

'Not that I know of. She's never mentioned anyone to me, anyway.'

A thought occurred to Hannah. 'What's going to happen to Bertie? Somebody's going to have to sort him out.'

'Well,' declared Maxine, 'there are only two people I can think of, and right now Miss Fabian hates the sight of both of them. But beggars can't be choosers, can they?'

The girl on reception greeted them with the sort of yawn that went with long shifts and having seen everything – several times. 'Name?'

'Clarice Fabian.'

'Date of birth?'

'Er . . . I don't know. Do you, Han?'

Hannah shook her head.

The receptionist looked at Maxine strangely. 'Are you telling me you don't know when you were born?'

'Sorry?' Maxine followed the look to her enormous belly and cottoned on. 'Oh, you thought I was the patient?' She laughed. 'No, we're here to book in the old lady they just brought in on the trolley. She was having her hair permed in our salon when she took ill.'

The receptionist sniffed the air. 'Ah, that'd explain the smell then. Address?'

'Ledyard Mansions. Flat forty, I think . . . no, forty-one.'

'Next of kin?'

'We don't think she has any,' replied Hannah. 'But she does have a couple of very close friends.' She crossed her fingers behind her back. 'Mrs De'Ath and Mrs Lorrimer. Shall I call the salon and get their phone numbers?'

Hannah was just spelling out Mrs De'Ath's name when Maxine let out a little 'oh' of surprise. A split second later, there came the sound of a small but enthusiastic waterfall, cascading onto the tiled floor of A&E.

'Hannah,' said a very small voice. 'I think I just wet myself.'

Even before she turned round, Hannah knew what had happened. 'Oh Max,' she exclaimed at the sight of the puddle. 'Your waters have broken!'

'What!' Maxine's face turned ghostly white. 'But ... they can't! I can't go into labour, I'm not ready, I've still got a fortnight to go!'

'Tough,' replied Hannah, grabbing the nearest wheelchair and plonking her friend in it. 'Have you got a midwife around here?' she asked the receptionist. 'I think my friend's going to be staying a little bit longer than she expected.'

Chapter 28

'Anyway,' Hannah gabbled into her mobile as she locked the car and walked towards the house, 'I'm really sorry I couldn't come out for that drink tonight, but it's been quite a day, one way or another.'

'Don't worry about it,' said Nick. 'I'm just glad Maxine and the baby are OK. She's not really going to call it Griselda-Mae after the receptionist, is she?'

Hannah giggled. 'No, that was just to wind Jay up! He actually believed her for about thirty seconds – you should've seen his face.'

'So how's he taking to fatherhood?'

'Well, he's totally besotted with the baby. But between you and me, I don't think he was too impressed about Max dropping the sprog at the General, when he'd forked out all that money for the Regency Clinic. She really is the cutest little thing though, all big eyes and curly blonde hair. You'll have to come along and see her soon.'

'I will. Oh – and what about the old lady? How's she doing?'

'Touch and go,' Hannah admitted. 'A heart attack's no joke at that age, no matter how much money you've got. Look, I'll have to go now but I'll see you at the weekend when you come to collect Lottie, yeah?'

'Of course. And don't forget, we're having that birthday drink soon.'

Hannah bounced into the house, full of the joys of vicarious motherhood. There really was nothing quite like sharing in a child's birth without actually having to suffer any of the pain, change any of the nappies, or go without chocolate for eighteen years so you could afford to send it to university.

'Lottie? Danny? Have I got news for you!'

A head poked round the banisters at the top of the stairs. 'Hello, Mum.'

'Hello, darling, how was the dance rehearsal?'

'Fine.'

'And Danny picked you up OK?'

'Yes.' The head disappeared.

Hannah climbed up the first few stairs. 'Are you all right?'

'Everything's fine, Mum, I told you. Can I go and watch telly in my room now? There's a programme about tree kangaroos.'

Slightly puzzled, Hannah made her way to the living room, where Danny was sprawled out across the sofa, fast asleep with a copy of 'Yachting' magazine open on his chest. Smiling, she bent down until her mouth was level with his ear.

'Boo!'

Danny shot upright. 'What the— For God's sake, Hannah, you scared me half to death.'

'Sorry love.' She perched on the arm of the sofa. 'Guess where I've been.'

'Out drinking with the birthday boy,' he replied, looking less than impressed. 'So – did he go mad and have a dash of lager in his lemonade?'

Hannah was too hyped up to be annoyed by Danny's silly digs at Nick. 'As a matter of fact I've been at the hospital,' she replied. 'Watching Maxine's baby being born.'

If she'd expected Danny to jump up and down and go 'wow', she was sorely disappointed. 'Oh,' he said. 'That's nice.'

'It was a bit of a surprise,' Hannah went on. 'I mean, it wasn't due for a couple of weeks yet.'

'Oh. Well, she's had it now, so everybody can stop worrying about it and get back to normal, can't they?'

'She's really pretty.' Hannah rummaged in her bag and extracted the Polaroid Jay had let her have. 'Look, isn't she the image of her mum?'

Danny glanced at the photo and grimaced. 'The image of a turnip, more like. Gawd but that's one ugly baby.' He laughed. 'Thank goodness we'll never have to put up with one of those, eh?'

Hannah looked into his eyes and saw that he really meant it. It wasn't the fact that they wouldn't be having any babies of their own that upset her – something she'd come to terms with long ago – but that he looked so pleased about it. As if only the very stupid could possibly want to do such a cretinous thing as breed.

'Yeah,' she said, feeling distinctly subdued now. 'I guess. Poor Miss Fabian had a heart attack today, too,' she went on. 'In the salon.'

'The old dear with all the money?' He whistled. 'Wonder who'll be coming into that little fortune, then?'

His crassness turned her stomach. 'She's not dead, Danny. Just very ill.'

'Still, it happens to us all sooner or later, doesn't it? That's why it pays to make the most of life while you're young – get out there and have some fun.' Danny pinched her cheek and playfully nibbled the end of her nose. 'Why don't I phone for a takeaway, and then you can play me at Gotham City Racing on the X-Box?'

She wanted to tell him exactly what she thought of that idea; but all at once she just couldn't be bothered.

'I'm tired,' she announced, picking up her handbag and heading for the stairs. 'You do what you like, I'm going to bed.'

Over the next couple of days, while Maxine and the baby were in hospital, Hannah made a point of visiting as often as she could. Far from putting an obstacle between them, shutting Hannah out the way brand-new mother-baby relationships sometimes do, the new baby seemed to have opened up a new dimension to their friendship. For the first time, Maxine could understand what it really meant to be a mother, to find yourself suddenly with sole responsibility for the life of another human being. And for the first time, they were able to share all the excitement and the fear of it.

If Hannah had arrived at the hospital a couple of minutes earlier that particular afternoon, she might have been in time to see two old ladies getting into the lift that went up to the Coronary Care Unit. And if she had listened outside the cubicle, she might have heard an interesting conversation.

'Ten minutes, ladies,' decreed the sister sternly. 'Miss Fabian is still very weak, you know.'

'There's nothing weak about her,' sniffed Mrs De'Ath. 'As tough as old boots, aren't you, Clarice?'

The wan figure in the bed opened its eyes and flicked them

270

from one old lady to the other. 'What are you doing here?' it demanded indignantly.

'Well if that's your attitude, we'll go,' said Mrs Lorrimer.

Mrs De'Ath swiped her with a glove. 'Don't talk nonsense, we're here because we said we'd do a job and we'll do it.'

'What job?' Miss Fabian struggled to sit upright, and the heart monitor gave a protesting 'peep'. Mrs De'Ath promptly pushed her back onto her pillows.

'Lie still, you daft old goose!' she commanded. 'Or do you want to drop dead with your hair looking like that? I mean, honestly, what a sight you'd look in your coffin.'

'It's not my fault if I took ill when they were doing my hair,' protested Miss Fabian.

'Nonsense, Clarice, it's absolutely typical of you – you never could organise yourself sensibly. Take that dog of yours.'

A look of alarm entered Miss Fabian's eyes. 'Bertie? What about him? What have you done to my Bertie?'

Mrs Lorrimer gave a long-suffering sigh. 'Killed him, skinned him and turned him into a very small hearthrug. What do you think we've done with him?'

'Where is he?'

'In my back kitchen, gnawing an enormous marrowbone I got him from the butcher's this morning.'

'But Bertie doesn't have bones! Not unless they're cooked. You did roast it properly, didn't you? He might get food poisoning, or—'

Mrs De'Ath leaned forward and put a hand over Clarice's mouth. 'For pity's sake Clarice, he's a dog, not a baby. Dogs lick their own bottoms, they couldn't care less about a few germs one way or the other. Oh, and we've been taking him for walks as well.'

'Long walks,' added Mrs Lorrimer.

Clarice looked even paler. 'You've been torturing my Bertie! My poor little Bertie, he's only got tiny little legs.'

'They won't look quite so tiny once he's lost a few rolls of fat from round his belly,' replied Mrs De'Ath. 'Now, apart from that, we've tidied up your window boxes and watered your plants, oh, and I washed the kitchen floor because it looked like it hadn't been done since VE Day. So everything will be quite in order when they send you home.'

Miss Fabian looked positively dazed. 'I don't understand,' she said. 'Why are you doing all this for me?'

'Because it needs doing,' replied Mrs De'Ath. 'And because, let's face it, nobody else is going to, are they?'

Miss Fabian looked sullen. 'I would have managed,' she said.

'No you wouldn't. Any more than we would have managed if we'd been ill, seeing as my no-good son and her useless daughter never even bother to visit us any more. And by the way,' Mrs De'Ath went on, 'for the last time let us make one thing clear: we did *not* kidnap your precious Bertie, and the less time we have to spend in his flatulent presence, the better.'

'Oh,' said Miss Fabian. 'Well, if you put it that way.'

'We do. And as for all that money you won, as far as we're concerned you can do what you like with it.'

'Really?'

'Really. All this wrangling is making my gastritis play up. So do you think there's any chance we could get back to talking to each other like civilised human beings?'

That evening, Grandad sat outside Maxine's hospital room with Hannah while Lottie went in to see the baby.

'Children,' mused Hannah as the door closed behind Lottie. 'They grow up so fast. You know, it hardly seems five minutes since I first held her in my arms and thought, "Help! What do I do with this?"'

'And you're still thinking the same thing now?' ventured Herbie.

'Too right I am. It's like, nobody can really tell you what to do because it's completely different for every parent and every child. Maxine's going to find that out pretty soon too, I guess.'

'Actually,' said Herbie, 'I've been meaning to have a word with you. About Lottie.'

Hannah felt the habitual pang of worry. 'She's not in some kind of trouble again, is she?'

'No,' replied Herbie. 'At least, not the kind of trouble you're thinking of. But I know you've noticed how quiet she's been over the last couple of days. Now I think I know why.' His expression darkened. 'It's all to do with Danny.'

'Oh Gramps,' protested Hannah, 'I know you don't like him much, but you can't blame him for everything.'

Herbie silenced her with a look. 'And you can't keep defending him every time he does something you know is stupid or wrong. Especially when it involves Lottie. Can you?'

She felt distinctly uncomfortable under Herbie's critical gaze. More than anyone, he seemed to have the ability to see right through to the very heart of her. He was right; when it came to Lottie's welfare, quite simply nobody and nothing else mattered.

'OK, what's he done now?' she asked.

'You know the other night, when you were supposed to be going for a drink with Nick?'

'The night Maxine had her baby, yes. What about it?'

'Danny promised to pick up Lottie from her dance practice, didn't he?'

Hannah frowned, puzzled. 'He *did* pick her up. She was there when I got home from the hospital.'

'Yes,' conceded Grandad, 'he did pick her up. Eventually. But only after she'd been standing in the dark, on her own, for the best part of an hour. He got "held up", apparently – somebody's stag do at a wine bar in Cirencester.'

'What!' Hannah's blood turned to ice. 'How do you know that? It can't be right, Lottie would've told me!'

Herbie ran a hand through what remained of his hair. 'No, Sprout, you were the last person she'd tell. She really loves her mum, does Lottie. She wants you to be happy. So she'd do anything to avoid upsetting you.'

'I just don't understand.' She was torn between fear, anger and resentment. 'How come you know all about it?'

'Oh, I think I just happened to be around at the right time. She was desperate to tell someone, but Danny made her promise not to, you see.'

'No!' gasped Hannah. 'He wouldn't do that!'

But she knew, in her heart, that he would.

'Bribed her by telling her he'd buy her that new mobile phone she's been after if she kept her mouth shut about it.' There was real contempt in Herbie's voice. 'But we were talking yesterday, and I asked her why she was so sad, and it all just spilled out.'

'Oh my God.' Hannah slumped back onto her chair. She was shaking. Eyes closed, all she could see was the image of poor little Lottie, alone and afraid and in danger, standing in the darkness waiting for Danny to come.

And that, she just could not forgive.

Danny could tell from the look on Hannah's face that she knew.

'Look, I didn't mean to,' he said, getting up off the sofa. 'I think the world of Lottie, you know that.'

That was like a red rag to a bull. 'Oh yes! You really care about her, don't you? So much that you left her standing on that road in the dark, on her own, where God only knows what might have happened to her!'

'But it didn't,' he pointed out. 'Anyway, she's a sensible girl, grown up for her age.'

'She's nine years old, Danny! And you had sole responsibility for her – just one little girl who needed you – but you couldn't be bothered, could you?'

They stood there in the middle of the living room, Hannah so angry and upset she could hardly get the words out, Danny defensive and sullen.

'It wasn't like that,' he protested.

'Oh really. So what was it like?'

'You know how it is – one thing leads to another, you lose track of the time.'

'And in the meantime, a nine-year-old girl is in danger. You make me sick, Danny. You can't even admit it was your fault and apologise properly; all you do is make pathetic excuses.'

'I'm sorry, all right?'

A cold clarity descended upon her. 'No, it isn't all right. It isn't all right at all.'

'For Christ's sake, Hannah, what do you want me to do, stick my head in the gas oven?'

'No,' she replied, looking him straight in the eye. 'What I want you to do is pack up your things and leave.'

He blinked. 'Pardon?'

'You heard, Danny. This just isn't working any more. I can't trust you to look after Lottie, and that means I can't trust you, full stop.'

She wasn't sure how she expected him to react, but it certainly wasn't with an unconcerned shrug of the shoulders. 'OK, whatever. Soon as I find myself another place, I'll move out.'

Her mouth was dry, her pulse racing. 'Right. As long as you understand that.'

'Well, it's not as if it was going to last forever between us, is it?' Danny went on, settling back down on the sofa as if nothing had happened.

'It isn't?'

He laughed. 'Of course not. I mean, you're older than I am for a start-off, and you've got a kid. And I'm hardly settling-down material, am I? We've had some fun though, eh?'

She sank into an armchair before she fell down, dizzy and angry and feeling as if the ground was dissolving beneath her feet. 'Fun,' she repeated flatly. 'That was all it was then? Just fun?'

'Sure. Nothing serious or anything – face it, you've had enough of serious to last you a lifetime. God knows how you put up with Nick for all that time, it must've been hell. And I'm not up for anything heavy; after all, once I'm thirty I'll come into the rest of my inheritance and then I can really start living.'

Hannah stared at him. 'What inheritance?'

'From my great-uncle, the sausage tycoon. Didn't I mention it? Nice big fat sum of money, trouble is for some reason he didn't seem to think I'd be mature enough to handle it before I was thirty. So I've been kicking my heels for the last few years, waiting until my ship comes in.'

The awful realisation of what he was saying hit her full in the guts. 'So I . . . we . . . this was just a stopgap then?'

Danny clearly didn't hear the anger in her voice or, if he did, it didn't trouble him. 'Yeah, if you like. Nice way of filling in time though. I've enjoyed my time with you, Han. Oh – and the kid, when she wasn't whingeing about something and nothing.'

The mention of Lottie turned the spark back into a flame. A cold, furious flame of controlled hatred.

'Listen to me, do you hear?' Her voice quavered with emotion. 'Just you stay away from me and my daughter, or . . . or . . . I don't know exactly what, but it'll definitely be something very, very bad. Now, get up those stairs and start packing. You've got until Sunday to move out.'

Chapter 29

Spring melded into a long, hot summer, so dreamlike that some days when she looked around the house, Hannah could scarcely believe she had ever shared it with Danny.

He might still be an investor in Split Ends, but not for much longer; only until Jay had raised the money to buy him out. It might leave the salon short of capital, but at least they wouldn't be beholden any longer to an irresponsible idiot who kept his brain in his trousers. That at least was what Jay thought about it all, but then Jay had hated Danny from the moment he set eyes on him.

Maybe I'm exceptionally stupid, pondered Hannah one day as she sat in the conservatory watching Lottie careering round the back garden with the ferrets and Doom wobbling in their wake. After all, practically everybody else had advised her to be careful not to fall head over heels for Danny on the rebound, but it had taken that horrible incident with Lottie to make her see that the flipside of carefree and fun was shallow and irresponsible.

A stopgap, she thought to herself; and it still stung. That's what he called me. All the time I thought he was serious about our relationship, he didn't even see it as a relationship at all.

'Penny for them, dear,' said her mother, bringing out two glasses of home-made lemonade.

Hannah started. 'Sorry?'

'You looked deep in thought. Something bothering you?'

'Oh, no. Not really.'

'You're not still moping about that Danny are you?' Eric looked concerned rather than critical. 'I know it hit you hard, him moving out.'

Hannah had been careful not to tell Erica the real reason why Danny had left. She had no particular desire to have her father go round to Danny's new place and try to beat him to a pulp. Particularly as Danny was twice his size and half his age.

'No, I'm fine. Just a bit tired – we've been really busy at the salon this month, what with all the bikini waxes, slimming wraps and tanning treatments. Everybody wants to look good on the beach.'

'Hmm.' Erica sat down on the other end of the rattan settee and took a sip from her glass. 'And what about you? Are you and Lottie going to head for the beach before the summer's over?'

'Oh . . . I don't think we'll bother.'

'You need a rest, you know. Both of you.'

'Lottie's had a good summer,' protested Hannah. 'She enjoyed that week at the adventure camp much more than she thought she would, and she went camping with Nick in the Lakes.'

'But what about you?' Erica looked at her sternly over the top of her lemonade glass. 'Even the strongest elastic snaps in the end if you stretch it too tightly, you know.'

Hannah had never seen herself as a length of elastic before, but she had to admit a certain aptness in the metaphor. There were days when she felt on top of everything – but rather more when she felt spread thinner than the butter on a dieter's round of toast; worn down by the sheer isolation of being a mother, and a businesswoman; and alone.

'Oh, I might get away for a weekend sometime,' she hedged. 'Maybe when Maxine's baby's older she and I will go on a city-break or something.'

Erica was plainly unconvinced. 'Hannah love, the way Maxine's going little Gemma will be doing her A levels before her mother's relaxed enough to leave her for a whole weekend. You should know what it's like being a new mum,' she reminded Hannah. 'So much to learn, and most of the time having to work it out as you go along.'

'I know, but she's doing a good job.'

'Of course she is. She's just convinced she isn't, like all young mums are. Every time Gemma cries Maxine thinks she's ill, and when she doesn't she thinks she's stopped breathing. So if I were you I wouldn't wait for Maxine, I'd get up and go while you can.'

'Well . . . maybe.'

'Wasn't Lottie talking about wanting to go to Disneyland Paris? I'm sure your father and I could take care of the animals for a week if you wanted to take her there.'

Hannah smiled at the thought of Erica and Derek struggling to regain control if things went wrong and anything escaped. She could just see her father pursuing a runaway ferret down Foley Road, trying to bring it to justice with his old handcuffs and police whistle.

'It's OK, Mum,' she assured Erica, 'if I want to go away Nick says he'll sort the animals out. He's used to it.'

Erica pursed her lips, looked as though she was about to say something, then didn't. Out in the garden, Lottie was giggling for all she was worth, chasing Doom round in circles while the ferrets whooshed in and out of a network of old drainpipes Nick had laid out for them on the lawn.

A couple of minutes later, Erica said: 'Nick's gone very furtive lately.'

Hannah wrinkled her nose. 'Furtive?'

'Whenever I see him, he seems to be in a hurry to get somewhere else, as if he's afraid I might give him the third degree. And don't say I'm imagining it,' Erica added, with a wagging finger. 'I've known that young man a long time. He's definitely hiding something.'

Shall I tell her? pondered Hannah. She'll have to know sooner or later. Sooner in fact, seeing as Miranda's baby was more or less imminent. She took a deep breath. 'Miranda's having a baby,' she said calmly; then waited for the storm.

'A baby?' Erica frowned. 'When?'

'In a few weeks' time.'

Erica's eyes widened as her brain did the calculations. 'You mean she's having *Nick's* baby?'

'Well . . . yes. Possibly.'

'What do you mean, possibly?'

'The thing is,' Hannah explained slowly, 'Miranda wasn't exactly faithful to Nick, and he found out. That's the main reason they split up. I don't think even she knows if the baby's his or not. Anyway, now she says she doesn't want the baby and she's going to have it adopted.'

Erica could not have looked more disgusted. 'How could he let himself get involved with a woman like that? And what about poor Charlotte, she must be so unhappy!'

278

'Actually,' Hannah admitted rather ruefully, 'the only time she's brought up the subject since we told her was when she asked if she could come and watch the birth, seeing as she'd missed out on the ferrets being born – and Maxine's baby. I'm afraid her interest's mainly biological.'

'Only on the surface, dear, only on the surface.' Erica tutted. 'You know, I bet that Miranda woman's out to get every penny she can from Nick. I take it he'll be insisting on a DNA test as soon as the poor thing is born?'

'There's no point,' replied Hannah, feeling curiously proud as she said it. 'Nick says he doesn't want to know; he's willing to take on the baby as his own, no matter what. Assuming Miranda doesn't change her mind, of course.'

Shell-shocked, Erica downed her entire glass of lemonade in a single gulp. 'Nick, bring up some other man's baby – on his own? And while he's trying to do a full-time job at the same time?'

'Obviously he'll need help with childcare and—'

'Hannah dear,' Erica said with concern. 'I hope he's not expecting you to get involved in this crackpot scheme in any way?'

'No, not at all,' answered Hannah. 'But it's not a crackpot scheme; I think it's a wonderful thing he's doing.

'And if he did ask me to help, well, why on earth shouldn't I say yes?'

In the end, it wasn't the momentous event it had threatened to be. It all came down to a brief phone call one late August morning.

'Nick? It's me.'

'Miranda – how are you?'

'As if you cared. Listen, the obstetrician says my blood pressure's too high, so he's booking me in for an elective Caesarian at the Regency Clinic tomorrow afternoon.'

Butterflies took flight in Nick's stomach. 'Tomorrow!'

'You can be there if you want, or not, it's up to you. I take it you still want your name on the birth certificate?'

'Of course I do, I—'

'Because if you don't want to go through with this, I'm going to hand it over for adoption straight away. The sooner I can put this horrible experience behind me, the better.'

'Don't do that! I told you, whatever needs to be done, I'll do it. I'll be there.'

'Fine. See you tomorrow then. 'Bye.'

It wasn't anything like Nick had imagined.

On the TV, in books, in films, giving birth was the most incredibly emotional experience: the culmination of nine months of excitement and longing. But Miranda just marched into theatre as if she was going into the dentist's surgery to have a troublesome tooth taken out.

'How long will it take?' she asked as the epidural took hold.

'Hardly any time at all once we've opened you up. And then we'll clean your baby up all spick and span and you can hold it. Are you having a boy or a girl?' the kindly Caribbean nurse asked Nick.

'I don't know,' admitted Nick, profoundly uncomfortable in his role as birthing partner, and grateful for the surgical mask that covered most of his face.

'Didn't want to know, eh? Keep it a surprise?'

'Not interested,' replied Miranda, flat on her back on the table. 'After all, I'm not keeping it.' She nodded at Nick. 'He is.

'Now, can we get this over with?' she demanded, ignoring the raised eyebrows. 'Only I'd like to have my body back, if it's all the same to you.'

A couple of evenings later, Hannah and Nick were sharing a glass of wine at the house in Foley Road, while little baby George Steadman slumbered away a touch of jaundice in his incubator at the General.

'Go on,' said Hannah softly, topping up Nick's wine glass. 'I'm listening.'

The tears were trickling down his cheeks, his fingernails digging into the arm of Hannah's sofa. The only other time she'd seen him cry like this was when Lottie was a tiny baby and she'd caught meningitis; and for one very dark night the doctors had warned them they might lose her. This, however, was a different kind of raw emotion.

His hand shook as he picked up the glass and took a drink. 'Then the baby was delivered, and it was the most beautiful little boy I'd ever seen. With these huge blue eyes, and this incredibly silky, flaxen hair.'

Hannah swallowed hard, imagining that moment; remembering back to the night she'd delivered Lottie, clutching on tight to her mother's hand and screaming curses at the absent father of her child. Wondering how it might have been if she, and not Miranda, had given birth to this new child.

Her silence made Nick look up. 'Oh God, Hannah, I'm sorry. The last thing you want to hear is me going on about Miranda's baby.'

Hannah shook her head. 'No, it's OK, I want to hear all about it. It's just a bit strange, that's all.' Almost as strange as it had been telling Lottie she had a new sort-of half-brother, and being greeted with an uninterested shrug of the shoulders. She gave his arm a squeeze and told herself to be grown-up. 'Go on, I'm listening.'

Nick took a deep breath. 'Well ... the nurse put him into my arms and I just couldn't stop laughing and crying like a complete idiot. I turned to Miranda, and I said, "Look Miranda, it's a boy! Don't you want to hold him?" But she just turned her head away and said, "I'm tired. He's yours now, you hold him." Can you believe that?'

'It's hard to,' Hannah admitted. 'But giving birth does strange things to women; when she's had time to think she might still come round and decide she wants to keep him.'

Nick shook his head. 'No. I don't think so, Han. Afterwards, when I went to visit her in her room, she was different; quieter, not so hard somehow. It was as if she was letting me have a final glimpse of what she was really feeling inside.

'"There are three things I can't let myself do, Nick," she said. "Fall in love, eat too much pasta, and change my mind. At least if I can keep to this one decision that'll make one out of three." Not too impressive, huh?'

'I said, "What's so bad about changing your mind?" but she wouldn't answer. She just said, "I know you think I'm a hard-faced bitch, Nick, but please remember one thing when I've sold up and gone back to London, and you're bringing up that little baby." And I swear there were tears in her eyes, the only ones I've ever see her cry.

'"Remember that I cared enough to give him to someone who would truly love him."'

*

281

Maxine loved baby Gemma with a ferocious, mother-tiger love that sometimes kept even Jay at arm's length.

She could never have imagined feeling anything so overwhelmingly strong if it had not actually happened to her. Many a time, Hannah had told her about the primal, protective surge that flooded over her the first time she took Lottie in her arms, and intellectually she had understood it. But never, until now, had she truly felt it; and sometimes it frightened her every bit as much as it filled her with joy and wonder. I'm not the person I used to be, she thought to herself. I really don't know myself any more.

As she sat in a shady part of the garden, watching Gemma sleep under a little lacy white parasol, she wondered how life could ever be the same again, and, more to the point, how work could ever take up as much of her energy and her thoughts as it had done before.

It wasn't that she didn't want to go back to the salon – though Hannah, Philomena, Claire and Raymond were doing a perfectly good job of keeping it ticking over. No, she loved her work and it was still important to her. It was just that if she did, it would be like betraying Gemma; like implying that there could be something else in her life remotely as important to Maxine as she was.

Besides, how could she bear to be parted from her baby, even for a matter of hours, when she'd only had her a few short weeks and they were still just getting to know each other?

There was the matter of ambition, of course; but even that didn't hold water. With Danny's money gone and Jay's enthusiasm distinctly lukewarm, little or no prospect remained of expanding the salon. And since it was doing perfectly well without her, and Jay was bringing in enough from the shopfitting business to keep all three of them, she had to admit he was right.

There really was nothing to stop her just staying at home and being a full-time mum. Of course, she hadn't quite made up her mind yet that that was where her immediate future lay, but the thought was always nagging at the back of her mind. She knew it was what Jay had been wanting all along.

The question was, if she decided it was what she wanted too, how was she going to break the news to Hannah? And what was to become of Split Ends?

Chapter 30

Maybe there was something in the air, or maybe it was just the season; at any rate, that year the first week of September seemed to signal even more new beginnings than usual.

'Delbert Mackenzie!' bellowed Nick at a diminutive, running figure in a dishevelled blazer and lopsided tie.

The figure skidded to a halt. 'Yes sir, what sir?'

'Don't give me that, you know what. No running in the corridors, and while you're at it I'll have that iPod – you can get it back at the end of the day.'

'Aw, sir, but—'

'Now. Or I'll confiscate it till the end of term. You know they're not allowed in school.'

Caught up in a never-ending cycle of round-the-clock baby feeding, Nick was more exhausted than he had ever believed possible, day nanny or not; but there was a definite hint of purpose in his step as he walked back down the corridors of Alderman Braithwaite Comprehensive. I'm coming home, he thought as he headed for the staffroom; doing what I'm meant to be doing – and this time I'm going to do it right, because this time, I know whom I'm doing it for.

'Sir,' said the boy as his iPod disappeared into Nick's pocket.

'What is it now?'

Delbert's urchin face split into a cheeky grin. 'Welcome back, sir.'

'Well,' said Mrs De'Ath with definite satisfaction, 'it's been a while since we did this, ladies.'

She was standing outside Split Ends with Mrs Lorrimer and

Miss Fabian, admiring the pictures of the latest styles displayed in the window.

'I think you should try that one, dear,' tittered Mrs Lorrimer, pointing to an outlandish competition-winning creation made up of a sort of basket-weave of blue hair extensions. 'It's very you.'

'Sometimes I worry about you, Nancy,' replied Mrs De'Ath witheringly, 'I really do.' But underneath the dour exterior she too was feeling a little bit silly, flirtatious even, as if she'd had a touch too much laughing gas at the dentist's.

Miss Fabian didn't bother trying to be dour or dignified. She was too busy beaming all over her face – which was no longer putty grey, but a nice healthy pink that matched Bertie's lolling tongue. After a strict fitness regime of long walks and proper food, they both looked positively rejuvenated.

'Come along, girls,' Clarice chivvied, her cheeks dimpling like a teenager's. 'We don't want to be late for our appointment, do we? Claire's put one of those lovely violet tints on one side for me, specially.'

And she pushed open the salon door and they marched right in: the Magnificent Three and a Half.

Claudette was so pleased to see Nick back that she even lent him her second-best coffee mug.

'Eet ees only for today, zough,' she cautioned. 'Tomorrow you breeng your own, *oui*?'

'And two pound fifty for the tea and coffee fund,' chimed in Mark, rattling the tin under Nick's nose.

'I reckon it ought to be double, now he's the big boss man,' declared Geoff, only half in jest. 'And he should buy chocolate biscuits all round, to celebrate being a new dad.'

'Watch it,' grinned Nick. 'Remember, I have the power to inflict 4C on you on a Friday afternoon.'

Everybody grimaced and made the sign of the cross. 'Oh God, I'd forgotten 3C had grown into 4C,' groaned Geoff. 'They're not even little buggers any more, they're turning into great big ones.'

'The way I see it,' advanced Mark, chewing on a toffee, 'we're supposed to be scientists, aren't we? Couldn't we arrange an unfortunate accident with an experimental death-ray or something? Nip 4C in the bud before they escape into the community and breed?'

'I think the school inspectors take a dim view of death-rays,' lamented Geoff. 'Downright unreasonable, I call it.' He eyed a lone figure on the other side of the staffroom. 'Now there's a man who could use a death-ray if anybody could.'

Harry Turnbull was looking more downtrodden and careworn than ever. Mind you, thought Nick, the man must have real grit and determination to have lasted a whole, ghastly year without actually letting the kids drive him over the edge. Nick really felt for him; it must be utterly miserable being a figure of fun, particularly when you were easily the smartest scientist in the school. But try telling that to a bunch of cocky kids who'd worked out that your disciplinary skills were nil.

'He's not getting on any better in the classroom then?' Nick enquired.

'Put it this way,' replied Mark, 'on the last day of the summer term, the second years tied him up and locked him in the greenhouse.'

Nick rubbed his chin. It wasn't as if he was short of things that needed sorting out, but he couldn't help thinking that some were more deserving than others. 'Got to do something about Harry,' he murmured. 'Poor old bastard.'

The question was: what?

Herbie looked furtively to right and left, pulled his collar up, and slunk across the road. If anybody he knew saw him here, any small remnant of street credibility would be right out the window.

Still, after that narrow shave with the police he'd promised Hannah he'd make a fresh start; and as Erica had so pointedly remarked, you couldn't make a fresh start without a decent haircut.

Mind you, he really didn't see why he couldn't just visit that cheap barber's behind the Lower High Street. He'd never been in a place like this before; nor had he wanted to. He had a horrible suspicion that he would emerge in half an hour's time looking – and smelling – like a perfumed ponce.

Gathering up all his failing courage, he pushed open the door and stepped inside.

'So how are you getting on with Damon?' enquired Gloria as Philomena snipped away at her hair.

Philomena reddened slightly. She still hadn't quite got over her guilt at stealing Gloria's man, despite the fact that Gloria seemed to have put the whole thing behind her. Nor had her old-fashioned Catholic sensibilities entirely adjusted themselves to Living In Sin.

'Well ... all right I suppose,' she said.

'Better than being with Bernard though?'

'*Anything*'s better than being with Bernard.'

'But?' hinted Gloria, clearly expecting more.

Philomena lowered her scissors. 'Do all men have annoying habits?' she asked.

'Mostly,' laughed Gloria, 'only you don't tend to notice them until the novelty's worn off the relationship. What sort of annoying habits?' she enquired, clearly intrigued.

'Believe me, you don't want to know.'

'Phil darling, I probably already do. I was with him for months, remember. It's not that thing with his toenails, is it?'

She didn't get a chance to find out, because just then the door of the salon opened and in walked an elderly man in a shiny suit, looking about as out of place as anybody possibly could.

Sitting side by side under the dryers, the three old ladies turned interested eyes on the new arrival.

'Ooh look – a man,' enthused Mrs Lorrimer, like a tourist on safari spotting an elephant.

'Well, sort of,' commented Mrs De'Ath. 'Not exactly a prime specimen, dear.'

Clarice didn't say anything. Her gaze had locked with Herbie's, and she was blushing like a sixteen-year-old.

Claire came forward to put the poor old chap out of his misery. 'Hello, you must be Mr Flowers.'

Herbie looked profoundly relieved. He took off his cap and fiddled with it. 'Hannah's granddad, that's right. I phoned up earlier ... about a haircut?' He looked around him doubtfully, then his gaze drifted back to Clarice Fabian. She wasn't a bad looker for her age. Quite nicely preserved. 'But er ... if you don't do men ...'

He wasn't escaping that easily. Claire guided him skilfully across to a chair in the waiting area. 'Of course we do, Mr Flowers. Don't you worry, we'll take good care of you. Won't we, ladies?'

Clarice Fabian beamed and thought, oh yes.

All summer, Harry Turnbull had been telling himself that this school year would be different: a whole new start. This time he would *not* let the kids intimidate him, or play him up, or just plain ignore him, the way most of them had last time round.

It wasn't so bad with the senior students – the ones who really wanted to learn. At least some of them seemed to appreciate his knowledge and experience. But when it came to a class of little thugs like this one . . .

He swallowed hard, straightened his tie and reminded himself of all the prestigious research projects he'd seen through to a successful conclusion. Surely a man who had discovered his very own molecule ought to be able to get the better of the subhuman species that was 4C?

Maybe he ought; but Harry still didn't believe a word of his own pep talk as he pushed open the door of the lab and went inside. Instinctively he flinched, waiting for the inevitable rain of missiles; but to his astonishment it never came. Even more peculiarly, the kids were all sitting down at the workbenches, not screeching at each other and rampaging around the place like they always did.

He filled his lungs with air, ready to yell a pointless 'Quiet please'; but as he opened his mouth, the lab fell completely silent.

Harry instantly felt more insecure than ever. What was this – some cruel new ploy to trick him into thinking he was in control, then turn the tables and humiliate him yet again? But what could he do? He had to play along with it.

'Morning, 4C,' he ventured.

'Morning, Mr Turnbull.' Two rows of attentive faces gazed back at him.

'Gather round. We're going to do a dissection today. Reproductive organs of the insect.'

This, he calculated, would be the moment when everything fell apart. Actually inviting them to stand up and move around was asking for a riot. And as for mentioning reproductive organs in a mixed class like this one . . . But – to his astonishment – they got up almost like civilised beings, and meekly gathered round his bench as if they were genuinely interested in what he had to offer.

A few of the girls went 'Ewww' when he got a pair of forceps and took the specimen out of the jar, but you could hardly blame them. To be frank he felt rather nauseous himself. He'd never been much of a pickled cockroach man, and this was a particularly vile-smelling one.

Rather disturbingly though, he was beginning to feel like the object of study himself. When he looked up from the dissection table, he saw that all eyes were on him, not the cockroach. What have I done now? he wondered. Has someone stuck a label on my head when I wasn't looking? It was all most unnerving.

Nervously he cleared his throat. 'Right. Yes. Well. Watch carefully, class, I'm going to open up the abdomen.'

He lifted up the shiny, surgical steel scalpel and, as he did so, every single member of the class took a step back – so suddenly that a couple of the smaller boys at the back tripped and fell over.

Yes, it was all unaccountably weird. But the very weirdest thing of all was the look Harry caught in the kids' eyes. If it hadn't been a ridiculous idea, he'd have sworn they were actually scared of him.

Hannah put her hand to her mouth as half a crisp went down the wrong way, and laughter turned into a coughing fit.

'No . . . you didn't!' she gasped between spasms.

Nick patted her on the back. Lottie was at her after-school drama club, little baby George was with his day nanny, and Nick and Hannah were having a quick after-work drink before going their separate ways. Funny, it was turning into something of a routine – a several-times-a-week ritual that both of them secretly looked forward to.

'Let's just say rumour's a wonderful thing,' he replied. 'It's amazing how quickly you can get an entire school to believe something if you tell it in confidence to the right people.'

Hannah took a sip of white wine spritzer to wash down a recalcitrant fragment of crisp. 'It must have been some rumour!' she commented. 'I mean, it takes a lot to impress a cynical bunch like 4C. Whatever did you tell them about Harry?'

Nick leaned closer, as though confiding a great secret. 'Oh, just a few things about his distinguished war record in the Falklands,' he said casually. 'With the Special Forces of course.'

'The Falklands!' spluttered Hannah. 'When did Harry Turnbull ever go to the Falklands?'

'How do you know he didn't?' retorted Nick. 'And of course I
might just have mentioned how he can snap a man's neck with
one hand . . . or something of the sort. And how dangerous he can
be if anybody makes him angry.'

'Nick Steadman, I just don't believe I'm hearing this!'
Hannah was definitely starting to see Nick in a new light.
However much he might have sympathised with Harry in the
past, the old strait-laced Nick would never have dreamed of fab-
ricating an entire alternative life history for his benefit.
Whatever happened to "science means the facts and nothing
but the facts"?'

'Ah well, there are facts and there are facts,' said Nick with a
wink. 'And as every good scientist knows, everything is relative.'

'All right then,' declared Hannah, sitting back with folded
arms. 'Here's some facts you'll never believe. You know our
three old ladies down at the salon?'

'The bingo lady and her two sidekicks? Are they still at each
other's throats?'

'They were until Miss Fabian had her heart attack, but now
they've made it all up and they're thick as thieves again. Anyhow, they came into the salon today and asked to speak to me,
and do you know what they said?'

Nick pondered for a moment. 'They've been offered half a
million quid to pose nude for a *Playboy* centrefold?'

The sheer ghastliness of the thought made Hannah feel quite
nauseous. 'No, even more unlikely than that. They heard that
Maxine and I wanted to expand Split Ends, but didn't have the
capital to do it, and they've offered to use some of Miss Fabian's
bingo winnings to invest in the salon!'

'Blimey,' said Nick, 'that's a stroke of luck. Maxine must be
over the moon.'

'That's what I thought,' agreed Hannah, 'but it's really odd.
When I rang her and told her about it, it was like she couldn't
wait to get off the phone and get rid of me.'

'So you think there's something wrong?'

Hannah flicked half-heartedly at a beer mat. 'I don't know. It
felt as if there was, only now I'm beginning to wonder if I was

imagining it.' She looked up at Nick. 'We're best mates, Nick. Wouldn't she tell me if there was something I should know?'

Erica was just about to dish up a nice lamb casserole when the doorbell rang three times, in swift succession.

'Somebody's in a hurry,' commented Derek, discarding his napkin and hauling himself up out of his chair. 'We're not expecting anyone, are we?'

He turned his gaze on Herbie, as if to add silently, 'The police for example?'

'You sit down and eat your dinner, dear, I'll get it,' said Erica, taking off her apron and glancing in the mirror above the fire place to make sure that there weren't any gravy-smears on her nose. The bell rang again, even more insistently. 'All right, all right, I'm coming!'

Naturally the door stuck (it always did after it had rained), and when she finally did manage to get it open the young man on the doorstep snapped, 'You took your time! Were you planning to leave me standing here all night?'

Erica was about to point out that it was right in the middle of dinnertime and that politeness cost nothing, when she suddenly realised who the stranger was. It was perhaps hardly surprising that she hadn't recognised him straight away: not with a daft hair cut that made him look like thirty-five striving desperately to be fifteen. But as soon as he opened his mouth, she knew him by his voice.

She clapped a hand over her mouth. 'Rhys!'

'Yes, Rhys,' said the visitor sarcastically. 'Who were you expecting – King Kong?'

'I . . .' Erica felt distinctly light-headed. She retreated a couple of steps up the hallway and squeaked, 'Derek – it's Rhys!'

Rhys pursued her into the hall and slammed the door shut behind him. He waved a typewritten letter in front of her face and she recognised her signature and Derek's at the bottom.

'Now,' he said angrily, 'perhaps you'd like to tell me what the hell you think you're doing, sending me threatening letters?'

Chapter 31

First thing the very next morning, Hannah rescheduled a couple of appointments and headed round to Maxine's house.

The side gate was standing open, so she went straight through into the garden. As she'd expected, she found Maxine sitting out in the September sunshine, baby Gemma fast asleep in her arms.

'Hello stranger,' said Hannah with a smile, kissing a fingertip and lightly touching the baby's face. 'And that goes for you too,' she added with a reproachful look at Maxine. 'I haven't seen you in ages – are you avoiding me or something?'

'Of course not,' said Maxine, but she looked uncomfortable. 'Do you want a coffee?'

'It's OK, don't get up, I'll make it myself.'

Hannah returned a couple of minutes later with two instant coffees and some biscuits she'd found on top of the bread-bin.

'Those are a bit soggy,' apologised Maxine. 'Sorry, I haven't had a chance to get out and buy some more. I seem to spend all my time here with this little one.' She gazed into her baby's face and Hannah saw that the love affair between them was more passionate than ever.

'No worries, Max, I eat far too many biscuits as it is.' Hannah stretched herself out on the bench that stood on the other side of the little white cast-iron table. 'But hey, you must get out of the house sometimes. Staying in all the time can't be good for you.'

'It's not about me,' replied Maxine. 'It's about Gemma. I can't bear to leave her, you see. Not even with Jay unless there's absolutely no alternative. Does that sound silly?'

'Not silly exactly.' Hannah hunted around for words that were tactful but honest. 'A bit overprotective, maybe. You'll have to leave her sometime, after all.'

'Not yet though,' whispered Maxine. 'Not just yet.'

'All right then,' suggested Hannah, 'let's all three of us go out together one day. The trip out'll do you both good. We could take a picnic. Or go to the wildlife park or something.'

Maxine looked alarmed. 'What – take Gemma out for the whole day? Would she be all right? Wouldn't the car make her ill?' She stopped and thought for a moment. 'Oh God, Han, I sound a bit mental, don't I?'

'You're just worrying too much, that's all,' said Hannah. 'Everybody does when they have their first baby. Well, nearly everybody – except the ones who don't give a toss, or haven't got the imagination to think anything might go wrong. It's only natural.'

'Really?'

'Really. For the first few weeks I checked on Lottie every five minutes. For some reason I was worried sick she'd stop breathing. But that fear gradually went away. Like I said, it's natural to worry,' she went on. 'You just don't want it to end up ruling your life.'

'No. I know you're right.' Maxine gently stroked Gemma's tiny pink fingers. 'But so's Jay, when he says this baby's the most precious thing in the whole world and we have to do everything we can to keep her safe.'

'Of course he is,' Hannah nodded. 'But I'm sure he doesn't want you cutting yourself off from everything.' Or at least I hope he doesn't, she mused. Jay had, after all, been displaying the odd prehistoric tendency lately. She picked up a very bendy malted milk biscuit, thought what the hell, and dunked it in her coffee. 'So – what do you think about our old ladies then? Offering to invest all that money in the salon?'

'Oh, Hannah.' Maxine looked positively unhappy now. 'I'm sorry, you must really think I'm messing you around, but I just don't know.'

'Don't know what, exactly?'

'How I feel about it. About anything. My head's all confused.'

'All right then, what does Jay think about it?' Hannah hardly needed to hear Maxine's answer: she'd always been able to read her friend's expressions. 'Oh Max, you have told him, haven't you?'

'Not yet,' she admitted. 'I'm a bit ... well ... afraid to.'

'Now that *is* silly!' exclaimed Hannah, through a mouthful of soggy biscuit. 'How can you be afraid of talking to your own husband?'

'Not afraid, exactly. Just a bit apprehensive.'

The reason wasn't hard to guess. 'You mean, you think he won't take it well?'

'Maybe. I don't really know.'

Hannah felt a strong urge to scream in utter frustration. 'Look, I know Jay wasn't keen on expanding Split Ends before, but this is different, surely? Danny's not involved any more, and our old ladies aren't interested in meddling in the business. I think it's just a bit of an adventure for them.' She leaned forward, her own enthusiasm getting the better of her. 'It would be an adventure for us, too.'

'I know.' Maxine stroked Gemma's cheek. 'But I don't know if this is the right time for me to be thinking about having adventures.'

'You mean Jay doesn't think it is.'

'No, not just Jay,' insisted Maxine. 'Since Gemma was born, I just don't seem to know myself any more, let alone what I want. I was so sure I'd be keen to rush back to work straight after the birth, but now she's actually here, I'm not sure about anything. It's all so confusing.'

Not for the first time a worrying thought entered Hannah's mind. 'You are going to come back to work though, aren't you? You're not going to pull out of the salon altogether.' Maxine said nothing. 'Oh Max, tell me you're not going to shut yourself away and forget all about your career.'

'I don't know,' repeated Maxine, haplessly honest. 'I love my work, you know I do – it's just that I love being a mum too.'

'The two things aren't mutually exclusive you know,' pointed out Hannah. 'Lots of mums work – I've worked pretty much ever since Lottie came along.'

'Yes, of course,' agreed Maxine. 'The thing is ... I haven't made up my mind if I actually want to.'

Hannah spent the rest of the day working and worrying – mainly about Maxine, but about pretty much everything else in the world too. It was always the way with her: some unresolved thing would start bothering her, develop into an obsession, and the next thing she knew she'd be agonising on behalf of the dispossessed pygmies of the Amazonian rainforest as well.

Not that there was much point in worrying. If Maxine made up her mind to detach herself from the salon, Jay certainly wouldn't try to dissuade her; and whatever arguments Hannah might come up with wouldn't carry much weight compared to a new mother's desire to be with her baby twenty-four hours a day.

But what would happen if Maxine stepped down and then Jay decided to sell his share of the business too? Hannah certainly couldn't afford to buy him out. Maybe she'd have to sell up her share as well, and start all over again.

More change. Yet another new start. She was beginning to hanker after the boring days when nothing ever changed.

That evening, after Nick had come round to collect Lottie, Hannah was sprawling across the sofa, fretfully eating Kettle Chips, when the doorbell rang. She very nearly didn't bother answering it, but curiosity got the better of her after the third ring, and she grudgingly heaved her carcass to the front door.

'Hello Sprout,' said Herbie, grim-faced and determined. His father and mother were standing on either side of him, but for once they were the ones who looked like naughty children.

'What's happened?' asked Hannah in alarm, visions of ambulances and fire engines flashing into her mind.

'Go on, tell her,' said Herbie, 'or I will.'

Erica and Derek exchanged uneasy glances. 'I . . . er . . .' began Derek. 'That is, your mother's got something to say to you.'

'It's a-about Charlotte's father,' stammered Erica.

Hannah frowned. 'Nick, you mean?'

'No dear. Charlotte's *father*.' She swallowed. 'Rhys.'

At the sound of that name, Hannah's stomach turned over. 'What about him?' she demanded. 'And why should I care anyway? He's nothing to do with me.'

'Actually . . . Can we come in, dear?' asked Erica with forced brightness. 'Only it's a bit . . . public, talking on the doorstep like this.'

Hannah had a horrible, doom-laden feeling as she followed Herbie and her parents down the hallway and into the living room. Resurrecting ghosts from the past was never a good idea in her experience, and even talking about this particular one gave

294

er the jitters. What's more, her parents had that furtive look they'd worn on her seventh birthday, the day they'd told her that Grandad Flowers would be 'working abroad for the Government' for the next few years.

'OK,' she said when everyone was sitting down. 'What's this about Rhys?'

'We had a little chat with him,' blurted out Derek.

'You spoke to him! When? What sort of "little chat?"' demanded Hannah, horror-stricken.

'We thought we ought to,' said Erica. 'For Charlotte's sake. That's why we wrote to him, you see.'

Hannah was too dumbstruck to express the blind fury she knew she would feel later. A kind of numbing haze seemed to surround her, making everything seem fuzzy and unreal. 'You *wrote* to Rhys?'

'Yes, dear. Don't be angry.'

'After I specifically told you I didn't want any contact with him? Ever?'

'We knew you'd be a wee bit upset,' conceded Derek. 'That's why we didn't mention it to you.'

A spark of anger managed to cut through the numbness. 'How dare you! How dare you go behind my back and then say it's all "for Charlotte's sake"! She doesn't need anything from that man.'

'Every child needs a father,' said Erica, gently but firmly.

'She's got a—'

'A *real* father,' interrupted Derek.

Hannah turned her gaze on Herbie, who was glaring stonily at his daughter and her husband. 'How long have you known about this, Gramps?'

'The first I knew was when he turned up on the doorstep last night,' replied Herbie. 'And that's the gospel truth. Soon as I realised what they'd been up to, I told them we were all coming round here tonight and—'

'Hang on.' The words were just sinking into Hannah's consciousness. 'What did you just say – he turned up on the doorstep? Rhys actually came to your house?'

'That's right, dear,' nodded Erica. 'And I must admit we were a little surprised that he didn't give us any notice. To be honest, he seemed a little ... well ... tense. But I'm sure things will be much more relaxed when he comes back on Saturday.'

'Saturday!' A whole world of unimaginable horror exploded in Hannah's head.

'Yes, he said he'd be coming back up on Saturday, and he definitely wants to see you and Charlotte. You see? I told you he would.'

The waiting was agony, but Hannah had to pick her moment. At last it came, after tea the following day.

'Lottie.'

The little girl looked up from the latest Harry Potter, legs curled under her as she snuggled in an armchair with one of her rabbits. 'All right, Mum, I'll clean my room as soon as I've finished this chapter.'

'It's not that. I just wanted a word with you about something.'

Lottie looked wary. 'Why, Mum? I haven't done anything wrong have I?'

Hannah smiled. 'No, at least not as far as I know. What I wanted to speak to you about is your . . . er . . . father.'

'Daddy Nick, you mean?'

That was the name she and Nick had agreed upon as a compromise for the time being. Hannah wondered if they'd ever make it all the way back to just 'Daddy' again, or whether Rhys Donoghue's unasked-for intervention would blow everything they'd rebuilt right out of the water. Thanks, Mum, she thought.

'No, not Daddy Nick. You know he and I got married after you were born, don't you?'

Lottie nodded solemnly. 'You and me were all on our own, and then Daddy Nick came along and then we were a family.' Her face fell. 'Only now we're not any more.'

Hannah felt a twist of pain at her daughter's words – so simple, so matter-of-fact, so true. 'Yes, well, remember what I told you – that before Daddy Nick came along, there was another man, the man who was what people call your biological father?' The only way Hannah could keep her cool was to be as clinically detached as possible. 'The one who put the seed in Mummy's tummy that grew into you?'

'Oh,' said Lottie unconcernedly. 'You mean sex. We did that at school with Mrs Perkins.'

'Right. Well. Anyway . . . Like I told you, when this man found

296

out that I was going to have a baby, he was angry and he went away.'

'But why did he go away?' demanded Lottie. 'Didn't he like me?'

Hannah put an arm round her shoulders. 'He didn't know anything about you, sweetheart, how could he not like you? He was just very young and scared, because being a father is a really hard job and he knew he wasn't strong enough to do it. So he ran away and left us. And I haven't heard anything from him from that day to this.'

'Why are you telling me all this again now, Mum?' asked Lottie, as usual going straight to the heart of the matter.

Hannah steeled herself. 'Because Granny and Grandad wrote to him and told him all about you, and now he wants to come up to Cheltenham to see you.'

Lottie's mouth dropped open, her eyes huge and round as gobstoppers. 'My real daddy wants to see me? He really, really does?'

Hannah nodded. 'But you don't have to see him if you don't want.'

'What's he like?' demanded Lottie. 'I want to know all about him. Is he nice?'

'I don't know what he's like now,' she confessed. 'He used to be quite bossy when I knew him, always telling me what to do.'

'Is he handsome?'

'Yes,' she admitted. 'Very handsome. And clever.'

'And is he a teacher, like Daddy Nick?'

Hannah laughed. 'Oh no, he's got a much more exciting job. He has his own kids' music programme on TV.'

This was like telling Lottie she'd just won a chain of sweet shops in a competition – only better. She clapped her hands and bounced in her chair. 'He's on TV? My daddy's on TV! Can we watch him, can we?'

'Sorry, sweetheart, he's only on cable and we don't have it. Maybe at Auntie Maxine's, if you ask very nicely. But in any case, you'll be seeing him in the flesh very soon.'

More's the pity, she thought; not so much afraid that Rhys would be a monster, as that the years might have turned him into exactly the kind of nice, reasonable, responsible person who could insinuate himself back into her and Lottie's lives without her say-so. Maybe even steal Lottie's heart away, all for himself.

'When?' asked Lottie eagerly.

Hannah swallowed hard. 'This Saturday,' she said.

Jay arrived home from his latest shopfitting job covered in plaster-dust and smelling of beer.

'Only had the one,' he assured Maxine, giving her a dusty peck on the cheek. 'Just to keep in with the lads – keeps morale up, you know. How are my two princesses?'

Gemma yawned, displaying a fine double row of pink gums. 'Fine,' said Maxine, though in point of fact she'd been bored rigid all day. Now that they were moving into autumn and the weather wasn't so dependably warm, more of her time was spent sitting in the house watching daytime TV than enjoying lazy times in the garden with Gemma. It didn't help that the latest daytime hit was a reality show about a top London hair salon, where the stylists were even more fascinating, glamorous and wealthy than their clients.

'Good, great. No need for a big meal tonight, anyhow. Got to go out again later to check up on the lads. They're working late on site, so I said I'd bring them round a Chinese.'

'You mean I'm going to be on my own all evening? Again?'

'Aw, don't look at me like that, princess!' Jay pinched her cheek playfully. It hurt. 'I'm only doing this to get extra money to look after the two special ladies in my life.' He patted her slowly diminishing belly. 'And the next one.'

Maxine gave him a sidelong look. 'What next one?'

'The next baby Maxine or baby Jay of course! Got to get that production line in full swing, eh, now we've got the hang of this breeding lark.'

'Oh we have, have we?'

Jay ignored her sceptical expression and blustered happily on. 'I mean, now you're at home all the time anyway, you might as well have three or four kids to look after as one, mightn't you? I wonder if we might have twins next time. There's a couple of sets on my dad's side of the family.'

Maxine listened to her husband with mounting horror. It wasn't that she hadn't known Jay wanted several kids, or that she objected to the idea in principle. But the thought of sitting here at home doing nothing but producing them, one after another, until she turned into a big, mindless, lardy blob, was the straw that broke the camel's back.

'Actually,' she said, sitting up straight in her chair, 'I won't be here all day after all.'

'What? Why?'

'Because I've decided to go back to work part-time.'

Jay was aghast. 'But I thought ... You can't! What about Gemma?'

'I'll take her with me.'

'To the salon!'

'Why not? She'll be perfectly safe in the staffroom and she'll have lots of company in between clients. And I won't have to be parted from her at all. Isn't that just the perfect solution?'

She could see from Jay's face that it wasn't, at least not from his point of view. But that was just too bad.

'Oh, and by the way,' she went on while she was on a roll, 'I forgot to tell you. Those three old ladies say they want to invest some of their big bingo win in the salon.'

'We decided against expanding, remember?' replied Jay tartly.

'No, love, *you* decided. We just stood there with our mouths open, like brain-dead goldfish. I think it's time you, I and Hannah got together again and really talked about the future. Like proper equals.

'After all, Jay, you've said it yourself often enough. The future's about moving forwards. If you try to stand still, all that happens is you go backwards.'

Chapter 32

'Nick,' said Hannah, 'I'm scared.'

He was sitting next to her on a bench in Sandford Park, watching her carpet-bombing the pigeons with big lumps of bread.

'I know you are, Han,' he sympathised, 'but hey, don't take it out on the birds.' He nudged her. 'Look at that fat one, wandering round in circles. He's probably concussed.'

'Sorry, Mr Pigeon,' she sighed, emptying the rest of the bag of bread onto the ground. She turned to Nick. 'Do you think I'm being childish too? My mum and dad certainly do.'

'Of course I don't,' Nick replied. 'Or put it this way – if you're childish, so am I.'

That was hard to believe, and Hannah said so.

'Ah, but at least you're Lottie's biological mother,' Nick pointed out. 'Nobody can ever take that away from you. But what am I? A sort of semi-separated stepfather.'

'Come on, Nick, you're much more than that and you know it.'

He shrugged. 'Not in the eyes of the law. And maybe not in Lottie's eyes any more, either. Not that it stops me *feeling* like I'm her real dad, though. Or hurting like crazy when she won't let me get close. And then some flash bloke pops up from nowhere after the best part of ten years, and suddenly he's her father and I'm nothing.'

Hannah swung her legs back and forth. It made her feel like a child again, momentarily free of the cares and responsibilities that weighed so heavily upon her. 'You'll never be nothing, and Rhys can't expect to swan in and take over Lottie's life, just because he and I happened to have sex ten years ago. Being a dad's about more than biology. You of all people should know that.'

'Knowing it and feeling it are two different things though, aren't they? And it sounds like he has different ideas.'

'I suppose he might have changed,' pondered Hannah, forcing herself to accept the possibility. 'Maybe he's not so selfish any more; it was a long time ago after all. People do grow up.' Unless they're Danny, she mused; but Rhys was a hundred times smarter than Danny would ever be.

'Yeah, maybe you're right.' Nick stretched out his long legs, closed his eyes and let the autumn sunshine do its best to relax him. Hannah leaned her head against his shoulder. It felt good. 'Either way, it's not for me to interfere, is it?'

'Actually . . .' said Hannah.

Nick opened one eye. 'Actually what?'

'I was wondering if you would interfere. Just a little bit. Could you arrange to be around when Rhys comes to the house?'

Nick shifted uncomfortably on the bench. 'Oh, Han, I don't know. He might not like it.'

'It would mean a lot to me.'

'But you won't be alone,' he reminded her. 'Your mum and dad will be there.'

'Yeah, the Rhys Donoghue Fan Club, Cheltenham branch. I was rather hoping there might be somebody there who's on *my* side. Well, Lottie's side,' she corrected herself. 'I guess it doesn't really matter that much how I feel about it.'

'It matters a lot,' objected Nick. 'You're her mum, that makes you the most special person in Lottie's life.'

Hannah's hand sought out his. Compared to his big paw, it felt tiny, fragile and vulnerable. 'Will you be there then?' she pleaded.

'Your hand's all cold,' he said. 'You really are scared, aren't you?'

'Will you?'

Nick let out a long sigh of resignation, then capitulated. 'All right. But if he hits me you can call the ambulance.'

Meanwhile, across town, an unscheduled confrontation was already taking place.

'What the hell are you doing here?' demanded Damon as Bernard pushed his way into Philomena's house, clearly the worse for wear.

'I'm here to see my wife.' Bernard swayed and made a grab for the hatstand to steady himself. '*My* wife, geddit? Till death do us part?'

'She's not your wife any more,' sniffed Damon. 'And she doesn't want anything to do with you, so you might as well just go away. You ought to be ashamed of yourself,' he added, 'turning up here in that condition.'

'What condition?' demanded Bernard, shoving his face into Damon's in a blast of beery breath. 'You insulting me or what?'

'I hardly need to. You're an insult to the human race as it is, you pathetic piece of shit.'

Philomena appeared at the top of the stairs. 'Oh God, it's you. What do you want, Bernard?'

'You. I want to come home. You're my wife, you belong with me.'

'No she doesn't,' snapped Damon. 'She's mine now, get that into your thick head. And why the hell would she want you back?'

'Let me talk to him,' said Philomena.

Damon waved her away. 'Leave this to me, I'm dealing with him.' He seized Bernard by the back of the collar and gave him a shove towards the front door. 'Go on, get out before I call the police.'

But Philomena had already started down the stairs. 'Leave him alone, Damon.'

'Leave him alone?' Damon's lip curled. 'But he's pond slime, we don't want him anywhere near us.'

With a confidence she didn't entirely feel, Philomena drew herself up to her full five-feet-nothing and declared: 'In case you've forgotten, this is my house, Damon. It may not be as smart as your house in Prestbury, but I can still decide who I want in it. Go into the front room and sit down, Bernard. I'll make you some black coffee. And when you've sobered up, you can tell me what this is all about.'

A pint of strong black coffee later, Bernard had gone from bellicose to maudlin.

'You're my angel,' he said, with tears in his bleary red eyes. 'My little Irish angel. I've always loved you, you know.'

'Which is why you used to smack hell out of me whenever

your horse didn't win or the dog peed on the carpet?' she enquired coolly.

'I never meant to lay a finger on you, I swear.' Bernard's voice was full of a drunkard's cast-iron sincerity. 'An' if you'll let me come home, I'll never lay a finger on you again.' He belched. 'Honest to God I won't.'

Damon looked on in evident disgust. 'Phil, you're surely not going to listen to the ravings of an alcoholic wife-beater? For God's sake just let me throw him out and have done with it.'

Philomena looked at him sharply. 'Back off, Damon. Whatever he is or isn't, he's still my husband. And you know I don't believe in divorce.'

It was obvious that Damon could scarcely credit what he was hearing. He bent down and brandished a gold-ringed fist in Bernard's face. 'I know people,' he said in a voice that exuded menace, 'do you hear me? People who can make other people disappear.'

Bernard stared at him blearily. Philomena turned white at the sight of Damon's thin-lipped smile. 'That's not funny, Damon!'

'Good. Because it's not a joke. You'd be amazed how quickly somebody can vanish,' he went on. 'One minute they're there, the next – gone. And nobody ever hears from them again. It's just like they never existed.' Damon's face was so close to Bernard's that his spittle spattered the other man's skin. 'And let's face it, Bernie-boy, the world would've been a whole lot better place if you'd never existed. Isn't that right, Phil?'

Philomena didn't have a chance to get a word in edgeways, because the very moment Damon stopped speaking Bernard erupted into life. With a roar of drunken rage, he seized Damon by the shoulders, lunged forward, and head-butted him – so hard that Damon's nose exploded in a crimson starburst, all over the Laura Ashley wallpaper.

'Take that, you fucking smug-faced creep!' roared Bernard, as Damon slumped to his knees beside the couch, blood spewing between his clasped fingers.

'You . . . bastard,' he mumbled through the pain. 'You'll pay for this, I swear you will.'

Bernard lumbered groggily to his feet and made a grab for Philomena's arm. 'Come on love, we're goin' home to my place.'

'Get off me!' shrieked Philomena, wresting her sleeve from his grasp.

'Phone the police,' commanded Damon, his words somewhat muffled by the scatter-cushion stemming the flow from his nose. 'I'm going to have him for GBH.'

'Yeah, phone the police,' retorted Bernard. 'An' I'll tell them how you threatened to kill me, so I will.'

Philomena took in the scene in a moment of unparalleled clarity. Two grown men acting like children, trading insults and punches over her, and neither one of them caring what she actually thought about any of it. That's it, she thought, at last certain what she must do.

Picking up the phone, she dialled the number. 'Hello – police? There are two intruders causing a disturbance in my house, and I want them removed. Both of them. Now.'

The following Saturday morning, the suspense in Hannah's house was unbearable. Erica was knitting for Britain, Derek kept pacing up and down in front of the living room window, and Hannah huddled up to Lottie on the sofa, wondering if she would ever feel in charge of her own life again.

When the doorbell finally rang, everybody jumped. Herbie was the only one with the presence of mind to actually answer it, and when he came back he didn't have Rhys with him anyway.

'Look, Lottie, it's Daddy Nick and baby George,' said Hannah brightly. 'Don't you want to give George a kiss?'

Lottie gave her mother a long-suffering look. 'Do I have to? He smells funny.'

'What on earth are you doing here?' demanded Derek, stiffening at the sight of his former son-in-law – not so much with anger, thought Hannah, as with sheer terror. Her poor old dad just didn't possess the emotional equipment to deal with estranged sons-in-law who wouldn't stay estranged, or semi-maybe-step-grandchildren who were too darned cute to be disregarded.

'Hannah asked me to be here,' replied Nick, entering the living room with baby George strapped into his tiny car seat.

'It's all right, dear.' Erica laid a hand on her husband's arm. 'I suppose he does have a right to know what's going on, all things considered.' There was no mistaking the softening in her voice as her eyes lighted on George's gurgling face. 'He has known Charlotte and Hannah a very long time, even if he isn't part of the family any more.'

'Not part of the family!' exclaimed Hannah. 'Mum, Nick's as much a part of *my* family as Lottie is, and like I've told you again and again, nothing's going to change that.'

'Things move on, Hannah love,' said her father. 'Marriages break up ... blood ties are different. That's why Rhys is coming here today, because he realises he's got responsibilities towards his daughter.'

'Really?' said Nick. 'I got the impression he was only coming because you pestered him with letters.'

Derek scowled. Erica went back to her knitting. Lottie lost interest. Baby George fell asleep.

'Can I just put the baby to sleep in the other room?' asked Nick. 'I don't want him disturbed. And don't worry, I won't cause a disturbance either,' he added for Erica and Derek's benefit. 'I'm just here for Hannah and Lottie if they need me.'

'I don't know why you had to ask him to come,' grumbled Derek once Nick was out of the room. 'It'll only complicate matters.'

'No, Dad, you and Mum already did that,' retorted Hannah. 'Everything was going just fine until you decided to interfere.'

'But Mum,' protested Lottie, 'I *want* to see my new daddy.'

'There you are, dear,' said Erica, beaming. 'Sometimes Grandma knows best. You'll realise that one day.'

The doorbell sounded again. Hannah thought she was ready for it this time, but when she stood up her knees turned to jelly. 'That'll be him.'

Erica started plucking at her pink mohair cardigan. 'Do I look all right, dear?'

Derek blew his nose with a sound like the Grimethorpe Colliery Band.

'All right, I'll get it,' said Herbie, as everybody stood staring at one another and willing somebody else to go to the door. 'Gawd help us, anybody'd think we were expecting a royal visit or something.'

The man on the doorstep might not be royalty, but he certainly had a way with commoners. 'Here,' he said, thrusting his jacket into Herbie's arms. 'Hang this up, and be careful. It's Paul Smith.'

A few choice ripostes sprang to the tip of Herbie's tongue; then he thought better of it. Starting a slanging match on the doorstep might not be the best course of action, all things considered.

'Hannah and Lottie are through there,' he said, pointing down the hallway to the living room door. 'I'll make some tea.'

'Coffee,' corrected the woman who had just followed Rhys into the house. 'Colombian, decaffeinated, low-calorie sweetener.'

No better taste in girlfriends than he has in haircuts, thought Herbie as he watched the hefty woman in the red suit following Rhys.

Hannah held her breath as Rhys strode into the room. What if she didn't recognise him after all this time? Worse, what if she fell head over heels in love with him again the moment she set eyes on him?

She needn't have worried. He was instantly recognisable, even if his haircut did make him look as if a series of red and green tramcars had run backwards and forwards over his peroxide blond head. But fancy him she most certainly did not.

'Hannah,' he said, taking her in with one critical sweep of his green eyes.

'Rhys.'

Erica fussed and burbled something about it being very good of him to come all this way again, and hoping he hadn't got lost in the one-way system. Derek hung around in the background, hands in pockets. Lottie gazed up in wonder at the tall, incredibly glamorous figure in the shiny designer suit. 'I'm Charlotte,' she said. 'Are you my daddy?'

Rhys glanced down at her as though he had just discovered a bug on his lettuce. 'Get that child out of here, will you? We need to talk business.'

Hannah gaped. 'Get her out of here? But she's the whole reason you've come!'

'Just do it, will you?'

'But Daddy,' protested Lottie.

'It's OK, sweetie,' said Hannah, though it patently wasn't 'You go with Great-Gramps and get yourself some juice.'

Reluctantly Lottie allowed herself to be led away, casting yearning looks back over her shoulder. Only when the door had swung to behind her did Rhys look marginally less uptight.

'Mercedes.' Rhys snapped his fingers, and the woman in the red suit stepped promptly to his side. 'This is Ms Suarez, my lawyer. Now Hannah, you can start by telling me how much.'

She frowned. 'How much what?'

'Don't give me that. How much money you want for you and the kid to get the hell out of my life and stay out.'

The internal walls weren't that thick, and Nick had heard every word.

He'd meant to put the baby down to sleep and then go straight back to the living room, but once Rhys arrived it seemed like the wrong moment to go barging in and complicating matters still further.

So he'd listened. And with every word he overheard, he grew more and more angry. He hadn't yet set eyes on the cretin, but he could picture him as clear as day in his mind's eye: slick as an oil spillage, perma-tanned, utterly devoted to the worship of himself. Never mind that one little girl had spent her whole life wondering who he was, hero-worshipping the very idea of him. Never mind that her mother had never asked for anything from him during the whole of the child's life.

No, as far as Rhys was concerned the whole thing was a crude blackmail scam: a demand for a big share of his hard-earned media cash, or else Hannah and her family would put the boot in on his TV career.

Hannah's voice rose in angry protest. 'But why on earth would I do a thing like that?'

'Why?' laughed Mercedes Suarez. 'Because you know very well that Mr Donoghue is in discussions to take over the *Sunday Groove* teenage God-slot on Channel Six. And you also know very well that his image depends on his being young, free, single and of impeccable morals.'

'In other words,' cut in Rhys drily, 'a bastard sprog in the closet could really ruin my reputation. Not that you need that explaining, do you Hannah?'

'A what! How dare you call your daughter that!'

'My daughter? Well, I suppose she may be ... or then again not. I mean, how do I know you weren't screwing half the campus ten years ago.'

Tears of fury pricked the underside of Hannah's eyelids. 'You know damned well I wasn't! I was hopelessly in love with you back then, God help me.'

'Jealousy's a terrible thing,' added Rhys. 'Just because you've

307

fucked up your own life, you and your family want to fuck u
mine too and make a nice fat profit into the bargain.'

'Now steady on, young man,' cut in Derek, belatedly stirre
into life. 'What are you saying? Are you accusing us of trying
blackmail you?'

'Oh, cut the crap,' snapped Rhys. He snapped his fingers aga
and Mercedes Suarez produced a cheque from her briefcas
'This is my best offer. If I were you I'd take it, 'cause there'll
no more. And if I hear another word from you or that kid—'

The door opened. And in walked Nick.

'You sick, contemptible little git,' he said, with venomous pr
cision.

Rhys's meticulously tweezed eyebrows collided in the midd
of his forehead. 'Who the hell are you?'

'Nick Steadman.'

Hannah stepped forward and slid her arm through hi
'Nick's my husband.' Her parents' faces registered mild su
prise. 'Lottie's stepfather.'

'Oh really? I thought from the letter that you were divorce
How cosy. So Nick, I suppose you were behind this little scam a
along, were you? Egging on Grandma and Grandpa to write be
ging letters to the big TV star? Hoping to get your hands on
share of the loot?'

Three long strides took Nick across the room. Face to fa
with Rhys, and half a head taller, he exuded the kind of controll
menace Vinnie Jones could only dream of.

'You make me sick,' he said. 'And do you know why? N
because of what you've said about me, or the things you'
accused my wife's family of. But because of what you've done
Lottie.'

'Done to her?' laughed Rhys. 'I've done nothing. And what
more, I've no intention of doing anything either.'

'Nothing. Precisely. That's what you are for all your flas
clothes and your lawyers – a big fat nothing, who doesn't give
damn that he's broken his own daughter's heart, who doesn
give a damn about anything or anybody, just as long as he gets
ponce about on some crummy cable TV show.'

Hannah had never seen him like this before: so angry, so
control, so ... magnificent. Is this really Nick? she thought.
this really the mild-mannered man I thought was so boring? Th

was a revelation. All the same, she didn't want him to get hurt, or fetch up in court on the receiving end of some horrible lawsuit; so she tried to pull him back. 'Leave it, Nick. You said it yourself, he's not worth it.'

'Maybe he's not, but Lottie is. She's beautiful and she's clever and she's funny, and she deserves someone a thousand times better than this jerk for a father.' Nick gently but firmly detached himself from Hannah's grip, and took another step forward. He was virtually nose to nose with Rhys now. 'Have you any idea what it's like for a nine-year-old girl to dream about some day meeting her real father? And then one day he turns up and doesn't even want to know her?'

Rhys shuffled uneasily from one foot to the other. He might have tried retreating if he hadn't already been backed up against the fireplace.

'May I remind you that if you lay one finger on Mr Donoghue's person—' began Mercedes Suarez.

'Oh shut up,' snapped Nick; and to her own surprise, she did. 'Well, have you?' he demanded of Rhys.

'Look, this isn't about her,' protested Rhys. 'Not . . . specifically.' His voice rose to a whine. 'I didn't start this, did I? It's nothing personal.'

'Nothing personal!' exploded Hannah. 'How dare you say that!'

Erica got to her feet, looking flushed and not at all serene. 'Yes, how dare you? I used to think you were a nice young man all those years ago, Rhys Donoghue, but obviously I was having a brainstorm at the time.'

Exasperated and under siege, Rhys stepped to one side and brandished the cheque under Hannah's nose. 'Just take your money and get out of my life, right?'

She grabbed it from his hand, tore it into a dozen pieces and let them flutter down onto the carpet. 'Wrong script, Rhys. I'm writing this one. What happens now is, you take *your* money and you get right back out of *my* house and *my* life. I never asked you for a penny before, and I wouldn't touch it now if you begged me. Got that?'

'B-but—'

'Just go, Rhys. Now. And if you ever, *ever* try to contact me or *my* daughter again—'

Nick looked him hard in the face. 'Believe me, it won't be just your reputation that's in pieces.'

Lottie sat halfway up the stairs with Herbie, not wanting to hear any of what was going on downstairs, and yet desperate not to miss a single word. Because all of it, absolutely all of it, was about her. And as she listened, the fairy-tale world she had built up so carefully around her fell away, turret by turret, brick by brick, until all that was left was the person she really was. Not a princess; not a TV star's daughter; just Lottie.

Herbie had his arm round her, but he knew she was trying not to cry as she huddled against him.

'It's OK,' he whispered. 'He's gone now. And he's not coming back.'

Lottie looked up into his face and said, 'I know, Great-Gramps.' Then her face crumpled and she couldn't hold back the sobbing any longer.

Chapter 33

The door of Lottie's bedroom slammed shut, and then there was a horrible silence.

'I must go to her,' said Hannah, heading for the door. 'Poor kid, she must be beside herself.'

Herbie caught her gently on the way past. 'Don't, Sprout. Not right now. She needs to be on her own for a bit. She's got a lot of things to sort out in her mind, and I don't think she's ready to talk just yet.' He turned his gaze on Erica and Derek. 'Thanks to some people who ought to have known better.'

White-faced, Erica sank heavily onto the sofa. 'What have we done, Derek? What have we gone and done?'

Her husband patted her shoulder, rather awkwardly. 'We meant well, love. It seemed like the right thing to do at the time.'

Herbie let out a snort of disbelief. 'Only to a pair of idiots who thought they knew better than everybody else.' Erica and Derek squirmed. It must feel weird, Hannah mused, being told off by Herbie of all people. 'I hope the two of you are ashamed of yourselves.'

Hannah half expected her parents to defend themselves indignantly, point out that Rhys might have turned out to be a perfectly lovely man who wanted nothing more than to build a relationship with his daughter. But Derek just said, 'Yes. We are. We really screwed up this time, didn't we?'

'Oh Dad.' Hannah felt weary and shaken. All the anger that had seethed in her while Rhys was there seemed to have evaporated with his departure. 'It's done now. Let's just see what we can do to repair the damage.'

Erica fiddled with the hem of her tweedy skirt. 'I think we owe you an apology, Hannah,' she said. 'We're so, so sorry – aren't we, Derek?'

Derek nodded glumly.

'Don't apologise to me,' said Hannah. 'Save it for Lottie. She's the one who's hurting.'

Another uncomfortable silence imposed itself, as Hannah's mother and father drank in the bad consequences of their good intentions. Nick cleared his throat and stood up. 'I think this is where I make my excuses and leave.'

He was halfway across the room when Derek called after him: 'Just a minute, Nick.'

'Yes?' Nick turned round.

'Before you go, Erica and I have got something to say to you.' He nudged his wife in the ribs. 'Haven't we, love?'

'Y-yes.'

'Go on then,' prompted Derek, clearly crushed by embarrassment and shame. 'You know I'm no good at this sort of thing.'

Erica gave him a withering look. 'After today, I'm not sure either of us is much good at anything.' She turned to Nick. 'We just want to say we're sorry, Nick. We were wrong – not just about Rhys, about you too.'

It was Nick's turn to look uncomfortable. 'I . . . you really don't have to say this, you know.'

Derek raised a hand. 'Oh yes we do. Me and Erica, all this time we've been telling ourselves that a "real" father's got to be better than a stepfather for Charlotte, and look how wrong we turned out to be. What do a few genes matter, when she's got someone who loves her the way you do?'

Hannah felt as stunned as Nick looked. She couldn't recall her father making such a lengthy speech since her wedding day – and then he'd been reading Herbie his rights. 'I tried to tell you often enough, Dad,' she pointed out gently. 'Nick's Lottie's father, and always has been. And he's a damned sight more to her than Rhys could ever be, that's for sure.'

'It all just goes to show we're not very good at listening. And another thing, Nick,' added Erica. 'That baby of yours—'

'Mum!' warned Hannah, afraid that her mother was about to spoil the détente by launching into a disapproving tirade about Miranda and the appalling state of modern morality.

'He's a little darling. An absolute delight. What's more, he's a very lucky boy to have you as his father.'

Nick raised an eyebrow. 'Whether I really am his father or not?'

Erica smiled ruefully. 'Let's just say I've learned a very big lesson today.'

Hannah followed Nick into the back room where George was still slumbering peacefully, one small pink fist jammed into his toothless, dribbly mouth.

'Just look at him,' she declared. 'He must have slept through the whole thing.'

'Like father like son, eh?' ventured Nick, taking a tentative sniff at the baby's bottom and heading straight for the changing bag.

'How do you mean?'

'Well, you always did say I could sleep through an earthquake. And that I never got worked up about things that sent other people into a frenzy. In fact, as I recall that used to really drive you mad.'

'Not mad exactly,' protested Hannah, though she knew he was right.

'No?' Nick's mouth twitched into a smile. 'What about that time the chimney caught fire on Christmas Day and the firemen ate all the turkey and mince pies? And I said, "What's the problem, we can have beans on toast," and you hit me with a marzipan stollen?'

'I was overwrought!'

'You were hopping mad!'

Hannah pouted. 'Maybe just a bit. Whatever. I'm not mad now though. I'm really proud of you. And I bet George will be too, when he's old enough to hear about what happened.'

George yawned, blinked and burped as Nick went to work on his smelly nappy. 'Proud of me?' enquired Nick. 'You mean you didn't mind when I came over all . . . caveman?'

'Not a bit.'

'You would have minded in the old days.'

'I don't mind now.' She watched Nick changing the baby, almost offered to help, then realised that he was doing the job as competently as she ever could. 'Nick.'

'Hmm?'

'What about you? Did you mind when I told Rhys you were my husband?'

Nick looked up. 'Why should I? I still am, aren't I?'

'Well, yes. At least until we . . . you know.'

'Yes.' He paused. 'Not that there's any hurry, is there? I mean, lawyers cost money,'

'And why should they have our hard-earned cash when we can put it to so much better use?'

'Couldn't have put it better myself.'

He smiled, relieved perhaps that she had found a practical reason not to rush the divorce. Otherwise he might have blurted out some other, far less rational motive.

Hannah watched his face, trying to read behind the kind eyes, beyond the friendly smile. Was there something more there, or had she been utterly mistaken?

If she reached out to touch him, would he draw away?

And how would he react if she were to confess that when it came to lawyers, she wasn't sure she wanted to see one at all any more? She longed to ask him, but she knew she couldn't take the pain of rejection. Not right now.

Yes. For now at least, not knowing was better than knowing and wishing she didn't.

Possibly for the first time in his life, Jason looked truly confident.

Claire shook her head in wonderment. 'I don't believe it, I just don't. All morning she's been grizzling, and as soon as Uncle Jason picks her up, she's all smiles again.'

Jason tickled Gemma under the chin, and she wriggled and giggled with glee. 'Oh, it just comes of being second eldest in a family of eight,' he explained modestly. 'You learn fast when you've got six younger brothers and sisters. It was like Regent's Park Zoo in our house.'

'Well,' declared Maxine, 'if you don't make it in hairdressing, you've got a great future as a nanny.'

Jason looked quite crestfallen. 'If I don't make it? Do you think I might not, then?'

'Don't be daft, you did really well in those last exams.' Maxine reached out her arms. 'Now, give me that baby back and you can get on with blow-drying Mrs Emerson.'

Once Claire and Jason had left the staffroom, Maxine started breastfeeding Gemma. 'How's it going, kid?'

'I'm finding it a bit knackering,' Maxine admitted. 'And Jay hasn't quite got over the sulks yet. But it's not working out too badly so far, is it? Me bringing her to work with me, I mean.'

'Not when you've got Nanny Jason in attendance,' chuckled Hannah. 'But you're still going to stick with part-time for the moment?'

'Oh God, yes. I mean, people tell you how tiring it is having a new baby, but you never really understand, do you? Not till you've actually had no sleep for weeks on end.' She rubbed a bleary eye. 'How do we manage, Han? Mums I mean. What with the exhaustion and the worry and everything else.'

'I don't know,' replied Hannah. 'I guess we manage because we want to. Because when it comes to the crunch, it's more important than anything else.'

Maxine nodded. 'You're right. You know, I think Jay's nose is a bit out of joint since Gemma came along. He loves her to bits, he really does; but he used to be so sure that he was number one in my life, and now he's wondering!'

'Things'll sort themselves out. Before you know it, you'll be the jealous one, when you see how close little Gemma is to him. Little girls and their daddies . . . it's a special bond.'

'So Lottie and Nick . . .?'

Hannah sighed. 'Let's just say he's still working on it. Come to that, so am I. Trouble is, since that business with Rhys Lottie's not in the mood to talk to anybody about anything, poor kid. Sometimes,' she added, 'I could throttle my parents.'

'Ah well, everybody makes mistakes. I'm sure they meant well.'

Hannah motioned strangling Maxine. 'Not you as well! If anybody else says that I swear I'll run amok, and it'll be all over the *Courant*. Then you'll be sorry.'

Maxine gently switched Gemma to the other breast. 'Oh, I don't know. Any publicity is good publicity and all that. Especially if Jay does agree to go ahead with the expansion plans.'

'You think he will?'

'I'm ninety per cent sure.' She winked. 'No, make that ninety-five; he always was a sucker for home-made lasagne and an early night.'

'It'll mean a lot more work,' pointed out Hannah. 'Long days, loads of disruption, no guarantees of success . . .'

'Don't tell me *you're* going cold on the idea!'

'Of course not.' Hannah stretched out her arms and legs, and felt her tired muscles crackle and pop. 'But if you're staying part-time and we're taking on more staff, we're going to need somebody who can take on a lot of the admin and management side of things.'

Their eyes met.

'Actually, I had an idea about that,' admitted Maxine.

'So did I.'

'You first.'

'No, you.'

'OK, I was thinking, why not Philomena?' She looked at Hannah. 'All right, all right, stupid idea.'

'No, not stupid at all.'

'So why are you pulling that face?'

'I'm not! I was just thinking the same thing. Phil's come on a hell of a lot since she kicked out Damon and Bernard; and if we don't offer her a chance to broaden her horizons I've a feeling she'll go elsewhere. Herr Kutz in Gloucester is looking for an assistant manager – I heard her talking about it with Claire the other day.'

'That's settled then,' declared Maxine.

'Only if Jay comes round to the idea, and only if Phil says yes!'

Maxine bent down and kissed baby Gemma on her tiny button nose. 'Never underestimate a woman's powers of persuasion, Han. You leave it to Gem and me; we've got the whole thing sussed.'

When Hannah next came down into the salon, she found Gloria holding court as Philomena put the finishing touches to a rather avant-garde style that reminded Hannah of a thicket of pampas grass.

'What do you think, Hannah darling?' she enquired, tossing her head so that all the individual tufts danced in different directions.

'Very . . . you,' decided Hannah.

'Yes, I thought so.' Gloria beamed and patted Philomena's

316

arm. 'Isn't she a treasure? She always knows exactly what I want without my having to tell her.'

'Gloria wanted something really special today,' explained Claire, leaning over to take a handful of curlers from Philomena's trolley. 'She's got a hot date with her new boyfriend tonight, haven't you, Glor?'

Gloria slid her feet out of her Jimmy Choos and wriggled her toes deliciously. 'We're going to that fab Art Deco restaurant near Suffolk Square – the one that used to be a cinema.'

'Wow,' sighed Claire. 'He must be loaded.'

Hannah laughed. 'Gloria's boyfriends are *always* loaded.'

'Well, I always think I go to all this effort to look good for them, the least they can do is have the wherewithal to show me a good time,' Gloria agreed.

'So who is he?' demanded Claire. 'What's he like?'

Gloria tapped the side of her nose. 'Wait and see, he'll be here to collect me any time now.'

Philomena was flicking off the last few hairs with a soft brush when the door jangled and a figure entered, bearing an enormous bunch of flowers.

'Gloria love, you look amazing!'

He was silhouetted against the light, but Hannah didn't need to see him clearly to know who he was. Nor did Claire or Maxine or Philomena. They drew in a collective breath.

'*Gramps?*' gasped Hannah.

Herbie stepped forward, looking positively jaunty in his wedding suit, matching shoes and blue fedora, executed a little bow and presented the flowers to Gloria. 'Hannah love, how're you doing?'

'Er . . . not as well as you are, by the looks of things!'

A titter ran round the salon.

Claire nudged Herbie in the ribs. 'Who's a dark horse then, eh?' She winked at Gloria. 'Better make sure he has the oysters and asparagus tonight, know what I mean?'

Herbie looked most indignant. 'I'll have you know there's plenty of life left in this old dog,' he protested.

'This is a turn up for the book,' commented Hannah as Herbie went off to fetch Gloria's coat.

'Ah well, you know what they say: carpe diem, gather ye rose-buds,' replied Gloria, her eyes meeting Hannah's in the mirror.

317

'Yes, I know he's old enough to be my dad, but he's a nice man. And yes, I know he's hardly got a penny to his name, but you never know when he'll pull off that big bank job, do you?' She giggled. 'Anyhow, for the time being I've found a kindred spirit, and that's good enough for me.'

'So where do you go from here?' wondered Hannah.

'Who knows?' Gloria grinned. 'I'm just going to chill out, do whatever I feel like and be totally irresponsible. Maybe you should do the same.'

'Been there, done that,' replied Hannah. 'And believe it or not, it ain't all it's cracked up to be.'

Chapter 34

'I just don't know what to do about Lottie,' confessed Hannah as she let Nick into the house the following Friday evening. 'She's still exactly the same.' She glanced upwards as they passed the bottom of the stairs. 'As soon as she comes home from school she goes straight up to her room, and it's all I can do to get her downstairs for her meals.'

Nick rubbed his chin. 'She still doesn't want to talk then?'

'She's hardly said a word all week. At first I thought she just needed time to get over the shock, but now I'm getting seriously worried.'

It might only be a week since the Rhys Donoghue debacle, but it felt like a month: seven grindingly difficult days of Hannah trying to get through to Lottie, and Lottie dodging every attempt to penetrate the wall of silence she had built up around her. To Hannah, it sometimes felt almost as if her daughter had been kidnapped, and replaced by a half-finished robot. Even Herbie had had little success in getting Lottie to open up, beyond making her laugh a couple of times during an almost silent game of Pass the Pigs.

Hannah called up the stairs. 'Lottie.'

No reply.

'Lottie, he's here – are you ready?' She waited a little longer, then started up the stairs. 'Maybe she's got her headphones on and she can't hear me.'

'Or maybe she doesn't want to?' ventured Nick. 'Look Han, if she'd rather not spend this weekend with me, I understand.'

Hannah shook her head. 'She can't just avoid things by hiding herself away; she's at least got to come down and talk to you.'

At the top of the stairs, she knocked on Lottie's bedroom door and went straight in. Lottie was sitting on the edge of the bed, chin on her hands, elbows on her knees. 'All right Mum, I'm coming,' she said, getting slowly to her feet.

'You're going to have a great weekend,' Hannah said with a brightness she didn't feel.

Lottie didn't answer, but followed her out of the room onto the landing.

'A little bird told me you're going to that new theme park near Burford.'

'Oh,' said Lottie. Well, at least it was something.

Hannah led the way downstairs and Lottie followed with obvious reluctance, her overnight bag bumping its way down the stairs behind her like a fat sausage dog with no legs.

'Hello, Lotpot.' Nick held out his arms for a hug but she didn't take him up on the offer, so he dropped them to his sides again. 'Ready for the off?'

Lottie hung her head, avoiding his gaze. She looked, thought Hannah, unutterably miserable; so dejected that she longed to scoop her up in her arms and cuddle her and make everything warm and safe, the way you could with a baby. But Lottie wasn't her baby any more, she'd be in double figures soon; and as puberty slouched ever closer, problems grew too complex to be wished away with love and kisses.

If only you knew how much I love you, thought Hannah. If only you really *knew*. You'd either have a smile as wide as the moon, or you'd die of embarrassment. Maybe both.

'Are you sure you want to come?' Nick asked Lottie.

She shuffled her feet and made a few unintelligible noises. Still standing part-way up the stairs, she was almost on a level with Nick, and had to stare resolutely down to avoid catching his eye.

'Only if you don't, it's OK.' Hannah cast him a despairing look, but he went on. 'Really it is.' He waited a little while, but Lottie still didn't respond. 'OK then,' he declared. 'Let's leave it for this weekend, eh? We can try again next week if you're feeling more like your old self.'

'Nick—' began Hannah, only too aware of the sadness in Nick's eyes. He and Lottie had been making progress in recent weeks, she was sure they had; especially since Miranda moved away. But now it felt like they had taken a dozen giant steps backwards.

'It's no problem, honestly,' he assured Hannah with a smile that might have convinced anyone but her. 'George and I will find plenty to keep us occupied. See you next week, Lotpot, have a nice time with your mum.'

He had just reached the front door and was about to open it when the thunder of small footsteps made him turn. Lottie was running towards him full-pelt, her arms stretched out.

'Please, Daddy,' she blurted out, 'please don't go.' And she flung her arms round his waist and buried her face in his chest.

Momentarily stunned, Nick gently stroked the tangled mess of her hair. 'Hey, Lotpot, don't worry, I'm not going anywhere.'

Still squeezing all the breath out of his body, she looked up at him with eyes that were dry but very, very bright. 'Oh Daddy, I've been horrible to you.'

'No you haven't.'

'Yes I have! I wanted to stop, but I just couldn't.'

'It's OK, really it is.'

'And I know baby George smells funny, but I do like him all the same.'

Nick held her close.

'I know that. And none of it matters now.'

'Please stay, Daddy. Please don't go away again. Not ever.'

Her words found an echo in Hannah's heart, and she found herself thinking again: if only you knew how much I love you.

Both of you.

Nick smiled in a way she hadn't seen for a very long time. 'I don't know about ever, Lotpot, but we could start with this weekend. How's about you, me, George and your mum all pile into the car and go to the seaside? It's far too long since we had a proper adventure.'

Time had moved along – only a couple of months, but with each day that passed, Hannah felt a perceptible readjustment in her relationship with Nick.

It was so strange ... just like old times in some ways, yet at heart totally different. Why? Because the people they had once been were gone forever, and their places had been taken by strangers they had to learn to grow into. Their marriage all those years ago might have been a mistake, entered into unthinkingly, too easily destroyed; but this new way of being together was slowly building up into something that Hannah dared to hope might last.

The question remained: in what way? Could the future bind them together as anything more than devoted friends, or was that just too much to hope for? I'm too old for fairy-tales, thought Hannah; better to accept what I've got and be happy.

And curiously enough, she was.

Gradually they fell into a routine. Instead of Nick taking Lottie away for the weekend, he brought George round to the house and they spent the time together. It was almost like being a family, but not quite. Not many husbands went home at night to their bachelor flat round the corner, or bedded down on the futon in the guest room.

The really remarkable thing was the way Hannah felt towards baby George. For a scary moment, just after the birth, she'd had a horrible fear that she wouldn't be able to respond to the baby, that every time she looked at his cherubic little face it would remind her of what Nick had done with Miranda, of a relationship that had produced the new life their marriage had failed to create.

But it wasn't like that at all. She'd loved him from the moment she first set eyes on him, and day by day was rediscovering all the wonders of new motherhood, the kisses and cuddles and first smiles, without so much as an episiotomy scar to show for it.

Even Lottie had to admit that a baby brother could be even more interesting than a baby ferret. Certainly he was more fun to dress up and feed, and Hannah had a hunch that before long Lottie would also be discovering the joys of having somebody younger to blame. Most of all, it warmed Hannah's heart to see Lottie sitting by George's cot for hours on end, telling him silly stories he couldn't possibly understand, and pulling faces to make him giggle. It felt right – like family.

Only it wasn't.

Yet Hannah was glad of the situation, weird though it might be. It gave her a chance to begin again, to discover aspects of Nick she'd never suspected existed in all those years of being Mrs Steadman. She wondered if it was the same for him, or if he aw her as just the same hapless Hannah he'd married ... and was eventually going to get round to divorcing.

One evening, when the children were asleep and they were sitting on the sofa watching a video, Nick announced: 'Julian's coming back from Madrid.'

Hannah stopped chewing on a toffee. 'Oh no. When?'

'Not for a few months, but when he does, he's going to want his flat back and George and I will have to find somewhere else to live. Somewhere cheap,' he added. 'I've a feeling it won't be easy.'

'Will you ... buy somewhere?'

'Not on the budget I've got at the moment.' Then he said the words she'd been dreading. 'We'd have to sell this house and split the proceeds.'

The thought ran through Hannah like an ice-cold shiver, but she tried to behave like an adult. 'I suppose that would be the sensible thing to do,' she said flatly. 'And you always were the sensible one.'

'Ah, but that was the old me.' Nick stretched out his long legs. 'Before I turned my life upside down. I'm not so sure any more that sensible is always the right way to go.'

Hannah ran her tongue over her lips. Her mouth and throat felt dry and dusty. 'There's room here,' she said quietly.

Nick frowned. 'Room, maybe. But you wouldn't want me and George here all the time, cramping your style. Would you?'

'You wouldn't be cramping anything. And Lottie would love to have you here,' added Hannah hastily, in case he thought she was propositioning him.

'Really?'

'Really.'

'So you're seriously suggesting that I move back in?'

'Yes. But you don't have to decide right away, do you?' Hannah went on. 'I mean, you said yourself Julian's not coming back for a few months.'

Nick scratched his chin. 'Maybe I've got some thinking to do,' he remarked.

They looked at each other.

'Maybe we both have,' replied Hannah.

*

323

It was the day before Lottie's tenth birthday, a chilly autumn Sun day afternoon when no one in their right mind would want to ea ice cream. Well, no one but half the kids in Cheltenham, though Hannah, handing Lottie some money and watching her gallop of towards the queue for the Mr Whippy van.

They were walking by the lake in Pittville Park, Nick wheelin George in his stroller and Hannah entertaining the baby with he repertoire of silly faces. Lottie had always loved them when sh was tiny, and from George's chuckles it seemed she hadn't los the knack.

'You'll stay like that if the wind changes,' commented Nick easing George's fleecy bobble hat down to keep his ears warm.

'Never mind, you can sell me to the circus and make loads o money.'

'Nah, they wouldn't take you – you'd scare the elephants.'

'Hark who's talking!' She swiped at Nick with her handba, and he lost his footing on the muddy bank. If she hadn't grabbe the sleeve of his jumper, he'd probably have ended up waist-dee in the lake. As it was, they just laughed until they ran out o breath.

They strolled on a little further, very slowly so that they coul keep Lottie within sight. Despite the chill of the day, and th heavy, grey skies, a robin was singing on a branch overhangin the lake, its red breast all fluffed up and its little lungs working fi to burst. I know how he feels, thought Hannah. It could be rain ing in torrents and I'd still be smiling from the inside out.

So why do I feel this irresistible urge to ruin it all?

Her heart was racing, pounding so violently against her rib that she was sure Nick must be able to hear it. You don't have t say this, she told herself; you can just keep your mouth shut an let everything go on happily, exactly the way it is, forever an ever, amen.

But the very next moment, she heard herself blurt out: 'Nick, have to tell you something.'

He halted in his tracks. 'That sounds ominous.'

She could hardly breathe, let alone speak. But she'd begun now; there was no going back. 'I . . . I think I've fallen in love.'

Nick's face fell. 'Oh.' There was a whole world of disappoint ment in that one small world. He swallowed. 'Who with?'

Hannah could hardly believe her ears. The question was s